ISBN:978-1499200133

Cover art by Johanna Tarkela - lhuin.deviantart.com

The Wolf's Cry / Natalie Crown

THE WOLF'S CRY

BOOK ONE IN THE SEMEI TRILOGY

Natalie Crown

For Dad,

because you ignited my love for books in the first place.

For Mum,

because you always believed I could do it.

CONTENTS

PART ONE – SEMEI

PART TWO – EMIRE

PART THREE – ALASHDIAL

PART ONE

SEMEI

CHAPTER ONE

THE MOUTH OF THE FOREST

The stone bounced once before disappearing into the shifting water, and Kammy frowned. She looked down at her boots and scooped up another, this one smooth and light. She pulled back her arm and flung it out to sea. Normally her stones would skim the surface, setting off a stream of ripples that granted her a second of satisfaction. Today her stones seemed to do nothing but sink. Kammy looked up at the sky and sighed. The clouds gathered, thick and dark with the promise of rain. The wind grew stronger with every gust and the sea began to churn, sending waves full of seaweed rolling towards her, each one bigger than the last. She wrapped her arms around herself and watched the storm grow, letting the wind catch her hair and carry it out behind her.

The mainland was a shadow on the horizon, a distant world to Kammy Helseth. Kammy squinted at it, pretending that she could see London. She pictured the Shard, an impossible structure to her mind. The tallest thing she had ever seen was the church steeple. She pictured the Thames running alongside the Southbank. Her home seemed an insignificant blot in comparison to such grandeur. She glanced to the western most point of her little island, just able to make out the dock from where she stood. It was the gateway to freedom. She glanced at her watch. The ferry was nowhere in sight, but it should have arrived five minutes ago. A drop of rain splashed at the end of her nose, disturbing her thoughts, and Kammy turned her back on the waves with reluctance. If she did not start home before the downpour she might end up stuck in the village, and that was not worth a few extra moments of solitude.

Kammy pushed London out of her mind and picked her way across the rock pools. Their surfaces reflected the furious sky until they were disrupted by the odd spit of rain. The crabs scuttled back and forth seeking shelter. The air tasted sharp with the tang of salt and Kammy sucked in long breaths as she navigated her way with ease. She quickly left the pools behind and started towards the sandy bluffs that were coated with patches of dry grass as tall as her knees. She heard a faint rumble overhead and quickened her pace, her attention focused solely on her feet and the steep climb ahead of her. When she reached the top she walked right into something. She jerked backwards and almost lost her footing.

'Watch where you're going.'

Kammy's cheeks flushed and she glared up at the girl before her.

Esme Cooper was proud to be the exact opposite of Kammy in every way. Tall and fair, she had bright green eyes that looked luminous in the growing darkness, eyes that were narrowed to slits beneath her hood.

'What are you doing here?' said Kammy, her small voice almost lost within the whistling wind.

'You don't own this beach, despite the fact that you spend most of your miserable existence here.'

Kammy's flush deepened. Thunder growled again and the rain fell more heavily. Kammy pulled her hood up and dropped her eyes to her feet, stepping towards the path that would take her home.

Esme's hand shot out and wrapped around her wrist, pinching her skin through her coat sleeve. 'I wish you would just do it and leave. I wish you'd stop thinking about it and that you'd actually go. It's a shame you don't have the guts.'

Kammy tried to twist away. 'Let go of me.'

Esme's grip tightened and her nails dug in deeper. She did not speak until Kammy looked her in the eye. Her lip curled. 'We don't want you here.'

She flung Kammy's arm away from her as if it were something rotten and Kammy stumbled, her boots slipping in sand and dirt, already turning to mud. Esme sneered and Kammy could feel every inch of her skin burning with humiliation.

'What the hell?'

Kammy sagged with relief. Jamie jogged towards them, his face twisted into a frown. Esme scowled.

'What's going on?' he said, a little out of breath.

Esme shot a dark look at Kammy and said, 'Nothing,' before rearranging her hood and stalking away from them, back towards the village. Kammy watched her go in silence, biting down on her bottom lip and avoiding Jamie's searching gaze.

'You okay?' said Jamie.

Kammy nodded and hid her trembling hands in her pockets.

'Are you going to tell me what that was about?'

Kammy sighed and tried to smile. 'The same as always. There's nothing to tell.'

'They're just jealous, Esme and the others. They're threatened by you.'

'Oh, sure, because I'm terrifying.'

Jamie grinned at her. 'You are, actually.'

Kammy felt the beginnings of a true smile and tried to stifle it, always aware that Jamie's ego needed to be kept in check. Even so, she eyed him with affection. He was a lanky thing, all arms, legs and terrible coordination. He towered over Kammy. His sandy curls had been ironed out by the rain and his jumper was already drenched.

'What are you doing out here anyway? I didn't see the ferry come in.'

He pushed his sopping fringe out of his eyes. 'I came back on an earlier one, because of this,' he pointed at the sky. 'Guess it's stuck at Felixstowe now. Anyway, I thought I'd come up and see you, and your Gran told me you were down here. I should have known, really.'

Kammy ducked behind him and started pushing him towards the path.

11

'Well, now you need to get home. You're not even wearing a coat.'

'Yes, Mum.'

'I'm thinking of your mum actually. She'll go mad when she sees you.'

Jamie spun away from her; his warm brown eyes sparkled with their usual mischief. 'I'll make sure to tell her that it's all your fault.'

Kammy punched his arm and he laughed before squinting through the rain towards the village. A boom cannoned overhead and Kammy looked up. The clouds were so black it looked as though night had arrived early.

Jamie ran a hand through his hair and pouted, 'It pains me to admit you're right. It looks bad. You're sure you're okay?'

Kammy offered him an assured smile. 'Yes, it's nothing I can't handle. Go.'

'Are you working tomorrow?'

'In the afternoon.'

'I'll pop in then.'

'Good. Now, go away.'

'But she's going to make me fill in more job applications,' he whined.

As though with a turn of a tap, the rain began to drive towards them like a river surging from the sky. Kammy let out a squeal and laughed while Jamie yelped and started to back away.

'Thank you,' Kammy shouted, 'for before.'

He shouted back, and she struggled to hear him, 'Always here for you, freak.' Then he tossed her a quick wave before leaping off down the path that led to the cluster of buildings that made up the village of Lumbersdale.

Kammy tried to watch him splash off, but he was lost to her in a few blinks of an eye. She turned the opposite way and she took a deep breath. Without him, her smile faded and the memory of her confrontation with Esme pushed itself back into the forefront of her mind. It was funny that they hated each other so much, yet both wanted the same thing; Kammy gone to the mainland. She glanced to her left, at the strip of ocean that divided the Isle of Daleswick from the eastern coast of England. The waves were slamming together now, shooting foam up into the sky. The water looked like black ice and Kammy felt her stomach turn. Just the thought of the crossing made her knees tremble. She did not have the guts, Esme was right.

A flash illuminated the sky and Kammy swore. She tried to move faster, but the path had turned into an oozing stream of mud. Her boots slurped at it, sticking and sinking. She pulled them free and struggled on, bowing against the wind that buffeted her.

She could see her home at the top of the hill, alone but for the forest behind it. It looked defenceless against the backdrop of the storm yet the flickering glow from the kitchen window promised a fire and warmth. Kammy jogged the final distance. Her Gran was incapable of remembering to lock the door so she darted inside quickly. The storm continued to rage just as loudly from indoors, but the log fire coated everything with a hazy heat that made Kammy smile.

The kitchen was a simple square of wooden surfaces and peeling yellow wallpaper. A vase of dying flowers sat on the dining table and stained mesh curtains hung on the windows. Kammy kicked her boots off, leaving them by the door so that the mud would dry, and hung her coat on the hook. She crossed the room to crouch before the fireplace.

The wind rattled the windows and Kammy glanced back at the darkness, entertaining the possibility that her grandmother was out in the storm. She let out a sigh of relief when she heard a muffled curse. Laughing to herself, Kammy straightened and started to fill the kettle.

Irena came striding into the kitchen, her trim figure clothed in a pair of old dungarees and a red jumper. 'Kam, I didn't expect to see you back so soon.' She had pulled her grey hair up into a scruffy bun and there was a line on her brow that told Kammy she was incredibly frustrated. She dropped herself into a chair at the table and huffed.

Smiling, Kammy pulled two mugs from the cupboard and asked. 'What's wrong?'

'That bloody wardrobe. Heavier than I thought.'

'*Gran*,' Kammy groaned, placing the mugs down with more force than she had intended. 'I told you that Harry offered to help, if you really must move the thing.'

Irena waved a hand, ignoring Kammy's words completely, and fixed her moss green eyes on her granddaughter. 'You look ill.'

Kammy snorted. 'Thanks.'

'Seriously Kam, you look ever so pale.'

The kettle began to whistle. 'I *am* pale. This is what I always look like.'

Irena's silence was not comforting, and Kammy focused on making the tea. She placed the mugs onto the table and Irena thanked her. Kammy sank into the other chair and curled her fingers around her drink.

She sighed, 'Go on, say it.'

Irena stared, and then shrugged her innocence. 'I don't know what you're talking about. Jamie stopped here by the way. Did he catch you?'

Kammy narrowed her eyes. Her Gran had always been quick to pick at the various aspects of Kammy's life that she disagreed with, namely her tendency to spend her time alone. Jamie and his importance to Kammy seemed to be the only thing they agreed on in that regard.

'He found me just as that started up,' she looked out the window. When she turned back to her Gran, she flinched. Irena's eyes were alight in a way that Kammy knew all too well. It was a look that made her feel as though all her thoughts and feelings could be drawn out of her on a string.

'You should have gone back to his for once. You're seventeen. You shouldn't be stuck around here all the time.'

'I didn't know you were so keen to get rid of me.'

Irena raised a thin eyebrow. 'It's my life ambition.'

Kammy laughed. 'I might have gotten stuck in the village. I had to come home.'

'You could have stayed at his.'

14

'Gran.'

'Kammy.'

Kammy wanted to be stubborn, but she had never been able to outmanoeuvre her grandmother when it came to stubbornness and she did not suppose she could start now.

'His mum hates me.'

Irena's eyebrows disappeared altogether. 'Helen? Why on earth do you think that?'

Kammy slouched back in her chair and mumbled, 'Because she does.'

'That is ridiculous,' said Irena, and her tone told Kammy that there would be no arguing such a statement. So, Kammy took a sip of tea and stayed silent. Her Gran could believe what she wanted about Helen Powell, but Kammy knew the truth. Jamie would never admit it, but he knew it too. *We don't want you here*, Esme had said. Kammy folded her arms on the table and rested her chin on top of them. She had never understood it and she knew that she never would.

'I'm just concerned, Kam. Since you finished school, you're either at home, at work, or at the beach. You're quite predictable.'

'You are full of compliments today.'

'I always thought you wanted to get away from this place.'

'I do.'

'Then do it.'

Kammy clamped her teeth together and stared at her lap. She made it sound so easy.

'Kam?'

'You hate it here too. So why don't you leave?' The words escaped her with more sharpness than she had meant and Irena's stare softened.

'I'm old.'

Kammy shook her head. She felt the years of bitterness filling her up from her toes. 'You weren't old ten years ago, we should have left then. Mum might have liked the mainland. There might have been something...'

'There wouldn't have been.'

Kammy caught herself and closed her eyes. After a long moment she said, 'Sorry.'

'Maybe you're right. Maybe we should have left anyway.'

Kammy peered up at her Gran and for a second Irena looked old and weary of the years behind her. Kammy felt an instant of blind panic and when Irena reached a hand across the table, Kammy took it and held on tight.

'I'm sorry Kam, I shouldn't push you.'

You should, Kammy thought, somebody needs to. But she said nothing. She stared at their hands clasped together, one small and the other lined. Irena's grip was firm and Kammy's eyes drifted up to her Gran's face as she felt the full force of her inadequacy. It was little wonder Irena did not understand her granddaughter's fears; Irena did not fear anything.

'Oh,' Irena pulled her hand free, 'look at the time.' She patted her hair as she glanced out the window and moved towards the door.

Kammy's eyes narrowed. 'What are you doing?'

'My shift starts in ten minutes.'

Kammy looked from her Gran to the window. The rain gushed against the shuddering glass in waves. The strength of the wind shook their house. If Kammy had not experienced such storms her whole life she might have been cowering beneath her bed, terrified that they would be blown away.

'You are not going out in that.'

Irena wound her thick scarf around her neck, 'I'm not?'

'Gran, *look* at it.'

Irena pulled on her coat. 'I can't afford to miss a shift, Kammy, but I promise I'll be very careful. I have a torch,' she patted a bulging pocket, 'and if it has not gotten any better by the time I leave then I'll get Harry to give me a lift home.'

Kammy knew that there was no point arguing. Irena stepped closer and tucked a stray strand of Kammy's black hair behind her ear. Kammy pursed her lips which only made Irena laugh so Kammy kissed her quickly on the cheek and shooed her away, defeated having barely begun to fight.

As soon as the door wheezed shut Kammy hurried to the window and squinted through it. Irena was a mauve blur against a world of black and grey, but she did not falter despite the strength of the wind. Kammy stayed at the window until Irena drifted out of sight, then she scooped up the two mugs and placed them in the sink. She opened the freezer to see what was available for dinner. When nothing took her fancy she hopped up the narrow staircase and pushed open the door to her room.

Kammy winced; she had forgotten how much of a mess she had left her room in. Her chest of drawers looked like it had exploded, spewing clothes in all directions. Books littered the floor along with scraps of paper ruined by half-hearted doodles that would never be completed. Her television still lay on its side beside her bed from when she and Jamie had tried to fix it a week ago. They had both been surprised to discover that they knew nothing about fixing televisions; Jamie had been convinced that he would be an expert at it. Kammy considered tidying for one second and then decided that it could wait another day or two. She collapsed face down onto her bed instead.

She felt miserable. She had had a rotten day in a week of rotten days and her Gran, though her intentions were always good, had only made it worse. Kammy groaned and flipped onto her back, staring up at the crack in her ceiling. A part of her wanted to stay there forever, on her soft bed that smelt of washing powder. She could lay there and dream of a life on the mainland. She closed her eyes and tried to picture it, but all she saw was the black depths of the ocean. Her stomach rolled and her eyes snapped open.

'Kammy,' she said out loud, 'you are pathetic.'

Kammy sometimes thought it would be better to live in a world without dreams. What was the point when they tormented you with false hope that would never quite die? Having no hope at all would save her a ton of disappointment.

Kammy pushed up onto her elbows, resisting the urge to spend the evening feeling sorry for herself. She scanned her room knowing that her misery was not helped by her intense boredom. Watching television would have been impossible, even if it was not broken, due to the storm. She could read, but the author had just killed off her favourite character and she felt incredibly bitter and petty about it. Her eyes fell on a shoelace, poking out from beneath the mountain of clothes beside her bed. A run would clear her mind. She glanced out of the window, chewing the inside of her cheek. The storm did not appear to be easing up, but her Gran had braved it. The forest would protect her from the full brunt of it anyway, and she had plenty of time to make it back so that Irena need never know.

Kammy grabbed her trainers and a hooded jumper from the floor and got changed, slipping her mobile into her front pocket. She threw in a few haphazard stretches as she went back downstairs and slipped into the poky bathroom. She turned on the tap and splashed some cool water on her face. Her hair was still drying and it hung in heavy waves around her face, thick and out of her control. She pulled it up into a hair tie and avoided looking at her reflection with a skill honed over the years. Doing so meant that she might avoid thinking about her eyes. It hardly helped. The deep blue shade was odd enough, even without the other abnormality.

A familiar discomfort scratched at the back of her throat and Kammy hurried out of the bathroom. She pulled her hood up and marched towards the door. When she turned the handle it swung inward, slamming against the inside wall. Kammy swore, but she stepped outside anyway, setting her shoulders against the gale. She struggled to shut the door behind her. Her fingers slipped on her keys, assailed as they were by the rain. Finally the door locked and she ran.

With the wind behind her she had no other choice but to run full pelt. She skirted the outside of her home and then hit the open hilltop, charging towards the shelter of the trees. Within seconds she was soaked. Thunder crashed around her. The ground swam beneath her feet and she slipped more than once, but the trees quickly engulfed her and it was as though she had been sucked into a vacuum. The pressure on her back lifted and she slowed to a jog. The rain could only fall in a drizzle and her trainers found grip on the forest floor. The trees were clustered together so tightly that the storm could not break through. Irena had always insisted that Kammy should stay away from the forest, but Kammy knew that it had a special power. That power being that it kept the rest of the island away from her. Kammy knew the trees as well as she knew the rock pools down at the beach. She did not need to think about where she was going. Her eyes could follow the familiar path in the gloom.

Of course, Kammy had another reason to love the forest. When she had been small she would watch her mother sneak away into the trees. Naturally, Kammy would follow her in secret. They would always end up at the same spot and Kammy would watch her mother laugh and cry in that place. Kammy had never understood why. She had never asked. She simply cherished it as a place that only she and her mother had known.

When Kammy felt the ground begin to rise she knew that she had reached her destination. She stopped and pulled out her phone. She had a message from Jamie:

Stop moping x

Kammy laughed; he knew her far too well. She decided that she would call him later, and then she used the light from her phone to illuminate the path before her. The earth dropped away and Kammy balanced herself as she stepped onto the sharp slope. She skidded as gracefully as she could to the bottom and looked ahead. She stood in a small clearing and stared into the mouth of the forest.

It was an animal's burrow, a nondescript thing carved out of the mud and coated with a fuzz of grass. She had never told Jamie about it because she knew it would make him laugh, and while his laughter was something she valued, this place was too special. Kammy followed the light of her phone to the rotting log that her mother used to sit on and she did the same, the storm now a distant whisper. She wrapped her arms around herself and closed her eyes.

Mary Helseth had died four years ago, when Kammy was thirteen years old, but she had been sick for as long as Kammy could remember. The day it had finally happened was lost to Kammy's memory, hidden beneath a haze of pain, and only flashes of the weeks that followed remained. Yet she remembered everything else about her mother so vividly that she sometimes thought it would be easy to conjure her up out of the air. Kammy tried it then and she could almost imagine that her mother sat beside her, no longer weak, but strong enough for the both of them.

A rustling sound sent Mary Helseth fading away, and Kammy opened her eyes. Something had sent a ripple through the tranquillity and Kammy tensed. Her palms started to itch and she scanned the shadows. The mouth of the forest watched in silence, the trees looming like sentinels behind it. There was the rustling again.

Kammy had just started to realise that she was afraid when a squirrel burst from the leaves to her right. It froze, staring up at her and Kammy laughed, feeling foolish. She squatted and held out a hand, trying to coax it forward. It was a red squirrel, larger than most that she had seen and with a distinct white stripe down its left forearm. Kammy thought it was quite cute.

'I won't hurt you.'

The squirrel's nose twitched. It stared at her, and then it darted away into the mouth.

Kammy jerked upright. It was as though the trees had parted beneath the pressure of the storm and a bolt of lightning had struck her. She had never entered the mouth for it had always been much too small. Yet, she had never seen anything else enter it either. The thought alone made her feel sick with excitement and fear. A small voice told Kammy that such a reaction was ridiculous, it was just a squirrel. But warmth spread to the tips of Kammy's fingers as they stretched forward. She could see now that it was not a burrow at all, but a tunnel large enough for her to fit through. Surely she would not even have to bend her head. The same small voice tried to speak again, but Kammy could not hear it through the rush of blood in her ears.

Kammy stepped inside the mouth of the forest and felt herself flipped upside down.

CHAPTER TWO

A PEBBLE

Kammy gasped, her knees crashing into the dirt.

She did not know how far she had fallen, but cool air had rushed past her cheeks. Now, she felt as though she had been dumped into a pool of cold water. Her skin prickled and she curled her fingers into the earth in a desperate attempt to bring some feeling back into her hands. She lifted her eyes to look ahead, but it was too dark for her to make much out. When she looked behind her she shivered. Her forest was still there, just inches away. She had not fallen at all.

Hands shaking, Kammy pulled out her phone and held it ahead of her, letting its light illuminate the darkness. A narrow tunnel stretched ahead, sloping gently downwards. Kammy frowned; how could she ever have thought this place so small as to be a burrow?

Her body began to thaw, and Kammy put out a hand to help herself up. Her fingers slipped in something wet, and she jerked them back towards her chest. Her first thought was that she sat in a pool of blood and she had stumbled across some madman's lair. She held her hand to the light, and forced a nervous laugh; it was only mud. Kammy stood, wiping her fingers on her leggings, and pondered what to do.

She knew that heading home would be the smart idea, generally the sort of idea that Kammy Helseth would embrace. But no matter how hard she considered it her body did not seem to turn, and her feet remained planted. Her heart raced, her palms were sweaty. Kammy glanced at her mobile; she had no signal. Ahead, there was only darkness. She could see nothing of what awaited her. She thought of all the things that could go wrong, like the tunnel collapsing on top of her. She should go home, crawl into bed, and call Jamie like she had planned.

Instead, Kammy took a step forward and smiled. She wondered if her mother had ever dared to enter the mouth? Kammy could not imagine it, for her mother had been just as timid as she was. But what if she had stood just inside the lip and had felt the same burning curiosity that compelled Kammy to take another step forward? What if it had made her feel brave for once? Brave, instead of hesitant and fearful. What harm could it really do to follow the path, when her whole being told her that it was the right thing to do?

Kammy hesitated as she ever did, that persistent small voice tugged on her consciousness. She felt hot and her head was heavy, so she shook it. Esme's voice rung clear in her ears.

Kammy started a steady march.

She kept her phone pointed at her feet so that she could avoid the larger stones lodged into the dirt. Her trainers had ample grip, and with every step she grew in confidence. The smell of the earth that surrounded her was overbearing and the narrow space was sweltering, but she breathed easily. She did not look back. Her trainers crunched in the soft dirt and she did not worry when the downward path grew steadily steeper. How far ahead had the squirrel ventured? Eventually she would find it at the end of the path, and she would have proven something to herself. No harm would come of it. She marched on.

Kammy could not have said whether she walked for a minute or an hour. Sweat pooled at the nape of her neck, but her legs felt fresh. She could just as well have not walked at all. Kammy laughed and the sound bounced around her, spurring her on.

Light touched her senses, thinning the fog in her mind a touch. Her confident steps faltered when she realised the light came from ahead. Behind, the darkness closed in. She took a deep breath to quell her uneasiness, forcing herself to relax. Had she somehow turned around? Had she walked so far that she had found another exit, into another part of the forest? Kammy started walking again. The light grew brighter and she wondered what had possessed her to enter the mouth in the first place. Her eyes had become so accustomed to the gloom that she could hardly see through the glare. She shielded them and stepped outside, blinking rapidly.

There was no sign of the storm. Light filtered through the trees, bright despite Kammy *knowing* that it was the evening. But then...the dry grass had clearly not seen rain, and the air which she drank into her lungs tasted fresh and clear. Kammy stifled the urge to giggle. She looked back at the tunnel, her mouth hanging open. Had she walked right through the night? She reached for her phone, already preparing a string of apologies to offer to her Gran. She had never sleepwalked before, but there was a first time for everything. Her confusion mounted. She still had no signal and according to her mobile, only half an hour had passed since she had entered the mouth. The screen flashed black; her battery must have died.

Kammy put her phone away, frowning. She needed to turn around and go home, but something held her still. Had the forest always been so beautiful? The leaves on the trees seemed that much greener. The smattering of daisies were surely larger than those she was used too? The warm air on her skin sent energy coursing through her. Had she fallen and hit her head? She walked further into the trees, the grass springy beneath her trainers. If she walked for long enough she would either wake up, or she would find a way out of the forest to discover where on Daleswick she had emerged. It was only a small island after all.

The flapping of wings signalled a bird overhead and Kammy smiled. She was not alone. There was no need for her to be frightened. She hummed softly to herself. Her eyes drifted upwards, towards the maze of leaves cracked apart by golden light. She was not watching where she was going and her trainer connected with something solid. She heard the dull thump and glanced down at her feet. An extraordinary stone rested there. It looked incredibly smooth, like the pebbles she would find at the beach. She gazed at it in wonder and picked it up, holding it out on her open palm. It was beautiful. It seemed to shine in the light, ringed with every shade of blue and then every shade of purple. The colours bled into one another without a blemish. Kammy ran her thumb over its surface. She had never seen anything like it.

Something rustled and Kammy dropped the pebble into her pocket, her eyes jerking upwards. She saw a flash of a bushy tail in the grass and she smiled. It was only the squirrel.

'Who are you?'

Kammy spun. She pressed her hand to her chest, startled. The fog in her mind lifted a touch further. She stared fearfully at the woman before her. Something was not right, she knew that instantly.

The woman was tall, much taller than Kammy, and her hair was a tangle of reds and oranges. Her amber eyes rested on Kammy's with burning curiosity and there was a soft curl to her lips. Kammy had never seen her before. Kammy had never seen anybody other than her mother in the forest.

'Who are you?' the woman repeated, taking a step forwards.

Kammy licked dry lips. She could not find her voice.

The woman's eyes narrowed, but she stopped moving. She had dressed strangely. She wore a leather jacket that looked incredibly old and battered. A belt, hung with a number of mismatched pouches, rested on her hips. Her feet were bare. She looked wild.

'I'm sorry,' Kammy croaked, 'I really should...'

'Where did you come from?'

Her accent was odd too. Kammy began to tremble. 'Sorry?'

The woman stared, her gaze cool.

'I...' Kammy could not look away from the woman, much less move. 'I came through that tunnel.'

'That is impossible.'

Kammy's throat worked, but her words dried up. The woman was granite, cold and immovable. The warmth and the light no longer entranced Kammy. She wanted to get away. She could see the tunnel and she knew that the woman's height would make it difficult for her to follow. If only Kammy could reach it quickly.

The woman's fingers flexed at her sides. 'I think you should tell me the truth.'

It was a demand almost disguised as a friendly suggestion. Kammy was rooted to the spot.

The woman took a step closer. 'How did you find this place?'

Kammy shook her head.

'*How* did you find this place?'

'I don't know what you mean.' The words tumbled out of Kammy in a rush and she jerked backwards. The woman simply drifted closer, her eyes sharpening with every step.

'It is impossible for you to be here.'

The woman was insane, it was the only explanation. Kammy stepped to her left. She needed to get back to the tunnel. 'I'll just leave and I won't come back.'

'You will have to come with me.'

Kammy's heart pounded. 'No, I have to go home now.'

The woman cut Kammy off with one long stride. She smiled a smile devoid of any kindness. 'I cannot let you leave.'

Kammy could not stop shaking her head. She stumbled backwards, 'I...I won't tell anybody I saw you. Just let me...'

'*Quiet.*'

Kammy shrunk away. Her Gran had been right all along; the forest *was* dangerous.

The woman's mouth twisted, 'It is so like your kind to beg and to whine.'

Kammy hardly heard her. Blood drummed in her ears. She had to run. Her muscles tensed and the woman laughed.

'If you attempt to flee then I shall be forced to hurt you.'

Kammy froze. Her voice was barely a whisper when she said, 'Won't you hurt me anyway?'

The woman's eyes flashed. 'Perhaps.'

Kammy swayed. Why had she been such a fool as to enter the mouth? She was not brave. She was a coward that hid in the shadow of others that were stronger than her. She felt tears sting her eyes, but then something brushed against her leg and she staggered sideways. The woman reacted, diving towards her, and Kammy threw her hands over her face and screamed.

Kammy heard a sharp intake of breath, and when hands did not claw at her flesh she peeked between her fingers. The woman had stopped mere paces away. She stared off into the trees with a manic smile on her face. Kammy gulped for air.

'For one of them?' The woman laughed, 'you are a fool.'

Kammy waited, shaking and crying and petrified.

Then she heard a voice behind her; '*Run.*'

Kammy could not move. The voice rang clear and her head screamed at her legs to do something, but she could only whimper. There was a snarl and a blow to her back that sent her sprawling forwards. She cried out as something huge and dark flashed past her. The woman's laughter filled the air. Kammy struggled to her feet and *then* she ran.

The shadows of the tunnel swallowed her and her head spun. She fell to her knees, wheezing, but she could hear snarling and tearing behind her. She dragged her ankles forwards, feeling phantom fingers clutch at them and she scrambled to her feet. Using her hands to propel herself forward, Kammy plunged into the darkness. She cried out when her knee crunched into a rock, but she limped on, clenching her teeth as tears filled her eyes.

She could not hear them anymore, only her own ragged breathing, but she did not slow down. Her fingernails dug into the dirt walls and she flung herself up the slope, gaining speed as it levelled out. She burst out of the mouth and did not stop. Cold gripped her. Wind whistled through the trees. Darkness loomed, but she could make out the log and the mound behind it. The storm still raged, but it was only half as strong as the storm within her stomach.

She ran and she ran. Branches tore at her and she thought they were hands. Roots tripped her and she screamed as she rolled away from them. The trees began to thin and she could see the silhouette of her home. The sky rolled above and the hill stretched before her. It was too open. The woman might swoop down and snatch her away. Kammy's knees buckled and she crashed into the mud. Up again, she sprinted. She knew that she would never make it home, but then her hands were jangling with the keys, struggling to crush them into the lock. Finally the door shut behind her. She collapsed into a heap on the floor.

Kammy held herself, but she could not stop shaking. The fire had gone out. The kitchen was cold and dark. She dragged herself over to a chair, seeking some comfort. When she closed her eyes she saw the woman's face. She could still hear that laughter and the sound of flesh tearing. Kammy clamped her hands over her ears, but it made no difference. Her eyes drifted to the window, half expecting to see her there, staring in with death in her eyes. Instead, she saw a bobbing light that grew steadily closer.

It was her Gran.

For a moment, warmth spread through her and she started to smile. Then she looked down at herself and groaned. Forcing her weak legs to stand, Kammy flung herself up the stairs and into her room. She pulled off her jumper and threw it on the floor where it landed with a thud. Swearing, Kammy grabbed it and pulled her phone out of the pocket. Her fingers brushed something else. Kammy pulled out the strange looking pebble. It was a terrible reminder of what she had just seen. It felt strange in her hand and Kammy wanted to throw it out of her window so that she would never see it again. She heard the door rattle and was jolted back into the present. She rolled the pebble under her bed and pulled off the rest of her sodden clothes. Her Gran's key rattled in the door at the same time as she pulled on her pyjamas.

'Kam?'

Kammy almost burst into tears at the sound of her voice. She choked them back and took a moment to compose herself before heading downstairs.

Irena's gaze fixed on the muddy footprints that Kammy had traipsed across the kitchen floor. Kammy wanted to kick herself.

'I cannot...' Irena's shrill voice trailed off when she saw her granddaughter perched at the bottom of the stairs.

Kammy braced herself. There was little point in trying to hide the fact that she had been in the forest, even without the footprints. Her hair was wet and her face flecked with mud. She waited for Irena's mouth to pucker and for her eyes to narrow, but Irena sighed instead. She looked very tired.

'Go clean yourself up and get into bed. I'll make you a hot chocolate.'

Kammy hesitated. She wanted to tell her Gran everything, but when she looked for the words they were not there. Her body drooped, heavy with exhaustion. She did as she was told, vowing to listen to her Gran more in the future. She would never set foot in that forest again.

CHAPTER THREE

SPIRITED AWAY

Kammy leaned on the bar, staring off into space, lost in her own thoughts. She had spent the day desperate to distract herself, but it was impossible. Every time she turned she saw wild red hair. She could not relax and she could hardly bear it.

A hand started waving in front of her face. Kammy jumped.

Harry Whistler laughed, 'You've been somewhere else all afternoon.'

Kammy forced a smile, 'Sorry, it's just so dead in here today...' her throat tightened and her voice trailed off. She had almost been dead herself the night before. Kammy grabbed the nearest dishcloth and ducked her head, hoping that Harry would not watch her too closely if she busied herself. She started polishing the glasses, but it was a vain hope.

'You okay?' he said, 'Irena told me you weren't feeling good last night.'

Kammy paused. 'She did?' Irena's lack of a furious outburst had already surprised her, but Kammy must have looked truly awful for her grandmother to be showing so much concern.

Kammy stifled a yawn, 'I'm fine, really.'

Harry nodded once, but the grey eyes set in his grizzly face looked unconvinced. His gaze swept over the empty pub, lingering on the door as if he could will somebody to step inside. The Woodcutter's was never busy, nowhere on Daleswick was, but the weather had even kept Vicar Howard away. Harry sighed, his belly bouncing as he disappeared into the cellar. Kammy watched him go, itching to tell him not to leave her. She stayed silent.

Her arms moved mechanically, wiping glasses that had already been wiped with the dishcloth. When she grabbed a fresh cloth to run along the bar, the hairs on the back of her neck stood on end. Her stomach flipped and she turned slowly to look out of the window onto the road. There was nothing there; only the old church behind the village and its overgrown cemetery. She felt like a fool, but the sick feeling did not go away. She clutched the cloth to her chest as her eyes darted around the pub, into every shadow. Then she squeezed them shut and took a deep breath. She had felt sick ever since she had slammed the door on the nightmare from the night before. Kammy pressed a hand to her aching head.

'You look horrendous.'

The door clattered shut and Kammy let out a strangled cry, gripping the bar so tight that her knuckles whitened. Jamie laughed and hopped up onto one of the bar stools.

Gathering herself, Kammy said, 'Between you and my Gran, it's no wonder I have such an inflated ego.'

Jamie grinned at her. He slapped a hand onto the bar, 'Tap water please, no ice. It's bloody cold out there.' He dumped a small plastic bag onto the green leather top of the bar stool next to him.

Kammy snorted. 'You're an idiot.' She got him his water and nodded at the bag, 'What's that?'

'Cold medicine. Mum's not feeling great.'

'Doesn't she have all that stuff already?'

Jamie gulped down his drink, wiping his mouth with the back of his hand. 'Just because she's a doctor doesn't mean we have some gargantuan stash of drugs at home.'

Kammy raised an eyebrow. 'Gargantuan?'

'Gargantuan.'

Kammy was halfway to smiling, but something tugged at her attention. Her eyes were drawn back to the window and she shivered. She glanced at Jamie, spinning himself on top of the stool. 'I guess you'll be heading straight home then?'

29

'Yeah, but I had to check in here first.' He stopped spinning and stuck his finger into her face. 'You didn't text me back last night. I was wounded.'

'Sorry,' she mumbled.

'So everything's okay?'

Who was that woman? And that second voice, the man?

'Kammy?'

Where could she have been, that the weather had changed so abruptly?

'Oi, Helseth.'

'Huh?' Kammy blinked, forcing herself back into the present. Jamie eyed her with concern.

'You're acting strange,' he said.

Kammy managed a laugh. 'I'm always strange.'

'True enough, I guess.'

Kammy did not like the way that Jamie was looking at her, like he was her best friend that knew her inside out and so knew that something was definitely wrong. Kammy cleared her throat, hoping that her voice did not sound too strained. 'How come you're not working today?'

Jamie took a sip of water, but his eyes never left her face. 'They said I could write from home.'

'That's great,' said Kammy, staring at the sparkling wine glasses and hoping Jamie might ignore the burn in her cheeks.

'Oh come on Kammy. I may be an idiot, but I'm not stupid. Spill.'

Heavy footsteps announced the return of Harry. He emerged from the cellar wiping large hands on the dishcloth that hung over his shoulder. He grinned at them before scanning the pub once more with a frown. Then his eyes fell on the almost empty glass of water in front of Jamie.

'You drink water on a day like today? Are you trying to force me out of business?'

30

Jamie shrugged and grinned, 'Sorry, sir. I'm all for healthy living.'

Harry threw the dishcloth at him. Jamie caught it and made a face.

'Healthy living, my arse,' said Harry, but he was still smiling.

Kammy peeked at Jamie hopefully, but his eyes immediately focused back on her and her shoulders slumped. She pouted at him and he knew that he was victorious.

Kammy looked at the clock over the door. She still had twenty minutes of her shift left. 'Harry,' she said, 'do you mind if I head off a little early?'

Harry laughed, 'Sure. I doubt I'll struggle to handle this lot,' he waved at the empty tables.

Kammy patted his arm. 'Thanks. I'll see you tomorrow.'

Jamie hopped off the stool, grabbed the cold medicine and plucked Kammy's coat off the stand. Kammy threw Harry a wave and followed Jamie outside. The bruises on her legs ached with each step, but she refused to let herself limp.

The rain had stopped which was a welcome change. Kammy turned her eyes upwards and thought that the sky even looked a little brighter. It was cold though, colder than it had been for a while. Kammy pulled on her coat and stuck her hands into her pockets.

'I thought you said you had to get home,' she said, lightly.

Jamie folded his arms. 'I said I was going to go home, not that I had to.'

'But your mum...'

'She has a cold. She'll be fine to wait a little longer. I'm concerned for you.'

Kammy shook her head. 'Don't be.'

'You're not meeting my eye.'

Kammy stared at him.

'Now you're just being stubborn.'

'I'm always stubborn.'

31

'But you're clearly keeping something from me, and you never keep things from me.' Kammy saw the flash of hurt in his eyes and felt a bud of guilt.

She glanced around, looking up and down the narrow street, but there was nobody about. It was the middle of the afternoon and most people in the village were at school, on the farms, or working in Erinsdale, the only town on the island. Kammy gnawed at the inside of her cheek. 'It's not that I don't want to tell you, it's just that you'll think I'm insane.'

'I already think you're insane, have done for a while. So hit me with it.'

Kammy shot him a look, but his smile in response was half hearted. He was trying his hardest to be flippant, but he really was worried. First it had been her Gran, now Jamie. If Kammy did not have such a strong aversion to her own reflection, she would check and see what all the fuss was about. Her eyes drifted over the village, the rooftops that dipped and rose with the rhythm of the earth beneath them. She could see her home on the top of the hill, but she saw the trees too and felt a chill despite her coat. The forest had never scared her before, but the thought of walking towards it alone made the sick feeling in her stomach that much stronger.

In a small voice, she said, 'Walk me home?' She did not tell him that she wanted him there because she was afraid; she knew that she did not need too.

Jamie fell into step beside her.

They walked away from the pub and the flowered vines that crawled along its walls. They walked down the road in silence, past houses of all shapes and sizes painted in a rainbow of colours. They listened to the distant waves, running across the stony beach. They trod through dirty puddles , past the crooked paths that zigzagged up towards the largest houses. Jamie lived in one of those and Kammy flinched when she saw his home, imagining that Helen watched them and hated the company that her son kept. The smell of fresh bread filled the air, but Kammy kept her gaze averted from the bakery. She did not need to see Esme on top of everything else. She took a deep breath. Her mouth was dry and she had to swallow a few times before she could speak.

'Last night I went into the forest for a run...'

Jamie's voice went up a few octaves. 'In that storm?'

Kammy ignored him. 'There's this spot there that mum used to go to and I...I like it, so...' Kammy glanced at him. She had never told him about the mouth, but if he cared that she had kept it from him, he did not show it. He nodded for her to continue. 'There's this burrow. At least, I thought it was a burrow, but then it was a tunnel. It was big enough for me to fit inside so I went in,' Kammy could feel her face burning. It sounded ridiculous. 'I kept walking and walking for...I don't know how long. I came back out into the forest, but it was...warm, the sun was shining.'

Jamie looked up and Kammy knew what he was thinking. He was feeling the heaviness of the air; he was looking at the expectant clouds. Daleswick had not seen sunshine for days.

'Were you *high*?'

Kammy pushed her hair off her face, 'Honestly? I wish I could say that I was.'

They passed the post box and stepped off the road, onto the dirt track. Jamie was not looking at her and Kammy groaned.

'This is why I didn't want to say anything. It's crazy.'

'No,' Jamie grabbed her shoulder and squeezed it, 'hey...I believe you. I mean, it *does* sound crazy, but I know you wouldn't be telling me this if you didn't think it was real.'

'*Think* it was real?'

Jamie looked abashed, 'There wasn't any sun yesterday and definitely not in the evening. Maybe you were tired...maybe you weren't...seeing things right.'

Kammy bit her tongue. Seeing things? Wouldn't that make her crazy? Could she have imagined the sun? She could not decide if the idea that it had all been in her head was more terrifying than it being real. They reached the gate that led down to the beach. Jamie pushed it open and held it for Kammy. She slipped through with her head bowed.

'Kam...'

'There was a woman too,' she blurted.

'What?'

'In the forest. There was a woman. I think she tried to attack me.'

Jamie grabbed her arm, stopping her before she could start up the hill. 'Kammy, that's...who was she?'

Kammy shrugged, looking beyond him and out to sea. 'I didn't recognise her. She was strange, different.'

Jamie looked utterly perplexed. 'And she attacked you? Why was she even in the forest? I thought you were the only one that ever went there.' His expression hardened as her words finally sank in, 'She *attacked* you?'

'She asked who I was and how I had gotten there. She didn't believe anything that I said and then she...she threatened me. I thought she was going to hurt me.'

Jamie's grip on her arm tightened. 'You told Harry, right?'

Kammy shook her head.

'What if she *had* managed to hurt you? Jesus Kam, if there's some nut job living out there in the forest, she might still.'

Kammy shuddered, 'I know...'

'You have to tell him, Kammy.'

Kammy tried to imagine how she would feel if Jamie were ever in danger, if their roles were reversed. The thought made her skin crawl and she stepped closer to him. 'I can't. Telling you is one thing, but everyone else? They already think I'm weird. Imagine what they'd say if it came out that I've been digging through rabbit burrows in the middle of a storm? They won't believe me.'

'Harry would.'

'The others won't.'

'I don't give a damn about them. You don't need to tell them everything anyway. Just tell them about the woman.'

Kammy paused, thinking it through.

'What if she hurts someone else? This is a small island, she won't stay hidden forever.' Kammy had never heard him sound so serious, 'How would you feel then, if you had kept it to yourself?'

34

Kammy pulled her coat tight around her. 'What if they don't find her?' If Jamie thought it possible that she had imagined the sunshine, could she have imagined the woman too?

He shook his head, looking a little guilty. 'If you saw her then she's on the island somewhere.'

Kammy found herself staring at the forest. The clouds hung close to the thick gathering of leaves. No light could break through. 'Somewhere...' Kammy whispered.

Jamie ran a hand through his curls, a sure sign of agitation. He puffed out his cheeks. 'Don't worry about it right now. Let's just get you home.'

'Are you sure your mum...'

Jamie shook his head, 'Honestly, she'll be fine.'

Kammy felt like she should tell him not to worry, and that she could manage the walk home just fine. But then she would be alone, so she said nothing. Kammy kept her eyes on her feet, doing her best to avoid the worst of the mud and pondered whether she felt better for telling Jamie. She could not help but think that, for the first time, they were on different wavelengths. How could he understand when he had not been there?

Something prickled the back of Kammy's neck and she swiped at her hair, but the prickling continued. She froze, Jamie stopping beside her. He looked confused and then his eyes grew round when they landed on her face. Kammy *knew* that somebody was watching them. She blinked back frustrated tears.

Jamie stepped towards her, 'What...'

It exploded out of the grass. Kammy screamed, flinging herself backwards. Her boots slipped in the mud and she landed on her back, the breath bursting from her lungs. She saw a flash of red. Feathers brushed her face. Her gaze followed the bird as it flew up into the sky. She closed her eyes and lay still, feeling the coolness of the mud seep through her hair.

'Kammy...' Jamie dropped to his knees beside her.

'I'm okay,' she said, letting him help her up.

She was not okay and they both knew it. Jamie threw an arm around her shoulders and she held on to him, trembling from head to toe. It was only a bird. Maybe she really was crazy.

'Come on,' said Jamie, giving her a squeeze.

It did not take them long to reach her home and the door was not locked. Jamie had to stoop so as not to bash his head against the low ceiling, so Kammy pulled away from him and sank into a chair, tugging off her coat as she did so. Jamie pulled a piece of paper off the fridge and held it up to her. It was a note from Irena.

'She's in town,' said Jamie.

Kammy nodded. It was okay because Jamie was with her. He started to boil the kettle and took two mugs off the draining board before settling down opposite her. Their eyes met and danced away. He seemed to be struggling to find something to say and Kammy squirmed. It had not been awkward between them for years, not since the day her mother had died.

Kammy's heartbeat started to return to normal, and she tried to grin. 'After all these years of everyone telling me, I really am a freak.'

Before Jamie could answer, his phone rang. The Superman theme music blasted out and it made Kammy smile. Jamie's belief that he had a lot in common with Superman was something familiar, something comfortable.

'Mum?' Jamie answered, 'Yeah, I'll be home soon. No, I...right, but...' he rolled his eyes at Kammy and her smile faded. It never took long for Helen to call. 'Fine,' he said, hanging up. He looked up at Kammy with two red spots blossoming in his cheeks.

'It's okay,' said Kammy, 'go.'

'She says she's feeling worse.'

'Seriously,' she held up her hands to show that they were no longer shaking. 'I'm fine.'

'Are you sure?' Jamie looked pained. 'Tell me honestly, because I'll stay if you want.'

Kammy waved him away, 'I feel like lying down for a bit anyway.'

'Okay, but I'll ring you tonight. We can talk about you telling Harry, if you want. You should definitely tell your Gran at least.' He stood, still looking torn, 'and if you need me at any time, just call. I'll come back.'

Kammy smiled. She wondered what she would ever do without him.

Jamie planted a quick kiss on the top of her head. 'I'll see you later.'

As soon as the door shut behind him Kammy leapt to her feet and locked it. It was an old, rusty lock that would give under little force, but it was still a small comfort. She left the tea and grabbed a glass of water instead, rolling her shoulders as she moved. She had mud in her hair, but she could not be bothered to wash it. She would try and sleep for a bit. She needed a break from the constant tension.

Kammy turned and almost dropped the glass onto the floor. A bird landed on the windowsill. Its eyes peered at her through the glass and its feathers were a reddish-brown. Kammy knew instantly that it was the same bird that had flown at her.

'Go away,' she shouted at it, not wanting to get close enough to rap her knuckles against the window. It did not move and continued to stare.

Kammy had never been afraid of birds and she resolved not to start. She turned her back on it and hurried up the stairs, all the while her skin burning. She glanced over her shoulder and the bird was still there, its beady eyes fixed on her and bright with intelligence.

She pulled her door shut behind her and her gaze flicked straight to her bedroom window. She half expected the bird to be sitting there waiting for her, but all she could see were the clouds floating over the hills.

Kammy slouched towards her bed. It looked soft and inviting, but for some reason she found herself crouched beside it and squinting into the darkness underneath. She stretched out an arm and pulled the pebble out. She sat back on her heels and gazed at it.

In all her life she had never seen anything so beautiful. She scratched at it with a nail to see if the colours had been painted on, but nothing flaked off. She had not seen such a stone in the forest before and she decided that she wanted nothing more to do with it. She pictured herself flinging it out of her window or dumping it into the bin. Instead she rolled it back under her bed and her brow pinched in confusion.

Something cold touched the back of her neck.

Kammy spun and shot to her feet. Her window was open. Kammy swallowed. Her window had been closed just moments before.

Kammy crept towards it, her eyes jumping over every inch of her room. There was nobody there. She was alone. Perhaps her window had been open all along and she had simply not noticed it? Her Gran often complained that her teenage pit was forced to sit stagnant. She might have opened it to let some air in. Kammy darted forwards, reaching out and yanking the latch to slam the window shut. She hooked the latch in place and laughed at herself.

A hand clamped down over her mouth and something hard smashed into the back of her head.

CHAPTER FOUR

DEATH SENTENCE

Kammy opened her eyes and regretted it immediately.

She groaned. It felt like a thousand needles were being jammed into the base of her skull. She heaved and tasted bile in the back of her throat. Closing her eyes again, Kammy lay still on the cold floor and took a few deep breaths. Her head throbbed.

The wave of nausea began to subside and Kammy attempted to open her eyes once more. The brightness made her stomach roll, but she clenched her jaw and forced her eyes to stay open. It was only then that she remembered what had happened in her bedroom. Her vision swam. She sat up slowly and she stared.

She was sitting in a large square room. The floor looked like white marble; spotless and polished to a glare. The walls were the same, stretching high above her. There were no windows, but one door; a thick grey door of solid looking metal.

'Hello?' Kammy's voice croaked into the silence. The word echoed once, and was gone.

She tried her hardest not to panic. She told herself that there was no point. Wherever she was, whatever had happened was surely all part of some great misunderstanding. If she could just talk to somebody then it would all get cleared up. At least she had not been dragged into the forest by the wild woman. For all she knew, she was in Erinsdale. Maybe Jamie had told Harry what she had said and they had locked her up for own safety. Maybe it was for the best.

39

No matter what Kammy told herself, she could not slow her breathing. She reached a hand round to the back of her head and winced. Beneath hair still coated with mud rose a tender lump. Her stomach clenched when she touched it and she closed her eyes, gritting her teeth until the sensation passed. If the police had come for her, why had they they knocked her out first?

She struggled to her feet. Her legs almost melted beneath her. She reached out a hand to steady herself and moved along the smooth wall, blinking every second against the glare. When she reached the door she curled her hand into a fist and knocked.

'Hello? I need to talk to somebody.'

All she heard in reply was her knuckles scraping against the metal. She pressed her forehead against the door and let its coolness soothe her. She kept thinking of the red haired woman and the sun-lit forest. She thought of the pebble and its mysterious beauty.

This has nothing to do with all that, she told herself, *I'm in Erinsdale.*

Her head felt like it was crumbling apart. Her skin was clammy and she peeled herself away from the door. With a start she remembered that her phone was in her pocket. She pulled it out, but the screen was black. She frowned. She had made a point of fully charging it that morning, since it had died the night before. She glanced at her watch and her confusion deepened; it had stopped. She bit down on her lip and sucked in a shaky breath. She could not have been in this place for long. If somebody came for her soon she might even be back with her Gran in time for dinner.

Kammy faced her cell. She spotted a small bucket in the corner and walked towards it. When she saw that it was full of water she actually smiled, for her throat was painfully dry. She eased herself down beside it and scooped up a few mouthfuls. Then she splashed her face and wet her neck. Her mind sharpened and she sat back. She could only wait.

She did not have to wait long. The sound of clanging metal had Kammy struggling back to her feet. The door creaked open and two figures walked into the room. Their faces were hidden behind delicate visors. Their bodies were wrapped in armour that glinted blue. Kammy accepted with a crushing sense of certainty that wherever she was, it was not Erinsdale.

The first figure, the tallest, faced her. 'Come with us.' His words came out muffled, but Kammy heard him. Yet her body did not respond. Paralysed by dread, its touch rooted her to the spot.

'What is this?' she said.

'Come.'

'Where am I?'

The second figure, or guard, spoke up. Her voice was kinder than the first. 'It will be easier for us all if you do as you are asked.'

Still, Kammy remained frozen. Their voices were strange. Their armour looked ancient and alien to her. She wanted to ask them a million questions, but the taller guard lost patience. He grabbed her arm and yanked her forwards. The sudden movement made Kammy's world spin and she started to see spots, but his gloved hand lodged between her shoulder blades, pushing her ahead of him. Kammy simply had to bear it.

'Follow me,' said the faceless woman.

Somehow, Kammy's legs were able to manage and she stepped out of the cell onto a small platform that was part of a winding staircase. She paused, her eyes drifting to the shadows above, but the second guard nudged her and her gaze fell downwards. The stairs were narrow and the stone steps uneven. Kammy pressed herself as close to the wall as possible.

'Where are you taking me?'

The female guard had already disappeared and the man did not respond. Kammy started down the steps. She focused on her feet, trying her hardest to ignore the reality of her situation. Where ever she was, it would all be sorted out soon. She was being taken to talk to somebody who would clear up the whole mess and send her home.

The staircase twisted on and on, with no windows that Kammy could use to gauge how high up they were. Every ten steps or so there were flaming torches lodged into the rough stone walls, surrounding her with dancing shadows. When they reached the bottom, Kammy had to wipe the sweat from her face with her sleeve. The woman did not wait. She stepped through a thick red curtain and Kammy followed suit knowing that if she did not, the male guard would only shove her through anyway.

41

She found herself in a wide corridor and she faltered. The walls and floors were white like her cell, but there was a giant window opposite her and more windows evenly spaced in all directions. All she could see through them was the blue of a cloudless sky.

'Move,' the guard behind her grunted.

The female guard marched away, her armour whistling with every step, and Kammy forced her stiff and aching limbs to follow. Her eyes raked the walls. Huge paintings were hung on them. They loomed over Kammy, their colours swirling into unfamiliar images. There was a tapestry too, hanging down from the ceiling and right to the floor. Kammy's eyes landed upon it and the silver outline of a wolf howling, but then she was beyond it and stepping round a corner.

'Here,' said the female guard, stopping beside a simple door.

Kammy glanced at it fearfully, 'Please, can't you...'

'We are not permitted to talk to you,' said the woman before turning abruptly away. The two guards stationed themselves on either side of the door, silent and then still. They might as well have been empty suits decorating the corridor.

Kammy considered running. Their armour looked heavy enough that she might outpace them and there was nobody else around, but the thought was fleeting. Her head still pounded every time that she moved and besides, where would she go? Running would be an admission of guilt; she knew that from watching all those police shows that her Gran loved. Running would only make things worse. She pushed open the door and stepped inside.

It was like being dropped into a hole in the ground. Darkness swamped her, along with a strong scent of dirt and sweat. The room was windowless again, but this time the walls were not bright and only one torch lit the gloom. She blinked and slowly her eyes began to adjust. She saw a desk in the centre of the room and then she saw the hulking figure sitting behind it. His outline was all she could make out at first and she had never seen a person so large. Then she could see that it was a man. He dwarfed the desk and the tinted blue armour somehow looked even more threatening on him. His small eyes reflected the flame beside him, glaring out from a shining bald head. He waved her closer and Kammy shuffled forwards, shrinking in on herself with every step.

Somebody else moved in the shadows and Kammy knew who it was before she saw her face. She was surprised to note that she felt relieved. The woman from the forest stepped into the light and eyed Kammy with intense distrust. She had her hair pulled back and she wore armour too. It was a strange comfort, given how terrifying everything had suddenly become. If the woman was not insane, as Kammy had assumed, but instead part of some secret organisation, then Kammy might not need to fear her forest at all.

Kammy found her voice. 'I think there has been a mistake. I...'

'You are a human?'

The sense of relief shrivelled and died, leaving ash in her throat. She choked on it, hardly able to breathe. The man's voice boomed so loudly that there was no mistaking what he had said and the look on his face was deadly serious.

'I...'

'Yet you found the Gate?' His clenched fists came to rest on the desk top, each the size of Kammy's head. 'Well?' he barked.

'I...' Kammy felt as though her skull was being bashed against a wall, 'I don't know anything about a gate...'

The man's head turned, his size making even the smallest movement seem awkward. His neck was thick, but he had no extra chins. Kammy feared that his whole bulk was muscle.

He spoke to the woman who had still not looked away from Kammy, 'You saw her in the forest?'

'Yes.'

He turned accusing eyes back to Kammy, 'Then you travelled through the Gate.'

'I told her,' Kammy cried, 'I found a tunnel in the forest and I went through it. That's all. I never saw a gate.' She gazed at him with imploring eyes, hoping to break through and uncover some sense.

The woman spoke, her voice as soft as silk compared to his. 'She must not have known what it was.'

Kammy felt a twinge of hope. As long as they knew that her ignorance was honest, they would surely let her go.

The man's fists seemed to convulse and his eyes narrowed to almost nothing. Kammy wished that she could sit down before her legs gave way. She realised that she still wore her black apron from work and she clutched at it with sweaty palms.

'What of the Key?'

Kammy's mind blanked. A wave of sickness pulsed through her. 'I don't...'

'Do not try to deny it,' he snapped, 'we know you have it.'

'I felt it on you,' the woman nodded.

Kammy wanted to scream at them, to tell them to leave her alone and to let her go, but when she spoke she whispered. 'I don't know what you're talking about. The only key I have is my house key.'

'You are lying,' the woman hissed.

'*No.*'

'Yes. I am no fool. I felt the Key on you as you came through the Gate.'

Kammy felt a chill at the thought of this woman inside her home. She thought of her Gran and tears sprung to her eyes.

The woman exhaled sharply. 'We should have left her in the tower until he returns. He shall want to question her himself.'

'No.' The man's voice thrummed with a firm finality and heat flooded the woman's face. His jaw tightened. Her lip pulled back into a snarl.

'He would want...'

'He would not want his time wasted.'

'But if she knows...'

'She knows nothing, that is obvious. He will get no more out of her than us.'

The two of them stared at one another, the woman's eyes shining in defiance. Kammy watched them with her breath stuck in her throat. She did not dare make a sound.

After a long moment, the man said, 'He left me in charge, Ria, not you.'

The woman, Ria, looked like she had been slapped. Her nostrils flared and her hand twitched forwards. She seemed to struggle for a moment, then her shoulders relaxed and she took a step back, staring past the man and at the wall.

'Then what do you suggest?' she said.

'She is useless.'

It was as though they had forgotten that Kammy stood there. Didn't she have rights? Wasn't that how it worked? Should she demand them? She wanted to speak, to remind them, but the words stuck in her dry throat. She thought she might have been invisible, but then the man looked right at her without a shred of kindness in his eyes.

'Have her taken back to her cell and fetch Gareth. He can end this mess. She has seen too much now. You should never have brought her here in the first place.'

'You wish to kill her? Surely it would...'

'*Silence.*'

Kammy could no longer see or hear them.

'Please,' she choked, her voice sounding blurred in her head, 'just take me home...please.'

The man looked bored. He waved a hand, dismissing her.

'Please, I won't tell anyone anything...I don't know where I am...' she blinked as the woman stepped towards her. The room turned while she stood still. '*Please.*'

A hand grabbed her and shoved her towards the door. Kammy stumbled through it, dazed. The sudden light lanced her eyes and she threw her arms up to shield her face. She could hear the woman speaking, but the words merged together into noise. Only when somebody grabbed her again, did Kammy snap.

'No,' she screamed. She twisted free and ran, but strong arms wrapped around her chest and lifted her. She kicked out, struggling with all that she had, unable to see through her tears. She writhed in the guard's arms, screaming and screaming. 'I didn't do anything. I didn't do anything.' The guards did not speak. The one holding her shifted her weight, grunting when her knees clattered against his chest. She felt the other grip her ankles. They squeezed her, clamping

45

her limbs into place. Her head pressed against an armoured chest so that her screams were muffled. She pushed against it, but the fight was impossible and in one moment her energy had drained out of her. She sagged and the guards started to march back towards her cell.

Human, they had called her. They had said it with pure loathing as though being human was the worst thing that they could imagine. But they were human too; they had to be. Not that it mattered any more. Kammy's eyes stared at the joints in the guard's breastplate. There were etchings there, of wolves. Dimly, she was aware of the beauty of the armour and Kammy squeezed her eyes shut knowing that it would be the last beautiful thing she would ever see.

All too soon the guards were lowering her to the floor with surprising gentleness, prying her fingers loose. She crouched where they placed her, staring in mute horror as they walked away. She watched the door clang shut and as that sound reverberated around her she launched back to her feet. She threw herself at the door, kicking and punching it. She tore around the room, trying to dig her nails into the marble. But desperation was not enough. There was no way out and her stomach heaved. She fell to the floor and retched. Then she wrapped her arms around herself and cried.

She was going to die.

Jamie had promised to call. She wondered if he had tried. He would have been worried when she didn't answer, surely he would have gone to check on her? Was he with her Gran? They would never know what had happened to her.

She could picture her bedroom with its faded orange wallpaper and its scratchy floorboards. She walked through Lumbersdale in her mind, touching houses as she passed, taking gulping breaths of the salty air. It had always felt like a prison to her. She had hated all of Daleswick. She had dreamed of leaving to find excitement and adventure and now she felt like a fool. She would give anything to be sitting in her kitchen waiting for the kettle to boil. Even Esme would be welcome. Kammy wanted to take back every dark thought she had ever had. She wanted to go home.

She pressed her hands over her eyes as if she could hold back her tears, but they slipped through her fingers until she was empty, drained. She did not want to die. The idea that she would was preposterous. She had many fears, but dying had never been one of them. She felt a pressure build in her chest, trying to break free, but there was no way out of the cell.

Eventually she grew quiet and she heard a sound apart from her sobs. It was time already. Every muscle in her body clenched in terror, but the door did not open. The sound was softer than that. Kammy wiped the tears away from her eyes and sat up, blinking away her dizziness. Her breaths were short as she scanned the walls.

Kammy frowned. A trickle of dust poured out of the wall opposite the door. Kammy feared that she was imagining it, certain that it had not been there before. But the dust flowed faster and Kammy crept towards it. It came from a hole the size of a pea, a hole that was growing steadily bigger. Mesmerised, Kammy knelt in front of it and brought her eye level.

A pink nose appeared.

Kammy yelped and shoved herself backwards, but shock quickly turned into laughter. A mouse wriggled free of the hole and dropped to the floor in front of her. It looked up at her, still but for its twitching whiskers. It was a large mouse with warm red fur.

Kammy smiled at it, 'Come to keep me company?'

Its nose twitched and it began to glow.

Kammy rubbed her eyes, but when she looked again the mouse was growing. Kammy scuttled backwards, but her body did not seem to be working as it should. She slipped, slumping to her knees as the mouse twisted and stretched, its body contorting. The mouse disappeared and in its place stood a boy.

Kammy screamed.

CHAPTER FIVE

MICE AND MEN

His hand slammed down over her mouth, his face inches away from hers. Kammy's body snapped rigid with terror.

The mouse had gone and a boy stood in its place. Her eyes danced over him, but there were no remaining traces of fur and no whiskers. Instead she stared at a young face, one that was hardly older than her own. Her mind reeled as she studied him, mostly because he looked quite normal. She had no idea what a man that had been a mouse *should* look like, but there had to be something odd about his features. Yet she could see nothing odd about him at all, though his short hair was a particularly bright shade of red. He was taller than Kammy and his broad shoulders looked strong. His round face was dusted with freckles and his green eyes looked as stunned as Kammy felt.

'Promise not to scream,' he whispered.

Kammy swallowed and nodded. She did not really have any other options.

He looked unsure for a moment, before he stepped back and let his arms fall to his sides. Kammy kept her promise, but she did not relax. She did not think she could have found her voice to scream even if she had wanted too. They stared at one another and Kammy felt a strange sort of indignant rage. He looked at her with such deep suspicion and she felt that it was entirely unjustified. She was not the one that had first appeared with a twitching pink nose.

'What are you?'

He smiled, but Kammy was not at all amused. They had spoken at the same time and she felt a sick feeling in her stomach that was becoming all too familiar. *What are you?* Kammy had struggled all her life with the fear that she was different, but Esme and the others were wrong. She was the same as everyone else.

'I'm just a girl,' she managed.

He raised his eyebrows. 'I can see that.'

Kammy only stared at him.

He held up his hands and took another step back. 'Okay, I'll go first. I'm Semei, obviously.'

Kammy closed her eyes and sagged lower on the floor. She wanted answers, but perhaps they would only make her headache worse? When she opened her eyes again the young man watched her with a curious expression. The more she looked at him, the less normal he seemed. His rough shirt and trousers were strange. The scruffy looking boots he wore were not a style she recognised. Yet as alien as he was to her, she sensed that she was just as strange to him and that only added to her fear. Still, he did not frighten her in the same way as the guards, or the large man, or Ria. There was something about him that seemed warm. She had only just met him and she found herself wanting to trust that he would be good. Then she remembered that he had first entered her cell as a mouse and her head all but split in two.

'My name is Eric,' he offered into the stretching silence.

She took a deep breath. 'Kammy.'

'Well, it's a pleasure to meet you Kammy.'

He sounded genuine, but Kammy was not even close to being able to return such kindness.

Eric continued to smile at her. He dropped to the floor and crossed his legs beneath him, squinting at her. 'You don't feel Semei and your clothes are weird, so I'd say you're human.'

'Of course I am. What else could I be?'

Eric's eyes darted towards the door and he brought a finger to his lips. Kammy clapped her mouth shut. He did not seem surprised or annoyed by her outburst. He simply shrugged and continued to watch her in that same curious way.

'I'm not really sure,' he said, 'I've never met a human before.'

'But you're human. You must be human.'

'No,' Eric shook his head, 'I told you...'

Kammy pressed a hand to her forehead. 'No, it's impossible. You're impossible.'

'You saw it yourself. We're all Semei in this layer...'

'Layer?' Kammy had the sudden urge to laugh. She ran a hand through her hair, her fingers catching in the tangles, and she shook her head. If this was not a dream then it was surely some elaborate prank.

'Oh right, you wouldn't know. This layer of earth, beneath the surface.'

Kammy blinked at him. 'And what exactly is a Semei?'

'Well, I don't know if this word will mean anything to you, but centuries ago, your people called us shapeshifters.'

Kammy did laugh then. Eric's cheeks flushed beneath his freckles and Kammy knew that she had offended him. She tried to stop, to hold her breath, but it burst out of her again. All of a sudden she found the whole situation hysterical. Eric scowled at her.

'I'm sorry. I didn't mean...I just...' her shoulders slumped. 'I was taken from my home, thrown into a cell and sentenced to death. Now you tell me that I'm in a different layer of the earth, a layer which happens to be inhabited by shapeshifters?'

Eric's expression softened. 'You're upset...'

'Of course I'm upset...'

'*Kammy*...' Eric hissed.

With a start Kammy realised that she was almost shouting. She pulled her knees up into her chest and fell silent.

Eric eyed the door for a moment before resting his arms on his knees and turning back to her. 'This is madness for me too, you know. I can't even begin to wonder why you're here. I've never heard of a human in our layer before, but at least I know about humans and that they exist. At least I know about the surface. It's different for you and I get that. But Kammy, you saw me shift. You can't pretend that you didn't.'

'I can try.'

Eric chuckled, 'Alright, you can try, but it won't work. All I can say is that this is real, this is happening. You just have to go with it. If you can accept that then maybe your head will hurt less.'

Kammy managed a weak smile. 'Is it that obvious my head hurts?'

'It's very obvious.'

Kammy doubted that anything at all would soothe the pounding in her head, but the fact that they were smiling at each other took a little of the weight off her shoulders.

'So,' said Eric, 'do you have any idea why you were brought here?'

'No.' Kammy shrugged, 'Where is here anyway?'

'This is one of the prison towers of the palace in Alashdial. It's the closest city to the Gate.'

'Gate?' Kammy frowned, 'they kept asking me about a gate. They kept asking me how I had found it, but I had no idea what they were talking about.'

Eric's eyes widened. 'You found the Gate yourself?'

His surprise made her wary, but what else could she do other than talk to him? 'No, I have no idea what the gate is...but that's what Ria and the other man seemed to believe, even though they also seemed sure it was impossible.'

'It is impossible. I don't know what they're thinking. The Gate is the only way between this layer and the surface. The Semei know of it because it's taught in our history, but passing through is strictly forbidden. You can only do it with certain permissions. Humans, it is said, can't even see the Gate, let alone go through it.'

Kammy felt a wave of relief. 'So it *was* a misunderstanding.' She could hardly compute talk of layers and gates, but a tiny part of her clung to the idea that as long as she was innocent, she might still have a chance.

Eric nodded. 'It must have been. Did they ask you anything else? I still don't understand why they would take you like this.'

'They were convinced that I had some sort of key.'

Eric sat up straight. 'A key?'

'Do you know something about it?'

'No, but it's always good to have an idea about what they are planning. It must be very important if they were willing to bring a human here.'

Kammy smiled, still feeling uncomfortable. 'You make it sound like...humans...are something really awful.'

Eric looked sheepish and scratched the back of his head. He cleared his throat. 'So you really don't have this key then?'

'No. I don't have anything that they could want.'

Eric looked so confused that he appeared to be in pain. 'Then why do they want to kill you? Why would they go to the trouble of bringing you here, just to kill you?'

Kammy lifted her shoulders. How would she know? She still had a million questions flying around her head, breaking through the clouds of disbelief, but she could hardly bring herself to ask them. It struck her that they had been talking as though they had all the time in the world. Her sentence could be carried out at any moment, no matter how she pleaded for sense. She felt sick.

'Kammy?'

Her hand clutched her stomach when she looked at him.

'I'm going to get you out of this.'

In a small voice, she said, 'Why would you do that?'

He shrugged. 'Why would I not?'

Kammy's chest strained with the ache of keeping hope at bay. Eric's eyes were so full of sincerity that it was almost impossible. She did not want to believe him. Why would he risk so much for a stranger? No person could be that kind.

'Why are you even here?' she said, finally.

Eric's skin darkened to a shade just lighter than his hair. He laughed, 'I was actually supposed to break into a different cell. I must have miscounted on the flight up here. Which reminds me...'

He started to stand and Kammy felt a surge of panic. She lurched to her feet too. 'Don't leave me.'

Eric's eyes widened. Kammy's palpable terror made him step closer to her. He hesitated before placing a hand on her shoulder. 'I have to. I can't get you out of here on my own. But I promise I will come back.'

Kammy's insides were squirming. 'What if they come back before you do?'

Eric squeezed her shoulder. 'You really think I would have sat here talking to you all this time if I thought there was any chance they would come for you so soon? You'd be surprised how long it takes to organise an execution.' Kammy turned a deep shade of green and Eric's smile faded. 'Sorry. I promise, okay?'

Kammy did not trust herself to speak. She had no choice but to watch him go. She stepped away from him and nodded. Eric did not hesitate. Watching him shift was no less unbelievable than the first time. Kammy's heart started to beat faster, but she felt more curious than afraid. It looked as though he were folding in upon himself. It should have been impossible, yet it happened right in front of her eyes. In seconds he was a mouse again, with fur the same shade of red as his hair.

Eric looked up at her and Kammy knelt in front of him. He touched the tip of her finger with his nose and scampered away through the hole in the wall.

Alone again, and the cell shrunk around Kammy. Her eyes ached. They were raw from crying and from the brightness of the walls, but her body felt infused with sudden energy. Eric would save her and she would get a second chance that she would not waste. She yearned for her island, bleak and dull as it was. Pacing from wall to wall, she forgot about the bumps and bruises all over her body.

Her heart raced along with her thoughts. Every second was agonising and Kammy could not stop moving. If she stopped then there would be nothing to distract her from the fear that crept along the edge of her mind. The fear that the next sound she would hear would be that of the metal door opening. The fear of tinted blue armour, come to end her life within these white walls.

Perhaps Eric had no intention of returning? He had seemed honest and kind, but Kammy did not know him. If she did not know him then how could she trust him? The energy that had surged through her went out like a light. She stopped and stared at the hole in the wall. She willed Eric to appear, but he did not.

A different mouse did and it pushed free of the hole. This mouse was a chocolate brown colour with a vivid white stripe down its left foreleg. Its eyes fixed on Kammy with such intensity that it might as well have been a giant bear. The mouse began to shift and Kammy marvelled at the sight. Soon a second boy stood before her. She hardly noticed Eric appear beside him.

He was dressed much like Eric, though his shirt hung looser on his slimmer frame. His hair was a fluffy, chocolate mess. He was taller than Eric and he glared between them both before his eyes came to rest fully on Kammy. The first thing she noticed was the purple bruise on his cheek. The second was how bright his blue eyes were.

'What is this?'

His voice was cool and Kammy tensed. He talked to Eric while continuing to stare at her and there was nothing friendly in his expression.

Eric shrugged, 'We're not leaving her, Jad.'

Kammy edged closer to Eric, sorry for doubting him for even a moment. Although she did not understand why he was grinning. Nothing about the situation was amusing.

'We need to leave now,' Jad's eyes finally left hers and Kammy took a breath.

'I promised her.'

Jad's jaw clenched. 'And how are we supposed to get her out of here?'

Eric's grin widened and he curled a finger into his mouth. He popped something out into his palm. Kammy frowned; it looked like a ball of blu tack except that it was orange. He held it up between his thumb and fore-finger. 'Welm gave me enough.'

Jad fell silent and Kammy could tell from the way his brow lowered that he was thinking hard. He had an air of authority about him. Eric had seemed friendly from the start, but Jad was different. He was harder than his red-headed companion; cooler. He made her feel nervous.

His gaze drifted to the door, 'the Armours will be on us in an instant.'

'We'll have a head start, and there are only two of them.'

Jad scowled. 'There are only two of us.'

Kammy bristled.

'Eryn might...'

'Eryn might not be anywhere near here.'

Kammy clutched her hands together to stop them shaking. She looked up at Eric and he smiled at her. The coldness in Jad that made her shrink away did not faze Eric at all.

Jad sighed, pushing his hair back and shaking his head. 'Can we really risk everything for this?'

Eric's eyebrows shot up. 'Don't even try it.'

Jad stared at him. His mouth fixed open as though he wanted to say something clever but could not. Kammy looked between them with mounting suspicion until, to her surprise, Jad laughed and all her attention was drawn back to him. He looked much younger when his expression was not so severe. He rubbed a hand along his jaw. 'You have me there.'

Kammy was lost. Her tongue stuck to the roof of her mouth. She could not demand that they explain themselves; she could not make a sound. She could only stare at them both while her mind screamed that they should hurry the hell up.

'We'll do it.'

Jad spoke to Eric as if Kammy was not there. She was almost too annoyed to feel relief that he would help her.

'Can you manage it?' said Eric, 'you'll have to carry her.'

Kammy felt her heart sink. She did not like the idea of being carried by either of them, but she looked at Eric with his strong arms and thick chest and felt sure he was the safer bet.

'I can manage it.'

Jad sounded bored. Kammy had to rein in her irritation.

Eric nodded. 'Then let's not waste any more time.' He stepped towards the hole with the orange ball in his hands. 'This will be fun,' he winked and popped it into his mouth. He started to chew as he knelt beside the wall. Kammy had given up on trying understanding anything at all, ever again.

She felt a light touch on her wrist and Kammy looked up.

'You'll want to stand back,' Jad said, and then the touch was gone. He moved away from her as silently as he had approached. Kammy caught her breath. His sourness was infectious. She glared at his back, following him to stand beside the door. He turned to face Eric and she did the same, keeping a few yards of distance between them.

Eric glanced back their way with a grin as he continued to chew. Kammy was just starting to wonder whether he had any plan after all. Then he gave them both a thumbs up. She felt something move beside her and she turned to look at Jad, but he no longer stood there. Kammy let out a strangled cry and a piercing blue eye swivelled towards her. In Jad's place stood a giant eagle with a sharp beak and razor talons. Kammy took a step back, but then she heard Eric shout.

'Cover your eyes,' he roared, charging towards them. Quiet was no longer necessary.

Kammy dropped to the floor on instinct, throwing her arms up over her head as the wall exploded. Her mouth opened and she knew that she was screaming, but all she could hear was the ringing in her ears as she slammed against the wall behind her. She spluttered, choking on the dust that billowed around them. She felt a hand grip her arm and push her forwards.

'Go, Kammy,' Eric urged.

Kammy's senses reeled and she stumbled towards the eagle, towards Jad. She stretched out a hand, but she did not know what to reach for. She faltered and the sound of grating metal sent a spasm of terror through her.

'Go.'

Jad started to move and Kammy cried out, but then Eric's arms were around her. He half lifted, half threw her onto Jad's back and Kammy gripped clumps of feathers, clinging on with all her strength as Jad rocked beneath her. She heard a shout from behind them. A hole gaped in the wall ahead. She could see nothing but blue sky beyond it. Jad charged forwards as a much smaller bird, Eric, shot past them.

Kammy heard another shout and then she heard nothing as they plummeted over the edge.

CHAPTER SIX

FLIGHT

The floor disappeared from beneath them.

Kammy screamed. The air rushed around her and she could feel that she was slipping. She gripped with her legs as her hands tore at feathers. She tried to close her eyes, but they were forced open by the fall and they streamed as colours raced past her. Then Jad threw out his wings and soared.

The rushing did not stop and Kammy pressed her chest against him. Her face froze in a terrified mask. Her stomach had been left somewhere far above, but wonder kept her focused. A giant waterfall thundered down beside them, every drop glittering like jewels. It plunged down a cliff, lush with greenery, but Kammy could not follow its path. She could not look down.

She held herself still as Jad beat his wings, lifting them higher. The air was warm. She could feel heat on her back and sweat on her palms. She clutched at his feathers, but it was near impossible to hold on. His feathers were so soft, so smooth. Kammy groaned and closed her eyes, willing it all to end. She was lying on the back of an eagle that was actually a young man.

It did not end. In fact, it got worse. She heard more wing beats stirring the air and she knew that they were being followed. She took a breath, and another, but they were short breaths of hot air that did nothing to calm her. She tried to rouse herself. She should have died in that cell, but somehow she was saved and at least now she had a chance. That thought sparked a semblance of courage within her and

Kammy opened her eyes just a crack, lifting her head as much as she dared. She looked back over her shoulder and the breath was knocked out of her.

Kammy could see the palace built into the cliff face. It was a majestic construction. Its white walls stretched up into a cluster of turrets and towers. Its façade was broken by gigantic windows that reflected a rainbow of colours. Two waterfalls flanked the palace and filled the chasm running far below them; a chasm bridged by a staircase of monstrous size. But Kammy hardly noticed how far she would fall should her grip fail. The giant structure that speared out of the palace and up into the sky commanded all of her attention. It burned her eyes so she could hardly look at it, but at the same time she could not look away. It looked like a white diamond. Each of its countless edges sent off shards of brilliant light. It dwarfed anything that Kammy had ever known and she had never felt as alive as she did in that moment.

Jad turned and the moment fractured. Kammy gripped hard with her knees as she felt herself slide. Her eyes dropped from the palace to the sight beneath it. Two birds were racing towards them, towards Eric who had fallen behind. The guards were gaining on them and while they were smaller than Jad, they were larger than Eric. Kammy felt a pang of guilt; if they had not brought her with them, they would have been able to flee quietly. They would be safe.

'They're coming,' she whispered, leaning as close to Jad's head as she could. She did not know what else she could do.

She had no idea if Jad heard her, but he beat his wings again and they shot forward. Kammy glanced back to see the palace and its diamond-like adornment fall away. They were now flying over a sea of trees, but the guards were even closer. One of them was right on Eric's tail. He dived suddenly and Kammy gasped, but the second guard ignored Eric and headed straight for her. Its talons were outstretched. It was metres away. Kammy swore and flattened herself against Jad.

If he did not hear her then he sensed her fear. Jad pulled up and turned sharply, his large wing cushioning Kammy and stopping her from falling. The guard barrelled past, surprised at first, but it was smaller and faster. It came at them again and when Jad tried to turn it turned with them, darting between Jad's wings and sinking its talons into Kammy's shoulders.

Kammy cried out in pain as she was lifted. The talons dug deeper, tearing at her, and her shoulders burned. Jad beat his wings again and again, but he could not shake the guard off, not with Kammy on his back. Kammy could feel something hot trickling down her arm and her stomach rolled as Jad's feathers slipped through her fingers. She ground her teeth together. Then she clenched her hand into a fist and swung it up over her head. She swung both fists, shrieking as she struck again and again. The guard squawked and squawked and then Kammy felt something crunch. The talons released her and she dropped onto Jad's back as the guard spun away.

Jad straightened out and Kammy stared at her grazed knuckles in astonishment. Her shoulders stung and she could hardly breathe. She looked back again to see Eric sweeping towards them. His guard had disappeared and the other hovered for a moment as it tried to regroup. When it saw Eric closing in it darted away, back towards the palace.

Kammy had helped. A part of her wanted to squeal with delight because she had done something. The fact that she had not been completely useless made her giddy. She lay flat against Jad's back, breathing short and exhausted breaths. When she tried to move, her shoulders protested so she stayed still. Even the pain could not quench her euphoria. Eric flew alongside them and she felt Jad tip forward gently; they were descending.

From where she lay Kammy could still see the palace, but they had flown so far that she could also see the bottom of the staircase and the city that sprawled down the mountainside. Alashdial looked as beautiful as its name sounded, but with every second they were further away. Kammy could not make out details, only that the city was very large. It stretched beyond the mountains base, thinning out until it hit a wall that circled its entirety. Beyond the wall the forest that they were flying over spread, and Kammy thought of Daleswick compared to such grandeur. She had to remind herself that she would no longer wish to be brave enough for adventures and that she would be happy with her lot, but it was difficult with so much adrenaline shooting through her veins.

They were skimming over the thin tops of the trees. Kammy could have leaned a little to the side and touched the leaves. She thought she might be smiling if the flight had not frozen her face in place. As Jad ducked into a clearing and drifted to the forest floor, Kammy took a deep breath. The scent of the trees and the earth was so familiar. They hit the ground with a soft bump and almost immediately Eric was there, smiling at her, his hair less bright in the shade of the trees. He lifted her down with ease and Kammy gave him a quick smile of thanks. Then she sank to the floor, her legs not quite ready to function.

'Are you alright?'

The eagle had gone and Jad stared down at her. Kammy temporarily forgot how to speak. There were dark shadows around his eyes and the blue was even more pronounced. He waited in the silence and his eyes drifted to her shoulders.

'You're bleeding,' he said.

Kammy lifted a hand, but her shoulder hurt and she winced, letting her arm drop. She nodded, wondering why her tongue suddenly felt ten times too big.

'We're not far from the village,' said Eric. Jad turned away from her and Kammy felt like an idiot. Eric held out a hand. 'Once we get there we can talk properly about taking you home.'

Kammy took his hand and stood on weak legs. The adrenaline started to fade and while her pride at fighting the guard still lingered, the thought that it would soon all be over overwhelmed her. The word home made her feel weary. It felt like she had been gone a lot longer than a few hours. She nodded at Eric; nodding seemed to be all that she could manage.

Eric turned to Jad, 'Are *you* okay?'

Jad smiled, and it lightened the shadows on his face. His eyes swept over the trees that surrounded them and he clapped a hand onto Eric's shoulder. 'I was not expecting to see you or the forest again anytime soon. I'm more than okay.'

Eric gripped his arm and grinned, 'You're welcome.'

Kammy watched them both, but more often than not her eyes drifted to Jad. Now that she was out of immediate danger she found herself wondering why he had been locked up in the first place. What could he have done? Had she been rescued by a pair of petty thieves or something much worse? As if sensing her gaze on him, Jad looked at her. Kammy's cheeks grew warm and she looked away.

'Come on,' said Jad, slapping Eric's back, 'we should move in case they come after us.'

'I doubt they will,' said Eric, but his eyes drifted upwards and Kammy shivered despite the warmth beneath the trees.

Eric looked at her and Kammy did not need any encouragement. Her fear of the guards returning her to that cell spurred her leaden legs to move. The boys started along the rough path before them and Kammy picked her way along it, settling in behind them. Silence fell, with Jad clearly as exhausted as she was. Eric seemed to sense that neither had any energy to spare for conversation. Kammy knew that she should be asking questions and demanding explanations, but whenever she tried to think of something to say she found her mind full of dust and rubble. Her head began to hurt again so she discarded the notion and let the sounds of the forest lull her. She would be home soon enough and none of it would matter.

Amongst the trees, Kammy thought she might as well have been home already. The birds chirping overhead, if they were truly birds, sounded the same. The dips and rises coated in grass looked much the same. Only the heat and two boys marching ahead of her reminded her that she was someplace unknown.

Semei. Shapeshifters. Her first instinct to laugh remained strong, but she had *seen it*. She had flown on the back of an eagle. All logic repulsed the possibility, but it was real.

Kammy pulled her mobile out again and was not surprised to see that it was still dead. She hoped that Jamie and her Gran were not too worried. She would tell them everything, even if they thought she was mad. And she would tell them that she loved them. She would tell them that every single day. The thought of seeing them made her smile, even as the heat and the pain wore her down.

The next thing she knew, Jad's hand was clutching her sleeve. Kammy's heart jolted against her chest. Eric had frozen. He stared off into the trees while Jad stood taut beside her. Kammy heard a soft snuffling coming from a bush ahead.

She heard the clattering of hooves and a doe leapt towards them. Jad pushed Kammy back and she tripped, hitting the ground with a cry. Then Eric laughed and Kammy gaped.

The doe had vanished and in its place was a dark skinned girl who threw her arms around Jad's neck with a cackle of delight.

'You're okay,' said the girl, shaking him a little in her excitement.

Jad laughed and hugged the girl back. Kammy watched, stumbling to her feet and feeling more drained by the second.

'Of course I am,' said Jad.

The girl pulled back and beamed up at him, her amber eyes bright. She brushed her fingers over his bruised cheek and her smile faded, but Eric cleared his throat pointedly. She glanced at him and smirked. Hopping towards him, she punched his arm. 'You're the hero of the day then?'

Eric swatted her hand away and tugged playfully on the long braid that hung down her back. 'I told you I would be.'

Jamie always likes to call himself a hero, Kammy thought. She watched the three friends together and she felt more out of place and alone than she ever had. When the girl finally noticed her, Kammy shrunk away. The girl was tall. Her black braid hung to her waist and her eyes narrowed.

'Who's this?' she said, folding her arms.

Kammy watched their smiles fade and she tensed. She willed herself to speak, to show something of herself, but she was silent. She looked to Eric and he took his cue.

'This is Kammy,' he said, 'we're helping her get home, Tayah.'

Tayah wrinkled her nose. Her eyes moved slowly over Kammy and she sniffed. Suddenly, her eyes bulged. 'She's *human*?'

Kammy's hands curled into fists at her sides. Hatred blazed on Tayah's face, hatred that she did not even attempt to hide. The diamond structure over the palace, the waterfalls and the city had been beautiful, but the people in this place, this layer, were rotten. Except for Eric, who watched her with an apology clear in his eyes.

'She's had a rough day. So let's get back quickly, all right?'

That was Jad's voice. Kammy peeked up at him from behind her thick hair to see him holding Tayah's arm, his mouth close to her ear. He had not expected Kammy to hear him and she wondered if the Semei thought that all humans were half deaf or if it was just her. Tayah shrugged Jad off, shooting Kammy one last glare before turning back the way she had come.

'Everyone will be so relieved to see you,' she said, 'both of you.'

Jad started after her with a contented smile on his face. Eric glanced back to check that Kammy followed. She nodded at him and forced her feet to move. The thought of lying down and sleeping appealed, but she rubbed her eyes and ignored the stiffness in her shoulders. She did not want to be any more of a burden.

There was no longer silence. Tayah's arrival had improved Jad and Eric's moods immensely. Kammy's eyes fixed on Tayah's, walking between the boys. She had her arms hooked through theirs for a while, and then she jumped on Eric's back. The next moment she gripped Jad's arm and giggled, whispering something in his ear. Their laughter bounced from tree to tree and Kammy drifted behind them like a ghost. She knew that Jamie would not have stood for it. He would have forced them to talk to him, to include him. Then she remembered the way Tayah had looked at her, simply for being human. Even Jamie's charms would not be enough to break through that wall of judgement. Kammy had always insisted to herself that Esme alone could make her feel small; she had been kidding herself.

The air hung heavy beneath the thick cover of branches and leaves. It filled her lungs and her nose. She did not feel the same euphoria she had experienced when she had unknowingly stood in this forest the first time. She was too drained. Kammy wiped sweat off her brow and pushed her dirty, tangled hair back off her face in an attempt to get cool. Her head swam and she stumbled. She felt sick, but she kept moving, afraid that if she stopped none of the others would notice. When she heard the faint tinkling sound of water, Kammy wondered if she had started to hallucinate.

'We're here,' said Jad, and his face lit up.

He stood beside a small stream, little more than a trickle of water winding beneath the trees and skipping over stones and twigs. Tayah clapped her hands and started running, with Jad close at her heels. Eric remained, a broad smile slapped across his face.

'Follow me,' he said, and so she did.

She felt very nervous. Eric moved slowly at first, following the course of the stream at a pace that Kammy could easily match, but Jad and Tayah soon disappeared from sight. Excitement got the better of Eric. He moved faster and faster, Kammy tripping and swearing behind him as she pushed her muscles to keep up.

When the trees began to thin, and a village appeared before them, she felt relief. Eric did not stop so Kammy did not either, but her eyes drank in as much as they could manage.

The village was quiet, the soft sound of the stream cut right through its middle. The birds still chirped around them. Kammy could hear other sounds too: laughter, shouting, a dog barking. It smelt of baking bread, like the Cooper's bakery. There was nothing majestic nor terrifying about the simple stone buildings. Jad and Tayah stood beside a wooden well. Tayah pulled herself up to sit on its edge, kicking her long legs and laughing. People were beginning to gather around them, most of them were old. They pulled Jad into hugs and planted kisses on his forehead. Face after face split by a smile. Jad's did too and his eyes shone. Kammy had doubted that he was capable of such emotion. Eric joined them and he was swamped as well. Kammy hung back as the village welcomed Jad home. She decided that he could not be a criminal unless the whole village was part of his gang.

Thinking too hard about anything made Kammy's head swim, so she stopped thinking and she swayed. She watched as an old woman placed a fair haired boy into Tayah's arms, and then froze when the woman looked directly at her. Kammy braced herself to see the accusation in her eyes; *you're human*. But it never came. Nobody seemed to notice as the woman slipped away from the crowd and walked towards her. As she got closer Kammy realised that she wasn't really that old; no older than her Gran at least. Her hair was as grey as her eyes, a few strands escaping from the headscarf that she wore. She was short and broad with a weathered face, but she moved easily. Her back was straight and her eyes glimmered with life.

'Charming young men, aren't they?' The woman spoke with a thick accent and a smile, 'Leaving you alone over here.'

Kammy decided that she liked this woman, though for some reason there was two of her.

'Come, I think you need to rest.'

Kammy started to nod. She stepped forward, but the woman multiplied. *How odd*, Kammy thought, right before she fainted.

CHAPTER SEVEN

OUTLAWS

Kammy's cheek squashed against something soft. She blinked, hardly able to comprehend the fact that she felt cool and comfortable. Her body still ached, but it was more of a distant pain that she could push to the back of her mind. She remembered stumbling into the arms of that kindly woman and she cringed. She had fainted and despite the coolness of the dark room, Kammy felt her cheeks grow warm. She was grateful that she had been brought inside to save her from embarrassing herself further.

The only light in the room crept beneath a curtain in the corner and between the shutters over the window. Kammy lay on her front on a bed. Somebody had thrown a thin sheet over her, which had bunched around her feet. She lifted a hand to touch her hair and found it damp, clean and free of tangles. Her head still felt groggy and her shoulders stiff, but she sat up and scanned the small room. The stone walls and floor were bare. There was a dressing table, a stool, a wardrobe and the bed, but nothing more. It was all very simple and plain. Truly, she had hoped to open her eyes and find herself home, but her new reality surrounded her still. Although, now she had rested, a part of her yearned to ask questions. While she was here she might as well learn as much as she could about this world she had discovered.

The smell of something cooking wafted through the long curtain that acted as a doorway and Kammy could hear voices from behind it. She stood, tentatively at first, until she was sure that her legs would carry her. Her work apron and her boots had been left at the end of her bed. She slipped the boots on, for the stone floor chilled her, and moved quietly across the room. She pulled the curtain back an inch and peeked through.

She looked into a large kitchen, or so she assumed for she could see no oven or fridge. A long table ran all along the back wall and a rusty tap in the corner dripped over a metal bucket. A smaller table sat at the centre of the room with a fruit bowl placed on it. Tayah was sitting there with the fair haired little boy bouncing on her knee. Eric had his back to her and Jad leant against the wall, staring out the window.

Kammy was about to pull back, not wanting to draw Tayah's attention, when she noticed a fifth figure sitting on a stool beneath a rail of cooking utensils. It was a scrawny little man. He had tufts of white hair sprouting from the sides of his head, leaving a bald strip down the middle, His hands moved with incredible speed over a chunk of wood that he held up beneath the faint light from the window. He chipped away at it with a knife, his eyes large behind thick rimmed glasses. His eyes did not seem to blink and his pale skin was practically translucent. Kammy looked away only to find that Jad had straightened to look right at her.

Kammy snapped the curtain shut and swore under her breath. She clapped a hand against her forehead. 'You're so *stupid*,' she hissed at herself.

She heard chairs moving and then footsteps. Kammy backed up towards the window. She peered through the shutters and watched Jad jog away from the house, followed closely by Tayah. Kammy shook her head and padded back to the bed.

She had left the shutters open and the added light bounced off a jug of water that she noticed for the first time on the dressing table. There was a glass beside it and Kammy poured herself a drink. She gulped it down, hoping it would sweep away the last cobwebs of sleep. Her eyes returned to the window and she told herself to get out there and talk to somebody. That was what Jamie would do, but the thought alone made her insides squirm. She could see people outside. They were all strangers, with that same odd accent. They would stare at her and they would judge her. She would rather wait. She gulped down some more water and leaned back against the wall.

She noticed that a little face was watching her. The blonde boy peeked through the curtain, his amber eyes round as he stared.

Kammy smiled at him. 'Hello.'

He took a quick step into the room, his hands clasped together in front of him. His fringe hung into his eyes and he shook it away. Kammy did not think he could be much older than five. Surely she could handle interaction with a five year old.

He grinned. 'Hullo.'

'What's your name?'

'Boo.'

Kammy laughed, 'I'm happy to meet you, Boo. My name is Kammy.'

Boo wiped his nose on his sleeve and stared at his feet. He rocked onto his heels before looking up at her from beneath his long lashes, 'What's a human?'

Kammy started to speak, but no words sprung to mind. She was saved by a shout from the kitchen. The curtain was pushed back and Eric stepped into the room with a steaming bowl in his hands. He smiled warmly at Kammy, then turned stern eyes to Boo.

'What did we tell you, Boo?'

'But I didn't disturb her,' Boo pouted, 'she was awake.'

'It's fine, really,' said Kammy, earning a beaming smile from Boo.

'You're off the hook then little man,' said Eric as he ruffled Boo's hair. Boo pushed him off and scowled. 'But didn't Welm say he needed your help with something important?'

Boo's eyes lit up. 'He *did*?' Without another word he scampered away, almost tearing the curtain down in his eagerness to get out.

Eric laughed and sat down next to Kammy, handing her the bowl. 'Here,' he said, 'made you some soup. Well, it wasn't just me, Jad helped. It's not much, but we thought you should eat something. I was going to put some chicken in it, but then I thought you might not eat meat so...'

Kammy took it, her stomach growling. 'Thank you.'

'You're welcome.'

Kammy waved the spoon towards the curtain. 'His name is really Boo?'

Eric snorted, 'Yeah, it stuck.'

Kammy was going to laugh, but after one spoonful of soup she was ravenous. She glanced at Eric in apology as she stuffed spoonful after spoonful into her mouth, her Gran's insistence on proper table manners forgotten. She was relieved to find that shapeshifters did not eat strange food, at least not all the time.

Eric laughed. 'There's more if you want.'

'Oh, no...' Kammy managed as she scooped up another loaded mouthful.

'I suppose now is a good time to fill you in then,' said Eric, resting his elbows on his knees. 'Jad's gone to get Fii. She's the boss around here. I think she wants to ask you a few questions. She's the one that treated your shoulders. That was really impressive you know, the way you fought the Armours.'

'Armours?'

'The ones that came after us. It's what we call them. They've not been around for long. You did well. I thought we were finished when they grabbed you.'

Kammy felt a flush of satisfaction. 'I just got lucky.'

'I reckon that all luck is accompanied by some skill.'

'I really don't think that punching a bird in the face requires that much skill.'

Eric shrugged, 'Thousands of feet in the air? I'd say it does. And it definitely takes some courage.'

Kammy glanced at her grazed knuckles and grinned, She *had* fought back, though she certainly had the cuts to show for it. 'What is that on my shoulders by the way? It feels weird.'

'It's a cream, an antiseptic. It will stop your wounds from getting infected. That numb sensation will wear off and it will probably start to hurt again, I'm afraid, but it should help the healing process. Fii also suspects you might have concussion and we don't know how the atmosphere here will affect you. So if you start feeling sick at all, just let me know.'

Her desperation for food started to wear off and she placed the bowl down at her feet. 'Is Fii a doctor?'

'No,' said Eric, 'but she is an incredible woman; strong and very intelligent. She takes care of us all. She washed your hair too, thinking you might feel better if you woke up fresh.'

'And she wants to ask me questions...like an interrogation?'

'No interrogation. She's just curious about you,' he smiled, 'we all are. You don't have to answer anything if you don't want too, we'll still get you home.'

Kammy nodded. She would try her hardest to help these people, though she did not really know what she could tell them.

'When will that be?' said Kammy, 'When will you take me home?'

Eric placed a hand on her arm, 'Soon. You were out of it for a couple of hours. Fii didn't want to wake you. I think she just wants to see that you're okay first.'

'So then, I have time to ask a few questions of my own?'

Eric hesitated, '...sure.'

Kammy took a moment to organise her thoughts. 'Won't the guards, the Armours, come after us? It doesn't seem like this place is very well hidden.'

'They might, it's a bit complicated,' said Eric, with a surprising degree of calm, 'Dorren had been left in charge and he's a fool. We would never have risked saving Jad otherwise, he would have been guarded much more securely. Even if they do come after us, they don't know where we are and we have our ways of disappearing. We'll be fine.'

Kammy's hunger became a hunger for knowledge. 'But why do you have to hide? Why was Jad in the palace in the first place? And where are we anyway?'

'Whoa,' Eric held up his hands, 'slow down.'

'I'm sorry,' Kammy blushed, 'I just have so many questions now that everything is less life threatening.'

Eric nodded, 'That's understandable.' He took a deep breath. 'Let's do this one at a time then. *Here* is a village called Littlebrook. Alashdial lies to the north, and Emire is the next closest town to the east. Other than that, there are lots of villages and smaller settlements dotted about. If you meant *here* even more literally, then this is Fii's house; as modest as the woman herself. As for your other questions, I'm not really sure how much I should say...'

'It's not like I'm going to tell anyone,' Kammy laughed, 'and if I did, who would believe me? I don't have any way of proving any of this.'

Eric looked at her and she could tell that he was weighing it up. She bit her lip and crossed her fingers in her lap. 'Okay,' he said, 'I guess I can tell you the condensed version. Jad is, well, wanted.'

Kammy blinked. 'I didn't think that he seemed particularly nice, but I had actually scratched out the possibility that he was a legitimate criminal.'

Eric chuckled and shook his head, 'He's not a criminal. Well, technically he's an outlaw but he's not the bad guy. His full name is Jadanim Ollarion; he's part of the last royal line. The Ollarion's founded Alashdial long, long ago.'

'So he's a prince?'

'In a way. We haven't had a monarchy for centuries now so those titles died out, but the Council has always been headed by an Ollarion. His grandfather, his father, and then it was supposed to pass to him.'

'Oh...' Jad was descended from royalty? Somehow it did not surprise her. He certainly seemed haughty enough.

'Two years ago, something happened. It's a long story that only Jad can truly tell, but a man named Bagor took over rule of Alashdial. He bribed men and women that were once loyal to Jad's family and he manipulated the people. He locked Jad up. He told the people that he was merely assuming the role of regent until Jad was of age, but the Council had already been abolished.'

Kammy took a moment to think. She was still tempted to reject everything that he said. Shapeshifters and royal bloodlines combined sounded like some sort of fairytale. Yet her mind ignored all sense and raced ahead of her. 'Even I can see through that lie. If he was only going to hand power back to Jad, then why would he get rid of the Council thing?'

Eric looked impressed. 'Exactly. Everybody saw through it but, in a way, he was doing the people a favour.'

'How so?'

'If he had told them the truth then they would have felt even more guilt when they did nothing to act against him.'

'But shouldn't they have done something? Revolted or...I don't know, something?'

'It's not that simple. We Semei...we have been a peaceful race for as long as anyone can remember. The people don't know how to fight.'

'You fought. You and Jad did.'

'That was a scrap, nothing more, and we've been preparing ourselves for a long time now. No, to rise against Bagor would have been civil war. Nobody was, or is, prepared for that. Besides, life under Bagor's rule did not change, not at first. The people had to look out for their own interests, above all else. They had to carry on with their lives.'

'While Jad rotted in a cell...'

Eric nodded. 'But there were people still loyal to him within the Palace. They helped him escape. It was a great victory for us, but Bagor hardly seemed to care. He has never put much effort into getting him back.'

'Why? Wasn't he afraid that Jad would turn the people against him?'

'As long as Jad was locked up, he was a reminder to the people that what Bagor had taken was not his. With Jad forced to remain outside the city walls, he can at least spread the tale that Jad had abandoned his people and that Bagor is just doing what is right by ruling in his place.'

'But that's rubbish. Can't you just tell them the truth?'

'I suspect that they know the truth Kammy, or that they did once. It's just not worth the fight. Not now.'

'Then why are you here? Why do you fight at all?'

Eric's eyes grew bright. 'Because Bagor is evil. His words are his greatest strength and they are poison. He cannot be allowed to get away with what he has done. I fight for Jad, but also because I know that it's the right thing to do. There must be justice. One day we will find something. We will find his weakness and when we do we will exploit it and Jad can take back what is his.'

Kammy heard the tremor in his voice. He believed what he was saying with a passion that she had not yet seen in him. He looked more a man than a boy and his conviction was almost enough to sweep away her own doubts.

'So, if Jad had been free for this long why was he in the palace today?'

'They got him yesterday. There has been a lot of activity near the Gate recently so Jad took it upon himself to check it out. We wouldn't even have known he was gone if Welm hadn't been out in the forest and seen them take him. We only had one shot to get him out. We were scared that we were finished. I never expected it to go so well.' Eric paused and his eyes shone with mischief, 'I shouldn't tell you, but when I got into Jad's cell he explained what had happened. He got into a tussle with Ria and before he could get away, Armours swamped him. He was caught because he saved some human girl. Of course, he wasn't expecting to see you again.'

The room around her fell away. Kammy stood in the forest with Ria bearing down on her, but then there was a voice; a deep voice that told her to run. And further back, she was outside the Mouth and there was something rustling just ahead. It was a squirrel with a white stripe down its foreleg. It had been Jad all along.

'You can't tell him you know. He might murder me.'

'I just...' Kammy shook her head, 'I just thought that he was really rude.'

'He *was* rude. One act of chivalry doesn't change that. But he's a good man. He wouldn't be my best friend if he wasn't.'

Kammy frowned. 'And Tayah? Is she good?'

Eric scratched the back of his head. 'Ah, she's complicated. I'm sorry if she...well...'

There was a tightness to his expression that told Kammy he would not elaborate, no matter how hard she might press him. She snatched at the first thought that floated through her mind. 'Are they together?' She quite liked the idea of pairing them off as one bulk of rudeness.

Eric's eyes widened. 'Jad and Tayah?' He threw his head back and roared with laughter.

'Sorry,' Kammy felt her face redden, 'are *you* and Tayah...'

'No,' Eric choked, his whole body shaking, 'by the Mother, no. Jad and Tayah would kill each other, and Tayah isn't exactly my type. We're just friends, all of us. We have been for years.'

Kammy kept her mouth shut, feeling stupid. That only made Eric laugh harder and before she knew it, Kammy giggled too.

'So,' she said, 'what is your type?'

Eric smirked. 'Blonde haired, blue eyed men.'

'Oh.'

'Is that surprising?'

'A little...' Kammy admitted. She still giggled. 'I prefer dark hair myself.'

Eric snorted and nudged her gently, 'I'll keep that in mind.'

Kammy beamed at him. She had only ever had one friend but, looking at Eric, she thought she might like to have two.

'May I come in?'

Kammy glanced up. The woman she had fainted on stood beneath the curtain, smiling at her. Kammy nodded, glancing at Eric. He patted her knee in reassurance. The woman stepped inside and the bug-eyed man followed after her, his gaze latching onto Kammy immediately. She squirmed, inching closer to Eric.

'How fascinating, that we understand one another. After all these years, humans and Semei speak the same tongue. How...' the woman trailed off and shook herself, 'my apologies, I can't help but wonder.'

Kammy had not even considered how lucky she was that she and Eric had been able to communicate when she had been in that cell. Ria too, had spoken the same language. It *was* fascinating, now it had been pointed out to her. Before she could ask more about it the woman spoke again.

'My name is Fii and this is Welm.'

Welm bowed his head and said nothing.

Kammy clasped her hands together, 'Thank you for looking after me. I really appreciate it.' She started to stand, 'Would you like to sit?'

Fii waved her away, 'Do not be ridiculous dear. I only wish to know how you are feeling.'

'Much better, thank you.'

'I filled her in,' said Eric.

'Good,' Fii nodded. Welm stood behind her shoulder, his stare fixed on Kammy in such a way that it made her shiver. 'We are all very sorry that this has happened to you and we want to get you back to the surface as quickly as possible, but we would also like to understand why you're here. Do you mind if we ask you some questions?'

'No,' Kammy's voice was small, 'of course.'

Fii smiled at her and pulled up the small stool beside the dressing table. 'Don't worry yourself. If you can't answer, you can't answer. It's not a problem.'

Eric shot Kammy a look as if to say I told you so and Kammy forced herself to relax.

'Now,' said Fii, 'Eric told me that you do not recall passing through the Gate so I wondered, what is the last thing you remember before waking in your cell?'

Kammy took a deep breath. 'I was in my bedroom. I was on edge and the window was open so I closed it. But there must have already been someone inside. They hit the back of my head and that's it.'

Fii looked thoughtful. 'But you had already found your way into our layer once before that?'

Kammy kept her eyes on Fii, but she was constantly aware of Welm watching her. 'I guess so. I mean, I didn't know that I had but I saw that woman, Ria, in the forest.'

'How did you get there?'

'I run in the forest, when I need to think. There's a place I go to, an animal's burrow. I'd never entered it before, it had never really looked big enough. But all of a sudden it seemed the perfect size. It makes no sense when I try to explain.'

'Interesting,' Fii mused, 'humans cannot normally see the Gate. Perhaps your exposure to it, having spent so much time nearby, is the reason it appeared to you...'

'Why can't humans see it?'

'We do not know for sure. It is taught that humans have long forgotten us Semei, and with those lost memories they refuse our existence. They do not see it because they do not wish to see it.'

Kammy frowned. 'That sounds...'

'Ridiculous?' Eric suggested. 'Maybe we will never understand the truth of it, but denial is a powerful thing.'

Fii nodded and fixed her gaze back on Kammy, 'Continue, if you will.'

Kammy pulled her mind back on track. 'The tunnel led me out into the forest again. I thought I was still on Daleswick. I think I might have known, deep down, that it wasn't my forest but I just couldn't believe it.'

'That is understandable,' said Fii. She fell silent for a moment and then glanced at Eric. When she looked at Kammy her eyes were more curious than before. 'You escaped from Ria with Jad's assistance?'

Kammy shot an alarmed look at Eric.

'Eric told me,' Fii rolled her eyes as she laughed. 'Protecting Jadanim's ego is not worth keeping something so important from me.'

'Right,' said Kammy, wondering what happened when a person disappointed Fii. She had a feeling that the outcome would be quite horrific.

'You really know nothing of this Key?'

Welm's voice sounded as small as he looked. Kammy could not help how her eyes narrowed as she looked at him and how her tone became defensive. 'No, I don't.'

Fii gazed out the window, 'This Key might be the only explanation as to why you're here.'

'It was a misunderstanding,' Kammy insisted.

'Yes,' Fii nodded, but she hardly sounded convinced. She stood suddenly, 'You've finished your water. Welm shall fix you a hot drink,' she looked at him and he hurried off. 'Eric and I will gather the others soon enough. Then we shall take you home and you can forget all of this.'

Kammy was so stunned by the abrupt end to the conversation that she spluttered, 'But I thought you wanted to ask me things...more questions?'

Fii stepped closer and after a moments hesitation, she placed her hand on Kammy's cheek. Kammy stiffened, but Fii's eyes warmed. 'There is nothing more to ask of you. Relax and we shall fix this.'

'But my Gran...how can I explain?'

Fii smiled, 'That is your decision. If you wish to be honest then there is nothing we can do to stop you.'

Kammy nodded despite her surprise. Fii turned away and Eric followed her. He looked back when he reached the curtain and smiled. Kammy thought that he looked sad. Then she was alone with her confusion.

Seconds later she heard somebody clear their throat. Welm stood before her, his pallor interrupted by blotchy red patches. He looked as awkward as Kammy felt when their eyes met. He held a mug in his hands and he held it out to her in silence. Kammy took it, noticing how the reflection of the light on his glasses meant that she could not see his eyes. She did not thank him, she only stared.

He backed away from her slowly. Kammy dropped her eyes to the mug, willing him to go away and wishing that Eric was still beside her.

'It's hot lemon,' he whispered, and Kammy suspected that was how he always talked.

She could smell the lemon in the vapours. She closed her eyes and sipped it, taking care that it did not burn her tongue, but Welm was still there when she looked up.

'I'm sorry for everything that has happened to you.'

The blotches in his face spread and darkened, his whisper grew even fainter. Kammy realised that he was embarrassed.

'Thank you,' she said, and he bobbed his head before scuttling away. Kammy watched the curtain fall shut with a frown. The way he had looked at her made her squirm with discomfort. She stepped over to the window and watched Welm hurry away from Fii's cottage. She had never met a person that made her feel that way before.

Kammy took another sip of hot lemon, savouring the way it soothed her throat. She stayed at the window, though she could not see much from where she stood. There was another house next door and a path that led towards the well. She could hardly believe how calm she felt considering all that she had seen and heard, and all that she could not see. She noted that there were no cars and no streetlights. This world was different to hers in so many ways and she felt a little like she had stepped back in time. It was serene. Nature pressed in around the village and there was barely a sound to disturb it. She wondered how long it would take to get home, and what else she might see on the way.

The door of the house opposite opened and Jad stepped out with a broad smile on his face. Kammy ducked, not wanting him to spot her, but he did not look her way. The bruise on his cheek shone like a beacon as he disappeared round the corner. Eric said that he was royalty, that he was important. He was a mystery that had begun to unravel, but soon she would be gone and she would never know any more about Jadanim Ollarion.

Kammy yawned and her eyelids fluttered. She felt so tired. Her arms and legs weighed her down. She floated back to the bed and felt herself sinking down onto it with a sigh. She could hardly keep her eyes open. She looked at the mug in her hands, but her vision started to blur. The mug dropped onto the floor with a clatter. Welm had brought it to her and he had seemed so nervous.

Kammy tried to stand again, but her head was resting on the bed. She tried to call out but her eyes closed, no matter how hard she fought against it.

CHAPTER EIGHT

A SHATTERED WORLD

Kammy shivered and pulled the covers up to her chin. She could hear something whistling in the distance. She yawned and rolled onto her back. Her shoulders burned and she gasped, falling back onto her front with a sigh. She sank into the pillows. Her legs were splayed. Her toes clung to the sheets. Forget Jamie, her bed was her true best friend.

Kammy started. She was in her bed.

She squeezed her eyes shut and counted to ten, but when she opened them once more it made no difference. There was her peeling orange wallpaper and her plain white duvet. She sat up slowly, her eyes wide. There was her bookcase, there was the mess that she had left on the floor and outside the closed window rolled puffy dark clouds that could only belong to Daleswick. Kammy pressed a hand to her forehead, but she did not have a temperature. She was home. Maybe she really had been dreaming?

Kammy kicked off her covers and sat up, but a pain shot through her back. She reached a hand up to her shoulder and felt the tears in her top. She still wore her work clothes and the wounds on her shoulders were very real. She remembered the hot lemon and the fear she had felt as she slipped into unconsciousness. The memory of Welm chilled her, but she focused on the overwhelming positive; she was safe. Eric had accomplished what he had promised.

Kammy stood and laughed as she felt the familiar roughness of the floorboards beneath her feet. She stretched as well as she could without it hurting and walked over to the window. The sun was rising and the village below bathed in its orange light. Beyond it she could see the road winding away to Erinsdale, and a lone bus trundling along. She blinked back a surge of emotion. She was home and safe. She could boil the kettle and sit at the kitchen table with her Gran again.

Her heart clenched and a smile split her face. '*Gran...*'

She dashed from her room and leapt down the stairs. The clock above the kitchen sink told her that it was not even seven in the morning, but she did not care. She threw herself past the bathroom and against Irena's bedroom door.

'Gran,' she burst inside.

Her grandmother's bedroom was empty. The bed had been made. The layers and layers of sheets and mauve blankets had been made immaculately. The one eyed teddy bear that had once belonged to her mother sat in its place between the pillows. The wardrobe stood at an awkward angle, having been dragged out of its usual corner. Harry had not been up to help yet. Kammy stepped out of the room and huffed. This was a record early time for Irena to be up and on her way to town, but she did like to get her shopping done early. Kammy did not want to have to wait. She wondered how long she had been back in her bed. If her Gran had found her sleeping she might not have noticed that she had ever been missing. Still, Kammy thought as she turned into the bathroom, she would tell Irena the whole truth. She needed to or she thought she might explode.

She had a quick, somewhat awkward, shower as she tried to keep Fii's dressings dry. She towel dried her hair and scrubbed her face. She ran upstairs to throw on jeans and a t-shirt and then she returned to sit at the kitchen table. She felt refreshed and happy. The aches and pains made as much of an impression on her as a sleeping ghost.

The first ten minutes or so passed quickly. Kammy stayed still, content to sit on the same rickety chair she had sat on for seventeen years. She smiled at the crack in the window. The memory of Irena's fury when faced with her granddaughter bouncing a tennis ball indoors was so distant that Kammy could now find the humour in it. She noticed the faded corners of the green kitchen tiles, the last splash of their original colour. She tried not to think of how the green was the same shade as Eric's eyes. She thought it might be best not to think of

Eric at all. She had the only friend that she needed. She did not want to see Eric again.

Kammy thought of returning to her room and reading a book, but she did not move. Now she had stopped to wait, she could do nothing else until she heard her Gran's voice. For the thousandth time she cursed Irena's refusal to buy a mobile phone.

Kammy's gaze latched onto something and her smile froze. A solitary mug sat beside the kettle. Her Gran liked to keep the kitchen spotless at all times; mugs belonged in the cupboard or on the draining board. Kammy frowned and went to pick it up, but she pulled her hand back when she saw that the mug was not empty. Stone cold tea filled it and the teabag had not been removed. The microwave door was ajar too. She pulled it wide to find a bowl of soup inside. The soup was cold and lumpy. It must have been there all night. It was unlike Irena to waste food. Kammy took a long breath and a chill passed through her.

She walked to the phone on the wall. If Irena had been worried about Kammy then that might have been enough to put her off her food. That was what Kammy told herself as she dialled the number for the pub. She listened to it ring without breathing, but nobody picked up. It was still too early. The clang of the phone as she placed it back on the hook echoed in her ears. She shot upstairs to grab her phone. It was working again. She had no messages, but she did have signal. She pulled up Jamie's number, accompanied by a picture of him wearing nothing but a pair of Superman pants, and called him. The line beeped three times and went dead. He must have turned his phone off when he went to bed; so much for him being worried about her.

Indecision gripped Kammy. She was sure that her Gran was in Erinsdale and that she would be home soon enough. She did not need to worry, but she could not help it. She needed to see the face of somebody she loved so badly it hurt and all the while she felt that something wasn't right. She told herself to stop being paranoid and that she should just wait. Instead she slipped on her trainers and pushed open the already unlocked front door.

She stepped out into the cold and her feet moved automatically. Her eyes were not tempted to the trees at her back. As the clouds parted above, they remained fixed on the village of Lumbersdale. For the first time in weeks the island saw the blue sky of morning and the sea watched, quiet and still. It was going to be a beautiful day, Kammy insisted to the fear that lay siege to her heart.

But the fear was strong. With every step she moved faster until she sprinted, her hair whipping up behind her and the cool air snapping at her lungs. She shot down the path and past the gate. She hit the deserted road that cut through the village and raced on. The colourful walls seemed to glow beneath the sun, making everything look more vibrant. Kammy was sure everything as okay because why would the world look so captivating if it was not? The pub loomed before her and she ducked into the back garden that led to the side of the building where Harry lived with his wife.

Kammy trampled the weeds that sprouted through the cracks in the patio floor. She slammed against the door and pounded on it with her fist. She knew that she was going to look like a fool. She knew that Harry would be angry, but she did not care. She grabbed the door knocker and slammed it over and over again until she heard a muffled grunt and a lock being unbolted.

Gasping for breath, Kammy stepped back and patted down her still drying hair in an attempt to make herself look less dishevelled. Harry opened the door and glowered at her through tired eyes.

'Is my Gran here?' Kammy blurted, 'Have you seen her?'

Harry blinked a few times. His morning stubble and his bed hair would have made Kammy laugh had she not been so desperate. To her surprise his eyes widened and he beamed down at her. He grabbed her in a bear hug and lifted her off the ground with a laugh.

'Kam,' he cried, 'you're alright.'

He placed her down again when she squirmed and Kammy took a step back. 'Is she here?'

'No,' he said, laughing again and gazing at her in wonder, 'she called last night to fill us in. She's probably out looking for you. What happened?' His gaze grew stern. 'You can't just disappear on us like that.'

'But...'

'All day yesterday we were out looking for you. We had the police down from Erinsdale and everything. Where were you? Irena was frantic.'

Kammy stared at him. All day? But she had worked at the pub that afternoon. She had only been gone one evening.

The longer she stood there, the more Harry moved beyond happiness at seeing her and into anger. 'How could you do that to her? You're all she's got.'

'But she's really okay?'

Harry took a breath. 'Yes. Now, where is Jamie?'

'What?'

'Helen hasn't left that house since you both disappeared. We kept telling her you'd turn up, but she didn't believe it. Kept saying she always knew this would happen. Poor thing...'

'I...' Kammy felt the world shift beneath her feet, 'I haven't been with Jamie.'

Harry trailed off. He laughed once as though he thought she was joking. Then the colour fled his face, 'You haven't?'

A sharp noise split the air and Kammy jumped. Harry swore. He pulled her inside and shut the door. Only then did Kammy realise that the sound was the phone ringing.

Harry looked lost. 'I have to take this, it's important. But...damn. You wait here. I'll be right back.'

Kammy nodded. She kept nodding even when Harry had disappeared upstairs. She drifted back to the door and outside again. She could not wait. She needed to get back home and she needed her Gran to be there. She needed somebody to tell her what to do because Jamie was missing and no matter how hard she tried to ignore it, a voice in her head told her that it was her fault. The mouth of the forest loomed in her mind. She had to do something, but she did not want to face the truth. She did not want to think of the Semei and the layer beneath the surface.

She did not look where she was going. Instinct carried her forwards while she focused on fighting panic. She walked into something that smelled of fresh bread and perfume. She muttered an apology and continued on.

'Kammy?'

She had never heard that voice sound so small and it broke through the fog. Kammy blinked as she looked up at Esme. The blonde girl hugged a bag of bread to her chest and her eyes were red-rimmed. They stared at one another as silence pushed in around them.

84

'You're alright,' Esme whispered.

Kammy's throat tightened. She could only watch the warring emotions dance across Esme's face.

Esme finally dropped her eyes to her feet. Her own throat worked. 'I'm glad,' she said. The air stilled around them and Esme's words disappeared as quickly as they came; Kammy could not believe that they had existed at all.

Esme gathered herself. Her bright eyes snapped back up to Kammy's. 'And Jamie?'

Kammy felt a fist close around her heart and tears rushed to fill her eyes. What had happened to him?

Esme took a step forward, her eyes round. 'Kammy...what about Jamie?'

Kammy shook her head and took a step backwards.

'Kammy,' Esme's expression hardened. 'Where is Jamie?'

'I don't know. He wasn't with me.'

Esme looked as though she had been punched. 'But he's always with you. Always.' Her fingers swiped away a tear and her lip curled. She started to look more like the Esme that Kammy feared. 'Where the hell were you anyway? Esme spat. 'We were out looking for you all day yesterday while he...why weren't you with him?'

Kammy turned away from her.

'You should have been with him, Kammy.'

'I know,' Kammy moaned. She staggered forwards, but Esme grabbed her arm and jerked her back.

'Don't you care?'

'Of course I care,' Kammy tried to pull free, 'how can you say that?'

'Then why are you here? Why aren't you looking for him?' Esme howled, 'Why weren't you with him?'

A deep growl reached their ears and Esme let go of her with a yelp. Kammy blinked through her tears and felt her breath catch. A wolf sat in the road behind her. It was as tall as she was, its fur shone silver in the sunlight and its bright blue eyes glittered. It bared its teeth as it padded closer and Kammy stared at it in wonder. Somehow she did not feel afraid. Esme dropped the bag of bread and screamed. She tugged at Kammy's elbow but when Kammy did not move she swore and ran, shouting something that Kammy did not hear.

Kammy sniffed and wiped her eyes with her sleeve. She drew in a shaky breath. This was no ordinary wolf.

'Eric?'

The wolf held her stare. It was a beautiful creature, spotless but for the white stripe that ran down its left foreleg.

Her heart thumped. '*Jad?*'

The wolf's head bowed and she knew then, for sure, that Jamie had been taken. Taken somewhere beneath the surface and it was all her fault for ever entering the forest's mouth.

'Help me,' she whispered.

He turned away from her and leapt forwards. With a cry Kammy jumped after him. They were going to go back. She was going to have to swallow her fear, for Jamie's sake.

Kammy was suddenly grateful that it was early, and that the village still slept. She focused everything on the steady rhythm of Jad's loping bounds. She no longer felt sore or stiff, she felt nothing other than the air on her cheeks. They left the village behind them as the sun climbed the sky. Kammy fixed her eyes on the forest, more determined than she had ever felt before, but Jad veered away. She followed him, confused, as he sped towards her house. Her head had cleared and purpose drove her on. She felt a flash of indignant fury and she aimed it at Jad. If the Semei had not drugged her, she might have had time to help her friend. Jad charged through the front door of her home and she clattered in after him. By the time she had pulled the door shut, he stood before her.

He looked strange inside her kitchen; awkward and out of place. Kammy opened her mouth to ask what they were doing, to tell him that Harry would come after her at any moment and that they needed to leave, but she said nothing. He was even more intimidating now that they were alone.

He did not hesitate. 'Where is the Key?'

Kammy was so surprised that she found her voice, 'What?'

'Oh, you *can* talk.'

Kammy glared at him. 'You drugged me.'

'*What*?'

'The drink. It knocked me out,' the words tumbled out of her, 'why did you do it? I might have had more...'

'We drugged you out because we wanted you to know as little about us as possible. Eric shouldn't have answered your questions. We wanted you to forget about us. We wanted you to be angry.'

'Well, I am angry.'

He held himself still. 'That was when we did not think we would see you again. Now, things are different. Where is the Key?'

'I don't know and I don't care. They've taken Jamie. They've taken my friend and we have to go now, we have to go and get him.'

'We are not going anywhere until I have the Key.'

'I don't have it.'

Jad's eyes sharpened, 'I felt it the moment I came through the Gate and I feel it even stronger now. It's how I knew this was your home. I can sense it so you must have it. You must have something from our world.'

Kammy felt a pain in her head that was becoming all too familiar. 'I don't...' Her eyes widened and Jad took a step towards her. She dashed past him and up the stairs. She left him behind her as she ran into her room and threw herself down beside her bed.

'What are you doing?'

He stood over her as she fished around beside her bed. Then she grasped the pebble from the forest. The pebble that she had not been able to throw out, no matter how much she had wanted to. She held it out to him. He took it, but the disappointment etched into his features made Kammy's heart sink.

'Is that not it?'

'It must be,' said Jad as he held the blue and purple pebble up to his eye. 'It is certainly from our layer. I just...thought it would be something more impressive.'

Kammy shrugged, 'I *did* find it on the floor of a forest...'

He looked her in the eye. 'I can feel something though. It does not belong on the surface. Do you have something to carry it in? I can't pull it into the shift.'

Kammy nodded. She grabbed her old school bag from the end of her bed and dropped the pebble inside.

Jad stepped back towards the door. He scowled, 'Come on then.'

Kammy held the bag to her chest. 'Wait.'

'But you just said...'

'I know,' Kammy shot a dark look at him. 'But I wasn't thinking. I have to wait for my Gran, she's worried enough as it is. I can't...'

Jad's jaw clenched. 'We don't have time.'

'Why?' Kammy's voice shook, but she held her ground, 'Why don't we have time? What happened?'

Jad's nostrils flared. His eyes threatened to break her with the force of their intensity, but Kammy pressed her lips together and refused to let it happen. A muscle twitched in his jaw and then his eyes fell away, hidden beneath dark lashes.

'Ria sent word to Bagor and his response reached the palace while you were in Littlebrook with us.' He spat Bagor's name with venom. 'They had already taken your friend. They came for him as soon as you escaped.'

'But why? Why Jamie?'

'We underestimated how much they wanted you. We thought that once you had gotten away they would give up. We thought that they only wanted you dead because they did not know what else to do with you, but they started searching for you almost immediately. They expected us to bring you straight here and Ria lay in wait. Your friend came looking for you,' Jad shrugged, 'and found Ria instead.'

Kammy sank onto the edge of her bed, 'I still don't understand...'

'Did you tell him about that stone, Kammy? About Ria?'

Kammy looked up at him.

'Because he knew about it. He told Ria and they took him as leverage, so that you would hand over the Key.'

'Then they can have it,' Kammy cried, 'I'll give it to them. I don't care what happens to it. I don't care about them, or you. I need to get Jamie back.'

'No.'

'Didn't you hear me? I don't care about you or what you think.' She tried to push past him. She did not know where she would go without him, but she knew she did not want to look at him anymore. Something about him made it hard for her to think.

He stepped in front of her. 'This is not about me.' His voice whispered power. Kammy stopped, keeping her eyes averted. 'This is not about any of us. It is about you. They will kill you if you stay here and they will kill you if they catch you. You have to come with me.'

Kammy trembled, 'Why do you care if they kill me?'

'Because Fii and Eric insisted, of course.' he said, with the faintest of smiles.

Kammy puffed out her cheeks. 'But Jamie...'

'I promise,' Jad held her gaze, 'we will work something out.'

Kammy looked into his eyes and wondered if she could trust that promise.

'My Gran...'

Jad placed his hand on her wrist and Kammy shivered. He did not seem to notice. 'She might worry, but I am sure she would prefer you to be alive rather than dead.'

'Will she be safe?'

'They already have their leverage. They do not need more.'

That was no answer.

Kammy looked at her bed and the covers all bunched at one end. It felt like seconds ago since she had woken and sprinted down the stairs to see her grandmother's face. She glanced out the window at the clear blue sky. How could such a glorious day hold so much horror?

'Okay,' she murmured.

'Then we have to go right now.'

He tried to hide his urgency, but she could still hear it. Her eyes drifted around her room one last time and landed on her mother's face. She lurched forwards.

Jad reached for her, 'What...'

She danced around him and snatched the picture frame from her bookcase. Her fingers brushed her mother's smile as she placed it inside her shoulder bag and zipped it shut. Kammy squared her shoulders and took a deep breath.

'I'm ready.'

Jad paused, watching her, and then he nodded. She followed him down the stairs, her heart thumping and her hands clenched to stop them shaking.

'I'll shift here.'

'Why not when we reach the Gate?'

Jad shook his head, 'We'll be quicker if I carry you.'

Kammy remembered the flight and the terror that had accompanied it. Her stomach turned, 'No...'

'Kammy,' Jad closed the distance between them and gripped her shoulders. Her voice shrunk to a squeak. He was not as tall as Jamie, but somehow he seemed much bigger. 'We have to go now, but I need you to promise that you can hold it together. If you fall, I might not be able to help you.'

Kammy swallowed, 'I promise.'

It scared her that when he shifted it did not affect her. It scared her that she was already growing used to it. She did not want it to become normal. Then again, she did not want to go back to the Semei world and to live in constant fear, but she had too. She had no choice.

The silver wolf led her out of her home and Kammy did not look back. If she had, she did not think she would have been able to find the strength to leave.

She looked ahead and her heart sank. Harry Whistler puffed up the path, his head bowed as he jogged towards her. He looked up and jerked to a halt. Kammy wondered what he thought seeing her standing there, her hand on the wolf's neck with the glow of the sun behind them.

'Kammy...' the fear in his voice carried towards her and she flinched.

'Tell my Gran I'm okay,' she shouted back as she pushed herself up onto Jad's back.

She did not know if Harry shouted again or if he tried to run after them. She could not bear to look and as soon as her hands gripped the scruff of fur around Jad's neck, he took off. Kammy clung to him, pressing her knees into his flanks and her face into his neck, keeping as close as she could. It was better than the eagle. His fur was thick and soft beneath her and he no longer had wings that threatened to beat her backwards. He smelt like wood smoke and grass. She inhaled and tried to relax, but it was impossible. She was ridden with guilt for the people she was leaving behind and for the danger that she had placed Jamie in.

The shade of the forest cooled the morning and Kammy shivered. She ignored her body's yearning for more layers as she remembered the strange heat of the Semei world. She would not be cold for long. She watched the trees flash past. Jad did not trip or hesitate; he ran so smoothly that Kammy felt sure he glided over the earth. They quickly reached the mouth of the forest and Kammy had to bite back her fear.

'Wait...'

Jad ignored her as she knew he would. They did not have time for hysterics. She had already wasted enough. Jad leapt down the bank towards the burrow, now large enough for a wolf and its rider to fit through with ease. Jad did not pause, but as they passed through Kammy felt them spin and her hands slipped free. The mouth was the Gate, she knew it surely then. Kammy felt like she had fallen, but when the world righted itself she still sat on Jad's back and he still ran down a path just wide enough for their passage.

Kammy held on and closed her eyes. There was no turning back now.

It was strange being with somebody yet feeling so alone. She could talk to him, but he could not respond so she kept silent as he carried her forwards. To what, she was not sure. She had no control over what was happening. He could take her anywhere and she would have to trust him. She trusted Eric and if Jad had come for her at his request, then she supposed she might trust him a little.

Before she knew it she hung upside down again and then they burst out into the heat of the Semei layer. Jad did not slow and for a moment everything was still around them. Kammy felt something stir inside her as the warmth of the air kissed her skin. Light glanced through the trees and Kammy threw up a hand to shield her eyes. A weight crashed into Jad's side.

Kammy almost flew from his back but Jad righted himself and ran once more, away from the dog that snapped at his tail. There were more dogs around them, snarling and gnashing their teeth, but there were other animals too. A large cat jumped onto the back of a hound that blocked Jad's passage. Jad swerved and the muscles in Kammy's legs burned as she struggled to hold on. An ambush had been laid for her and Jad had been expecting it. She did not look back as Jad left the fight behind. The trees swamped them and the forest grew quiet. Only then did she notice they were not alone. A doe ran alongside them, and a fox bounded at their heels. They ran together, never slowing. Kammy's knuckles ached, but she clung on.

It came as a shock to Kammy when Jad stopped abruptly, but the doe and the fox were already changing. Within seconds Tayah and Eric stood beside them. Tayah turned away, her shoulders tense and her eyes scanning the trees. Eric smiled at Kammy and held out his hand. She took it and slid off Jad's back; she was happy to see him, but he did not look quite as pleased.

'What's happening?' she asked, breathless.

'They reinforced the guard on the Gate, four instead of two. We thought that they would.'

'Won't they come after us?'

'We had help.'

Kammy turned when he spoke and struggled to hide her alarm. Jad leant against a tree, his hand pressed into his side and his breathing short. His white face looked furious.

'Some of the villagers offered to distract them so we could get you through,' he said with an effort.

'But,' said Kammy, 'won't they get hurt?'

Eric's eyes were on Jad, but he answered Kammy. 'They were only meant to keep the guards occupied while we got away. Then they were to disappear and lay low for a while before returning to Littlebrook. The guards were not expecting a large force, only me and you. The villagers have the greater number. They'll be fine.'

Kammy felt sick. She glanced back over her shoulder and pictured the dogs again, with their sharp teeth and their raking claws. Those people had risked their lives for her sake, for nothing.

Tayah paced, 'We don't have time to stand around talking. We must keep moving. They'll be in the forest.'

'I...' Jad scowled. His jaw clenched so tight it looked like it might break.

'We can walk from here,' Eric cut in, 'as long as we start now.'

Jad's eyes danced away, but Kammy caught the flash of relief in them. She watched him for a moment, but there was nothing she could say. Her life was in their hands, and so was Jamie's. She would do what they told her to do until they were, somehow, safe.

'Did you hear anything?' said Jad.

Tayah whipped around with a sharp shake of her head and Eric's lips thinned. Jad looked startled for a moment, and then his eyes flicked to Kammy and away again.

'We should move,' said Eric, his voice strained.

The three of them turned their backs to her, but Kammy's feet remained planted. Her eyes narrowed.

'What is it?'

The boys looked at each other, then at her, then at the ground. Kammy looked between them, her heart sinking. She saw something change in Jad's eyes and she stared at him, afraid to speak again. It was Tayah's voice that cut through the tension. She huffed and her braid swung behind her.

'Your friend is dead. Now, let's go.'

PART TWO

EMIRE

CHAPTER NINE

STONE THROWING

Just as they had during the flight from her cell, Kammy's eyes changed. The pupils were swamped and the irises filled until they were orbs of impenetrable midnight blue. Her skin, already pale, paled further. Jad watched as something inside of her withered away. She looked smaller, fainter somehow. Jad waited for the hysteria for he knew something about grief, about the screams of denial and the tears. Instead, Kammy stood, silent and still, and Jad did not know what to do. He looked at Tayah, but she would not meet his eye; for once, she knew that she had gone too far. Jad clenched his jaw and turned away from all of them.

'We need to go,' he said.

Eric's, his shock obvious, said, 'Jad, can't we...'

Jad stared up at the trees overhead. 'We don't have a choice, Eric. The longer we stand around the worse this situation will get.'

'But...'

Jad looked at his friend and shook his head. Eric hesitated, the doubt clear in his eyes. He nodded, reluctantly, but they both understood that cold logic needed to win this time. Eric looked back at Kammy and Jad chanced a glance too. She had not moved or made a sound. Her eyes were dry, but still in their changed state. Jad felt useless. Without thinking, he clutched his left arm. No matter how hard he tried, the people around him would always get hurt.

Eric scratched the back of his head. Twigs snapped beneath his boots as he took a few tentative steps towards Kammy. He reached out a hand.

'Hey,' he said, 'can you...'

Kammy flinched away from him, 'I can follow.'

Eric pulled back, his cheeks glowing and his expression lost. Kammy's eyes remained fixed on the same nameless spot. Jad knew that he should say something, but his mouth remained pressed shut. There was nothing that he could do; he knew that well enough.

'I'll take watch,' said Tayah, tugging on her braid like she always did when she felt guilty about something. 'I'm the most rested of all of us.'

Jad nodded. Her doe's hooves faded quickly, but the tension remained. So Jad did the only thing he could, he moved forward.

He started walking, knowing that lingering would only cause them harm. He turned his back on on Littlebrook, on Alashdial, and he led them away. His whole body burned with exhaustion that ran so deep his bones ached. He could feel the skin on his feet and his legs stretching with every step. Even so, he was tempted to sink into his Soul. He knew he needed to save the little strength he still had, but they were moving so slowly and being slow put them at much greater risk. Armours could be on them at any moment; *would* be on them at any moment. Jad knew that it would take a miracle from the Mother if they were ever to make it out of the forest.

The thought struck him that he had not been beyond these trees since his father had died. Then, when Bagor had stolen power, he had not wanted to leave. He had been so afraid that if he strayed too far from Alashdial's walls he might miss his chance. The villages surrounding the city had been far enough until they had settled, mostly untroubled, in Littlebrook. Jad could hardly imagine life away from it, from the shadows of the forest and the shelter of the mountains. Jad scanned the ground for the closed Akasi pods. They were still there; he could not remember how far from the Crystal they managed to thrive. He could not remember the last time he had sat and watched them bloom.

'This is it then.'

Jad started out of his thoughts. Eric walked beside him with a familiar smile on his face. He always smiled like that when he was

97

trying to pretend that he was not nervous. Jad gripped his friend's shoulder and said, 'It seems so.' He was grateful as ever that he was not alone.

Eric let out a low whistle, 'We've talked about this day for so long, dreamt of it so often, it feels odd that it is here; the day that we make a move against Bagor. It doesn't seem real. It doesn't feel like much of a rebellion.'

'It's more than we had yesterday.'

Eric laughed, 'True. It's just...different to how I imagined it.'

Jad smirked, 'Did you imagine us marching an army into Alashdial and reclaiming it as our own by force?'

'There is that,' Eric shrugged, 'but I meant...' he glanced over his shoulder.

Kammy had fallen back a little, but her legs continued to carry her forwards. She was still intact, still in one piece, but her quiet seemed unnatural. She moved like a doll on a string, stumbling every now and then. Jad wanted to shake her until she cried, then he might have some idea how to handle her. Not that he had ever handled tears particularly well.

Jad lowered his voice, 'We could move faster without her.'

'I wouldn't let you shift even if she wasn't here and you know it.'

Jad shot Eric a look, but pushed aside his frustration; he knew it all too well. 'It was as you said before. I couldn't just leave her, but...'

'She makes things difficult?'

'Not just that. She *makes* things, Eric. If you had not gone to her cell before mine then she would be dead by now and we would not know anything about the Key. We would still have nothing, and we would be doing nothing. She makes everything real. The risk is more than ever now. The risk that you and Tayah and everyone has taken by siding with me.'

Eric held up his hand. 'Please, not your speech again.'

Jad snorted, 'I won't bother. I know you will not listen.'

They fell silent and Jad lost himself in his thoughts once more. He could not help fearing the worst; that he had led his friends astray for a lost cause. That his dreams could never be realised. He was just a little boy playing at being his father.

'She should never have been able to find the Gate,' said Jad.

'I know.'

'And she should never have found the Key. It is Semei, I felt it.'

Eric scrunched up his nose, thinking hard. 'Maybe we've had it wrong all this time. Maybe humans aren't as dense as we like to think.'

Jad kept his voice low. 'Her eyes, Eric. Don't try to tell me you've not noticed her eyes; when she was afraid before and now, when she's upset.'

Eric looked at him.

'She must be Semei.'

Eric gaped and spluttered, 'What?' He saw that Jad was serious and laughed. 'That's impossible.'

'Why impossible?'

Eric leaned in close. 'Just because her eyes change does not make her Semei. I know that only Semei born from the lines have them, but maybe it's the same on the surface. How many humans have you met? How can you know there are no others like her?'

'There must be more to her,' Jad insisted.

'We don't go to the surface Jad. The few that do come straight back.' Eric shook his head, 'Besides, if she were Semei, then the years on the surface would have made her sickly and weak. Or she'd already be dead.'

'Then what is your explanation?'

'Like I said, maybe we know less about humans than we think. Maybe we've been arrogant fools to ever assume as much as we do.'

'Perhaps that is true,' said Jad, his fatigue making him even more stubborn than usual, 'but that does not change what I believe about Kammy.'

'Then why don't you talk to her about it?'

Jad shook his head, 'Not now, not after...' he trailed off, clamping his jaw shut when he heard a grunt from behind them. He whirled, crouching and scanning the trees for any movement. Kammy had fallen toher knees, her face hidden behind her hair.

Eric shot Jad an alarmed look and took a step closer to her, 'Kammy?'

Her head jerked up. She looked surprised to see them. She stood and clutched her hands to her chest.

'I'm fine,' she said, her voice as empty as her eyes.

'I'm sorry,' said Eric, his voice full of a warmth that Jad had never been able to mimic, 'we have to keep going.'

'We'll be safe when we reach the river,' said Jad, trying his best anyway.

Kammy pulled her bag back up onto her shoulder, 'I'm fine.'

Eric sighed and Jad knew exactly how his friend felt; helpless and guilty. Jad had to shake himself. Had they not rescued Kammy then she would be dead instead of her friend. That was something they could not have helped. That was to be blamed on Bagor. Jad scowled and kicked at a stone near his feet; it was all Bagor.

A keening sound announced Tayah's return. She skidded towards them on hooves that quickly faded, replaced by her grey boots. Her eyes were wide and her breathing fast.

Jad knew they had a problem.

'What is it?' he said.

'Four of them ahead,' she gasped, 'heading right for us.'

'Only four,' said Eric.

Jad nodded, thinking hard, 'Dorren hasn't worked out where we are headed. He's split the Armours up in an attempt to cover the whole forest.'

Eric grinned, 'He's an idiot. That's good, right?'

'Maybe.' Jad looked back at Tayah, 'We can't outrun them?'

She shook her head, 'Not with...'

100

All three of them looked at Kammy. She stared into her bag, showing no sign of having heard a word. Jad swore. He wished that they could leave her behind but she carried the Key and more than that, he knew he never would.

'We have to fight them.'

'How? You can't even shift.'

Jad glowered at Tayah. 'I can for this.'

'But Tayah is right,' Eric looked tired, 'There are four of them. We wouldn't be strong enough even if we were properly rested.'

'Then what else can we do?' Jad snapped. 'Do we sit here waiting until they stumble right on top of us?' Eric would not meet his eye. Tayah frowned at him, but neither spoke. Jad's voice softened, 'We might as well try.'

His words sounded hollow even to his own ears; he knew as well as they did that it was pointless. In saving Kammy they had surrendered themselves and their rebellion was over before it had begun. He had been kidding himself to think that they could ever succeed.

'We have minutes Jad,' said Tayah. Her eyes flashed at the thought; she had never been good at losing, but there was little chance of a different outcome this time.

'Shift and hide,' said Jad, 'maybe they will pass us by. If not, then we do what we can.'

Eric and Tayah nodded. She turned away, her hands clenched into fists. Eric tried to smile, 'We can always escape later. We're good at escaping.'

Jad smiled back, comforted by the knowledge that Eric and Tayah's lives would be spared. He turned to Kammy and she stared at him without blinking. Jad scanned the area and spotted a thick sprouting of bushes at the top of a small rise. They did not have time to talk so Jad grabbed Kammy's hand. She clutched at his fingers with surprising strength and Jad felt a stab of guilt. Jad's friends might be kept alive, but he doubted that Kammy would be afforded that luxury. The two of them were doomed.

Jad pulled Kammy up to the bushes and knelt before them. It would be incredibly uncomfortable, but there was just enough space for Kammy to crawl underneath. Jad turned to tell her so, but Kammy had already flattened herself against the earth. Jad placed a hand on her shoulder and she paused without looking at him.

'We will try and lure them away from you. When it's safe, run that way...' Jad heard Tayah huff. He was running out of time. He gave Kammy a gentle nudge. She started crawling again and he leant as close as he could so that she could hear him. 'Keep running straight until you hit the river. The land beyond it is Seeve's land. Bagor cannot touch you there; not yet.'

Kammy did not respond and Jad knew that she would be spotted easily should anybody look their way, but what more could he do? He took a deep breath, braced himself and touched his Soul.

The pain threatened to tear a scream from his throat. Jad clamped his jaw shut. He could see his wolf, as familiar as his own skin, but it resisted him. He forced his body to mould into its form while every bone, muscle and tendon roared in protest.

When he completed the shift Jad felt no relief. The pain remained and it took every ounce of his concentration to hold the wolf in place. He saw Kammy's eyes, dark and round, through the green. They shone, showing something other than deadness. Jad did not have time to ponder. His heightened sense of smell had caught their scent. They were mere metres away. He dragged himself behind the bush and lay silent, aware that he might slip and lose himself at any moment.

A rabbit scurried into his view and Jad knew instantly that it was no ordinary rabbit. It was too big, for one, and it moved with a careful precision not normally seen in such skittish creatures. Three other rabbits joined it and they huddled together. Their heads turned and their ears pricked. Jad could hear Kammy's rushed breathing. From the moment he had met her she had been frightened, but there would be no saving her this time.

One of the rabbits turned beady eyes towards the bushes and Jad tensed. Kammy smelt different. She smelt human. The rabbits ears twitched and it started to grow. By the time Jad burst from the bushes the rabbits were a pack of baying hounds.

Jad charged, forgetting the pain. He leapt at the closest dog with a snarl. The air rushed through his fur as he bowled it aside. He turned, landing on all fours, and a second dog bore down on him. Jad growled, swiping at it with a large paw, but the dog was smaller than his wolf and it ducked easily. Teeth sank into his foreleg and Jad howled. Adrenaline kept him focused. He had to lure them away from Kammy. He clamped his own teeth around the scruff of his attackers neck and he shook with all his strength until he tasted blood. He could see Eric and Tayah ahead. They had their backs to one another and were holding their own. Jad felt a surge of elation; maybe they were strong enough. Then he saw something crawling away from the bushes; Kammy. It was too soon, he thought, cursing her stupidity. She would surely be seen.

Something slammed into Jad's side. The dog in his jaws flew free and Jad hit the earth, skidding into a nearby tree. Winded, he struggled to stand. Two dogs padded closer to him, their tongues lolling and their teeth dripping. Blood oozed from the neck of one, but it did not appear weakened. Jad growled and bared his teeth, cornered and with no hope of aid from his friends. His moment of optimism passed. He crouched, ready to attack.

A jagged stone smashed into the side of the wounded dog's head and it slumped to the earth, unconscious.

Jad did not hesitate; he leapt at the second, clawing and swiping even as it felt like his muscles were tearing apart. His jaw latched on and he threw the dog high and far. It landed with a crunch and limped away without looking back. Only two remained and Jad spun to help his friends.

But they did not need his help. One of the dogs staggered from side to side, shaking its head and walking in uneven circles. A bloodied rock was still nearby. The final dog backed away from Tayah and Eric, surveying the scene. Tayah only had to trot closer and kick out to send it scampering away through the trees. Its companion tottered along behind, zigzagging as it went. They had won.

The wolf tore itself away from Jad, leaving him cold and wheezing on his back. The leaves of the trees swirled above him and he could hear the roaring of a wind that he could not feel. Jad closed his eyes and flexed his fingers to make sure that they were still there.

He heard Tayah's voice, 'By the Mother, what just happened?'

Then Jad heard Eric laugh, a great snorting laugh that seemed strange given all that had happened that day.

Jad opened his eyes and forced himself to sit up; then he saw what Eric had found so amusing.

Kammy had not run away; in fact she stood beside the bushes. There were twigs in her hair, dirt on her clothes and a huge stone in her hand. There were more stones at her feet too and Jad gaped at her.

It had been Kammy that had driven the Armours away.

Kammy had saved them.

CHAPTER TEN

THE CROSSING

They had walked through the day into the night and Kammy wondered how she would last much longer. She stumbled on, trailing behind the others. They were silent, exhausted, and all very much aware that they still were not safe.

Kammy's bag bumped against her thigh and its weight on her shoulder seemed to be all that stopped her from floating away. She had filled it with stones as she had walked and she kept a hand near it at all times. She remembered the look on their faces when they had realised what she had done. It almost made her smile. But then she remembered the blood and that moment of horror when she had feared that she had killed the first dog; a dog that had actually been a man or a woman. The nausea faded when she realised that its chest continued to rise and fall, but that impulse to smile dimmed. Then she remembered that Jamie was dead. Perhaps a heavy rock to the skull had ended his life? Any hope Kammy had of smiling was lost to her.

She could picture him so clearly that she was half convinced he would step out of her mind and breathe again. She could see his dusty curls and the steady warmth in his eyes. She could hear him teasing her, his lip curled and eyebrow raised. She could smell the scent of him and the way that his cheap aftershave never could completely mask the tang of the ocean salt on his skin. But what made it all so much worse was that Kammy felt nothing.

She stared at her feet and the old trainers that she had worn countless times in the presence of her friend. They took step after step without fail. Should she have fallen? Should she not be able to walk at all? Jamie was *dead*.

When her mother died Kammy had not been able to stop crying. She had not moved for days. She had cocooned herself in her room and she had sobbed until her tears had finally run out. But her mother had always been sick. In a way, Kammy had known that it was coming. She had been as prepared as any person can be, to lose somebody that they love. Jamie had been ripped away from her without warning. There would be no last joke and no last goodbye, but the tears would not come; Kammy felt nothing.

She thought of Helen, sitting alone in that big house waiting for her son to come home. All those years Helen had hated Kammy for no reason; at least she had a reason now.

Eric made her jump. 'That was quite impressive.'

Kammy looked at him and her face felt hot. He eyed her warily; guilt and pity and kindness clear in his eyes. He almost looked nervous. Did he see it too? How cold and heartless she had become?

Eric started to turn away and Kammy bit her lip. She did not feel much like talking, but she did not want Eric to be frightened of her either.

'I was picking them up,' she said, and to her relief he looked back at her. 'The stones and the rocks, I was picking them up as I walked. I spend...I used to spend a lot of time down at the beach skimming stones.' Her voice sounded strange. She cleared her throat. 'I thought that I might be able to help, somehow.'

'And you did,' said Eric, 'you have very good aim.'

'You just didn't see all the times that I missed.'

Eric laughed. Jad and Tayah, who had pulled even further ahead, glanced back in alarm for laughter was far from all of their minds. That only made Eric laugh harder. Kammy did not smile, but she thought that she felt some of the chill thaw. It was easy walking beside Eric. She looked up at him out of the corner of her eye and for one second he was Jamie. She closed her eyes and wrapped her arms around herself.

'Where is Fii? And Boo?' she asked, desperate to distract herself now that her tongue had loosened.

'Fii left with Boo as soon as we took you back. She had a feeling things would be getting more dangerous for us, and she was right. They should already be safe in Emire by now.'

'Emire?'

'A town in the Basin. It's a bowl shaped valley at the foot of the mountains, the second largest settlement on the continent, after Alashdial.'

'And it really is safe there?'

'It should be.'

Eric fell silent, but stayed close by her side and Kammy struggled with a thought that kept rising in her mind. It floated unwanted, but unrelenting. She hated herself for feeling nothing at all, but perhaps it was easier this way. Perhaps it was better to never ask.

She could not stop herself. 'What happened?'

Eric scratched the back of his head. He had been expecting the question, she could tell, but he had been as keen as she to avoid it. The words had fallen out of her mouth and she could not draw them back in.

'It was our fault. We thought they would focus on Jad, that he was the important loss.' Eric shook his head, 'we underestimated how much they wanted to get you back.'

'Jad told me some. How Ria was waiting for me, but took...' she swallowed, 'but how did you know?'

'We have people in the palace; spies, you could say. They got word to us quickly.'

'And the Key?' Kammy gripped her bag even tighter. 'Do your spies know anything about why they want it?'

Eric looked pained. 'Nobody does. They clearly want it desperately, but we have no idea why. I'm so sorry. You had no idea what you were getting into when you picked that thing up.'

Kammy's tongue sat thick in her throat. 'And how do you know for sure that he's...'

Eric moved as if to touch her and she flinched. He pulled back, his shoulders slumped. 'We have a witness. He saw them take him...I really am so sorry Kammy...'

'Don't...' She crushed her hands against her chest, fighting the pressure building inside. Eric took a step closer to her again and she turned away.

'It's here.'

Tayah's shout from ahead was a lifeline. Kammy clung onto it and pulled herself back from the edge. She sprang forward, away from Eric and his kindness. Her lifeless limbs managed to support her somehow. The trees thinned and she soon stood beside Jad looking down a short bank of patchy grass and mud. Eric followed and none of them spoke for a moment.

The river roared past beneath them and flecks of white froth were all that broke the silky black surface. The gathering night made the water appear opaque. Its mysteries were hidden from them and Kammy felt her stomach heave. She swallowed, lifting her eyes quickly. She could see the opposite bank. The trees seemed less dense and the earth sloped downwards, otherwise it looked much the same, and much too far away. Kammy heard the sound of waves breaking. She looked downstream before she could stop herself. Dark shadows rose like a wall of jagged shields. It took Kammy a moment to realise they were rocks. The water slammed into them and the current looked a lot stronger than Kammy felt. She was suddenly very cold.

'We have to cross that?' she said, her voice almost drowned out by the rushing water.

Jad looked at her. His eyes were a source of light in the falling dark.

'Can't we just fly over?' said Tayah.

Jad looked back at the river. 'Neither you or Eric can carry Kammy, and I...can't shift again.'

Kammy felt Tayah's gaze on her and she met it, her own eyes narrowing. She did not have the energy to feel intimidated.

Eric stared upstream. 'Why don't we follow the river until we reach a bridge?'

Jad shook his head. 'The roads will be guarded by now and we would be wasting time, asking for another attack.'

'Then how?'

Kammy watched Jad pull his sleeve across his brow. He took a deep breath before saying, 'You two fly and I'll wade across with Kammy.'

Kammy's stomach rose to her throat. 'What?'

'It's shallow enough. As long as we are careful then we can stand the current. It should only take minutes.'

He looked certain of himself, but Kammy did not feel reassured. She had noted, on some level, that he seemed to be making some sort of an effort. He was not being openly rude and he had come into her world with the intention of saving her life. But this was fast moving water and he looked dead on his feet.

'I hate water,' she said, lifting her chin and waiting for one of them to laugh or roll their eyes. They did nothing of the sort and they said nothing at all. Kammy understood that she was going to wade across the river even if they had to throw her in first.

'Are you sure?' said Eric, looking at Jad.

Tayah folded her arms, 'Yes, you're not exactly looking your best.'

'Go,' said Jad, with a tight smile, 'before I get offended.'

Eric and Tayah did as they were asked. Kammy felt the air stir behind her and then the two of them were flying and across. It took them no time at all and Kammy wondered what it felt like, to change oneself at will. She returned her gaze to Jad. His face looked hollow and his chest rose and fell faster that it should have. She had been so close to him when he had last shifted. She had seen that split second when his face had contorted in agony. She guessed it was not as simple as it looked.

'You can definitely do this?' she said, surprised at her own forwardness.

His shoulders tensed. 'I can.'

Kammy stared at the black water before her determined to ignore the rocks, but she could not help hearing them. Fear drove her, shooting through every part of her like a bullet train and the adrenaline that followed was welcome. It overwhelmed her and pushed aside the numbness. She could think of nothing else but the water; there was no ache of guilt or pain. She unclipped her watch and pulled her phone out of her pocket. Neither worked. She put them into her bag, zipped it shut and checked that it was secure on her shoulder. Then Kammy sat down on the bank and started to tug off her trainers. Any grip that they had once had had long been worn away. She peeled off her socks too and with Jad watching, she hurled them into the river. They were sucked away into oblivion with a faint plop.

'What did you do that for?' said Jad.

Kammy focused on steadying her breathing as she spoke. 'I thought that if I left them here the Armours would find them. Then they'd know exactly where we had crossed, right?'

Kammy was not certain, but she thought that Jad looked impressed.

He did not bother to take his boots off as he took a step down the bank. She was about to ask him if she could check the grip when he said, 'So, I get stuck with you again.'

Kammy started to follow him. 'You could always take the Key and leave me behind.'

Jad snorted, stopping when the water lapped at the tip of his boots. 'I'm tempted,' he said.

Kammy did not notice that a smile passed over her lips. He was a jerk, but he was a jerk with a fairly well adjusted moral code. He was not tempted at all. She stopped next to him and the imminent crossing commanded all of her attention.

'Stay on my right side,' said Jad, 'I'm stronger and will take the brunt of the current. We'll move slowly. All you need to do is hold onto my arm.'

Kammy nodded. She tried not to imagine the taste of the water in her mouth, the sting in her eyes and the smell up her nose. She grabbed Jad's arm and he tensed. She wished that there was some way she could hide her trembling from him.

'We'll be okay,' he said, sounding quite awkward.

'Let's just go.' She wanted to get it over and done with.

Jad stepped into the river and Kammy's bare feet followed. She gasped; ice filling the gaps between her toes. Her grip on Jad tightened but he eased her onwards without a word and she pressed into his side, as close as she could, with the water tugging at her ankles. She thought she heard Eric shouting something, but she could not make it out over the thundering in her ears. Her eyes were fixed on the black sheet before her and she imagined all sorts of terrors that might live at the bottom. Her feet sank into the mud, but with each step she feared something more horrific. Then she took another step and the water rose up to her chest.

Kammy cried out, throwing an arm forward and sending up a great splash. She gasped, losing her balance and the water rose up to swamp her, but Jad's strong arm gripped her shoulders and pulled her back to his side.

'Sorry...' she breathed.

He stood still, looking down at the top of her head. 'You okay?' His voice shook from cold.

Kammy closed her eyes and tried to remember how to breathe. Now that they were standing still she could feel the tension in Jad's body as the water buffeted him. Her teeth chattered and her skin tingled; it was freezing. Her clothes were weights, desperate to drag her down into the blackness. Something slimy brushed over the top of her feet. She did not want to be in the water any longer than she needed to be.

'Okay,' she managed, and they started moving again.

'You're halfway there,' shouted Eric, his words encouraging enough that Kammy looked up and caught a glimpse of his smile.

Jad groaned.

They staggered together and stopped. Jad's grip on her shoulder changed; he was holding on to her, she was the one supporting him.

'What...' she could barely talk, 'what's wrong?'

He shook his head and took another step. The water rose to Kammy's shoulders and panic rose with it.

'Jad...'

He turned his back on the current, his expression grim and his face tinged with yellow. His hands found her waist and he lifted her. For one moment she rose free of the water, but then Jad's eyes widened and that was not all. His bright blue irises swamped the rest of his eyes until that blue was all that she could see. Kammy gaped at him; she had watched the same thing happen to her own eyes her whole life. Then Jad slipped and Kammy screamed as his hands were torn off of her and she plunged into the water.

Ice filled her throat and she chocked. Her back slammed into the mud. Her hands clawed at nothing as her ears and eyes drowned in water. The current carried her backwards towards the rocks; rocks that would smash her to pieces. Kammy kicked and kicked against the weight of her clothes. Her head broke the surface. She tried to draw breath, she heard somebody shout her name, and she was pulled back under.

The darkness was absolute and the cold burned every part of her. Her brain told her to keep kicking, but her legs would not move. Her chest burned and a loud buzzing filled her ears. Was this how her father felt when he died? She pushed at the water with weak arms, but she could not stop the current from hurtling towards the rocks.

Something soft and warm curled around her side. She jerked but it held on, pushing her and lifting her; it was helping. Kammy knew that it was Jad and she blinked away the spots from her vision. She kicked again.

When her head broke the surface again the bank was close. Her feet struck mud as she coughed and spluttered. She dug numb toes into it, gripping on, and she crawled with tears of shock and pain in her eyes. The weight supporting her disappeared and the full force of the current slammed into her side.

Kammy could not move. It took all of her strength to stay rooted. Her toes and her fingers clung to mud that dissolved beneath her. The muscles in her arms and legs strained and she ground her teeth together. Her body began to rock and she whimpered; she could not hold on.

A strong hand hooked her arm and dragged her forwards. Kammy grabbed at it, flinging out her other arm and she was pulled free of the mud and the water's deathly grip.

Gasping and retching, Kammy stayed on all fours. She shook so violently that she knew her legs would crumble if she tried to stand.

She looked up and blinked several times to make sure that she was not seeing things. Tayah sat before her, not Eric or Jad; Tayah had pulled her from the river.

'Thank you,' Kammy whispered.

Tayah took that second to scowl at her and then she turned away, her expression changing to one of fear.

'I'm sorry...'

Kammy's eyes widened at the sound of Jad's voice. Eric cradled Jad in his arms, his face ashen and his eyes half closed.

'I'm sorry...' he said again, his body jerking in Eric's tight grip.

Eric stared at Tayah. He looked petrified. Kammy tried to crawl closer.

'What's wrong w-with him?'

Tayah shook her head, 'He's done too much. He's pushed himself too hard.'

Jad's breathing slowed. Eric clutched him, his mouth open in silent panic.

'What do we do?' Tayah's hand flew to her mouth.

Kammy rocked back on her heels, dazed. She looked between the three of them. They were no different to her really. They were frightened and they did not know which way to turn and now Jad was...what? Was he dying? Kammy felt hollow at the thought.

Eric heard the padding of footsteps first. His back stiffened and he pulled Jad closer, his eyes searching in the darkness. Kammy held her breath, wondering what other horrors her life could conjure.

Two hulking shadows loomed out of the trees. They were bears; their black fur long and thick. Their lips pulled back to reveal sharp teeth and they growled. Kammy shivered.

It was Jad that acted. He pushed Eric away and staggered to his feet, drawing on the last of his strength. He shook his head as he sucked in rattling breaths. He started to roll up the sleeve on his left arm.

'Jad...' Eric stood with him.

Jad ignored him, rolling his sleeve up to his shoulder. Kammy gasped, her fingers fluttering to her throat.

Jad's left arm was split by a gruesome scar that ran all the way from his wrist to his shoulder. The skin around it had blackened and the flesh was raw and raised. He held it out before him and Kammy thought of the white stripe that was to be found every time that he shifted.

'My name is Jadanim Ollarion,' he said, his voice a ghost in the night, 'Seeve will...Seeve...'

He paused and raised a hand to wipe away the blood from his nose. Then he toppled forwards and his body lay limp on the grass.

CHAPTER ELEVEN

THE CRYSTALS

'What if he doesn't remember you?'

'He will.'

The voices swelled around him the moment he snapped back to awareness. He felt sore all over but the searing pain of the shift had passed, and while his head felt heavy it no longer pulsed. He lay on something soft and he felt warm and comfortable. It was enough to make him smile.

'Oh, thank the Mother.'

Jad heard chairs scraping back and then a hand held his. He opened his eyes slowly to find Tayah beaming from where she crouched beside him. Her eyes darted over his face, checking for any signs of permanent damage. Eric stood behind her shoulder, just about managing to look as though he had not been worried at all.

'Welcome back,' said Eric.

Tayah gave his hand a squeeze, 'How are you feeling?'

'Stiff,' Jad croaked.

Tayah grabbed his shoulder and helped him ease into a sitting position. He looked around and wondered if he had been transported back in time. He recognised the small room with its grey stone walls and its rough wooden floors. He was in one of the guest rooms of Emire's keep. It was not as grand as the chambers he had been granted when he had visited with his father, but the windows were the same narrow ovals and the brown rug that had been thrown over the end of the bed was adorned with the leaf crest. Jad almost expected his father to burst through the door demanding that he leap out of bed with one of his roaring laughs. Jad shook away the memory. He spotted a fresh white shirt and a platter of food beside it. His stomach rumbled, but he turned back to his friends. With every second came greater alertness.

'How long have I been out?'

'Last night and most of the day,' said Eric.

'What happened?'

Tayah's expression sharpened. 'Not much.'

'The watchmen that found us brought us to Emire. We were each given a room through the night. We were allowed to wash, eat and we were handed fresh clothes. Then we were brought in here with you.'

'We haven't heard anything since,' Tayah finished with a frown.

Jad rolled his shoulders, 'Seeve?'

Tayah shot a dark look at the door, 'He hasn't shown himself yet.'

Eric sighed, ' He isn't in Emire. Or at least he wasn't when we arrived. We just have to wait.'

Tayah made a face at him.

Jad was still too drowsy and comforted by familiarity to worry much. He pushed the sheets away and moved his heavy legs. They were safe; for now at least. They could have been left to fend for themselves outside the town walls, they could have been taken by the Armours. Then a thought struck him and he remembered being swamped by the ice water of the river.

'Kammy?'

'I'm here.'

She appeared from behind Eric and stood at the end of his bed. She met his gaze and it surprised Jad to see her eyes look so normal. Now that they were out of immediate danger she was not angry or upset. She looked different, calmer; though there was still a sad curve to her mouth. She had been given Semei clothing; a white shirt with lace ties and a pair of simple cotton trousers. If it had not been for the bag draped across her shoulder there would be nothing about her to suggest that she was human. Even the smell had faded. Her eyes danced away from him and only then did Jad remember that he was shirtless. His own eyes jerked to the shame that branded onto his left arm and his cheeks burst into flame. He leant forward, snatching the clean shirt from the end of the bed, and yanked it over his head. He thanked the Mother when he realised that it was long-sleeved and he kept his eyes averted from Kammy.

'They were a bit wary of her,' Eric said to Jad, throwing Kammy a quick smile, 'but kind enough.'

'Well, I don't like it,' said Tayah, folding her arms and getting to her feet, 'They locked us in here which means they don't trust us. They haven't sent anybody to check that you're okay for hours. You were almost frothing at the mouth when they found us Jad.'

'The doctor did say he just needed rest.'

'I don't care Eric,' Tayah shook her head, her braid flying through the air, 'Jad, you haven't seen the General for years and we turn up out of the blue with a *human*.' Jad cringed at her exasperated tone. 'Who knows what Bagor might have offered him?'

Jad plucked some cheese off the platter. Tayah's concerns had merit, but he could only shrug, 'Seeve is a good man. Besides, what choice did we have?'

'We had no other choice,' Tayah grumbled, 'but that doesn't mean that I can't complain.'

Jad laughed. He reached forward to pat her on the head. She swatted him away, but her expression softened.

'It's good to see you smile,' she said, 'we were really worried for a moment there.'

Before he could crack a joke about her becoming soft he heard something click in the door and all four of them turned and held their breath. Jad dropped the cheese back onto the platter. The General of Emire *had* been a good man, years ago.

Tayah spoke under her breath. 'About time.'

Seeve strode into the room and Jad stood, again feeling a strange sense of displacement. The man had not changed at all. He was as big as ever, both tall and broad of chest. His skin was black and his head bald. His small eyes swivelled to meet Jad's and he froze in the doorway. Jad stared back, trying to find meaning in that gaze. If Seeve had accepted Bagor as king of Alashdial, then it would all be over.

Seeve crossed the room and the others stepped back to let him pass. His eyes were bright with emotion and he placed a large hand on Jad's shoulder.

'Is it true about your grandfather?'

The images came unbidden, flashing through his mind, each more painful than the last; his grandfather screaming, falling to the ground, his grandfather's dead gaze. Jad bowed his head.

Seeve's grip on his shoulder tightened. 'Then we shall make him pay.'

Jad closed his eyes as a weight lifted from his shoulders.

Seeve released Jad and a broad smile washed away the brightness in his eyes. He turned to face the others and the tension eased its way out of the small room. His eyes fell to Eric first and he grinned, cuffing him softly around the head. 'I remember you,' he said, 'Jadanim's shadow; always following him into trouble.'

'Not much has changed,' said Eric, looking very proud of having been remembered. Jad grinned at his friend.

'And this is?' said Seeve, holding out a hand.

Tayah tilted her chin and shook his hand once before quickly letting go again. 'Tayah.'

'Ah, the little one's sister. Fii mentioned you.'

Some of Tayah's haughtiness deserted her. 'They're okay?'

'Yes, yes. All fine. I've sent Karl to bring them up.' His eyes still watched her closely, 'I remember your mother. She was a good woman. I was sorry to hear of her death.'

Tayah's face tightened, but Seeve did not seem to notice. He moved on to Kammy.

'The human,' he said, and his welcoming smile openly curious.

Seeve dwarfed Kammy. She had to crane her neck to look up at him and her fingers plucked at the cloth covering the small table in the centre of the room. Jad felt oddly defensive.

'This is Kammy Helseth,' he said, 'she's under our protection.'

'Of course,' said Seeve with a short laugh that made Jad feel quite foolish.

Seeve held out a hand and Kammy took it, her tiny fingers disappearing into his. 'Thank you for helping us,' she said. Jad's eyes flickered towards her. She did not sound at all daunted by the meeting; she did not sound *anything*. He quickly looked away.

Seeve lowered himself into a chair that was much too small for him. It creaked, but his loud voice drowned out its protests, 'My watchmen explained all that they could. I can only apologise for my delay. I was down in Folston. There have been some strange reports from the coast recently.'

'We've been locked in here for hours without a single enquiry into our well-being,' Tayah interjected.

Seeve did not acknowledge the hostility in her voice. 'Again, I apologise. My people were not sure how to act given the circumstances. It is not every day that an Alashdian outlaw of royal blood turns up on your doorstep.' He turned to Jad, 'I trust you are feeling better?'

Jad sat back down on the edge of the bed and nodded, 'Much better.'

To his surprise Seeve pointed an accusing finger at him and frowned. 'You are far too reckless. I thought your father taught you that action for action's sake is not always the best course.'

Jad felt heat rise in his cheeks. It had been a long time since anyone other than Fii had scolded him. 'I did not have much of a choice.'

'You might think that,' said Seeve, his stare unflinching, 'but what use will you be to anyone if you push yourself to death?'

Jad could say nothing to that. He could see Eric's smug smile out of the corner of his eye. Eric had been saying as much every day for the past two years.

119

'Why did you not come to me sooner?' Seeve barked, leaving Jad no time to dwell.

'I couldn't. I was a prisoner for nearly half a year.'

He heard another chair being pulled out and he looked up. Kammy sat down and watched him intently. Jad, inexplicably, found himself thinking of Ania and the vacant look in her eyes whenever he had spoken about anything serious. Her smile had always been well practiced. Jad shook himself, he had not thought of Ania in months.

He cleared his throat. 'I still had friends in the Palace, but early on it was impossible to get word out. I was cuffed and unable to shift. I was constantly guarded and did not receive visitors. Only when Eryn managed to clinch one of the positions as my guard did I have any chance. Bagor was distracted by his plans and had grown complacent. Eryn and some others smuggled me out to Welm. Yet I dared not contact anyone. I was too frightened to stay in one place for too long. I was afraid that any message would be traced back to the people that were helping me and that they would suffer. Eventually it became clear that Bagor was not devoting his time or resources to finding me. As long as I stayed away from the city and was not stirring trouble then he did not seem to care. He might have preferred to have me locked away, and I had to be careful, but he did not go out of his way to catch me.'

'So why did you not come then?'

'I...I did not want to come to you seeking protection. I wanted to have something on Bagor. I wanted to have a goal. I thought that if I stayed close to Alashdial, I was more likely to find a weakness or some way that I could stop him. It would have felt like giving up had I come to you with nothing at all. I tried to send the others on ahead of me,' Jad smiled at the memory, 'but Fii laughed in my face.'

Seeve did not smile; he looked thoughtful. 'Why now?'

Jad glanced at Kammy's bag.

'How do we know that we can trust you?'

Jad cringed. Tayah glowered at Seeve. She had straightened to her full height and her hands were on her hips. Jad looked back at the General, bracing himself for the backlash of indignant rage.

Seeve did not look angry at all, rather, he looked amused. 'A fair question,' he said, nodding to Tayah, 'it has been years after all.'

Tayah glanced over her shoulder at Jad and raised a pointed eyebrow. Seeve continued, 'I will tell you of my encounters with Bagor, but first you could all do with some fresh air before the light fades.'

Seeve stood, holding Tayah's gaze as if waiting for her to protest. When she nodded he took two strides to the door and held it open for them. Jad grabbed a bread roll, for his stomach still grumbled. He heard a sigh and Kammy shuffled past him. Her hair shielded her face and he saw her plunging beneath the water again. She had almost died because of his weakness.

'I'm sorry,' he said quietly, remembering the terror in her eyes when he had let her go. Kammy said nothing, but she glanced at him quickly and shook her head. The fact that she did not blame him did nothing to ease his guilt. Jad followed her towards the door and tore off a mouthful of bread.

Seeve stopped him before he could step out into the corridor. 'I had forgotten that you are a man now. Your father would be proud.' He gripped Jad's shoulder again and then he swept after the others, throwing a light-hearted insult Eric's way. Jad stood very still, waiting for the strange mix of pride and guilt to settle. He threw the bread back onto the bed, no longer hungry. His father had been a great man and a great leader. Physical appearances aside, Jad did not compare. He pulled the door shut behind him and followed the others.

The keep was centuries old, its dark halls were narrow and brimmed with shadows. The stone kept the interior cool and the flaming torches were the only spots of light. Jad followed Seeve's bulk, trying not to linger on the memories of those who were gone. Vengeance was all the good that he could find for those memories. He paid little attention to the conversation. He yawned and rolled his shoulders. He felt better already, but he was still looking forward to his next bout of sleep. Sheltered within these walls he knew that he would not need to shift. That thought comforted him. He forced his eyes to stay open; soon, he would have had so much rest he would be sick of it.

The keep was busy and Jad looked from face to face, recognising many that hurried past. It became clear that even the strangers knew who he was for they stared unashamedly, some of them not even bothering to smile.

Seeve led them to an old staircase so narrow they had to climb the uneven steps in single file. Jad followed Kammy, who echoed his silence, while Seeve chatted easily to Eric and Tayah. He heard the

121

crunch of a heavy door and felt fresh air spill onto his face. They stepped out onto the wall that surrounded the keep and Kammy gasped. Jad felt a swell of pride. He had not seen much of the surface, but the world of the Semei, *his* world, was beautiful.

Jad stepped to the parapet and looked out over the town of Emire. The buildings looked more crooked than ever, piled on top of each other and so close that the rooftops nearly kissed. Their burnt red walls had not dimmed over the years. The ground was barely visible from above, but he knew there would not be an inch of green. The streets were so cramped that what once had been grass had been trampled to dust. It was a stark contrast to Alashdial, but it had its own charm. He could remember days spent on the rooftops, leaping from one to the next, eluding capture for as long as he could; often with Eric in tow. Their punishment had always been lessons in the library and Jad's eyes swept to the east. There was the library's Time Tower stretching high above the mazy town. Its face was turned to him and Jad smiled. It shone golden in the evening light.

The true beauty lay beyond the towns crumbling walls. The land surrounding Alashdial was uneven. Its slopes and inclines were carpeted by tight clusters of trees. The Basin, on the other hand, was almost flat. It was circled by the mountains, but they were distant shadows. Then came the farmland before fields of colour that surrounded the town; reds, oranges, purples and yellows. There was barely a tree in sight. The fading light touched everything with an ethereal glow. In the distance Jad caught a glint of something bright; the Crystal. His hands gripped the parapet and he glanced at Kammy's rapturous expression. He smiled; he thought it was breathtaking.

Seeve stepped up beside him, looking out over the town he had governed for three decades. 'The word from Alashdial was that your grandfather had had a heart attack, and that Bagor had been granted the position of regent until you were a suitable age to rule.'

Jad's grip on the parapet tightened, 'When it first happened the city was in lockdown. You might have heard the truth otherwise. By the time the people were free to move, he had weaved his magic. Nobody was sure what the truth was any more.'

Seeve nodded, 'He wished to contain the truth, but it was a needless exercise. Anyone with half a mind could see that it made no sense. If Rogan had truly had a heart attack then the Council would have continued to lead without him at its helm. They would not have appointed Bagor, especially not so abruptly. When I heard nothing from the Council it was clear that something was wrong, but I could not leave Myra.'

Jad bowed his head. Myra had been an indomitable woman with a heart as big as her husband. 'I heard. I am sorry.'

Seeve spoke on. 'His first visit came three months later. Myra had just passed and I did not trust myself to meet with him. I hated the man regardless, but I was grieving and feared any confrontation would have ended with my hands around his throat. It may not seem so, but that would not have worked out well for anybody. Karl and a few others went in my place. By all accounts he was charming. He only wished to offer his friendship and his condolences.'

Jad could feel his insides burning at the thought.

'His next visit came two months later and he brought a much larger retinue. This time I did meet him.' Seeve's eyes narrowed to nothing. 'I asked after you Jad. He told me that you were still crippled with grief and that you were being well looked after. I knew that he was lying and he knew that I knew, but there was nothing to be done. He simpered and he smiled, but I heard the threat behind every word.'

Eric had pulled himself up to sit on the wall. He leaned back against the parapet. 'But he could not have hurt you here.'

Seeve looked surprised, 'Surely you have heard that he is building an army?'

Jad frowned, 'We realised that he was attempting to, once he started forming the Armours, but other than those few loyal to him, who would fight? There has not been a Semei war since the old years of kings and queens. The people do not know how.'

'True enough,' said Seeve, but Jad did not like the look in the General's eyes. Seeve turned his back on the basin and looked up at the sky, 'but people can be trained, if they want it badly enough.'

Tayah snorted, 'Who would want war?'

Seeve grimaced, 'Greed feeds the idea. Even those with good intentions can be taken in by the promise of war. You would do well to remember that.' He looked around at each of them. 'You must know that Bagor spends hardly any of his time in Alashdial. He travels across our world, from continent to continent and back again. He has met with countless leaders, bribing some, threatening others, whichever is necessary. He has brought many around to his vision of war.'

'But they know what he did.' Jad snapped.

'Wait,' Tayah waved him to silence even as he seethed, 'if he is roping in leaders all over the place, who is he warring with? Jad?'

'He wishes war against humans, not Semei.'

Jad faltered. He gaped at Seeve, but the General did not start laughing at the joke he had just made. He looked very serious. A confused silence fell. Jad pushed a hand through his hair, his eyes drifting back to where he thought he had seen the Crystal. He heard Tayah sniff and the clatter of her boots as she strode away from them. Jad let out a breath.

'Why?'

Kammy stared at Seeve with wide eyes and Jad's sense of dread thickened.

Seeve glanced at her, his expression grim. 'He has a convincing argument. What do you know of the connection between our worlds?'

'I...' Kammy shook her head, 'I don't know anything.'

'You saw the Crystal, didn't you?' said Eric, his freckles standing out more than usual for he had turned very pale.

Kammy's eyes lit up at the memory. 'Yes,' she breathed.

'There are five such Crystals in our world. The one in Alashdial is the second largest. They grow from the centre of the earth, from the Mother, and they sustain us. Our world lies beneath yours; *inside* it. We need the Crystals to survive. Look at the sky, Kammy. Do you see anything?'

Jad watched her. She pushed her hair back and squinted, no doubt wondering what she was supposed to be seeing. She scrunched up her nose and Jad almost smiled.

'I don't see anything,' she said, dropping her hands in defeat.

'Exactly,' Seeve clicked his fingers. 'Where is the setting sun? Or as the night is coming, where are the stars? Where is the moon? They sky is cloudless so why can't we see them?'

Kammy looked again and her lips parted in wonder.

'We don't have those things here. The Mother provides for us through the Crystals alone. They give us light. They make the water flow and the air pure to breathe.'

'But that's...'

'As impossible as a mouse turning into a man?' Eric smiled.

She stared at them each in turn, then back at the sky. Jad could almost feel her willing a star to pop into existence.

'You humans do not know of the Crystals because they do not break through to the surface, though the largest does come close. The irony is that you need the Crystals too. Should they cease to exist then you would certainly last longer than us Semei, but soon enough your sun and your atmosphere would not be enough. The Mother would die and so would all that she fights to sustain.'

Kammy shrugged, 'I don't see what that has to do with...'

'The Crystals are dying.'

Jad's stomach turned to lead.

'*What*?' Tayah hissed.

'Have you not noticed the weather?' said Seeve, his voice solemn, 'The heat?'

Jad suddenly felt very weary, as though every bone in his body was a weight he could no longer carry. It had been unnaturally hot for close to a month, but he had hardly given the weather a second thought. Now that he stopped to think, he had only ever felt such warmth beating down upon his skin on the surface.

'There are storms further north,' said Seeve, 'which is why I was in Folston. They are concerned.'

Kammy looked confused. 'Why does it matter that it's hot? Or that there are storms?'

'Our climate is mild, it always has been,' said Seeve. 'As far as I am aware, our seasons are similar to yours, but our summers are simply warm and our winters not much cooler. Rain is rare and unheard of at this time of year.'

Jad could barely comprehend what he was hearing. 'But how can the Crystals be dying?'

Seeve shot Kammy an apologetic look, 'The Humans are killing them.'

'That's ridiculous,' Kammy snapped. She looked a little surprised at herself. She swallowed and took a breath. 'How can it be our fault when we don't even know the Crystals exist?'

Seeve shook his head. 'They do not realise what damage they are doing, or they do not care, but I once visited a human city and I never wish to return. It was a grey place. There were fumes that choked me, lights that burned my eyes. Each breath I took tasted like poison.'

'But that's...' Kammy looked flustered. 'That's just how the world is, isn't it?' Her cheeks were bright and Jad could see her pupils shrinking. He straightened; he did not want Seeve to notice, not yet.

If Seeve saw anything, he did not say. He held up his hands. 'Whether or not the humans meant for this to happen, it has.'

Kammy turned away from him, her back taut with tension.

'So, the weather changing is a sign that the Crystals are growing weaker?' said Jad, drawing Seeve's attention back to him.

'Yes. The effects might only be mild for many years, perhaps decades or even centuries. Many would not notice it, but I am convinced.'

'How do you know all of this?' said Tayah.

'Bagor.'

Jad felt a flash of fury. 'Then how can you believe a word of it?'

'Because it makes sense.'

'So you are siding with him?'

Seeve barked a laugh. 'No, I could never ally myself with such a man. I hope and I pray to the Mother that he is lying, but I fear this is one of those rare occasions where he is not twisting the truth. It is not my opinion that should concern you, for if I believe him then so will others. Those are the opinions that matter. Age-old prejudices are already in place and all Bagor must do is fan the flames. They may not like Bagor, but this is not about him, not the way he is selling it. He is telling them all that this is about the future of our people.'

Jad wanted to tear at his own face. He could feel their eyes on him, but he would not meet anybody's gaze. Of all the fears that had tormented him over the last two years, Bagor gaining support from outside Alashdial had not been one of them. Everybody knew what a monster he was.

'Bagor has always hated humans.' Jad spoke into the silence, 'For as long as I can remember.'

'I never thought this would go beyond Alashdial. Maybe it was naive, but...' Eric sighed, 'I never imagined anything more than winning Alashdial back for Jad.'

'Look,' said Tayah, 'I hate Bagor, you know I do. But if this is true...if we need to save our people,' Jad looked up at her slowly. Her eyes were bright. 'Then why should we stop him?' she said in a rush, 'why shouldn't we save our future?'

'How can you...' Kammy's hands were clenched into fists and her eyes were gone. She was so furious that she could hardly talk. 'That is...they're *trying*.'

Jad closed his eyes. They would all side with Bagor now.

'Bah,' Seeve waved a hand, 'Bagor is a murderous bastard. Even if war was the only answer, I could never follow that man. Besides, there must be more to this. There *is*.'

'What?' said Jad, latching onto hope.

'What is his true objective?' No matter how large his army, the humans have weapons that we could never compete with, weapons that would do more to harm the Mother. Bagor is no fool. He knows that a war against humans would be impossible to win. So, why? I'm afraid that I do not know the answer, but the last time that Bagor came to see me he mentioned something; a Key.'

Jad looked at Kammy and licked dry lips. 'We have it.'

Seeve sounded stunned. 'You do?' Then he laughed and slapped his hand on the stone wall, 'I was not expecting to hear that.'

'Do you know what it is or why he wants it?' said Jad.

'I am afraid not. Bagor did not give me much information. He wants me to vocalise my support for his campaign, but he will never trust me. Still, it can only be a good thing that you have it and he does not. May I see?'

Kammy glanced back at them. Her eyes had settled again, but her mouth remained an angry line. She clutched her bag close, but then she sighed. She unzipped it and pulled out the purple and blue pebble. She handed it to Seeve in silence.

'This is it?' said the General, rolling it over in his hands, 'it hardly looks like anything special.'

'I thought so too,' said Jad, eyeing the smooth stone, 'but I could feel its pull on the surface and so could Ria. It must be the Key.'

Seeve handed it back to Kammy. She tucked it away and turned her back on them again.

'This is why you have made your move,' said Seeve. 'Does Bagor know you have it?'

Jad nodded.

Seeve did not hesitate. 'I can shelter you here. He will not dare move against me yet. Doing so would lose him much of the support he might have gained. We can think things over and work out our next move. That is,' he looked at Tayah, 'if you trust me?'

Roused from her thoughts, Tayah smirked, 'I think so.'

Seeve laughed. 'That is a relief.'

The door crunched behind them and they heard a small, familiar voice.

'*Tay.*'

Tayah's smirk dissolved into a watery smile. Jad turned and despite everything, he smiled too. Boo flung himself forwards and Tayah snatched him up, swinging him through the air and then pulling him in close. Fii followed behind at a gentle pace and Jad stepped towards her, glad to have her calm head near.

'Littlebrook?' he said.

'We received word this morning. They are fine.' She hugged him tight, but when she pulled back her eyes were fixed over his shoulder.

Kammy stood apart, staring at Tayah and Boo. Their happiness at having been reunited shone from both of their faces. Kammy's eyes were lifeless and with the news of Bagor's war, Jad could not see how things were about to get any easier for her.

Fii clicked her tongue, patted Jad on the arm and stepped towards the human that was trapped amongst them.

CHAPTER TWELVE

THE STORY OF THE MOTHER

Fii led Kammy away from the wall.

Kammy was barely aware of where she was going. She let Fii steer her back towards her room. She did not see where the others went, she did not notice that Fii disappeared for a moment. Only when Fii returned with a plate of food did Kammy realise she had ever left. Not long before, Kammy had felt ravenous, but she had lost her appetite. She stared at the slab of meat and the vegetables before her and felt sick. Slowly, sense returned and she became conscious of Fii's eyes on her, watching as she pushed her food around her plate. Kammy kept her gaze averted. She did not want to be rude to Fii but every time she imagined talking, words failed her. The Semei wanted a war against humans and she was stuck in their world; a world so ridiculous it did not even have a sun. She hurtled towards another night away from her home, another night without her Gran, without Jamie.

'You know,' said Fii, when it became clear that Kammy would not eat, 'I am ever so glad to see you safe.'

Kammy placed her fork down carefully. She felt a stab of irritation. She hardly felt safe, stuck within walls full of people that hated what she was. Even Fii was not without blemish, for she had been part of the plan to drug Kammy back in Littlebrook. Perhaps there had been no bad intentions, but the memory still rankled. Yet when Kammy looked up to tell Fii so, she saw that the old woman looked wretched. Her hair crawled out from beneath her shawl and her eyes were rimmed with red.

'We should never have left you alone, not when we could not be certain of what would happen.'

Kammy still felt mutinous. 'You should have explained what you were planning,' Fii's expression dropped and Kammy sighed, fumbling for something kinder to say, 'But I wanted to go back. If I hadn't, then you guys wouldn't have the Key.' She patted her bag and tried her best to smile.

Fii, rather than looking mollified, looked furious. 'I do not care about the Key,' she said, 'I care about you.'

Kammy dropped her eyes, 'Why? I'm human.'

Fii stood, her chair scraping back against the floor. She bustled closer and took one of Kammy's hands into both of her own. 'You are a young woman who has had to deal with far too much over these past few days. That is all that I see when I look at you.'

Kammy closed her eyes, but held onto Fii's hands. She could not help but think of her Gran, her brilliant Gran. She could not help but think that she was gone too, just like Jamie, and Kammy felt burning behind her eyes. She was in constant war with that feeling. She yawned, hoping that Fii would attribute fatigue to the redness of her eyes.

Fii patted her hand and let go. 'You're tired and it's getting late. Sleep now and I will come to see you in the morning.'

She started to turn away and Kammy felt a bubble of panic rise in her chest. It was silly, she knew, but the thought of Fii leaving her alone with all that she was avoiding left her paralysed with fear.

'Wait,' she cried, 'please, I...'

Fii looked back at her, her smile encouraging.

Kammy blushed. 'Would you stay? Just until I fall asleep...' Fii started to speak and Kammy blurted, 'It's just, last night I was so exhausted that I passed out, but now...'

Fii's eyes shone with understanding. 'Of course.'

Kammy's relief was tempered by awkwardness. No matter how kind Fii seemed and how much she wanted her to stay, Kammy barely knew her. She stood and rocked on her heels, unsure of what she should do. Would Fii think less of her if she crawled straight into bed without even changing her clothes?

Fii laughed as if reading her thoughts. 'Sleep. Don't worry about me.'

Kammy felt sheepish and her cheeks were still warm, but she kicked off the boots she had been given and placed her bag beside the pillow. Then she crawled under the sheets of the strange bed and stared up at the strange ceiling. It was not only this world that made her uncomfortable. She hardly felt like herself any more.

'Would you like me to put out the torches?'

'No,' said Kammy quickly. She did not need more darkness to deal with.

Fii settled herself into one of the chairs again. 'And you don't mind if I finish your food?'

Kammy smiled, 'Go ahead.'

'Goodnight then.'

'Goodnight,' said Kammy, 'and thank you.'

Kammy took a deep breath. She pulled the soft sheets up under her arms and closed her eyes. Jamie's face loomed out of the darkness and her eyes snapped open again. Gnawing the inside of her cheek, Kammy turned to face the wall. Her hands were shaking so she bunched the sheet up between her fingers. It was no longer just Jamie that haunted her. *A war on humans.* She could still see all their faces so clearly, even Eric's, accepting it. None of them would look at her. No wonder Tayah hated her if this was what the Semei believed. Kammy did not like many humans herself, not the ones she had met anyway, but she still felt a cold sense of injustice. Should the mistakes of a few condemn the rest? Seeve did not seem to believe that the Semei would have a chance, but could they do it? Could they destroy her home and all the people she knew? And what would happen to her? Her mind clicked and whirred and every passing second seemed to make her head pound harder.

'Fii?'

'Hmm?'

Kammy lay very still. 'Can I ask you something?'

'Of course.'

'I've been wondering for a while, but there was never a good time to ask. How do you shift? How does it work?'

'That is quite the question Kammy. It doesn't *work*, it is our nature. It would take a long time to explain.'

'That's okay. even if I can't understand. I'd just like to listen.' She waited, blinking at the wall and hoping that Fii would not think her childish.

'There is a tale, a legend that mothers tell their children when their minds first turn to curiosity. It is the story of the Mother and the child that she loved most of all.'

Kammy closed her eyes. She needed something to stop her from thinking, just for a little while. 'I'd like to hear that.'

'All right,' said Fii, clearing her throat, 'it's quite appropriate really, with the Festival of the Mother coming so soon.'

'Festival?'

'We shall have many days to tell you of the delights of the Festival. All the Semei in the world celebrate it on the same day every year. This tale may actually help you understand some of its importance to us. It begins many years ago, hundreds and thousands of years past. The Mother existed in an endless ocean of darkness. Newly born, she was a bright spot that floated on and on, and she was entirely alone. One day she decided that it simply would not do. She did not want to be alone any more so she started to build. She toiled for centuries, crafting a shell around herself until one day it was complete. Her creation was Earth and it was an extension of her, infused with her energy and strength.'

'At first, pride in her creation was enough but as the years wore on the Mother became restless. There was something missing, for her creation was a dead thing. Earth was a bleak shell that had no purpose for being. It needed life. Now, creating life was much more difficult than creating the shell that life would inhabit. It needed sacrifice. The Mother had to give up parts of herself to the life that she moulded, in turn putting her own life into the hands of the nature she constructed.'

Kammy did not want the soothing rhythm of Fii's voice to stop.

'The Mother sacrificed five parts of herself. That was enough to give her children and the world around them life to last for billions of years, so long as they did not misuse it. Her life force manifested itself

133

into five Crystals and soon after the grass began to grow, water began to flow through rivers and fill the oceans. The first five were also born; the Mother's favourite children, for they lived alone with her for many hundreds of years. They were crafted with such care that it is said that their blood was drawn from the Mother's own heart. For many generations their bloodline was considered royalty.'

'One of them was Ollarion?' Kammy whispered.

'Yes,' said Fii, 'the Ollarion bloodline is the last to maintain prominence. The other four names are buried in our histories and most no longer remember them, beyond knowing that there was one for each Crystal. No doubt there are still some descendants roaming these lands.'

'Oh.'

'When the Mother realised the extent of the love she felt for her first five children, she resolved to create many more. She wanted to fill her world with life. She wanted to be overwhelmed by colour and noise at every turn. Man and animal began to roam. There were no Semei then, and no humans; every creature lived as equal. They moved between the surface and this layer, relishing the life they had been given. They were the same, Kammy, in the beginning.'

'Even amongst the five, though she loved all her children, one was very special to the Mother. Lyssa was her first creation and her favourite of all. The two of them would often be found together. One day, they were sitting on a hillside when a flock of ravens flew past. Lyssa remarked, "Why is it that I cannot fly?" The Mother was surprised, but she was proud of the diversity she had created. "There must be balance, Lyssa," she said, "if you could do all that others can do, you might grow to dominate the rest." Lyssa smiled, "Dear Mother, would I ever wish to dominate? No, I only wish to fly." Now, though Lyssa had tried to hide it, the Mother could see the sadness in her daughter's eyes and it pained her. So, she told Lyssa, "If you can prove to me that you truly wish to fly, that you understand the ravens and that you appreciate all that they do, then you may have this wish."'

'A week passed and when Lyssa returned the Mother was stunned. Lyssa had drawn diagrams and built models. She talked of all the ways in which the air moved and how the birds themselves were constructed. She knew everything that there was to know and the Mother, though she harboured a bud of anxiety, could not go against her word. She revealed to Lyssa the secret of her Soul; how it had always and would always be a part of her. Through it, she was granted the power to fly. She could shift into a raven, but there were limitations. The process was not easy. It took a great deal of concentration and energy. Lyssa could not hold the form of the raven for too long, especially not when she was tired.'

'Is that why Jad collapsed...' said Kammy, still wide awake, 'because he was already tired?'

Fii paused, 'Jad is strong, stronger than most, but yes that is why. He constantly pushes himself to be stronger, past the realms of possibility.'

Kammy thought of the dark shadows on Jad's face. She thought of his scar, then of his eyes and she was overtaken by a wave of curiosity, but Fii took up her tale again and it swept over Kammy like a blanket.

'The ability to shift did not mean she could suddenly become any bird either, not unless she studied them with the same diligence that she studied the raven. Lyssa saw little point in doing so. She had only wanted to fly and that gift had been granted to her. She soared as she had dreamed she would. She saw sights that she could never have seen before and she skimmed the waves of the oceans, enchanted by the possibilities she saw beneath. So, when she returned to the Mother some time later, she asked, "Why is it, dear Mother, that I cannot swim deep beneath the sea?" The Mother laughed this time and told Lyssa that if she could find the answer, her Soul would once again grant her the power. The Mother simply could not believe that Lyssa would demonstrate the same dedication a second time. But when Lyssa returned one week later, she brought diagrams and models with her and they were just as detailed as before. The Mother felt a growing sense of unease. Lyssa was granted the power that she craved, but the Mother made it clear that she could not grant her anything else. Lyssa was happy and grateful. She promised the Mother that she would not ask again and she was true to her word.'

'For a while there was no trouble. Soon, however, others began to notice that Lyssa would disappear for days on end. One of those days she was followed, and her secret was uncovered. Some thought that Lyssa was an abomination, while others were consumed by jealousy. The envious ones stormed to face the Mother, accusing her of favouritism and demanding the same treatment. How could she deny them? She loved all of her children and she felt guilty for what she had done. She should never have treated Lyssa so. She told the jealous ones the same thing that she had told her favourite daughter.

If they could return to her with complete understanding of a bird, of a fish, or of any kind of animal that was not too small or so big that it would be impossible to master, then she would reveal to them the workings of their Soul. They returned in their droves and even though the Mother was consumed by trepidation, she kept her word. And so, the Semei were born. The others, the ones that regarded the shape-shifters as unnatural, moved to the surface and abandoned the Mother. They called themselves humans and there was war. The Mother grieved, and she was sure that her grief would kill her. She watched her children die, killing their brothers and sisters, and she knew that she had caused it. She could only think of one way to end it; she sealed the Gates between the worlds, cutting the surface off and bringing the war to an abrupt end.'

'But...there is a Gate?'

'That one was only discovered just over a century ago. Nobody knew how long it had been there. At the time, people believed the Mother was about to return to us. I wonder if the simple truth is that she is not strong enough to hold the seal forever.'

Kammy imagined the two worlds colliding once more.

'So the war had ended, but the Mother's grief had not. She was disappointed in her children, but most of all she was ashamed of the conflict she had caused. The Mother decided it would be best to leave her children. The humans had abandoned her, and the Semei, still bitter despite being granted all they wished, barely argued for her to stay. Only the first five fought to remain beside her. They had all followed Lyssa and become Semei, but they had held themselves above the feud. They could not bear the division and they decided to leave with the Mother. Only, at the last possible moment, Lyssa refused.'

'Why?'

'She told the Mother, through her tears, that as the first Semei she could not abandon the others. She believed that it was her fault the world was divided and that it was down to her to heal the rift between the humans and the Semei. The Mother pleaded and begged, but Lyssa would not be moved. So, the Mother left, leaving the Crystals and her favourite daughter behind.'

Kammy turned to face Fii. 'She just disappeared?'

136

Fii nodded, 'And as soon as she was gone, the Semei felt her absence. Within days our world became duller. The air was less pure, the water less refreshing. Over time our lives have become shorter. Once we would live for centuries, now we cannot even reach one. Lyssa's death was another blow. As long as she lived the people had still felt a connection to the Mother and a hope that she would return. When a simple sickness took the first of the Semei, the people lost that hope. More horror was to follow. Sometimes our children would attempt their first shift and they would not be able to shift back. It was our punishment, they believed, for not begging the Mother to stay. These children were named the Abandoned and they are a cruel reminder of the war that split this Earth in two.'

'Why didn't they just stop trying to shift? Then nobody would have been abandoned.'

Fii chuckled, 'Ah, I can only imagine what they thought and felt back then. But I can tell you that shifting can be exhausting, but the thrill never fades. I can believe that nobody was strong enough to give that up. No, their only hope, and ours too, was that by caring for the Crystals the Mother might come back to us one day.'

Fii fell silent and it took Kammy a short while to realise that she had finished. 'That's a strange bedtime story,' she said, 'it's sad.'

'It is sad, but it is also important. This war that you fear, that Bagor wishes to pursue, is utter stupidity. If only people would remember the story of the Mother, then they might realise what fools we would be to make the same mistakes again.'

Kammy let that thought sink in. 'The Mother...it's all very different to what humans believe.'

'It is a story, and to many it is no more than that. Do you know what I think? I think that people may believe what they want to believe as long as they are driven to do good. You see, morality is what matters most. It does not matter how our lives came to be, it is what we do with them that is important. As long as you try your best and strive to help those around you, what higher power could condemn you?'

Kammy had never believed in much of anything. Her Mum and her Gran had never spoken of such things, but Kammy felt better for having heard the tale. Maybe Eric, or one of the others, could find a way to remind the Semei of the story of the Mother, and then there would be no war.

'I'm not very sleepy now,' said Kammy.

Fii laughed, 'Perhaps another tale would be better suited to helping you sleep?'

Kammy smiled and closed her eyes. 'Yes, please.'

But Fii did not start up straight away. There was a short silence before she spoke again, and her voice was soft and hesitant. 'It will get easier, Kammy. I promise.'

Kammy's fingers curled tightly around the sheets. Fii's intentions were good, but Kammy did not believe her.

CHAPTER THIRTEEN

THE WANDERER

Peace reined on the rooftops. They hung so close together that the noise and bustle of Emire lay trapped below. Only a sliver of sound escaped and it faded to nothing, set free into the sky. Jad smiled and closed his eyes. The tiles were warm against his back and even though they were scratchy and uneven, he was comfortable. The air stirred, a little more restless than usual, but not unruly enough to disturb him. He yawned and let his mind wander.

Fii had insisted that he spend his first day in Emire in bed. At first, Jad had been wholly accepting of the idea. When the morning's light had peeped into his room he had groaned and rolled away from it, feeling stiff and un rested. When he had awoken again a few hours later, he had found the thought of staying rooted to his bed much more repellent. Eric and Tayah had not been to see him and when Jad had slipped out of his room to find them he had bumped into Seeve instead. The General had practically dragged him back again, informing him that his friends were in the library and that they would undoubtedly visit him later. Seeve, it appeared, feared Fii's wrath even more than Jad did. So, Jad had called upon one of his oldest tricks. He had peeked out the door to make sure that nobody was watching. Then he had weaved his way through the shadows of the keep and up onto the wall. Ignoring his aching muscles, he had hoisted himself up onto the rooftops. If he was going to be forced to rest, he might as well do it with his lungs full of air and day light on his face.

What Seeve and Fii could not understand was that even when comfortable, there was no real rest to be had. Jad's mind churned, grinding relentlessly in his skull, chewing over all the problems that he faced. Whenever he felt his body starting to relax he would remember that the Crystals were dying and he would be shot through by panic. Whenever a fond memory of past rooftop adventures tried to push its way to the surface, it would be beaten back and drowned by the knowledge of Bagor's intended war; a war against the humans that would eventually kill them all. Jad scowled. If a war had justification, did that make it the right course? Could the right course ever be followed by a man such as Bagor?

He thought of Kammy and his scowl etched itself deeper into his face. She would continue to argue that there was no justification, but then she did not understand. If their roles were reversed she would think much the same as he did, would she not? Or would there be no question in her mind at all? War meant death and destruction; surely it could never be right?'

'Thought you'd be up here.'

Jad glanced up. Eric strode towards him with an easy smile on his face. Jad sat up and grinned. He had been so bored all day that seeing his friend quickly banished his scowl.

'You know I can't be contained for long.'

Eric snorted. 'I do.' He dropped down beside Jad, rattling the roof tiles, and leaned back on his elbows with a sigh. 'Tay's coming...slowly.'

Jad laughed, 'Let me guess, you told her that she didn't have to climb up here...'

'...So she insisted that she would.' Eric finished for him with a smirk.

They heard her grumbling before they saw her. Then ten bitten fingernails appeared over the far edge, closely followed by Tayah's face. She was concentrating so hard that her tongue was poking out. When she spotted them laughing at her, her eyes narrowed. With one last heave, she pulled herself up and over and started to crawl towards them.

'Forgotten how to walk?' Jad inquired.

'Shut up.'

She picked her way across the tiles and when she finally sat still beside them, she relaxed. 'I don't know why you insist on coming up here.'

'To get away from you,' said Eric, nudging her gently.

She gasped and her fingers clutched the tiles. The boys laughed and Tayah glared at them, 'You do it so you can show off.'

'And the only reason you do not like it,' said Jad, 'is because you *can't* show off.'

'Don't worry,' Eric mumbled through a yawn, 'we won't let you fall.'

Tayah pressed her lips together and Jad tried to fight down another burst of laughter. He made the mistake of catching Eric's eye and they both spluttered with mirth as Tayah muttered. Teasing her excessive amounts of pride had always been an enjoyable pastime.

She rolled her eyes. 'All right, all right, let's change the subject, shall we? Fii will have your head when she finds out you're up here.'

Jad winced at the thought, but he shrugged, 'I needed to get out of there. I'm fine anyway. She is just being overprotective.'

'Can't blame her,' said Eric, rapping his knuckles against the tiles, 'with everything that is going on.'

'And you were bad, Jad,' said Tayah, 'really bad.'

The urge to laugh was fading fast, but Jad forced another smile. He hated to think of his weakness. He hated to think that he was the one they all worried for, the one they felt they needed to keep safe. He was supposed to be the protector, not the protected.

'So,' he said with forced brevity, 'did you find anything? Seeve said you were in the library.'

Eric made a face, 'I hate that place.'

'I quite like it,' said Tayah, 'shame that the old beanstalk is still there. I'm sure he was due to pass on about a thousand years ago.'

Jad grinned, 'If only.'

'But no,' said Eric, 'we haven't found anything yet. At least, not anything useful. I'll be honest, looking for information about a *key* doesn't really narrow down the search.'

'Still,' Tayah offered an encouraging smile, 'we have plenty of time. We'll find something eventually.'

'Or we won't,' said Jad.

Eric and Tayah had nothing to say to that.

Jad lay back again and stared up at the blue sky. 'All we know is that we have something Bagor wants. We don't know what it does or what it's for. What if we don't find anything in the library? What do we do then?'

'I guess...' Tayah trailed off and puffed out her cheeks.

Jad shook himself, 'I'm sorry. There's no point in thinking like that, I know. I guess I just can't stop thinking about what Seeve said, about this war...'

'Is there any point in thinking about that either?' suggested Eric, 'There's nothing we can do about it right now. We should focus on what we can do.'

Jad shrugged, 'We'll have to think about it at some point.'

'Could he really do it?' said Tayah, sounding doubtful, 'Go to war against humans?'

'He could go to war,' said Jad, 'whether any Semei would come back from it is another question entirely.'

'Well,' Eric frowned, 'I hope it doesn't come to that, for Kammy's sake as well as everyone else's.'

Jad stared at his boots, 'Even if war was the only way to save the Semei?'

'I don't think war should ever be the answer. There must be another way.'

Jad stared out over the red rooftops and towards the Time Tower. He hoped his friends would not notice the flush of shame on his face. Eric was right, of course, there had to be something else. A way where Bagor did not lead anybody and where people, both human and Semei, would not die.

'I went to see Kammy this morning,' said Eric. Jad looked up, but did not speak. 'I tried to get her to come into town with me, but she wasn't feeling up to it. Not yet.'

'Well,' Tayah huffed, 'I hope she doesn't think she can avoid the library work all together. The more of us there are reading, the quicker we will find what we need.'

'Tay,' Eric looked appalled, 'she's grieving.'

'I know, but she can still read at the same time, can't she?'

Eric stared at Tayah, seemingly in shock at her complete lack of sensitivity.

'She's been through a lot...' Jad started.

Tayah rounded on him, 'Oh, sure. Because you're a bundle of sweetness whenever you're around her?'

Jad's cheeks burned. 'I saved her life.'

Tayah raised an eyebrow.

'She has a point,' Eric spoke over them both. 'You both need to go easier on her. She didn't ask for any of this.'

Jad still felt the urge to protest. He had saved her life more than once and he had tried to be kind. It was not his fault that he had never been good at dealing with certain things, like emotions. Eric fixed him with a look and Jad sighed, 'Fine, I'll try.'

Tayah wrinkled her nose, 'I suppose she is less whiny than I thought she would be. Plus, the stink when I'm near her isn't as strong anymore.'

Jad and Eric shared a look.

'What?' Tayah cried, 'it's not like I'm going to tell her that.'

Eric shook his head, 'Tayah...'

'Anyway,' Tayah spoke over him, looking a little put out, 'if you want there to be any chance that Fii hasn't noticed you've gone, we should head back.'

'One can only hope,' said Jad, stretching as he pushed himself to his feet.

Eric followed, patting his stomach, 'Plus, I'm hungry.'

Jad looked back towards the keep, and his prison for the rest of the evening. 'Tomorrow, I'll come to the library with you.'

Eric nodded and the two of them started to walk, comfortable traversing the slight incline of the rooftops. Tayah crawled along behind them, her knuckles clenched as she held on tight. When they reached the edge they hung themselves over it and dropped onto the wall below with ease. Tayah shimmied close and paused.

Jad held up his hands, 'Want some help?'

Tayah kicked out at him, 'No, I do not.'

He laughed as he ducked away. She backed towards the edge and dangled over it, unable to stop a soft whimper. Then she landed beside Jad and wobbled before she steadied herself. Tilting her chin, she said, 'it's only because you two have had more practice than me.'

Eric looked back at them, having already started along the wall. 'Of course Tay, of course.' She stuck her tongue out at him just as he disappeared around the corner. Then they both heard him swear.

Jad glanced at Tayah in alarm. He scuttled after Eric, unfazed by the drop on his left. Tayah followed more slowly. When Jad rounded the corner and stepped off the parapet to stand beside Eric, he saw the problem. He tried his hardest to craft an innocent looking smile, but it withered away before it had fully formed.

'Clambering over the rooftops like a cat is your idea of rest, is it?'

Fii stood before them, beside the door that led back into the keep, carrying both Boo and a very severe expression. Seeve was there too, with his arms folded across his barrel chest. Jad felt like a little boy again under the combined force of their gazes.

When Tayah finally caught up to them, Boo's eyes lit up. He pointed at them with glee. 'You been naughty.'

Fii rolled her eyes, 'Rest means rest, Jadanim,' she said, placing Boo down.

Jad bowed his head, 'I know.'

'When it is prescribed to you, it is done so for a reason.'

'I know.'

Fii speared him with a sharp stare and Jad squirmed. Then her eyes snapped to the others. 'And you two should not encourage him.'

144

'We didn't...' Tayah started.

'Since when have we been able...' spluttered Eric.

But Fii held up her hands. 'I don't want to hear it,' she said, with Seeve nodding silent agreement at her shoulder, 'now be off with you. This little one wants his dinner.'

'Food,' Boo moaned, tugging at Tayah's leggings.

'As do I,' boomed Seeve, relaxing when he realised that Fii was not about to launch into one of her more spectacular tirades.

A few words from Fii had successfully planted seeds of guilt in Jad's stomach, but they were not enough to quell his hunger. Led by Boo, they began to file past in silence. Fii's expression did not come close to softening.

As Jad passed her Fii spoke through clenched teeth, 'You might want to eat later. Tamsin is waiting in your room.'

Tayah froze and looked back at him with wide eyes, 'The Wanderer?'

Jad could see his own shock reflected there. Fii nodded at him and he said to Tayah, 'Come with me?'

For a moment her eyes sparkled with excitement. Then Boo tugged at her hand again and her gaze dropped. Suddenly she looked very shy and so unlike herself that Jad almost laughed. He understood; Tamsin had always left him feeling awed when he had met her as a boy.

'No,' she said, 'I should really get this little monster fed.'

Eric threw an arm around her shoulders and grinned, 'And this one.'

She shrugged him off and looked back at Jad, 'We'll come find you later, okay?'

Jad nodded and the three of them disappeared through the door with Seeve close behind. Jad made the mistake of revealing to Fii the full extent of his boyish grin and her face remained a mask of stone.

'Yes, Jadanim, I am still mad,' she said, as a muscle in her cheek started to twitch.

Jad's grin grew wider, 'Sorry Fii,' he said as he darted off. He heard her sigh behind him.

Back inside the keep, Jad no longer felt contained as he had done earlier that day. Now, he had a reason to be indoors. A chance to speak to Tamsin was an opportunity one should never pass up. He could not help, but feel nervous. Tamsin's reputation was intimidating enough, even before meeting her in person. Jad had only met her twice, both times with his father and both times memorable. More than anything, he was pleased that she remembered him at all, let alone wanted to talk to him. He scurried down the stairs and saw the others disappear around the corner. He turned the opposite way, any thoughts of food banished. Soon, he charged back into his assigned room, hoping his eagerness did not shine too brightly on his face.

Tamsin was leaning against the wall, her limbs long and clearly muscled beneath her simple clothes. She turned away from the window and looked him up and down. She had not changed. Her skin was bronze and her eyes silver and cat like. She wore her golden hair cropped short. There was something quite remarkable about her appearance. She took a step towards him, her graceful movements disguising her famous strength.

She smirked. 'Did I get you in trouble, kid?' Her accent was strange, a blend of all the places she had been.

Jad tried not to frown at her use of the diminutive. 'So it was you that told Fii I was out of my room?'

Tamsin shrugged, stepping around the table and reaching to ruffle his hair. Jad was not quick enough to dance away from her and she laughed. 'She told me you would be here and you were not. That means you broke the rules.'

Jad raised an eyebrow. 'I thought you lived a life outside the rules?'

Tamsin sat down and Jad followed suit. Her eyes twinkled at him. 'I do. You do not.'

Jad almost pouted. Tamsin was, and always would be, something of an enigma. She had first arrived in Emire ten years before and had quickly come to Seeve's attention as an intelligent and invaluable woman that could serve him well. The problem had always been that she did not believe in serving anybody or in staying still. She would not speak of her home on the eastern continent, or of her life

146

before. And while she had grown to harbour a certain amount of loyalty towards Seeve, she would disappear on a whim, sometimes for a year or more. Seeve had been the first to grant her the moniker of *The Wanderer*, and he had said it with a mixture of affection and irritation.

'I am honoured that you wish to speak with me,' said Jad. 'The last time I saw you was when you refused my father's offer of a place on the Council, insisting that you were about to embark on some great adventure.'

Tamsin smiled at the memory, 'He was furious.'

'But you would not back down,' said Jad, smiling too, 'I think you were the only one he could not break down by the force of one of his rages.'

'He was a good man, if a little too loud at times.' Her smile turned, 'It was only a year ago that I heard about everything that has happened. I have thought of you often since then.'

'One year?' Jad's eyes widened, 'you really must have been on a great adventure.' He tried to imagine what she might have seen. He had only ever crossed the sea twice when he was young and he could hardly remember it.

'I was on the surface.'

Jad gaped, 'For five years?'

'About that. Though time passes differently between our layer and the human world.'

'But why?'

'Why not? I thought it would be interesting.'

'Did you not get sick?'

'I started to. In the last year I began to feel a strange weakness. That was when I realised that I must return.'

Jad could not stop gaping, 'But was it not hard? Leaving the sun and the air behind?'

Tamsin lifted her shoulders, 'I did not want to die, so it was easy enough.'

'So you have seen what the humans are doing? How they are killing the Crystals?'

Tamsin stilled. She closed her eyes and sighed. 'I saw a great deal of awful things. I saw gallons of oil poured relentlessly into oceans, choking the life therein. I saw cities so full of toxic air that it hung in the streets like a vapour. But you must understand that the surface is full of wonders Natural wonders yes, but man made ones too. And there are many people that are doing all they can to help their planet. I offered my aid to these people.'

Jad frowned, 'You know what Bagor plans?'

'War? Oh, yes, I know. Rather than waiting centuries for the Crystals to die and to drain the life from our world, he wishes to eliminate our whole race now by sending us into a war we cannot hope to win.'

'So you do not agree with it?'

'I think that something should be done.'

Jad mulled that over. Tamsin had a tendency towards the mysterious.

'Something like what?'

'The answer is not killing humans, kid. Bagor will gain support because people will be scared or greedy enough to ignore sense. We can only imagine what he hopes to gain personally. He will argue that this war is for our people's sake, but that is not true. Whatever the true answer is, I do not know.'

'Then how do you know that there is another answer at all?'

'Because I believe it. When I returned to Emire I found this place a shambles. Myra was gone and there was no noise coming from Alashdial. There had been a break-in down at the library near Folston and Seeve could hardly bear to deal with any of it. It was chaos and for the first time in a long time I realised that I had to stop. Seeve needed me and I hoped that, one day, you and I would meet again and that you might need me too. Once I learned of all that Bagor had done and all that he intended, I vowed to be ready. I have never felt so at ease when still. For me to feel this way, for me to want to fight against him so strongly, I have to believe that there is a reason. There must be an alternative to war, a way that we can heal the world instead of hurting it. My last year here must have had purpose.'

'It sounds like Seeve was lucky to get you back.'

Tamsin laughed, 'Of course he was. He is lucky to have me at all, I am sure you will agree. But he is too stubborn to ever be broken completely. He would have pulled through. Besides, he has Karl.' She laughed again. 'No, my purpose is something more. I have heard of this Key. I will do all that I can to aid you.'

Jad was certain he did not deserve such loyalty from her but he nodded, grateful all the same. 'Thank you, but I am afraid I don't have much to tell you. We plan on reading every page of every book in the library until we find something that sounds like our Key.'

'Perhaps the Key should not be your only focus.'

Jad's gaze sharpened. 'What do you mean?'

A soft smile played across Tamsin's lips. 'Look to the last war between the Semei and the humans. Look to the history of the first five; your ancestors and the ancestors of the other royal lines.'

'Why?'

She shrugged, 'Because history repeats itself. Bagor wishes to repeat the war, perhaps the Key is a repeat as well.'

'But those histories are little more than legends.'

'All legends are born from truth, I have found. Regardless, it is always sensible to begin at the beginning, correct?'

'I guess,' said Jad, thinking hard. He did not see how history lessons would help them at all.

'The human girl; Kammy, is it?'

'Yes,' said Jad, more sharply than intended.

'What does she think of all this?'

Jad hesitated. He had not really spoken to her about it, not properly. He had not spoken to her properly about anything at all. Eric was right; he did need to try harder. 'I know she does not agree with the war.'

'That is not surprising. Look to history and talk to her, perhaps things will become clearer.'

Tamsin got to her feet and Jad rose with her. When she held out her hand he shook it, feeling the strength in her grip and trying to work out what it was that she was barely telling him.

'I don't...'

She cut him off, 'I am sure you do not want to hear it again, but you should...'

'Rest,' Jad sighed, 'I know.'

Tamsin smiled, 'I tease you, kid, but I stopped by here because I want you to know that I am with you. For all that it is worth.'

'It is worth a great deal,' said Jad with sincerity, 'the whole town will hear Tayah's joy when I tell her that the Wanderer is on our side.'

Tamsin grinned as she pulled open the door, her feline eyes bright. 'Talk to Kammy.'

Jad watched the door close and he frowned. He had the distinct impression that Tamsin knew something he did not, and that she was going to enjoy watching him struggle to figure it out.

CHAPTER FOURTEEN

EMIRE

The next day did not feel any better. Kammy did not leave her room, no matter how much Fii and Eric urged her too. Seeve had appeared and promised her the freedom of the town, but she felt no inclination to take advantage of his kindness. It was on the third day that Eric had threatened to throw her over his shoulder and carry her through the streets of Emire if she did not leave her room. Reluctantly, she had followed him and, reluctantly, she had agreed to do so the next day, and the next.

A week had passed and Kammy found herself alone in the town centre. The last traces of her concussion seemed to have passed and her shoulders had almost fully healed. Eric's insistence had done the trick, for she realised that doing *something* was a helpful distraction. Scouring the library looking for any clue about the Key kept her occupied. She had struggled at first, used to typing a word into Google and becoming an expert in minutes. But after a few hours she had started to enjoy browsing the heavy books. She had not found anything yet, but every book she had opened fascinated her. She had read tales of kings and queens from centuries past. She had discovered the horrors that could befall a Semei that tried to stretch their Soul too thin, or tried to squeeze themselves into a form too minuscule. She learned that the Semei called English 'Alash' and that there *were* other languages beneath the surface. Each book left her hungry to learn more. Things were not exactly *better*, but she could almost pretend that they were.

Emire was overwhelming. The streets were narrow and the rooftops hung overhead, so close together that only a thin strip of light burst through. Kammy had to remind herself that it was not sunlight every few minutes. There was a heavy heat to the day, held in by the walls and the sheer number of people between them. The smell was strong too; the scent of bodies pressed together, dry dirt mixed with sweat. And then there was the noise. The only town Kammy had ever seen was Erinsdale; a dull place with a few shops and not much else. Emire moved constantly. There was a hum in the air. She had never heard anything like it. It was somehow oppressive yet inviting and Kammy thought she might love it.

Still, Kammy kept her eyes on her feet. She had not forgotten that first evening on the wall and what Seeve had said. She was terrified that somebody would stop at any moment, that they would point and shout and then chase her beyond the town walls. Nothing of the sort had happened yet. The Semei of Emire were busy with their own business. They paid her no attention, but Kammy would not let herself relax.

She did not look very different from them, she realised, now that she was dressed the same. On the second morning in Emire, Fii had arrived with a bundle of clothes and shoes. She had been quite enthusiastic, holding shirts and dresses up against Kammy. At first, Kammy had not shared that enthusiasm, but as the days had passed she had started to pick her clothes more carefully. Her bag was the only thing that might look different. She had been told to keep the Key on her at all times, in case they had to leave suddenly, so she kept it tucked beneath her arm, hiding it as well as she could.

Kammy paid little attention to where she was going and when she took a left turn she walked into a wall of scents so strong that she almost stumbled backwards. She grinned, delighted that she had chanced upon Market Street. Stalls spilled out of homes onto the dirt. People were shouting at each other as they haggled over prices, their voices getting louder and louder as they struggled to be heard. Kammy took a deep breath and walked into it.

She passed fish stalls and had to pull her shirt up to cover her nose. She had to duck underneath the meat that hung overhead. She passed crates of vegetables and fruits, and her nose was assailed by the pungent smell of old cheese. A gaggle of children ran underfoot, followed by two chickens. In the blink of an eye the chickens were gone and two young girls sat giggling where they had just disappeared. A man, their father, scolded them half-heartedly and Kammy laughed. She let the sights and the smells flood her senses. She could forget everything when there was so much going on.

Her eyes fell onto a stall that she had not seen before. Her smile stretched wider at the sight of it. This stall was something quite different; a variety of pots and urns sitting atop an old table. Each pot and urn filled with some sort of powder. There seemed to be every shade of brown, but one was also a bright red and another a bruised purple. Between each pot sat a variety of small plants whose leaves Kammy did not recognise. It smelled exquisite and alien to her. She had never seen such things on Daleswick.

'Ah,' said a voice, 'you're not the only one entranced by the lost spices of Danorrah, child.'

Kammy looked up. A small woman stood behind the stall, her face a mass of wrinkles that hung over filmy eyes. Her yellowing teeth disappeared as her carefully prepared smile faded. She stared at Kammy, making no further sound. Kammy was so frightened that she could not move.

The woman's eyes filled with tears. She flitted out from behind the stall and her clawed hands gripped Kammy's wrist. 'Simbassi.'

Kammy's mouth dried, 'I don't...' she tried to step back, but she knocked into the wall of bodies behind her.

The woman only held on tighter, '*Simbassi.*'

The smell and the heat was suddenly cloying. Every breath burned and Kammy wrenched free, knocking into people as she tried to run against the tide. It was happening. She had been found out. She heard voices cry out in alarm as she pushed past. Then a strong grip held her and pulled her from the mass with a scream on the tip of her tongue.

'Are you all right?'

Kammy almost laughed. '*Eric.*' She pressed a hand to her chest, 'I thought...'

Eric fixed her with a look. 'How many times will I have to assure you, just because you're human does not mean you are going to get lynched.'

Kammy looked past him, at the crowd over his shoulder. Not a single person looked her way and the little woman was nowhere to be seen. She was out of immediate danger.

'It was just...' she paused. Eric already thought she was far too paranoid. 'Never mind.'

Eric eyed her suspiciously and then he seemed to relax. He clapped her on the shoulder and said, 'I'm impressed. You went out on your own.'

Kammy snorted. 'Self high five for that.'

'What?'

She laughed, 'Nothing. I was actually trying to get to the library, but I got a little distracted. Walk with me?'

She knew she did not need to ask. Eric seemed quite happy in the role of her babysitter. He beamed as they walked and Kammy felt like laughing for the second time in quick succession. That was another sign that Fii had been right; Kammy had started to laugh again.

It was Eric that drew attention. People nodded towards him or smiled as they whizzed about, ignoring Kammy. By all accounts, Jad and Eric had left a lasting impression on Emire when they were boys.

'I've been wanting to ask,' said Kammy, 'can you sense each other? Like, if a chicken ran out in front of you, would you be able to tell if it was a real chicken?'

'A chicken?' Eric laughed, 'It depends. If we concentrate then we can tell, but I wouldn't really call it sensing. A chicken that is actually Semei will move differently to a real chicken. Its instincts and behaviours will be different. Camoflaguing yourself as an animal is incredibly difficult, if you're attempting complete subterfuge.'

'So they can't sense that I'm human?'

Eric looked her in the eye, his green pair darker in the shadowed streets. 'Maybe when you had first arrived, there was...well, a smell.'

Kammy's jaw hung open, 'I smell bad?'

'Not bad,' Eric nudged her, 'just different. And not any more. So no, nobody will know you're human from looking at you.'

Kammy was still a bit ruffled by the smell revelation, but she nodded, feeling assured. Eric continued to stare at her. 'What?'

154

'I know what Seeve said upset you, I understand; it upset me too. But you have to understand, that Semei don't hate humans, not really. They don't hate you.'

'Tayah does.'

Eric sighed, 'Tayah has had to deal with some things. She shouldn't treat you the way she does, but she...she thinks that she needs to be strong for Boo's sake. She doesn't hate you. She just feels like she should.'

Kammy wanted to say that a person could be strong without being rude. She wanted to say that pretending to hate a person was no better than actually hating them, but Eric already looked uncomfortable enough. 'They look nothing alike.'

He shrugged, 'Different fathers...'

'Right,' said Kammy, itching to ask more. She bit her lip and glanced at Eric. It was clear that he did not want to talk about Tayah, no doubt because it was not his place. So Kammy changed tack. 'Tell me how this all started then. How did you all meet up with Jad when he first managed to get free?'

She had meant to lighten the mood but, if anything, Eric looked even more reluctant. 'It was pretty easy for Tayah. She just grabbed Boo and walked away from Alashdial. I had to sort things out with my family first.'

'I'm sorry,' said Kammy, 'we don't have to...'

But Eric shook his head and chuckled. His expression lightened and Kammy relaxed. She could not imagine ever seeing Eric upset and she did not want too.

'It's alright,' he said, 'it's a bit hard to talk about because I haven't seen my parents or my sisters in so long, but it's okay. They support me in what I'm doing, or trying to do. It was only difficult because I feared Bagor might target them should I leave for Jad. Me and my Da had a huge fight outside of our house, both of us shouting as loud as we could so everybody could hear. I told him he was a silly old man for believing in Bagor and he disowned me. It was all staged of course, but it did the trick. Bagor has left them alone,' he frowned, 'at least, as far as I know...'

Kammy smiled at him. Her curiosity was not sated, but she did not want to push him further. No matter what he said, his expression had darkened and she did not want to make him miserable. They carried on walking in silence and Kammy realised she had lost her bearings completely. The streets were so full that their progress was slow. She rummaged in her mind, trying to change the subject.

'Have you known Jad for a long time then?'

To her relief, Eric grinned. 'Feels like forever. We met here, actually. My Da came to Emire on business. I didn't understand any of it, but I begged him to let me come along anyway. I got bored quickly and managed to sneak away. I met Jad on the library rooftop. I already knew who he was, of course, and was surprised that he wasn't a stuffy brat. We were close from then on. We met Tayah two years later, through Fii. We didn't like her much at first, because she was a girl,' Eric smiled at the memory, 'but she soon showed us that girls could be just as good company as boys.'

Kammy could just picture a miniature version of Tayah, perhaps with two braids instead of one, kicking the boys until they let her join their fun.

She was pulled from her thoughts when the throng of bodies loosened around them. They stepped free of the dark streets into Tower Square. It was one of only three squares throughout the whole of Emire, and it looked like an ocean of space compared to the density that surrounded it. At its centre sat the library, with the tower sprouting out of its middle. Eric had told her that the round, glass face at its top was how they tracked the time of day. She had spent a whole evening watching the colour of the glass change as the light faded. It made her miss her simple watch.

'I'm not coming in,' said Eric, making a face, 'it was my turn yesterday. Will you be able to get back?'

Kammy nodded. The route between the library and the keep was a simple one as long as she did not allow herself to become distracted.

'Right, see you tonight then,' said Eric with a smile. He tossed her a wave before dashing off, his bright hair visible amongst the crowd until he turned a corner and passed out of sight. Kammy started to cross the square alone and she smiled as a gentle breeze lifted her hair. For the first time since she had entered this layer there were clouds in the sky, a few fluffy white ones, but the warmth still soothed. It would have been a very rare day to have such weather on Daleswick.

The library was not a particularly spectacular building. Apart from the tower and its size, it looked much like all the other buildings surrounding it. Still, it was Kammy's favourite place in Emire. The tall doors were open because of the heat and just beneath them Kammy spotted a familiar face staring at her. She slowed, glancing around, but Welm's magnified eyes were fixed on her face. She felt a chill that had nothing to do with the breeze. It was the first time that she had seen him since Littlebrook and she had not even considered that he might be in Emire. He started to walk towards her and Kammy looked for an escape, but he moved with surprising swiftness. He stopped a couple of paces away, shorter even than she. He tried to smile. Kammy did not smile back. She knew it was unfair to blame him when they had all been a part of it, but she had not forgotten that mug of hot lemon.

'I was hoping to see you,' he wheezed, his eyes fixed on her with an odd stillness. He held something out to her and Kammy blinked at it. It was a belt. It had a large pouch attached on one side, fastened by a metal clasp, and beside that was what looked suspiciously like a slingshot.

'Sorry?' she said.

'It is for you,' Welm pushed it towards her.

Kammy could hardly push it back. She stared at the belt that was now in her hands and spluttered. 'Why?'

Welm shuffled on his feet. Kammy had the impression that he was not much of a fan of talking. 'Your bag is too conspicuous. Plus, Jadanim told me of your show with the stones. I thought that, if you practice, the slingshot might be useful. For self defence.'

Kammy gaped at him. Was he giving her a weapon? Stunned, she did not notice Welm slip away until it was too late for her to thank him. Had the belt not been solid in her hands she might have thought that she had imagined the whole encounter. She scanned the square, but could not spot him and her eyes fell back to his gift. He was such a strange little man and he made her feel uncomfortable, but how could she possibly think badly of him when he had been so kind? She ran her fingers along the leather strap until they brushed the clasp on the pouch. She held it closer and she gasped again. Etched into the clasp was an image of a lioness; it was beautiful.

In a contented daze, Kammy stepped into the shade of the library, holding her belt tight to her chest. The head librarian was a severe-looking old man of impossible height and he was not happy that Seeve had granted Jad and the others full use of the library. He sneered, but said nothing as he watched Kammy mount the nearest staircase.

The library's exterior was quite plain but the interior was beautiful, full of dark wood and dark leather. The low burning torches on the walls cast a soft, hazy glow about the place. It smelt like its books, musty and old. The only sounds that could be heard, once you had stepped away from the entrance, were hushed whispers and the rustle of pages turning. Kammy took the next staircase, heading straight for the history section. She was met by rows and rows of shelves and with a happy sigh Kammy drifted between them, waiting for a title to jump out at her. She had never left Daleswick, never seen the world that she had learned about in class or from the internet. Now, a whole new world had opened before her. A world with a different history, a world with different cultures. There was so much to learn. When she reached the end of the row she stepped out into one of the quiet study areas and she froze.

Jad was sitting at a long desk with his neck craned over a huge book. He looked incredibly grumpy and Kammy wanted to duck away and pretend that she had not seen him, but something held her still. She wanted to talk to him. She had wanted to all week, but the thought alone made her feel awkward. He fascinated and frustrated her in equal measure. She felt comfortable with Eric and she was happy to avoid Tayah, but with Jad she was unsure of herself. He was royalty, which was intimidating enough. He had clearly been through a great deal in the past few years and he approached everything with an intensity beyond his nineteen years, an intensity that dwarfed Kammy. She never knew if he would smile or glare at her, and the whiplash made her reluctant to face him. She watched him turn a page and run a hand through his scruffy chocolate hair. She noted how much better he looked. His face held a healthy flush instead of a sickly pallor, and the dark circles around his eyes had gone. She had still not mentioned his eyes, and what she had seen in the river, to anybody. If only she could find the courage, she wanted to ask *him*. That thought decided her. Kammy squared her shoulders, ignoring the flutter of nerves in her stomach. She crossed to his desk and sat down in the chair opposite him.

'Found anything?' she whispered.

He jumped, his eyes jerking up to hers as he slammed the book that he was reading shut and pulled it close to his chest. Kammy raised her eyebrows.

'What?' he said, his cheeks reddening.

'You're looking for stuff about the Key, aren't you?'

'Oh, right. No.'

'No, you're not?'

'No, I haven't found anything.'

They stared at one another. Kammy felt her heart sink; was he *angry*? Angry with her? She had thought that their relationship had at least progressed beyond open hostility. She considered turning around and leaving without another word, but then she realised that she was angry too. Since his visit to her room he had ignored her all week. Surely she was entitled to some basic decency? So she stayed where she was, determined not to back down and to make things easy for him. She placed her new belt onto the table and Jad's eyes flicked down to it.

'What's that?' he said, after a long pause.

Kammy's eyes dropped to the lion clasp again and she smiled. When she looked up again Jad's book had disappeared into the pile beside him and he looked a lot more composed. Kammy looked from the pile back to his face, but he continued to stare at the belt.

'Welm gave it to me. I don't know why.'

Jad eyed it for a moment longer. 'He made it.'

'*What*?'

Jad shrugged.

Kammy frowned at him. 'Well, does he always make things like this?'

'He's always making *something*, though he focuses mainly on alchemy. He is a genius. That belt is more the sort of thing he would make in his spare time.'

'An alchemist?' Kammy leaned forwards, 'Like making gold? Potions and stuff?'

Jad looked at her. 'You know, we are in a library. We're not supposed to talk.'

Kammy folded her arms. 'We're whispering, that's allowed.'

159

They glared at one another, jaws clenched in mirrored stubbornness. Kammy wanted to know more about Welm. She knew nothing about alchemy, but she had read the word once or twice in books. She thought it was something like magic. Was it the same here, or did it mean something else to the Semei? Her mind jumped ahead, delighting at all the possibilities.

Jad sighed, 'Can I help you with something?'

Kammy jolted out of her imagination. She steadied herself. 'I would like some answers.'

'About alchemy? I'm not the person to ask.'

'About all sorts of things.'

'Well, I would need a question first.'

Kammy's nostrils flared. His unpredictability was *infuriating*. She took a deep breath and blurted, 'Are we right beneath my world? Under the surface?'

Jad looked surprised. Kammy was equally so. That was not what she had meant to say, not at all.

'Not directly. We are thousands and thousands of miles beneath the surface, as far as anyone can tell.'

Her curiosity was piqued. 'But that's impossible. We'd be too close to the centre and we'd burn.'

'Who says?'

'Common sense.'

'Then common sense is nonsense.'

Kammy narrowed her eyes. 'Could a human...dig deep enough to find this place?'

'I don't think it would work that way. The divide between the worlds is more than a physical one.'

'So it's what?'

He shrugged. 'How would I know?'

'Okay,' she took a deep breath. She had to stop being so afraid. She had to ask him about his eyes. 'Why do the Semei know about humans when humans know nothing about the Semei?'

He took a moment to think, and Kammy thought his expression started to soften. 'Some humans might know, somewhere. Otherwise, I cannot know why the knowledge was lost to your people. I suppose it might have something to do with the Gate. Ever since it appeared we have seen what was on the other side, so it's hard to forget humans. How can our history forget when we know what we could find there?'

'Could find?'

'You won't have noticed, not yet, but the air, for one thing, is different on the surface. It's fresher, more invigorating. The feel of the sun on your skin is...it is incomparable.'

'That's depressing.'

'It's why the Gate is restricted. It's off limits to most because the surface can be addictive. Most Semei fear it anyway, and would not pass through. But our past is dotted with Semei that did dare and that stayed too long on the surface.'

'Too long?'

Jad nodded, 'we cannot survive there.'

Something struck Kammy and she swallowed a sudden lump in her throat. 'Can I survive here?'

Jad looked up at her from beneath dark lashes, 'I don't think you need to worry.'

'Why? Are you going to take me back soon?' Then the bitterness she had harboured all week rose up and she lost control of her mouth. 'Is this because of the war? The humans all need to die anyway, so what's the point in keeping me around?'

Jad tensed, 'What?'

'Do you hate humans, Jad?' she heard herself say.

'No,' he said, without hesitation.

Kammy wanted to stop herself but the words were irrepressible and then she thought, why should she stop? Why shouldn't she tell him what she thought? 'But if it wasn't Bagor...if it was Seeve suggesting this war, you'd support it?'

Kammy saw it start again. Was this why she was pushing him, so she could check one more time that it was real? His pupils began to drown, besieged by bright blue. He was angry. She wondered if her eyes had done the same. She wondered why he was not asking her about it either.

'My people will die.'

'Or mine will.'

'I wouldn't be so sure about that,' Jad hissed.

'What does that mean?'

Jad shook his head. His hands were balled on the desk and people were starting to stare as their voices rose. 'Nothing,' he ground out, 'we shouldn't talk about this here.'

'Talk about what? Killing humans? You *would* fight, wouldn't you?'

'If it came to it, you think I should just stand by and watch my people die?'

'My people are innocent.'

'Ignorant.'

Kammy had never felt such heat burn through her. 'Then maybe you're no better than Bagor.'

Jad's face turned deathly white. His eyes jolted back to normal and his anger fled. He stared at her for a second that lasted an eternity and then he stood, drawing more eyes towards them as he started to walk away.

Kammy's own fury deserted her and her heart sank. 'Wait,' she said, pushing her chair back, 'Jad...' she grabbed her belt and darted after him, 'I didn't mean that, okay? I just...' faintly, she heard the clattering of footsteps, but Kammy ignored it and grabbed Jad's arm, making him face her. He looked sick.

She gazed up at him, 'I just want to understand.'

Jad swallowed, looking down at where her small hand held his left arm.

A shout went up from behind them and they both turned to see Tayah bent double with her hands on her knees. She was breathing

162

heavily. When she straightened her eyes sought Jad's. She looked petrified.

'He's here,' she said, 'Bagor is here.'

CHAPTER FIFTEEN

TICK TOCK

Jad laughed. He saw the wild look in her eyes and he laughed. Everything became very still, apart from Tayah's head which nodded slowly. Jad shook his own, unable to stop laughing.

'Jad,' Tayah took a step closer, 'he's here.'

Finally the shock passed and the laughter ceased. Jad felt something cold and dark descend over him and he shrunk beneath it. *Not now*, he thought. The nameless faces that surrounded them started to whisper. They all knew who he was. He should have stayed hidden.

'Where?' he said.

'Seeve is waiting to meet him at the keep.'

Jad grabbed Kammy's hand and started to move.

'Hey,' Tayah reached for him, 'you can't, Jad. You can't go up there.'

'Do you think I'm an idiot?' he growled as he strode past with Kammy following close behind. She did not speak, but held tightly on to his hand.

Bagor is here, he thought, *in Emire*. Jad could picture his face and his smile so clearly. His mind burned and he tried to hurry, but a crowd had formed. Word that the king of Alashdial was in town had already spread. The library was emptying and the faces of the people that passed looked bright with interest. Jad wanted to howl at them all. He bit down on his tongue, hoping that the pain might distract him. It did not. The cold anger rocked him closer to the brink. He had to shove against the crowd that rushed for the exit.

'Jad, *stop*,' he heard Tayah cry.

He ignored her. He had to see for himself.

'Jad, you're hurting me...'

Her voice seeped through. He looked down at his hand squeezing Kammy's and he realised he had been clinging to her. He let go immediately, distracted long enough by the thought that he had hurt her for Tayah to catch up.

'Thank you...' Tayah started.

Jad was still looking at Kammy. Her eyes were round with concern for him even as she pulled her hand back to her chest.

'I'm sorry,' he said. Then he slipped into himself and found his Soul.

The wolf fit around him like a glove and Jad savoured the familiar rush. He had not shifted for a week and he leapt forwards, feeling stronger than he had for a long time. He could hear Tayah shouting behind him, but he quickly pulled away from her. As a wolf, he no longer had to push past people. They parted before him, their eyes widening as they fell upon him, offering no hindrance. He did not run to the entrance, but to the next set of stairs. He bounded up them, relishing the wolf's speed. People had to dive out of his way for he could not stop. The staircase grew steeper and more uneven. He climbed, taking four steps with each bound. Round and round he ran until he reached the top and found himself in a small square room.

Jad let go of the wolf and hurried over to the glass face. Energy charged him and his chest heaved. He pressed his hands against the glass and stared towards the keep. The square in front of it was full of people and still more flocked towards it. A space in the middle had been kept clear and Jad could see a figure standing alone just in front of the steps; Seeve. Then a second figure broke free from the crowd and Jad felt ice shoot down his spine. His breath fogged the glass as Bagor strode towards the General. There was no doubting it was him. No other man held himself in such a way, as if he knew he was untouchable. Bagor held out his hand and Seeve took it. Jad could not tear his eyes away even as they burned.

'Are you *insane*?'

He looked back over his shoulder. Tayah glared at him as she clambered up the last few steps.

'Do you *want* to draw attention to yourself?'

'Please, they already know who I am.'

Kammy appeared behind Tayah, her breath laboured. While Tayah looked furious, Kammy only looked bewildered. He turned away from the pair of them. His eyes found the two small figures standing in front of the keep. They had not moved. He could see Seeve's mouth working and Bagor threw his head back, laughing. Jad swore and his fist clenched. He needed to know what they were saying.

Tayah sighed behind him, 'Okay, what's happening?'

'I don't know,' he growled, then the frustration became too much. He slapped his hand against the glass. 'Dammit, I need to be down there.'

'You *can't*.'

He rounded on her. 'He is here, right *here*. I will not just stand by and do nothing.'

Tayah grabbed his hands, holding on when he tried to pull back. 'You listen to me,' she said in a low voice, 'hey, look at me. There is nothing you can do right now. Do not be a fool.'

He stared at her. He remembered all those times that her rash actions had caused him problems and he wanted to throw each one of them back in her face. He opened his mouth to do so, but Kammy's voice stopped him.

'He looks so small,' she said.

She stood beside him, gazing out of the glass just as he had been. But her eyes were bright with curiosity and not anger. This was the man that had murdered her friend and torn her from her home, yet she looked calm as she gazed down at his form. Jad envied her.

He pulled free of Tayah and growled, 'He is a monster.'

Kammy turned her head towards him, but she did not lift her eyes. Quietly, she said, 'But you aren't.'

166

He stared at her, feeling the rage leak out of him. She was apologising for what she had said. He could see the regret on her face. His eyes dropped to his arm and the scar beneath his shirt.

'Am I not?'

Kammy turned fully to face him.

'Somebody's coming,' said Tayah, backing away from the stairs.

Jad heard the pounding of heavy footsteps. He held his breath and waited. He saw a flash of red hair and then Eric stood before them, catching his breath.

'Thank the Mother,' he gasped, 'I thought you might have taken to the rooftops.'

Somebody else came behind him, a wiry man with his hair slicked back in an attempt to hide the fact that he was balding. Karl had been Seeve's second in command for as long as Jad could remember. He had always been a stern man, but his expression as he looked at Jad was especially grim.

'We have to move, now.'

'But...' Jad could not bear it. He looked back over his shoulder. Seeve and Bagor had started to walk towards the keep.

'What do we need to do?' said Tayah.

'Bagor brought a small retinue, no doubt so that he could get close to Emire by staying off the roads to avoid being detected. Once the formalities are done, his people will have the freedom of the town. We must get you away before then.'

'That is pointless,' said Jad, shaking his head, 'he will know that we are here, or that we have been. There is no way to hide it.'

Karl's beady eyes narrowed. 'It is not pointless. If Seeve denies that you are within the town walls then Bagor can not question his word, unless he wishes to make an enemy of Seeve. In doing that, he would lose many of the followers he has worked so hard to gain. No, he will not question Seeve yet. But if Bagor's people find you and have proof of Seeve's lie, then he can denounce the General without concern. He can force Seeve to give you up. Is that what you wish?'

Jad clamped his mouth shut.

'Good,' said Karl.

Eric shook his head. 'Why is he here? Why now?'

'Dorren may be an idiot,' said Jad, his shoulders slumping, 'but Bagor is not. Seeve was my father's closest friend. It was obvious that I would turn to him.' His own idiocy made his stomach squirm. 'We should never have come here.'

'No.'

They all turned to Kammy. Jad had never heard her speak with such conviction. She looked thoughtful.

'We had no choice but to come here, Jad. If we had tried to go any further we'd probably be dead, and you surely would be. You needed to rest. We've been safe here and if we do what Seeve asks, then he can continue to keep us safe until an opportunity presents itself, right?' She offered him a small smile.

Eric tossed Kammy a wide grin before turning to Karl, 'So what is Seeve's plan?'

'There is an abandoned farmhouse in the Basin that is not far. It has been awaiting work for months,' said Karl. 'I can lead you there now, before Bagor's men are free to roam the streets.'

'Won't he look there?' asked Kammy. She had cinched her belt around her waist. Jad noticed how her fingers rested on the slingshot.

'We noted the faces of those that entered the town. The watchmen will not let anyone leave Emire without an escort for the duration of their stay, under the guise of their protection. As long as you are outside the walls, you will be safe.'

'How long...'

'We do not have time for questions,' snapped Karl. His face was flushed and his head shone beneath his thin hair. 'We must go, now.'

Jad looked again. Bagor and Seeve had disappeared and the crowd began to drain away from the keep. He did not want to walk away. He did not think it made him much of a leader. He thought it made him a coward.

'Come on Jad,' Tayah urged. They were all staring at him.

168

He closed his eyes and nodded.

Karl did not hesitate. He turned on his heel and disappeared down the stairs. Jad could not move. He felt a hand on his shoulder and looked at Eric.

'I will kill him,' Jad said, nodding slowly.

Eric's expression did not change. 'But not today.'

'Come *on*,' Tayah cried.

The flight down the staircase of the tower was very different from the rush Jad had felt as he had soared to the top as the wolf. The silence crashed around them and tension buzzed in his ears. He wished he could shift again, knowing that it would help to calm him and to make him feel stronger, but Karl refused. It would only draw more unwanted attention, he said. When they reached the main building of the library, Karl slowed their pace to that of a brisk walk. Jad thought it foolish. It would only take a quick glance for any of them to be recognised. They would either make it out of Emire or they would not, it would not make a difference if they cartwheeled along the way.

The library had emptied out when word of Bagor's arrival had spread, but people were starting to trickle back inside and they stared openly as Karl led the procession past. Jad kept his eyes on the floor, his jaw clenched so tight he thought it might snap.

'This is *stupid*,' he ground out.

Kammy was the only one that heard. She glanced back at him, her eyes wide and fearful. He wished he could reassure her, but all he could think was that once Bagor had the Key she would be of no more use to him. She would be thrown aside and killed.

'Keep going,' Jad urged as he started to walk faster.

They made it down the first set of stairs and then the next. The head librarian glared at them each in turn as they walked by. Then they were outside and Jad had to hold up a hand to shield his eyes from the bright light. Still, Karl did not pause. He turned sharply, his arms swinging at his sides as he marched. They followed him one by one and Jad glanced from left to right. The smatterings of people around were not paying them any attention, but they would start to if they continued to move so unnaturally. Jad pulled himself up beside Kammy.

'We should talk.'

'What?' Kammy sounded alarmed.

'Not about anything in particular...' Jad shrugged, 'it will just look a bit more normal if we talk. Rather than walking single file as if we were marching to our doom.'

'Oh, right. Sure.'

Karl led them out of the square. They plunged into the heart of Emire and its famed streets that were so often full to bursting. They were not full now, though more people were appearing by the second. Jad scowled, checking their faces to see if he recognised them. He wondered which traitors had accompanied Bagor from Alashdial, and how many of them he knew well.

'You still look like you're marching to your doom.'

'Huh?' Jad glanced at Kammy. She looked tense, but there was a glitter of mirth in her eyes. 'Oh.' He tried to relax and Kammy giggled. His scowl deepened and she laughed harder. After a moment he found he smiled despite himself.

'I didn't think you would find this so amusing,' he said, his eyes never ceasing to sweep over every inch of the space around them.

She shrugged, her short legs having to work hard to match Karl's loping strides. 'I'm terrified, but there isn't really much I can do about it, is there? Maybe hysteria will strike soon.'

Jad did not think so. He had expected hysteria from her once, but she was tougher than she looked. He glanced at her quickly out of the corner of his eye. Right now she looked resolute and determined; a far cry from the frantic girl Eric had first led him too.

'Will Fii and Boo be safe?'

'Yes.'

'And Welm?' she said, her hands resting on her belt.

Jad's mouth curved into a smile. 'Oh, he'll be fine.'

Jad spotted a flash of red and he tensed, ready to grab Kammy and to shout for the others to run. He blinked again and let out a breath. It was just a woman's scarf.

'What is it?' said Kammy, stepping closer to him.

'Nothing,' he said, but he placed his hand on her back anyway and they closed up to the others.

Jad had never moved through the streets of Emire so freely. It was normally a battle, which was what had first driven him to the rooftops when he was younger. They made quick progress, hitting the outer edge of town without any trouble. The buildings seemed to shrink around them, still pressing in close but growing shorter the further they walked. Jad could see the old walls up ahead. They had been built in a different age and had been a ruin until a decade ago. Seeve had been ridiculed for bothering to restore them, for when had the Semei fought a war? Jad suspected Seeve felt rather smug about his decision now.

'You're doing it again.'

Jad shook himself. 'What?'

'You look suspicious,' said Kammy.

'How are you so calm?' he asked, incredulous.

'I'm not, I guess I must just be hiding it well. Plus, we're almost there, aren't we?'

They were passing the stables, stray strands of hay sunk underfoot. Then the walls were before them, the gates open to reveal the fields beyond. Jad's gaze flitted up to the wall and he braced himself to find unwelcome eyes upon them. But there was nobody there that should not be, just two watchmen wearing the crest of Emire. They nodded at Karl, but said nothing as the small group piled past. With another look at Kammy, Jad forced himself to relax. He remembered the book that she had caught him reading. He would have to talk to her about that soon.

Karl stopped abruptly. He stared out over the Basin and Jad followed his gaze. There were countless cottages and farms dotted across the fields, but he spotted their farmhouse immediately for it was hard to miss. It sat alone at the top of a smooth rise. It's windows had been boarded up and it was clearly in disrepair, but it was close. They would be tucked away soon. They would be hiding from Bagor and Jad would be unable to hurt him.

'I must return,' said Karl, 'Bagor will notice my absence, but Seeve did not trust another to bring you here. Like I said, when the formalities are through, Bagor's people will be watched. You will be safe. Food and drink will be provided for you in due course. Do you understand?' He looked at Jad.

Jad felt a weight on his heart. He looked back, but he could not see the keep, only the crooked red houses of Emire.

'This is for the best,' said Eric, offering him a lopsided smile, 'if we can just be patient, then we can find a way to beat him, Jad. I promise.'

'We've found nothing in the library,' he said, feeling hopeless.

'But we will,' Tayah cocked her head to the side, 'so let's go settle in to our temporary home.'

Their confidence was hard to ignore. Jad looked at Karl and nodded, there was nothing else he could do. Karl managed a tight smile before he took off, leaving the four of them on the dirt track that led away from Emire and away from their farmhouse. Jad turned away from the road and looked out over the fields.

'We had better move then,' he said.

Tayah smirked at him, 'Lighten up tough guy,' she said, laughing when he snarled at her. 'I'll race you.'

'What...' Jad started, but Tayah spun away. Eric started running too, and even Kammy followed close behind. Shaking his head, Jad took off after them. The quicker they were inside, the better.

They hit the first field. The flowers were bright yellow and they reached up to Jad's knees. As the four of them tore through, the flowers trembled and Tayah sneezed. It was a great booming sound. Kammy snorted a laugh just ahead of him and Tayah glanced back with narrowed eyes. Jad watched as Kammy covered her mouth, but Tayah sneezed again and Kammy could not contain it. Rather than looking offended, Tayah looked wicked. She slowed and her hand trailed behind her. Then she turned suddenly and ran at Kammy. Kammy barely had time to blink before Tayah's hand, full of crushed flower heads, was in her face. Tayah whirled away, cackling as Kammy held her hands over her face, sniffing and gasping. Jad felt the last of his tension ebb as a laugh bubbled up in his throat. He slowed beside Kammy as she wiped her face clean and he was relieved to see that she still smiled. She glanced at him, her eyes sparkling and she leapt at him. Jad stepped back but could not escape her. He closed his eyes as she threw the flowers into his face.

'Hey,' he spluttered, his nose beginning to itch, but Kammy was already gone.

He tore after her. He sneezed twice and he heard Kammy laugh harder. He pushed his legs, running as fast as he could but he did not close in on her. She looked back at him, her hair flying up around her face.

Eric had already reached the cottage. 'She's faster than you, Jad,' he shouted as Tayah pulled up beside him.

Jad ran harder, his eyes fixed on the back of her shirt. She was so small, he thought, how could she possibly outrun him? But she scampered on and with a cry of delight Eric picked her up when she reached the cottage, throwing her up in the air in celebration. Jad pulled up beside them, shaking his head.

'You lost,' Tayah smiled.

'Yeah, yeah,' he muttered as Eric placed Kammy back on her feet. Jad pushed Tayah gently, 'Let's just get inside.'

They were breathless, with smiles plastered across their faces. They were safe now, and the release was exhilarating. Jad pulled on the door and it swung open easily. He held it for the others and followed them inside.

The smell of damp and rot struck him first. Kammy wrinkled her nose while Eric made a disgusted sound and Jad did not blame them. The cottage had clearly been left to fester for a long time. The downstairs was one large space. A sticky looking green film coated the walls. Cracks of light crept through the boards over the windows. All but one of them were covered and that one did little to illuminate the place. Other than a table, two chairs and an untrustworthy looking staircase at the back, the place was empty.

'Well,' said Tayah, lowering herself carefully onto one of the chairs, 'this is going to be fun.'

'At least we know Bagor will never suspect we're here,' said Eric, squinting at the walls. He stepped back, frowning, 'Who could stand it?'

'I'm sure Seeve will bring us some things,' said Kammy, her eyes bright as she dropped onto the second chair, 'to make it more comfortable.'

Jad watched her. It appeared that she could not stop smiling. The run had brought a glow to her cheeks and he found himself wanting to smile just looking at her. There, again, loomed Ania in his mind. He quickly looked away to see that Tayah watched Kammy too, a thoughtful expression on her face.

A rumbling sound made them all jump. Eric scratched the back of his head and laughed as he patted his stomach. 'I'm hungry,' he said.

Jad rolled his eyes, 'You're always hungry.'

Movement caught his attention. He looked away from Eric to see Kammy's smile disappear. She looked petrified. Tayah noticed it too and she turned to look at something behind Jad. She shot to her feet, her chair flying backwards.

'No...'

Jad turned and beheld what had them so terrified. A bird sat on the windowsill, a familiar one. Its eyes were turned towards them, its feathers a deep shade of red. It flapped out of sight as Jad backed towards his friends. The door creaked open.

Ria stepped inside. Her eyes met Jad's for the briefest of moments before finding Tayah's. She looked as though she were about to smile, then stopped herself. Jad wanted to check on Tayah, but he did not dare take his eyes away from Bagor's most loyal subject.

'How did you...' Eric started.

'I did not enter the city with the others, nor did I follow the procession to meet with Seeve. I waited for you to make your move.'

Jad closed his eyes. He *had* seen her when he had spotted that flash of red.

Ria looked over Jad's shoulder to where he knew Kammy sat, 'Come with me.'

Jad heard Kammy's sharp intake of breath and he stepped in front of her. 'No,' he said.

Ria laughed. She looked at him and she shook her head. She placed her hands on her hips. 'You are lucky that it is me that has found you. You should be more willing to cooperate.'

'Lucky?' Jad glared at her, 'Why? Because you won't lead Bagor right to us? Or us right to him?'

'Lucky because I might not tell him where you are hiding. Lucky because I ask only for the human and not for you, Ollarion.'

'Kammy is going nowhere with you.'

Ria stepped further inside. Jad had to tilt his head to meet her eye.

'I could take her.'

Jad tensed, 'Then we would fight you.'

Ria's sneer wavered. 'Then give me the Key.'

'He said no,' Tayah spat.

Ria's focus snapped away from Jad. Her aura of calm fell away altogether. She was distracted, and Jad tried desperately to think of a way that they could take advantage.

Ria spoke to Tayah with an edge to her voice. 'It is getting harder to protect you.'

'I don't care,' Tayah's voice trembled, 'I don't want your protection. You're worse than he is.'

'He will *save* us,' Ria cried, stepping closer still, 'don't you see that? He is the only one that can, the only one that has the courage and the vision. I know he has done wrong in the past, but he wants to make up for it. He wants...'

Tayah's eyes shone, 'I don't want to hear it.'

'Please, Tay...'

'Stop it,' said Eric, putting his arm around Tayah's shoulders. She leaned into him and Jad could see that she was shaking.

'Do what you came to do,' Jad said, 'or leave.'

Ria gathered herself. With one last look at Tayah, she drew herself up to her full height. She pushed her hair back off her face and smirked at Jad, though her eyes betrayed her simmering distress. She looked at Kammy again and Jad felt something cold uncurl itself in the pit of his stomach. Ria was alone, and she would not fight them. So why had she come?

'I will tell Bagor that I saw no sign of you in the city. This trip was not truly about bringing you home anyway. He will leave you a message, just in case. Your friend,' she nodded at Kammy, 'Jamie isn't it?'

Jad felt dread fill him. 'Get out,' he hissed.

But Ria ignored him. 'Jamie is alive. If you wish for him to remain that way then you shall return to Alashdial with the Key, and soon. You will be welcomed.'

With a burst she became a bird again, and with one shriek she was gone.

CHAPTER SIXTEEN

A SEA OF FLOWERS

Jamie was alive.

That knowledge set her whole body alight. The world looked brighter. Her fears of war and of children's tales no longer concerned her. As Jamie had come back to life, so had she. Every nerve in her body screamed for movement, for action, but the cottage was still.

She looked at Jad, ready for his wide smile to meet her own. He looked at her, but he did not smile. She felt the first spark of doubt when she recognised the pity in his eyes. She looked to Eric instead, attributing Jad's response to one of his strange moods. But Eric would not meet her eye and Tayah was lost some place else entirely.

'You all heard that, right?' Kammy tried to laugh.

They said nothing. Jad continued to stare at her. His throat bobbed and his lips parted, but he remained silent.

'Stop looking at me like that.'

He did as she asked. He looked at Eric instead and she could only watch as the pair of them seemed to come to some sort of silent agreement. Jad nodded and Eric started to lead Tayah back to her chair.

Only then did Jad start talking. 'I doubt Bagor will send anyone else for us after Ria, but we should still be careful. I'll take first watch outside. I 'm sure somebody will be along with food soon.'

Kammy could not believe what she was hearing. 'We can find food on the way,' she cried.

But Jad had his back to her and moved towards the door. She turned to Eric, incredulous, but he was talking to Tayah, his voice low. Jad was about to leave without even acknowledging Ria's words. They were acting like nothing had happened.

'*Stop.*'

Jad could not ignore that. He turned back to her, everything about him screaming his reluctance.

Kammy drew in a shaky breath, 'You heard what Ria said.'

'Yes.'

She blinked at him. She could not understand why he had suddenly become so cold.

'Then say something,' she said.

He laughed bitterly. 'All that I have to say are things that you do not want to hear.'

'Try me.'

He took a step closer to her. 'There is nothing that we can do.'

He might as well have slapped her. 'We can do what Ria said. We can take them this *stupid* Key and Jamie will be okay.'

Jad looked at Eric. His eyes were starting to change; she was sure hers had too.

'This is exactly what Ria wanted, for her to react like this.'

'Do not do that. Do *not* talk as if I'm not standing right here.'

'What difference does it make,' said Jad, with a shrug that made Kammy want to punch him, 'you're not going to listen.'

'Why are you being like this? I might listen if you would *talk* to me.'

Eric tried to interject, 'Jad...'

Jad's mouth snapped shut. His gaze fell to the floor and there were bright spots of red in his cheeks.

Kammy could only shake her head, 'Fine, I don't care. I don't know what's going on here, but I am going to save my friend.' She fixed her eyes on the open door and stormed towards it.

Jad stepped in front of her, 'You are not going anywhere.'

Her frustration burst out of her in an eruption of fury. She ripped her bag off her shoulder and she flung it across the room. 'There,' she cried, as it landed with a dull thump, 'keep the bloody thing. I'm leaving.'

She tried to step past him, but he blocked her again and she bounced off his chest. He wrapped a hand around her wrist and she glared up at him.

'Let go of me.'

Eric tried again, 'Kammy...'

But neither Jad nor Kammy heard him. They were held in a battle of wills, their eyes locked together by the force of the anger radiating between them.

Jad's voice was a low whisper. 'If you go back there you will end up dead. You are not leaving.'

'You do not get to tell me what I can and cannot do.' Kammy tried to pull away, but he held on and she laughed in his face. 'I see how it is. As long as we're all doing what you want, helping you deal with Bagor, then everything is fine. But the rest of us? Do we not matter? Or is it just me? I guess you don't mind leaving humans to die after all.'

He let go of her as if he'd been shocked. He nodded once, swallowing again and again as if choking something back. Then he turned and stalked away, slamming the door shut behind him.

Kammy started after him, but somebody else pulled her back. She spun, ready to scream in Eric's face, but he lowered his gaze to hers and she could not do it. She swallowed her anger and he smiled at her.

'Just take a moment and breathe,' he said, 'breathe.'

Kammy did as he asked. She let him lead her back to the table and push her into the seat opposite Tayah. Half her rage had left with Jad and in its place settled an uncomfortable numbness.

'I'm sorry about Jad. He didn't handle that very well, but he is just trying to look out for you.'

Kammy scoffed, 'No, he isn't. He just doesn't think I could do it.'

'You couldn't.' Kammy started to protest, but Eric knelt down beside her and took hold of her hand. 'You couldn't. Just as I couldn't, and Jad couldn't. None of us could, not alone. That is why we have to stick together.'

He gave her hand a reassuring squeeze, but Kammy continued to shake her head, 'I just don't understand. Jamie is alive. Why did he react like that? Why did all of you react like that?'

Eric shot a quick look at Tayah. She was slouched in her seat, staring at her lap and paying them no attention. He looked worried, but Kammy could not spare that a thought; she could think of nothing but her best friend. He was a prisoner somewhere and he had no idea what was happening to him.

'Okay,' Eric stood and held up a finger, 'for one, there is no point in rushing into anything and making rash decisions. If we were to act, we would need to think things through first. And for another...' he paused, and the look on his face told Kammy to brace herself. 'For another, Ria might have been lying. It's highly likely that she was just trying to entice you, to make it easier for them. I'm sorry Kammy, but we can't risk the Key for nothing.'

Kammy had not considered that possibility. It had not even floated close to the edge of her consciousness. She felt as though the air had been knocked out of her, but she held it together. There was still a chance and Jamie was *not* nothing.

'We don't even know what the Key is.'

'I know,' said Eric, his voice gentle with understanding, 'but it's all we have.'

Kammy's eyes sought her bag across the room. She took a deep breath and shook her head. 'Why did Ria just leave like that? Why didn't she fight us and force me to go with her?'

'Well, Ria is strong but four against one were not great odds for her and...' Eric shifted, looking uncomfortable. ' She won't fight us, not while...Well, she never has.'

'Why not?'

Her question hovered in the air for a moment, then Tayah stood, surprising them both.

'Because she's my sister.'

Kammy could only stare as Tayah marched past them and disappeared up the rickety staircase. She turned stunned eyes to Eric and he nodded with a sad smile on his face. Kammy could hardly believe it. Ria and Tayah? But then she pictured Tayah's amber eyes and realised with a jolt that Ria had the same pair.

Eric dropped into the chair that Tayah had just vacated. He ran a hand across his bristly hair as Kammy tried to make sense of it all.

'So, Ria just lets you go? She isn't really on Bagor's side?'

'Ria is fanatical about Bagor. She is hungry for his approval. When she found Jad alone, when he saved you that first time, she was happy to fight him. It is Tayah and Boo alone that she truly wants to protect. We have hardly seen her over the last two years. The few times that Bagor has sent people after us, he has never sent Ria. I suppose he is doing her some sort of kindness, by not forcing her to choose. But it is inevitable that she will have to eventually. She has this delusion that Tayah will...see the light one day and leave Jad, but that won't happen. Neither of us would leave him. Not for anything.'

Kammy did not doubt him. 'How does something like that happen? They're family, but they are on completely different sides.'

Eric shrugged, his eyes on the stairs, 'Blood does not make you family. Just ask Jad.'

Kammy's curiosity was piqued, but when she turned to ask him more he was still staring after Tayah. She could see that he was worried. His eyes danced from the stairs towards the door, and back again. If only he could split himself into pieces and comfort them all at once.

Kammy smiled at him. 'Go after her. I'll talk to Jad.'

Eric looked uncertain, 'I don't know if that's a good idea.'

'I'm fine,' said Kammy, placing her hands on the table. 'See? I've even stopped shaking.' Learning Tayah's secret had doused the remaining embers of her anger. 'I promise that I won't do anything stupid.'

'You're sure you're okay?'

Kammy nodded. Eric smiled at her, ruffling her hair as he hurried past. Kammy watched him disappear, off to be Tayah's shoulder to lean on. She found herself wondering, while Eric was supporting all of them, who was there to support Eric?

That thought was enough to steady her reeling mind. For Eric's sake, she would force herself to breathe and to think. She had not been completely honest with him, for she was not okay. She was shaken and terrified and excited. But she felt calm enough to face Jad again. She stood and stepped outside, not bothering to close the door. Jad's talk of keeping watch had been no more than an excuse for him to run away from Kammy. Ria's word in Bagor's ear would keep them safe in their cottage.

The sun, the *light*, was setting, or fading, she supposed. Everything it touched was kissed by a warm orange glow. Emire sat ahead of her, its red buildings looked like a maze of fire. The heat of the day had faded to something more comfortable and Kammy forced herself to focus. She could not see Jad so she started to walk around the cottage, crushing weeds beneath her feet. She spotted him as soon as she rounded the corner. He stood out clearly against the sea of red flowers that surrounded him. He had his back to her and just seeing him made the phantom of her anger rise. He had treated her cruelly, so she had returned the favour. He might refuse to talk to her ever again, for all she knew.

She pushed that thought aside as she remembered that moment just before, when she had been overtaken by daring. When she had thrown the flowers into his face she had felt a split second of panic, but he had laughed. They had all laughed, together. No matter how hard Jad might try to pretend otherwise, Kammy had become a part of something with these people. She had not known them long, but they were all she had for the moment. She could be afraid of anything else, but not them.

She started towards him, letting her fingertips brush against the soft petals at their tips. She stopped a few paces away. He stood so still that she did not want to disturb him.

'Have you calmed down?'

Her eyes narrowed, 'Have you stopped being an arse?' To her relief she heard him laugh and she relaxed. 'You know,' she said, 'for future reference, I'd appreciate it if you explained what you were thinking, rather than just expecting me to understand.'

At first he did not say anything. Then he turned to face her and her breath caught. Kammy felt foolish but bathed in the evening light he looked softer, somehow.

'I am sorry,' he said, 'I just...I knew what you were thinking and what you would want to do. I didn't know what to say to you,' he shrugged, 'I never know what to say. And the fact that Ria had given you this hope made me so angry because it's cruel. But I should not have taken that out on you.'

Kammy closed her eyes. She heard what he was trying to tell her; that Jamie was still dead and that Ria had lied. 'It's okay,' she said, 'I'm sorry too, for what it's worth.

'You had every right to say what you did. I can see why I might come across that way: selfish. I've thought it about myself often enough.'

Kammy closed her eyes, 'I don't really think that you are selfish.'

She meant it. She might have thought that Jad was rude, prone to foul moods, and incredibly frustrating - but he was not selfish. She had not forgotten everything that he had done for her, starting with the first time she had stumbled through the forest's mouth.

'I've been meaning to talk to you about something,' he said, 'about your eyes.'

Kammy's breath hitched and their eyes met. She started to laugh and Jad looked confused. She waved a hand in apology. 'I'm sorry, it's just...ever since the river, when I saw your eyes change, just like mine have done all my life, I've been dying to ask you about it. I could never get the words out and now...' she lifted her shoulders, 'I think I've had enough revelations today. Do you think you could tell me tomorrow instead?' She could hardly believe she was saying it. Her eyes had been the cause of so much pain and here was her chance to understand. Yet, somehow, it no longer felt important. They were only her eyes; a part of her, but not everything. Her eyes would not change whether Jamie was alive or dead.

Jad nodded. He stared at her in the same way that he had when they had rushed through Emire, towards the cottage. Her stomach flipped and she dropped her eyes, pushing her hair behind her ears.

'I really am sorry,' he said again and Kammy looked up, ready to insist that he was forgiven. Something in his gaze made her pause. 'Not just for today,' he said, 'for everything, for all of you. I...' He turned away again. She stared at his back, which was taut with tension, and he heaved a great sigh. 'I don't know what to do.'

Kammy did not know what to say, what she *could* say to reassure him. She did not know what to do either. She swallowed and took a step closer.

'Why do you hate him so much?' she said, her voice little more than a whisper.

He did not answer straight away and she feared that he would not. She feared that she had misjudged what was passing between them. But then he half turned back to face her and he started to talk.

'Eight years ago, I watched him kill my father.' He looked Kammy right in the eye and she felt horror seep beneath her skin. 'I saw it all and I heard his excuses. They believed him at first, you know? They brushed me off, saying it was grief making my imagination run wild. Nobody ever admitted that they had been wrong, but I always knew. He killed him, his own brother.'

'*Brother*? Bagor is your uncle?'

Jad flinched. 'He is no family of mine.'

The pain in his voice made Kammy's heart ache.

'Then, two years ago, Dorren helped him break free. I arrived in the Council Chamber just in time to watch him kill my grandfather too. He destroyed my family and then he took Alashdial. He took everything from me.' Kammy's hands were over her heart. She wanted to reach out to him, but she did not dare. He took a breath to compose himself. 'That is why I cannot give him anything, Kammy. I cannot risk that Key. But I do not know what to do. Eric and Tayah...I dragged them into this and I've got nothing to show for it. Fii too, and Boo. And now Bagor wants to save the Semei.' He laughed, 'All this time I thought I was going to liberate my people from a tyrant. But why would they want me if they can have him? He is charming and he is smart and he wants to fight a war for them. Should I not just leave

184

it? Should I not just forget what he has done, like they all have? I am nothing compared to him. I'm broken.'

'That is not true,' Kammy stepped forwards, her eyes blazing.

'Is it not?' He rolled up his sleeve until she could see his scar. 'Then what is this?'

Kammy's eyes followed its twisted path through his flesh, 'I don't understand...'

'Have you heard of the Abandoned?'

Kammy ignored his scar and locked eyes with him. 'Fii mentioned that sometimes Semei get stuck, but you're not...'

'I'm not stuck, no. But I came close. I am Ollarion, part of the royal line, descended from the first five and I came so close. This,' he jerked his arm towards her, but Kammy's gaze did not waver, 'this is what I was left with. A constant reminder of my weakness. Even when I shift, it's there. How can I lead anyone when I am only half a Semei myself?'

'You're not,' Kammy shook her head, 'you *are* a leader. You lead us.'

'Then why don't I know what to do next?'

Kammy bit down on her lip. He looked so miserable, she was afraid she was about to make it worse.

'Listen,' she said, swallowing the lump in her throat, 'maybe we should go back to Alashdial.'

'Kammy...'

'No, hear me out.' He shook his head, but fell silent so Kammy pressed on, 'We've been in the library all week and we haven't found anything about the Key, right? We could stay in Emire forever and not find anything. We'd be safe, but you'd never find a way to stop Bagor. It would be an endless stalemate. But if we go back, if we are careful...there might be something...'

'Kammy, please...'

'There might be a way,' she cried, feeling something sharp and bitter rise inside of her. Something that she had worked so hard to avoid.

185

'What way?' His pain had turned to pity, 'How could the four of us do anything on his doorstep?'

'You could contact your spies. We could be smart. There must be something...there has to be...'

'*Kammy...*'

She held up her hands to stop him. 'I know there's a strong chance that Ria is lying, but I...I can't risk it.' She could avoid it no longer. A solitary tear ran down her cheek and the cold lump she had harboured in her chest began to crumble. 'When I heard that he was dead I knew it was my fault, but there was nothing I could do about it so I forced myself to carry on. I felt unnatural, I thought there was something wrong with me because I could keep walking, because I could function knowing that he was gone. It was because I couldn't face it. But now...' Her chest tightened until she could hardly breathe. More tears began to crawl down her cheeks. '*Now* there might be a chance. And if he...if he is alive, and there is any way that I could save him, then I have to. I can't let him die again...I...'

She could not speak any more. Grief choked her. She pressed her lips together and squeezed her eyes shut, trying to hold it all back, but the first sob ripped out of her. 'I'm sorry,' she gasped as her whole body started to shake. She pressed her hands to her face, trying to hide herself from him as she cried.

When she felt Jad place a tentative hand on her shoulder, she stiffened, but then she sank into him, pressing her face against his warm chest. She breathed him in as her tears soaked his shirt. He stood rigid for a moment, but then he wrapped his arms around her.

'Maybe there is a way,' he whispered, 'maybe we can try.'

Kammy continued to cry, finally mourning the death of her best friend, fearing the chance that she might have to mourn him a second time.

'But if we do go,' said Jad, his breath ruffling her hair, 'we will all go together.'

CHAPTER SEVENTEEN

LITTLE FLOWERS

Seeve himself had appeared at the cottage that evening, grim-faced, but optimistic. Bagor only intended to stay in Emire for one night and he had not even asked after Jad or mentioned the Key. The only moment of note was a sealed letter that Ria had slipped to Seeve for Tayah. Tayah took it off him and tucked it away without reading it and Seeve had not batted an eyelid. He had laughed and said that they could be back in the keep the next evening if they wanted to and Bagor was clearly none the wiser as to where they were hidden. Jad had hardly been able to meet his eye. He had smiled and said that it was all great news, but his words rung hollow in his ears. He was certain that Seeve would notice and realise that there was something wrong. The others had remained silent, but somehow Seeve had not suspected a thing. Still smiling, he had passed each of them a small bundle containing bedding, fresh clothes, food and water. They had enough to last them a few days as, he explained, it might be prudent to stay in the cottage for longer than appeared necessary, just in case any of Bagor's people lingered. Seeve had cast an eye around their dingy little squat and apologised for the comfort that it lacked. Then he had disappeared again, with Karl close behind, fearing Bagor would soon become suspicious. He left Jad to wallow in his guilt.

Jad did not want to hide anything from the General, but he had no choice. If Seeve knew what they planned then he would stop them, no doubt questioning their sanity in the process. Not that their sanity did not deserve to be questioned; Jad questioned it himself. Regardless, they could not ask Seeve for help as he might lock them all in the keep until their insanity had passed.

Jad had expected Eric and Tayah to baulk at the idea; he almost hoped that they would. But they had only nodded solemnly, as if they had been expecting it. They knew him well enough to understand that his initial refusal had been little more than desperate blustering. Tayah had taken herself off for a moment and Jad knew that she was thinking about Boo. They left her in peace with her thoughts and Kammy had beamed at Jad with a new light in her eyes. He had tried to push his doubts aside. They had a chance, Jad told himself. Seeve might not be able to help them, but somebody else could.

So they had eaten in near silence and gone straight to sleep. Eric's soft snores rose instantly, but Jad took longer to drift off. He stared at the ceiling and realised that he was scared. He kept thinking of Fii and how furious she would be once she found out what they had done. They had to succeed for her sake; she would not survive losing them all. He dozed fitfully and cracks of light started to spear into his eyes. He felt like he had hardly slept at all.

The next day took an age to pass. Jad, Eric and Tayah spoke about what lay ahead and despite their uncertainty, a faint plan began to form. They then sunk back into a heavy silence as the hours crawled by. Jad had tried to sleep again, but one person was not feeling the strain of their desperate path; Kammy was reborn. When the first light had roused her from a deep sleep she had sprung from her sleeping mat. She spent the whole day behind the cottage with her slingshot. As Jad tried to force his mind to rest, all he could hear was Kammy's muffled curses and the thunk, thunk, thunk of stones hitting the wall. He had come close to begging her to stop, but he could not bring himself to do it. Their moment in the flowers clung to him, a slightly uncomfortable yet pleasant memory. She had finally broken, but it had not ruined her as he had feared that it would. She had pulled herself back from her despair and he decided that he liked seeing her happy. Tayah had done the deed for him anyway, in the end, shrieking her displeasure. Kammy had laughed, shouted an apology and stopped for all of five minutes before starting up again.

So, when the second morning arrived, they were all surprisingly eager to undertake their new mission. Anything was better than another day of mindless stewing in their rotting hovel.

Jad stood by the only open window. He slung his bundle onto his back, strapping it into place and it made him feel even worse. Seeve had unknowingly brought them enough supplies to make their trip back towards Littlebrook comfortable. Shaking his head, Jad sighed and frowned out the window. Dark clouds were rolling towards them from the north, the likes of which he had never seen before.

'Maybe it's an omen.'

Eric came to stand beside him with a small smile playing on his lips. Jad scoffed and turned his back on the unsettling sight.

'We don't need bad omens to tell us that we are making a very bad decision.'

'And here I was thinking that a leader is supposed to inspire confidence in his followers. Good job, Ollarion.'

Eric appeared relaxed, and his teasing made Jad feel better. If Eric had truly been worried, then he would be kinder.

'You think we can do it?'

Eric shrugged, 'You don't?'

'A part of me doesn't. That part thinks we should forget about the whole thing right now and stick with Seeve. But then, could we? Could we forget that he might be alive, and then die because of us?'

Eric shook his head. 'I don't think I could. And I couldn't do that to Kammy.'

Jad nodded, not quite meeting Eric's eye. 'Exactly,' he said, 'though this is a terrible way to repay Seeve.'

'He'll understand, Jad. He'll be angry, but he'll understand. Besides, it's not like we're going to waltz back into Alashdial without any sort of plan. We'll think of something, we always do.'

Jad nodded with a little more conviction. 'Let's not tell Kammy yet. I don't want her to get her hopes up any higher.' Eric nodded and Jad swept his eyes over the dank cottage's interior. He said, 'I think I'd prefer the cells of the palace to this place anyway. Come on, let's get the girls.' He started towards the door.

'You know, I think Tayah is actually starting to warm up to her,' said Eric, 'who would have thought it, with you as well. It's like the world has flipped upside down. If you're both nice, what's going to happen to me...'

Jad paused with his hand on the door. He did not like the look in Eric's eyes. 'What are you talking about?'

Eric started to grin, 'Just that I never thought I'd see you taking orders from Kammy.'

Jad's eyes narrowed. 'I am not...', but Eric started to laugh and Jad shoved him with a rueful smile, 'shut up...' He stepped outside and Eric followed.

'There, there my friend. It was only a matter of time before you turned soft.'

Jad stopped and turned, raising an eyebrow. 'Soft?'

Eric smiled.

With an overly dramatic roar, Jad charged. He swung an arm around Eric's neck, bearing down with all his weight and Eric almost buckled. But then Eric's arms gripped him and Jad was lifted clean off his feet. Jad twisted and slammed his feet into Eric's chest. Eric's grip loosened and Jad dropped, landing lightly on his feet. With a sweep of Jad's leg, Eric fell on his back in the dirt.

Gasping for breath as he laughed, Jad rested his hands on his knees and leaned over his friend, 'Still soft?'

Eric chuckled, 'You've started down the path now. There's no turning back.'

'Are you two finished?'

Jad glanced up. Tayah was standing by the wall with her arms folded and her braid immaculate. She watched them with raised eyebrows. Kammy knelt before her, her back turned to the boys. Jad straightened, holding out a hand to Eric to help him to his feet. The pair of them wandered across and peered over Kammy's shoulder.

'We're having an impromptu funeral,' said Tayah.

Kammy glanced up at her, her eyes narrowed, but it appeared that Tayah was right. Kammy had indeed dug a shallow hole in the earth. Her fingers were caked in dirt.

Jad frowned. 'What died?'

'My patience?' suggested Tayah.

Kammy huffed. She tried to shake her hair back off of her face without using her hands.

'Nothing died,' she said. She pulled her bag off her lap, holding it up before her with reverence. Ever since the crossing of the river it had looked a little worse for wear, worn and discoloured, but Kammy let out a sad sigh. Then she placed it in the hole and started to fill it in again.

Eric looked incredibly confused. 'What are you doing?'

Kammy was biting her lip, her eyes focused on her task. Within seconds, her bag was gone. 'If I want to blend in then I can't take it with me, and I can't get it safely to the keep. If I leave it in the cottage then anyone might find it. It was a birthday present from my Gran, as was my watch...I can't just throw them away, just in case...' Jad watched her, but to his surprise she smiled and pointed at the cottage wall. 'Five paces from that discoloured brick, six bricks from the right.' She patted the dirt down, then hopped to her feet, wiping her hands on her trousers. 'When we come back, I'll find it again.'

Jad found himself smiling, but then he noticed Eric grinning at him and he scowled instead.

'What's that?' said Tayah, pointing at a scrap of something beside Kammy's boot.

'Oh,' Kammy cried. She scooped it up and pressed it to her chest. 'Thank you,' she said as she opened the pouch on her belt and slipped it inside. 'I took it out of the frame because it was too bulky. It's just a photo of Mum, but I can't believe I almost...' She stopped and her head jerked up towards the sky. She held out her hands, palms turned upwards.

Jad was about to ask her what was wrong when he felt a splash of something cold on his cheek. It had started to rain. There were only one or two drops at first, but it quickly became a light drizzle and they all stared up at the sky in wonder.

'What the...' Tayah swore. She swung her pack off her back, dumped it in the dirt and started rummaging through it. They each did the same, pulling out the thin cloaks that Seeve had brought for them. He had meant for them to be used if it got cold at night, but Jad swung his around his neck and tugged up the hood. They were not made to withstand rain, but they were better than nothing.

'Looks like Bagor was right then.'

The rain threatened to wash away the lighthearted mood. Tayah glared and her eyes flickered towards Kammy, as if the weather was all her fault. Kammy did not notice for she was still struggling with the clasp of her cloak and Jad was grateful. Eric moved to help her with it and she laughed, but Jad felt each drop of water like an added weight on his shoulders. Rain like this would only strengthen Bagor's argument that their world was dying. If Tayah was so quick to realise it, then others would be too.

'Come on,' he said, grabbing Tayah's arm and pulling her away from Kammy, 'the quicker we get going, the more time we'll have to work this out.' Tayah sighed and relaxed. She was suddenly more concerned with tucking her braid safely into her hood.

'Shouldn't we wait for this to pass?' said Eric.

Jad looked up at the sky. 'I don't think it's going to pass. Better to get back to the forest in case it gets worse.'

'You realise what we are doing is insanity, right?' said Tayah, her amber eyes shining bright from the shadow cast by her hood, 'as in, we should probably be locked away for even considering it.'

Jad shot her a look. 'You are welcome to stay behind.'

'Ha,' Tayah snorted, 'you wouldn't last an hour without me.'

The tension had dwindled. Kammy was none the wiser and they were off, heads bowed beneath the light pattering of raindrops. Jad paused, letting the others pass him as he looked towards Emire. The colour had been sucked away by the clouds. No longer a bright red, the town looked like a mottled jigsaw, a haze of rusted orange. The fields too were dull, the flowers drooping beneath the weight of the water. He ignored the dread pooling in his gut and told himself that he would see it again, once more alight with fire.

'Come on, Jad,' called Kammy with a hint of laughter in her voice.

Jad pulled himself away from the sight and hurried after his friends. He tried to draw something from Kammy's enthusiasm. There was little point in mulling over dark thoughts. They had made their decision. Whatever was going to happen, would happen.

'So,' said Tayah, 'what do we do if we find Bagor lying in wait when we reach the bridge? Run?'

Jad smiled. 'I've told you, he won't be waiting. He knows that we will either take the bait or we'll stay in Emire. If we are heading to

Alashdial, why bother lingering here? If anything, we should be more worried about bumping into Seeve's watchmen.'

'At least we won't have to swim this time,' said Kammy, looking back at Jad. Was she teasing him?

'We'll be swimming the whole way home if this continues,' Tayah grumbled, casting a furious look at the dark sky, 'I wish we could shift.'

'We should save all our strength,' said Eric, before Jad had to, 'we don't know what we might need to do when we get there.'

Tayah continued to complain as the rain grew steadily heavier. Soon the downpour was so loud that Jad could no longer hear her. She stopped mumbling, falling into a mutinous silence as the earth began to swim at their feet. The walls of Emire disappeared behind them and the Basin started to rise as the mountains loomed clearer through the gloom. Their cloaks were soon soaked and Jad shivered. He could not help but think that the weather was trying to tell him something.

After the second hour Jad felt so miserable that he was convinced Seeve would be waiting for them when they reached the bridge and that their little adventure would be over before it had begun. When the ground began to rise more steeply and the first smattering of trees started to appear, he could not help turning every few seconds, expecting to find watchmen behind them. There was never anybody there. The sound of rushing water met their ears, even through the steady downpour, and then they were crossing the bridge. Jad stared at the river beneath them. It frothed and churned, charging past at a furious rate. He glanced up at Kammy, but she stared straight ahead until they were across and had set foot once more on Alashdian lands. The trees closed around them offering, for the first time, slight relief from the rain.

'Just one more day of this,' said Eric, attempting cheer.

'We should get off the road now, just in case,' said Jad, leading them deeper into the trees.

Tayah made a disgruntled sound, 'It's still coming through.'

Like Jad, she had hoped the forest would be enough to hold the rain off completely. But it drove towards them, cold and determined. It was gentle, but persistent.

Kammy laughed at them, 'It's just a bit of rain. You people would never survive in my world.' She marched off, looking back at them, 'Come on.'

Jad shared a look with Eric. Neither of them wanted to remind her that they really could not survive in her world. Neither of them wanted to pull her down from the high she had climbed to.

They started off after her, pulling their boots from the pooling mud. Tayah followed with her arms wrapped around herself. Jad had imagined feeling thrilled to find himself back on the earth of his home, but the fact that it was so unsteady beneath his feet made him feel uncomfortable. He had never seen the forest beneath sheets of rain. He could not remember it ever being so uninviting. The trees themselves begged them to turn back and to give up. It took all of his stubborn will to keep putting one foot before the other.

When the rain finally relented, even Kammy fell quiet. They decided to rest then, for it was almost dark. They sat in a huddle while they ate, then they rolled out their sleeping mats. They slept in a close square, their backs turned towards one another, hoping for some shared warmth. It was a vain hope; their clothes were so soaked that even though the night was mild, they lay as one shivering mass. Nobody sat watch for they were so far from the road that they were certain they would not be spotted, plus they were miserable. More rain woke them before morning's light and they dragged themselves back to their feet, their bones stiff and aching. Alashdial felt a world away.

'I can't even practice with my slingshot, 'Kammy complained, sinking completely into the same moodiness as the others.

Jad thought it a blessing that Kammy's weapon remained hooked to her belt. He suspected that Tayah might explode if Kammy started that up again.

On they walked with little notion of how much time passed. The grey sky meant that Jad could not tell when morning became afternoon. He kept his eyes fixed on the familiar terrain until he finally saw something that made him smile.

'What's that?' said Kammy with wide eyes.

From the base of a tree came a soft lilac light. Jad crept close to it, a look of wonder on his face.

194

'It's an Akasi flower,' he said, 'they are native to Alashdial and the land that surrounds the city, but they only bloom at night. It must be confused by the darkness.'

The flower had not opened fully, not yet revealing the true extent of it's beauty, but the glow was enough to lift their spirits.

'We're almost there,' said Jad, with renewed purpose.

From then on, the Akasi lit their way, their purple light like lanterns in a fog floating before them. The flowers remained half closed as the darkness and the rain continued to hang over them, but they were no longer constrained by silence. The others had started to talk again and when Jad spotted the stream he felt such a rush of relief that he laughed. They had made it.

'Excellent,' said Kammy, rubbing her hands together to warm them. She started to walk downstream.

'Not that way,' said Eric, smiling at her eagerness.

'Oh,' she looked disappointed, as though she had been proud of knowing the way, 'I thought...'

'That *is* the way to Littlebrook, but we're not actually going to Littlebrook.'

She pulled her cloak tighter around herself. 'We're not?'

'Follow me,' said Jad.

They did follow the stream, but they followed it upstream instead. The gentle flow of water glimmered purple beneath the light of the Akasi, making it easy to follow as it wound away from Littlebrook. Jad stopped when it disappeared into the mouth of a natural dam and he turned to face Kammy, enjoying the confusion on her face and hoping that it would not turn to disappointment.

'We're here,' he said with a grin.

Kammy narrowed her eyes at him. She pulled back her hood to see better and turned on the spot. 'Right...'

Eric laughed, 'You're cruel, Jad.'

Kammy actually stamped her foot, 'What is going on?'

Jad thought it best not to toy with her for much longer. He stepped towards the bowed tree beside the dam and he knocked on it twice quickly, and once again. Then he stepped back towards the others and waited.

Nothing happened.

'Seriously, what is this?' said Kammy, starting to sound impatient.

Jad shot a look towards Tayah and Eric, but they appeared as confused as he did.

'Maybe this is the wrong tree?' said Tayah with a shrug and no conviction behind her words. It was certainly the right one. They had seen it enough times. If they were in the right place and there was no answer then that could only mean one thing. He had never made it back. Jad bowed his head.

'Okay,' said Kammy, 'you're scaring me now.'

The ground shook violently and Kammy stumbled sideways. Jad grabbed her arm, holding her steady as he braced himself. Then they heard something crack.

'What the hell was that?' cried Kammy.

A patch of earth beside the dam began to shake and Kammy's fingers gripped Jad's sleeve. Then the earth, a perfectly shaped square of grass, lifted and showered dirt beneath it. Light burst out towards them, severe and temporarily blinding. Somebody coughed and a face appeared, mostly obscured by an over-sized pair of smudged goggles.

Welm grinned up at them, 'Hello.'

CHAPTER EIGHTEEN

THE MAD ALCHEMIST

Kammy's jaw hung open.

Welm scurried out of the hole, holding his grass covered trapdoor open and waving them closer. 'Quickly, quickly, get inside.'

Jad and the others did not hesitate and Kammy followed them, dazed. She had expected to spend the night in Fii's old home in Littlebrook, with a warm fire and a well kept roof overhead. She had not expected to find herself climbing down a steep wooden staircase that led beneath the earth. She hesitated at the top, glancing at Welm. He waved her on and she frowned. Her hand rested on the belt that he had made for her and then she felt guilty for still doubting him. She quickly ducked inside and out of the rain, reaching out a hand to steady herself. The walls of the narrow passage were panelled with wood and a strange buzzing filled her ears.

Welm hurried inside after her, letting the trapdoor fall shut. Kammy jumped, expecting to find herself plunged into darkness but the bright light continued to hover around them. As Welm tied the rope holding the trapdoor to a hook on the wall, Kammy studied the ceiling. The buzzing sound came from light bulbs that lit the way, hanging at even intervals along a wire.

'Electricity?' she said, stunned.

Welm clapped his hands together, his obvious excitement catching Kammy off guard. She had never seen him so animated. 'You really think so?'

'Well…it seems like it.'

'Oh good,' he pushed his goggles back onto the top of his head. His eyes were rimmed with soot. 'It isn't electricity of course, but that is what I have been trying to replicate.' Then he pushed past her without another word until he reached Jad at the front.

'I thought I might be seeing you,' he chattered away, 'As soon as I heard that Bagor was in Emire, I hurried back here. I've had contact with the city and there is much to talk about. Come, come, let's get you warm. Horrible weather isn't it? Quite horrible.'

Kammy gaped at the back of Welm's head. He was clearly more comfortable when he was hidden below ground. He led them down the staircase, skipping along easily at the front while they struggled with the thin steps, until he reached a door. Then he led them through into a cavern.

The space was huge and Kammy could hardly take it all in. A laugh of delight escaped her. The walls of the cavern were lined with shelves. They stretched so high that Welm would never have been able to reach the tops were it not for the crooked ladders leaning against them. The shelves were full to bursting with all manner of things that Kammy could not begin to describe. She saw a jar full of what looked like marbles, but fire glowed inside them. Beside those sat a vial of silver liquid that bubbled where it stood. Further along rested a block of orange putty, the same putty that Eric had used to blow open the wall of Kammy's cell. She backed away from that, but there were countless other wonders. She peered up at a jar of golden sand that glittered.

'Sandust,' said Eric, picking up the jar. 'It lights up darkness without drawing as much attention as a flame and without affecting your vision.' Kammy gazed at it, her jaw hanging off its hinge. Eric took her hand and poured a pinch into her palm. 'Try,' he said, 'you just have to blow on it.'

Kammy stared at the little golden mound. She blew on it gently and she gasped. The Sandust flew from her palm and hung in the air. Each grain glittered and shone as it spread further until the whole cavern appeared to be coated in light. Kammy laughed as she watched it. The light reflected off more treasures and Kammy turned on the spot. There was a large table at the centre of the room. It was covered in papers and contraptions such as Kammy had never seen.

'What is this place?'

'It's where Welm works his magic,' said Tayah, directing an affectionate smile towards him.

'I told you he was a genius,' said Jad.

Welm blushed and lowered his head.

'But how is it here? Underground?'

Welm smiled, 'It was Jad's grandfather that granted me this boon. I have always preferred working alone where I cannot be disturbed. Where better than beneath the earth in a secret location? He had this place built for me and we are all very lucky that Bagor was never party to its exact location.'

'So how did you know it was us?' said Kammy, 'That it was safe?'

'The tree above is hollow,' he pointed at a hole in the wall. 'Three quick knocks, followed by one more is the code. I hear it through there and I know that it is safe.'

'And all of this?' Kammy could not stop gawking.

'My work,' he shrugged, 'my experiments.'

'Alchemy?' Kammy breathed.

'Yes, mostly,' said Welm, clearly pleased by her enthusiasm. 'Now,' he waved for them to follow, 'the Oilblum on your boots will have been damaged by the mud.' He plucked a small bottle from a nearby shelf and stepped towards another door that Kammy had not noticed, 'Come, and rest.'

Kammy held her breath, barely able to imagine what might lay beyond the second door, but she was disappointed. Welm led them into a small room, as dark as the cavern behind them but plain. A bed took up one corner, a table with two chairs another and a fire pit dominated the centre, which made Kammy nervous seeing as they were surrounded by so much wood. A third door was closed to them and Kammy hoped desperately that it was a bathroom. She was fed up of squatting behind trees.

'Sit, sit,' Welm urged, still beaming at them, 'I'm afraid I cannot offer you fresh clothing, at least none that would fit, but I'll make some tea to warm you.' He handed the small bottle to Jad and dashed back into his cavern with a metal pot.

The thought of hot tea made Kammy almost delirious with happiness. She sank into one of the chairs and pulled off her sopping wet cloak. The rest of her clothes were not much drier, but she brushed aside the discomfort and watched Jad as he pulled the cork out of the bottle that Welm had handed to him.

'What's Oilblum?' she said.

Welm reappeared with water sloshing in the pot, 'My first invention,' he announced, before turning his back to them and settling before the fire pit.

'Oilblum is essential,' said Jad, 'pouring out a pea sized drop onto his finger and then handing the bottle to Tayah. 'Have you not wondered how our clothes are included when we shift?'

'I...' Kammy paused. She had never thought about it. She was struck by the notion of Jad with no clothes on and she began to blush. 'No, I...didn't.'

Jad rubbed the clear lotion into his boots. 'Long ago, the Semei did not care for modesty, back when we spent as much time shifting as we did in our natural forms. But as society changed, so did people's views.'

'Basically,' said Eric, 'people got sick of everyone running around naked.'

Tayah snorted.

'So, people looked for a way to deal with the situation, a way to include our clothes in our transformation. The silk moths were discovered. They live beneath the earth, where it is damp and warm. The silk that they spin can be used to craft clothes so supple that we can manipulate them into our shifts.'

'But,' said Welm, looking back over his shoulder, 'these clothes were very expensive. It took a long time to weave shirts from such fine silk and only the richest could really afford it. I was certain that there must be another way.'

'And there was,' said Jad, 'Welm created Oilblum, a much cheaper and easier way to maintain our modesty. He was in high demand after he delivered the goods and we were lucky that he was Alashdian. Our economy flourished because of this man. Every Semei needs Oilblum.' Jad sounded very proud.

200

Eric handed Kammy the bottle and she sniffed it, 'What is it made from?'

Welm spoke while he waited for the water to boil, 'The two main ingredients are the silk, melted down, and a mineral we call Blumite. There is more to it than that, but for now know that when it is rubbed into clothes; wool, cotton, leather...it makes them so supple that they can be manipulated.'

Kammy placed the bottle down beside her. She could not help staring at Welm. She would never have expected so much from such a man. She had begun to feel more comfortable in this world during her time in Emire. She had believed that she was beginning to understand its ways, but that was far from the truth.

'So,' she said, turning her attention back to Welm's hideaway, 'is this where you would all hide if Bagor ever sent his people to find you?'

Jad nodded, 'Correct. Welm came to us, actually. He offered its services should we ever need it.'

'You were already hiding?' said Kammy.

Welm nodded, his expression solemn. 'I came straight here on that dreadful day, when I knew that there was to be no stopping Bagor. For those first few months I did not dare contact a soul. I could not resist the occasional meander through the trees and it was pure chance that had me stumble across Fii. Otherwise, I might have remained alone here.'

'You were hiding because Bagor wants to use you,' said Kammy, understanding, 'your skills.'

'Yes. He has since used those that I trained, and through them has tried to train others. He had them create his Armours, but they could not achieve his aims and it became a pointless exercise. Bagor wanted the Armour to become a part of the shift, but the Oilblum only works on gentle materials. For now his Armours are little more than a fancy detail, which suits Bagor, I would say. He asks much of my old workers, but they are not innovators. They can do what I taught them and little more. Perhaps a bright spark will appear someday, but until then he seeks me out with growing desperation. He tells the people I am mad so that they might feel inclined to help the search. I sometimes think that he would rather I fall into his grasp than Jad.'

A small smile crept across Jad's lips. 'He will never have us.'

201

'Never,' said Welm, his eyes twinkling.

The water began to bubble and Welm shot to his feet. He placed some mugs on the table and made them all tea, pushing the boiling drinks into grateful hands. Kammy took a sip, not caring when it burned and savouring the sensation as it warmed her. The others seemed equally as relaxed, but as Kammy felt more and more comfortable, she wanted to ask more and more questions.

'I can hardly believe I haven't asked before,' she said, 'but how was it that Bagor escaped in the first place? Dorren helped him, right?'

Jad leant forward, sitting right on the edge of Welm's bed, and he glared into his mug. 'He tricked his way to freedom. Words have always been his greatest strength and they were all he needed. He spent all those years that he was locked up putting everything into place, manipulating any that were weak enough to be taken in.'

'He made deals,' said Welm, 'he bribed and he bartered with promises of power and wealth. The tried and tested method. Dorren sided with him quickly and he was the chief prison guard back then. So Bagor knew he had already taken a huge step towards freedom.'

'Dorren is a fool,' Jad spat.

'He orchestrated Bagor's escape,' Eric explained, 'under Bagor's careful instruction. He recruited more within the palace who were sympathetic to Bagor's way of thinking and he was the one that called the emergency Council meeting. It was that meeting that kept the leaders distracted while Bagor prepared to strike.'

'It was over before anybody had realised it had even begun,' said Jad, clearly lost in the distant memory. Kammy remembered what he had said about his grandfather. Was that the day that Jad had watched him die? For the first time Kammy thought of Bagor as more than just a shadow that lingered at the edge of her existence. She thought of him as a man that had hurt people she cared about. She felt a chill run through her. This man, this monster, had her friend. She did not doubt that he would hurt Jamie without a moments pause, if he had not already. She placed her mug of tea down as her stomach rolled.

'And he has ruled without interruption since,' said Welm.

'Because the people are too scared to stand up to him,' Tayah muttered.

'But not you,' said Welm, 'the four of you would never have come back here if you were too scared to stand up to him.'

Kammy gnawed at the inside of her cheek and her eyes flicked over to Jad's. He looked as anxious as she felt.

'Kammy's friend, the one Ria brought through,' said Jad, staring hard at Welm, 'we think he may be alive.'

Kammy expected some sort of strong reaction, some outward sign of shock, but Welm did not move.

'Yes,' he said, 'you wish to save him?'

Kammy jerked towards him, half rising out of her chair, 'It's true? He really is alive?'

'I have not seen him myself, but yes. That is what I have been told.'

Kammy sank back into her chair and covered her face with her hands. She thought her jaw might break as her smile stretched wider. It did not matter that they still had no idea of how to save him. The fact that he was alive to be saved was enough for now.

'Do you have a plan?' said Welm, not immediately trying to dissuade them.

Eric said, 'I had thought we might do the same thing as when I rescued Jad. That went well enough. If we could borrow some...'

Welm shook his head. 'That won't work a second time. It only worked the first because the erosive putty was a new invention of mine. Bagor will have put something in place to stop the same thing happening again. How is it that you know Jamie is alive?'

'Ria told us,' Tayah snarled, 'Bagor wanted to lure us back, so he can get his hands on the Key. He used Jamie as bait.'

'His plan worked, clearly.'

Kammy squirmed where she sat. They were doing exactly what Bagor wanted. She pressed her lips together; she had no other choice.

'That could work in our favour,' said Welm.

'How?' Jad frowned.

'Bagor will expect you to do one of two things. Most likely is that he thinks you will remain in Emire and so he will bide his time. Bagor has always been a patient man, particularly when he already has a plan in motion. Eventually, Seeve would not be able to shelter you and Bagor would be waiting. Or, he expects that you will do exactly what he asks and return with the Key. I doubt he anticipates a third option. Bagor's greatest weakness has always been his determination to underestimate those that he deems weaker than he is.'

'But what is our third option? What can we do?' said Eric.

'There is something, but it is risky.'

'Any course will be risky. We must still try.' Jad's steady voice made Kammy's heart swell.

'Then you do as he asks. Kammy goes to Bagor and promises him the Key.'

Jad shot to his feet. 'What?'

Kammy stared at Welm in disbelief. She would do anything to save Jamie, but there had to be another way. Could she really expect Jad to make that sacrifice? Could she ask him to give up the one thing he had that might help him overcome his uncle?

'You think we should send Kammy, alone, straight to the man that wants her dead?' Jad sounded furious.

'Bagor will not want her dead,' Welm said, with calm, and Kammy felt more confused by the second. 'Bagor will, in fact, be quite anxious to meet her.'

The mood in the room changed and Welm was the only one who met Kammy's eye. Jad's fury dissolved and he dropped back onto the bed, looking pale. Eric and Tayah looked between one another, confused.

Kammy tried to smile, 'Oh no, what now?'

Welm looked surprised, 'I thought you would have talked about this already.'

'Talked about what?'

'The fact that you are Semei.'

Kammy burst into laughter and expected the others to join her. They did not laugh, but they did stare. Jad looked apologetic, Eric stunned and Tayah's eyes shone with excitement. Kammy's laughter trailed off and her eyes bulged.

'You can't seriously think that?'

'It's more than that Kammy,' Welm spoke as though he were merely commenting on the weather, 'You are Simbassi.'

It felt like the shock had punched right through her chest. Her protests died in her throat. She had heard that word before, when the old lady from the spice stall had gripped her hand. Tayah shook her head in wonder.

'The Simbassi,' Eric gasped, 'I never thought...'

Jad looked pained, 'I tried to tell you at the cottage. I suspected it in Emire, but I wanted to make sure first. People don't talk of the other lines any more. I thought that they had all died out. I thought it might just be coincidence.'

Kammy tried to shake the ringing from her ears. 'This is ridiculous. How can you...'

'Your eyes, Kammy.'

She looked up at Jad and she felt like she was falling.

'Kammy, the descendants of the first five established the old kingdoms. There were five royal lines; Ollarion,' Welm nodded at Jad, 'being the last to survive. Each line could be identified by their eyes, the mark left to them by the Mother. The Simbassi supposedly died out around eighteen years ago, but you have their eyes.'

Jad spoke to Welm, 'When did you see...'

Welm smiled at Kammy, 'I saw her eyes change when I brought her that mug of hot lemon at Fii's home. She was afraid of me.'

Despite the shock, Kammy's cheeks still burned.

Eric turned to Jad, 'You mentioned the possibility once, but I didn't see how it could be.' He glanced at Kammy, 'But it explains how you found the Gate and the Key.'

Tayah gawked openly.

Kammy could hardly hear them. With shaking hands, she opened her pouch and pulled out the photo of her mother. She ran a finger over Mary Helseth's face, staring into the eyes that she had inherited. The Simbassi line had died out eighteen years ago, the same year that Mary had moved to Daleswick to marry John Helseth.

'The Simbassi,' Welm said softly, 'the lions that guarded the greatest Crystal.'

'Lions?' Her eyes dropped to the rampant lioness etched into the clasp of her belt. Tears sprung to her eyes. Could it be possible? Could her mother have kept such a secret?

'The city of Danorrah was the Simbassi's home until the sickness...'

'Stop,' Kammy cried, and they all fell very still. Kammy swallowed the emotion that had lodged in her throat. 'I don't want to talk about this.'

'But Kammy...'

'*Stop*. None of that matters. If this is what Bagor believes and if it will help us to save Jamie, then that is all that is important. Okay?' She glared round at them all, suddenly furious. How could they have kept it from her, even if they had not been sure? Even if it was not true?

Jad's gaze fell to the floor and Eric scratched the back of his head. It was Tayah that turned back to Welm without an ounce of sheepishness.

'So how does this help us?'

Welm's gaze was still on Kammy; he was not cowed. He crossed his legs beneath him and held his hands in his lap. 'Bagor will not harm Kammy, I am certain of it. She is a descendant of the Simbassi line and she is too important. She can walk through Alashdial, right up to the palace, and she can demand to see her friend.'

'Why are you sure of this?' said Jad, 'How can you know he won't hurt her? He has hurt important people before. He has hurt people that loved him, that he should have loved.'

'It doesn't matter,' Kammy muttered.

'Of course it matters,' Jad growled, 'we are not sending you in there alone.'

'If Welm says I'll be safe, then I'll be safe,' Kammy cried. 'I trust his word.'

Jad looked like there was much more that he wanted to say. His nostrils flared, but he slumped back and stared at the wall. Kammy felt a pang of guilt; he was only looking out for her after all. But she had never thought she would be much help in the rescue attempt. Hearing that she could be part of the action, even with the overwhelming circumstances, thrilled her.

Eric spoke up, sounding wary, 'I'm with Jad, Kammy. We can't send you in alone.'

'You wouldn't,' said Welm, as if that was completely obvious. 'You two,' he nodded at Eric and Tayah, 'you would be able to walk the streets of Alashdial with relative ease, correct? Ria's protection should be enough?'

Tayah looked uncomfortable, but she nodded.

'And Eric, your parents would shelter you tomorrow if needed, until the evening?'

Eric sat straight and his eyes brightened. Kammy could see the hope in them and she almost smiled. He would get to see his family again.

Then Welm turned to Jad, 'Do you believe that Ania would help you, if she could?'

Jad blushed and his eyes brushed against Kammy's before he wrenched them away and stared resolutely at the wall once more. Kammy frowned as she felt her own cheeks grow warm. Who was Ania?

Jad nodded once.

'Then we have a plan.'

'How is that a plan?' Jad snapped. 'How is that not just putting us all into unnecessary danger? Especially Kammy.'

'Because Bagor won't expect you to attempt deception, to attempt trickery. He will underestimate how strong you can be if you all work together. Bagor believes he is untouchable. The palace is hardly a stronghold. His mistrust of others means that he prefers the palace to be empty of all but those closest to him. If you can get inside, which you can, then you stand a chance.'

Jad pinched his nose, 'We won't even get past the outer walls...'

Welm walked towards Jad, who looked up at him in confusion, and he stopped beside the panelled wall. He crouched and with a grunt of exertion he pushed. After a second of silence, the panels started to move and soon a small, dark passage appeared.

The four friends gaped at it.

'It runs beneath the wall and leads into Alashdial. Rogan had it installed for me, so I could move quickly between here and the city without dealing with the formalities at the gates.' Welm looked at their stunned expressions with a smile. 'Let's eat and I shall explain everything.'

Dinner was a simple affair. Welm did not have much to offer them, but the others were so hungry that they wolfed down the broth he made and asked for more. While they were eating Welm explained the plan that he had formulated. Jad was still not happy, in fact he was furious. While he fumed, Kammy mumbled something about going to get some air and she slipped away, her appetite having deserted her. She felt their eyes on her back. She sensed Jad itching to say something and fighting down the urge to follow. But they let her go without a word.

She knew that they would not really want her to go outside on her own, but for that moment she did not care. She was so angry with them, but there was just enough anger to last one night, and to justify her decision to ignore sense. She hurried up the stairs that led to the surface. She untied the rope and cracked open the trapdoor.

Her breath caught. Darkness had fallen completely, but the forest was alight. The Akasi flowers that had looked so eerie in the fog of rain were radiant. Their purple petals had unfurled completely and the air smelled sweet. Kammy crawled out into the night, letting the trapdoor snap shut behind her. She walked across the damp grass towards a tree that overlooked the little dam. Then she sat down with her back against the trunk, not caring that the mud would stick to her clothes. She stared at the Akasi, but her thoughts were elsewhere.

Simbassi.

A coincidence, she thought, it had to be. She could not be the only human with eyes such as hers. She could not be a shapeshifter and she was certainly not royalty. Yet, a part of her stirred to the idea and she wondered why she had not thought of the possibility herself. It would explain why she had been shunned and isolated back on Daleswick. Perhaps Esme and the others had known that Kammy did not truly belong there? Perhaps all Kammy's dreams of a life far away had been a part of something bigger?

Of course, if that was all true then it would mean that her Mum and her Gran had kept it from her. That was what scared her most. That was what made her want to reject the idea with all her heart. How could her mother have held her as she cried, as she had cursed her eyes, and not explained? How could her mother have taken that to the grave? How could her Gran have let her?

A thought struck Kammy and she pulled her knees into her chest. She felt as though somebody had gripped her heart and crushed it in their fist. She remembered Jad explaining that the Semei could not survive in the human world. She pictured her mother's face, once so beautiful but in the end so shrunken. Helen, who had treated her for years, had never understood her sickness. There had been nothing she could do to help Mary Helseth.

Kammy's shoulders shook as she cried. The Akasi flowers blurred before her and she buried her face against her knees. She refused the truth. She refused to accept that her mother could have been saved, had she only found the courage to enter the forest's mouth. Mary had not been Semei. Kammy was not Semei.

She heard the trapdoor creak open. Kammy quickly wiped the tears from her eyes and sniffed, composing herself. She thought it would be Eric coming to check on her. So when Welm's tufts of hair appeared, haloed by the light behind him, she was surprised. He smiled at her, closed the trapdoor and started to wring his hands.

When he did not speak, Kammy said, 'I was going to come back in soon.'

Welm shook his head. 'We understand.'

His voice was a whisper again. He seemed to shrink in on himself and his eyes shot around the shadows. Outside of his own space, he became a different person.

'I only wanted to give you these,' he said.

He shuffled closer to her and held out his hand. In it was a small pouch. Kammy took it in silence, sitting a little straighter so he did not need to crouch.

'Open it,' he said.

She did so, loosening the ties, and she peered inside. At first she could not make anything out in the darkness. She held her eye to the opening and frowned. A flicker of fire shone for a second and disappeared.

'What...' she started, but there were more splashes of flame. Each sparked for a moment before fading. She felt the bottom of the pouch and she stared at Welm. They were the marbles she had seen in his cavern.

'Why have you given me these?'

He smiled. 'For your slingshot.'

'I...what do they do?'

'Upon hard contact the marble casing shatters, releasing the flame. The fire will burn through anything, though only for a short time, and some things burn more easily than others.' He stopped abruptly, his eyes flitting about as though he had only then remembered that he did not like to talk, 'To defend yourself,' he whispered.

Kammy sniffed. Tears were threatening again and she had to clear her throat a few times before she could speak. 'Why do you keep doing these things for me?'

Welm started to back away from her and Kammy slumped against the tree, sure that he was not going to answer. He knelt beside the trapdoor with his back towards her. He knocked on the tree and after a moment the trapdoor began to ease open.

'Keep them stored in that pouch. It is lined to absorb the flames should they smash accidentally.' He started to descend and only when his head had almost disappeared did he look back at her. 'Only Fii knows this, but I was born in Danorrah and lived my childhood there. That is why I remember the Simbassi, while others have chosen to forget. They were good leaders, fair. You are one of them, lost but now returned to us. I am sorry I did not tell you sooner, but you see, I did not believe you would have liked to hear it from me. Not until we...became friends. I did not know your mother or your grandmother, but I knew of them. If I can help you, I shall.' Then he pulled the trapdoor shut behind him, sealing away the harsh light.

He had not asked Kammy to come back inside so she stayed where she was for a while longer. She pulled the pouch closer and put it into the bag on her belt. They were all gifts from Welm that he hoped would make her stronger. Kammy took a deep breath and wiped the tears from her eyes. Simbassi or not, she was going to save Jamie. Now, she even had a weapon. With her fingers curled around her slingshot, Kammy stood and knocked on the tree, waiting to be welcomed back inside.

PART THREE
ALASHDIAL

CHAPTER NINETEEN

THE HOWDS

Eric wanted to laugh.

The five of them were pressed tightly within the small passage beneath the metal grate. He could see the tension on the faces of his friends, but Eric did not have room left within him to feel anxious or afraid. He brimmed with happiness and the only reason he fought back his grin was because he knew Tayah might punch him for it. He would see his family again and that was all that he could think about.

'Eric?'

He shook himself. 'Yes?'

Jad shot him a look but it was Welm that wanted his attention. 'You remember your part?'

He nodded. He had been more focused when the plan itself had been laid out. Only now, beneath Alashdial itself, did he start to struggle. 'Myself and Tayah will lay low at my home until the first hour of the light fading. By that time, Kammy will have been reunited with Jamie.'

'We hope,' Jad grumbled.

Eric ignored him. 'Myself and Tayah will head up to the palace and we shall demand to see Kammy before we will consider handing over the Key.' He patted the pack on his back. They had found a random rock out in the forest to play the part. 'Bagor will allow it because he will not expect us to deceive him, and because he still wants people to believe that he is good, somewhere very deep down inside.'

Welm turned to Jad.

Jad sighed and Eric could not help a small smile. He did not think he had ever seen his friend so reluctant to partake in a risky venture. The real Key was going to stay with Welm, so losing it was not his concern. No, Eric thought as his eyes drifted towards Kammy, the Key was not the issue.

'At the second hour of the light fading I will, hopefully, be inside the palace. I will ring the bell, hopefully, giving the others the chance to escape in all the confusion. I want to point out one last time that it is a very small chance. I know you will all ignore me.' He scowled.

'Jad,' Kammy looked him in the eye. 'We're doing this.'

Jad mumbled something unintelligible and slumped back against the wall, glaring at the earth at their feet. He had a satchel slung over his shoulder and his grip on the strap had whitened his knuckles. Eric found it highly amusing, though he suspected that he should really share the others' concern. There was little point in worrying, Eric told himself, so why not focus on the positives?

'Then there is little time to be wasted here,' said Welm. 'This grate will lead you into one of the guard posts in the wall. The young lady that is supposed to man it at this hour is one of our people and she leaves it empty for me. You should still hurry. Do not linger. It is positioned right behind a house so you should not be seen when you first emerge. I have never had any trouble.'

'Thank you, Welm,' said Eric, knowing that Jad's mood meant he would forget his manners. 'We would not have been able to do this without you.'

Welm's shiny cheeks started to glow and he looked down at his feet. 'You two should go first.'

Tayah glanced up at Eric and nodded. While he was ecstatic to be close to his family, she dreaded seeing hers. She hugged Jad while Eric turned to Kammy.

'Thank you,' she smiled up at him, 'for doing this.'

215

Eric waved her off. 'I wouldn't be anywhere else.' Her smile widened and Eric grabbed her, lifting her off the ground with a bear hug. She lauged as he placed her back on her feet, only for her laugh to fade away when she realised that Tayah was waiting to say goodbye to her. Without looking Kammy in the eye, Tayah placed an awkward arm around her shoulders. Kammy patted her back and Eric turned away from them with a chuckle. Eric placed a hand on Welm's shoulder and then stopped in front of Jad.

'Cheer up,' he said.

Jad glared at him before gripping his friend in a tight hug, 'Be careful.'

Eric nodded into Jad's shoulder. 'We'll be fine.'

It was time to leave. Eric turned his attention to the metal grate and reached up to it. It moved with ease. He pushed it aside, careful not to scrape it against the stone, and he took a deep breath. Then he reached up and hauled himself through the small gap, twisting his shoulders while the muscles in his arms strained. Welm was right, there was nobody in the small space. He scooted to the side and reached down to grip Tayah's hand. He pulled her up and then they were both crouched over the hole, peering down at Jad's face.

'Good luck,' said Jad.

'See you soon,' said Eric.

It was eerie how their roles had reversed. When they had been younger it was always Jad that had dared to take risks, while Eric had listed all the ways in which the risks were foolish. Eric did not have time to ponder such things. He pulled away from the hole in the floor and pressed his back against the wall beside the door. He started to ease it open.

'I cannot believe we are doing this.'

Eric glanced back at Tayah. 'You don't have to come. I'm happy to do this alone.'

She cocked her head to the side, 'Of course I'm coming, Eric. I...'

'Just like to complain?' he finished for her and she laughed.

The trepidation continued to swim in her eyes, but she focused on the door anyway, determined to go on. Their plan relied on chance, and chance was fickle; it did not always favour those that it should. Eric tried to draw on her fear and her focus. He pushed thoughts of his family out of his mind as he swung the door open. Without hesitation, he sprung towards the house opposite, his boots tapping against the cobbles. Tayah ran beside him and they both froze beneath a window, scanning the narrow space between Alashdial's outer wall and its first row of houses. The edge of the city had been built on flat ground and was fairly new. The buildings were not built of the same polished white stone as the old city, on the mountainside. These houses had been thrown together quickly and cheaply, and they had been built in uniform rows. It was not the Alashdial that Eric had grown up in, but it was enough.

Tayah sucked in a sharp breath. 'We're here.' She turned towards him and smiled. There was a spark of excitement in her eyes, at last, and Eric grinned at her.

They were home.

'Come on,' he urged, leading her along the edge of the house. He could hear the first rumblings of the morning. Families rose from their beds, doors were being opened and closed. The quicker they could get to Eric's home, the better. The more people that filled the streets, the more likely they were to be recognised.

Eric led Tayah onto the main road, a straight road that led all the way from the wall to the palace. It was wide and open, but they hoped that they would look less suspicious walking along it with their heads held high than they would if they skulked through the shadows. They slowed to a walk and Eric froze as he drank in the sight before him. There was no place in the world, not even on the surface, that was more beautiful than Alashdial. He was sure of it.

Tayah laughed at him, with him, for him. Her smile was just as wide. 'Are you okay?'

Eric elbowed her gently in the ribs. She laughed harder. Even the air felt different close to the Crystal.

'I know you.'

Eric's grin froze. A sallow skinned man stared at them. His clothes hung off his small frame and his teeth were crooked. The new city had been the poorest part of Alashdial when Eric had lived at home, but Eric had never seen a man that looked so wretched. He did not recognise him, but there was a spark of familiarity in the man's

217

eyes. Eric's own flitted to the open road behind the man. There was nobody else around, but the morning was growing steadily brighter. The city started to wake.

'I'm sorry, sir.' Eric spoke as calmly as he could, 'You must be mistaken.' He turned to Tayah who started to march away.

'The Armours have been telling us to look out for you. The Ollarion boy and his friends.'

Eric ignored him.

'I remember seeing you at the market with your Da. I know it's you. I'll call the guards.'

Swearing, Eric stopped. The man grinned and pointed up into the sky. Eric looked up and frowned. There were dark shapes moving through the air, high above them.

'Armours,' said the man, breathless with excitement. 'They patrol the skies these days so if anyone sends up the call, they can swoop down and be on you in seconds.'

Eric felt the hairs on the back of his neck stand on end. There were so many of them. He had thought that Bagor lacked men and women to serve him, but that could not be the case if all of those shapes were Armours. His attention was drawn back to the ground when the man clicked his tongue.

Eric scratched the back of his head. It was too soon for Bagor to know they were in the city, they would never be able to stall him for long enough. 'What do you want?'

The man shrugged. 'What have you got?'

Eric's head drooped; nothing. They had nothing to give and Eric had never been good at lying.

'Do you know who I am?' Tayah stepped past Eric with a sharp flick of her braid. Her chin tilted imperiously as she glared down at the man. 'Then you know my sister?'

The man's smile faltered. He looked a lot less confident as he blustered, 'So what?'

'So,' Tayah folded her arms, 'you know how patient and forgiving she is when people waste her time. We have been summoned by the King and it is very important that we make our way to the palace without fanfare.' Her voice grew louder with every word. 'If you call the Armours then everyone will know we are here and the King will be displeased. If you delay us any longer then we shall be late. I will inform Ria that is was your fault and she will come to deal with you personally. Your face is memorable enough. Would you like that?'

The man tried to sneer at her, but he only succeeded in making himself look even more like a weasel. Tayah fixed him with a ferocious stare and he stepped back.

'Pah,' he spat and wiped his mouth with his sleeve. He turned away from them, his shoulders hunched.

Tayah did not relax until he had passed out of sight. She shook her head and whispered, 'He looked like he was starving...'

Eric placed a hand on her shoulder. 'Thank you. You saved us there.'

'I hate doing that...pretending I'm like her.' She puffed out her cheeks. 'I didn't think anyone would recognise us and yet the first person we see knows who we are. We should have waited until it was busier. If we were part of a crowd then nobody would pay us any attention.'

'Or more people would recognise us, Tay. Plus, we would move slower. That man was a one off.' His eyes drifted back to the Armours in the sky. Their presence made him uneasy and for the first time he could not even use the dream of his family to make himself smile. 'So let's hurry and get there as quickly as we can. We don't want to push our luck now, seeing as we'll need plenty of it later.'

Somehow, they held themselves back from running. The encounter with the man had shaken them, so they pulled up their hoods. It was not raining, but it was still overcast so Eric hoped that they could get away with it. They hurried along in silence, sticking close together. Eric's excitement had dwindled.

They passed row after row of houses and the Crystal light grew brighter by the minute. More and more people began to emerge from their homes; men and women heading off to work, or taking their children to school. The cobbles began to slope and for the first time they heard the faint rumblings of the twin waterfalls. They left the new city behind and stepped into the old, the heart of Alashdial. Eric could not resist stopping to take it all in. He had flown overhead when he had rescued Jad, but that was not the same. The mountain rose up ahead of them. White buildings shone, each its own unique shape. The ground sloped and wide staircases sprouted off in all directions. Every inch of ground that was not paved with cobbles burst with green life. Vines crawled over walls and the musical tinkling of water surrounded them. These were the streets Eric had played on as a boy. These were the homes of old friends and enemies. The flags and the banners for the Festival had been put in place. He yearned for it. He had forgotten what he had given up, what he had sacrificed, but it was back within his grasp.

The people of Alashdial swirled around them as the dawn became morning. The mindless chatter of the mass buzzed and Eric did his best to keep his gaze averted. But as they got closer and closer to his home, it became much more difficult. They passed a familiar house just as the door opened and Eric could not stop himself from looking up. His eyes were pulled against his will. He saw a flash of blonde hair and something fluttered in his stomach. He jerked his eyes away and grabbed Tayah, trying to pull her past. It was too late.

'Eric?'

His stomach stopped fluttering and did a few flips instead.

Tayah tugged at his hand. 'Come on...'

But Eric's legs no longer seemed to work properly and he hesitated. By the time the shock had passed, Arren stood in front of him. They stared at one another in mutual shock, Eric having to look up to him just like before. Physically, he had hardly changed. The fair stubble on his jaw was the only difference that Eric could see. It was Arren's attire that scared Eric, for he was wearing Bagor's armour. Tayah gave up trying to pull Eric away.

'How did you know it was me?' said Eric, blushing at the breathless sound of his voice.

Arren shot him one of his crooked smiles. He lifted a hand and tugged Eric's hood. 'Even with this I could still see your hair.'

As Arren let his hand fall, his smile faded and his eyes fixed onto Eric's with an intensity that made him shiver. He seemed to be waiting for an explanation, but Eric could only think of one thing.

'You work for him now?'

Arren's gaze did not flinch, but his cheeks glowed faintly. He nodded. 'It pays well.'

Eric's gaze sharpened. He hoped that he looked angry because that was not really how he felt. He felt betrayed which made him feel foolish. Arren did not owe him anything. They had been neighbours once, that was all.

'What are you doing here, Eric?'

Eric said nothing and Arren scratched his jaw. His eyes drifted to Tayah for the first time. She held onto Eric's arm and glared at Arren.

'I should take you in,' said Arren, his armour rattling as he took a step closer.

'Then hurry up about it,' snapped Tayah.

Eric could feel the pressure of her fingers on his arm, but he could hardly hear her over the pounding of his blood in his ears. He saw Arren glance at her in alarm, and then he smiled again, his blue eyes twinkling.

'It's a good thing I'm not patrolling the streets today. My work is up at the palace. I'm off duty until I get there.'

Eric closed his eyes. They jerked open again when Arren gripped his arm. He smelt of bath soap and for some reason that made Eric blush once more.

'Whatever it is you're doing,' said Arren, 'be careful. The city is not the same as you remember.'

He pushed past them and strode off without looking back, leaving Eric struggling to recall where he was and what he was supposed to be doing.

'Eric?' Tayah whispered, stepping into the space that Arren had just vacated.

He blinked at her. 'We were stupid to ever think that this part might be easy.'

Tayah raised an eyebrow. 'I don't think I ever thought that, if I remember rightly.'

Eric managed a strained smile. He had been the only one to get carried away. But then, he always thought that things would be easy. He had thought the same when he had staged that fight with his father. He had been certain that he would be home again within the month.

'Come on,' Tayah slipped her hand into his, 'we're almost there.'

Eric let Tayah lead him from then on. They passed their old school and had to wade through a gaggle of small children. They passed Fii's old house, still empty as the day Eric had left. He thought Tayah would have wanted to stop, for it had been her home for a long time too, but she pulled him past. With each memory, the pain in Eric's chest grew. When they crossed the Founder's Bridge Eric wanted to swing his legs over the edge and throw a coin into the water. He had sat there with Jad and Tayah almost every day. They had thought that the three wolves carved into its side were symbolic. They were the three wolves and it had been on that bridge that they had made a pact to always be there for one another, no matter what. Somehow, Tayah continued to lead him without a moments pause until they had stepped onto the street; his street. That realisation brought Eric back to the present with a jolt.

His home looked exactly as he remembered. It was not much, a two storey box that had never really been big enough for five people, but it was home. His eyes fell to the small garden at the front. His mother managed to make it beautiful despite how little she had to work with. Then his front door opened and somebody stepped out of it. Eric grabbed Tayah and bundled her towards the nearest house.

'What...'

He pressed his hand over her mouth until they were hidden behind a wall. Then he held a finger to his lips and pulled his hand away.

'Ria,' he whispered.

Tayah's eyes bulged. 'Here?' Eric could hear the panic in her voice. 'Why?'

Eric did not know. He shook his head and held up a finger. He crept back along the wall and peered around the corner.

It was like somebody had taken a sledgehammer to his stomach. Ria was talking to his father, but - unlike his home - Bram Howd had changed a great deal. His once furiously red hair was frosted with white and there were countless lines on his face when he frowned. Eric could not remember seeing his father with a frown on his face; he had always been smiling. His father looked so much smaller than he remembered.

Eric pulled back and pressed his forehead against the wall.

'What is it?'

Eric swallowed. 'She's with my Da.'

Tayah pressed her lips into a thin line. Her gaze bore into him and he knew what she was thinking. Had the man from the wall informed the Armours after all? Had Arren? Had they already failed? Taking a deep breath, Eric looked back around the corner.

He was just in time to see Ria shoot upwards in a splash of feathers towards the palace. His father was nowhere to be seen and the front door was shut.

Eric looked back at Tayah and shrugged. 'She's gone.'

Tayah shook her head,'I don't like it. I don't know what we should do, but I don't like it.'

Eric rubbed his eyes. He hated making decisions. He had always been happy to let Jad lead.

'We stick to the plan. We lay low at mine.'

Tayah looked horrified. 'But what if she comes back?'

'I don't know, Tay,' Eric admitted. 'But we'll be safer in there than we are standing here.' He held out his hand to her and was surprised to see that he was shaking. They were so close.

Tayah looked unsure, but she took his hand anyway and managed to smile for half a second before it turned into a grimace. He gave her hand a quick squeeze and led her back out onto the street. They kept their hoods pulled low over their faces and forced themselves to walk. Eric could see the details of his mother's lace curtains and a crack in the window that had not been there when he was last home. He bumped into somebody and mumbled an apology without looking up. He held his breath, but nobody grabbed him or cried out his name. They reached the alley that ran down the side of his house, and then they were at the back door, the varnished wood chipped and faded.

'Go on then,' hissed Tayah, scanning the skies.

Eric blinked. He had lifted his fist and then frozen. Shaking himself, he knocked three times and stepped back, his heart pounding.

Bram answered immediately, his face set in an impatient scowl. 'What now?'

Eric tipped his hood back and stared wide eyed into his father's face.

The colour drained from Bram's skin until he looked grey. His jaw hung slack as his eyes focused on Eric's.

'Da?'

'Eric?' He croaked. Then Bram threw his arms around his son and held him tight, '*My boy.*'

Eric nodded, clinging to the back of his father's shirt as silent tears spilled down his cheeks.

Bram pulled back, remembering who they were. 'Get inside, quick,' he said, pulling Eric in after him. Tayah followed and Bram placed a gentle hand on her cheek. She smiled at him and pulled the door shut behind her. Bram turned back to Eric. He held him at arms length and gazed at him with shining eyes.

'Not a boy any longer,' he said, his voice gruff, 'a man.'

Eric did not feel like much of a man standing in his parents' kitchen, with tears on his cheeks. He tried to hold them back, but his father was looking at him with such pride in his eyes that a few more leaked out. Everything was as it should be. His father's chair still sat in the corner, so worn that it could not possibly be comfortable. Two dolls had been left on the floor, frozen in whichever game his sisters had been playing. He recognised them both; he had brought them from the market years before on a whim. Even the patchwork tablecloth was unchanged, with the same frayed edges. Eric coughed back a fresh wave of tears and Bram laughed, throwing his arms around his son again before turning to Tayah.

'And you, sweetheart,' he said, taking her hands, 'a young woman.'

Tayah grinned at him. 'It's wonderful to see you again.'

'Sit, both of you, sit.' He flitted around the table, pulling out chairs and laughing sporadically. He seemed unable to stand still and with every second that passed he looked more like the father that Eric had known. 'I'll get you some drinks,' Bram said, 'Would you like to eat? No, we'll wait for your mother. *Your mother.* Just wait till she sees you...'

Eric sank into a chair, beaming at his father as he moved about the kitchen. He felt like he could sit there and listen to his father talk until the end of time. And the others would be home soon. He could barely wait to see them again.

'Here,' Bram handed them a glass of water each, tweaking Eric's ear as he passed. He sat down with them and tried his hardest to adopt a serious expression over the top of his smile.

'Of course,' he said, 'I can't pretend that I am only happy to see you. I'm also confused. Why are you here?'

Eric wanted to forget about the life that existed outside of this moment. He stared at his father, silenced by his sudden need to ignore reality.

'We figured you might know,' said Tayah, 'we saw you talking to Ria.'

'Ria?' Bram frowned. 'She said nothing about you.'

Eric's curiosity was caught. He cleared his throat. 'Then what did she want?'

Bram shrugged, 'She comes by whenever she can. Every other week or so since...' he could not stop himself from glancing at his son, 'Well, work has dried up.'

Eric gripped the edge of the table. 'Because of me. Because I left.'

Bram started to shake his head, 'We don't know that...'

'Da, don't...'

Bram talked over him. 'Why it happened does not matter, all right? It does not matter. Things are hard for everyone these days. Ria has helped us, with money and with food. Don't be giving up on that one yet.'

Tayah looked dazed for a moment before she mustered the most contemptuous look that she could. 'As long as she supports Bagor, it does not matter what else she does.'

Eric shot his father a look and Bram bit back his words.

'Still,' said Tayah, composing herself, 'it's good to know that we don't have to worry about her coming back.'

Bram's thick brow lowered. 'She might still, if she hears you are in the city. Which brings me back to what you're doing here. How the hell did you get in? Where is Jadanim?'

The glow of his sons reappearance was starting to fade and Eric could see his father's mind working. The lines on his face were so much more pronounced when he wasn't smiling.

'Welm has a way into the city. He helped us.' Eric began. 'And Jad is safe. He's in Alashdial too.'

'He's *what*? Have you all gone soft in the head?'

'Da...'

'What is it son? What's going on?'

Eric was reluctant to talk. He did not want to think about what was to come. He did not want to burst the bubble of happiness that encapsulated the small kitchen. But Bram had never been a patient man and Eric knew that he had no choice.

'Bagor has a prisoner, a human boy.'

Bram nodded. 'I've heard the rumours, we all have. There are rumours of a human girl too, but she got away somehow.'

'We know her. She's with us. The boy is her friend and we are going to save him.'

Bram turned his eyes to the ceiling and clasped his hand together, 'By the Mother, what did I do to deserve this?'

'No,' Eric started, 'it's okay...'

Bram slammed his hand onto the tabletop, making it tremble. 'It is madness. An impossible task. The moment the King gets his hands on you you will be thrown into a cell for the rest of your days, or worse, you will be killed. Two years ago, I lost my son. But I was comforted by the knowledge that you were out there, you hear? That you were free. If you try this, I won't even have that.'

'But we have something Bagor wants,' Tayah said, as soon as Bram stopped for breath. Eric was grateful for he had lost the ability to speak. Guilt squirmed through him.

'Bagor is searching for a Key and we have it,' she said. 'It will be enough to protect us. It's our bargaining tool. And maybe we can learn something. You see, we have no idea why he wants it or what it does. Perhaps Bagor is the only one who can tell us. Then we might find out how to hurt him, to beat him. That's why this is a risk worth taking.'

Bram scoffed, 'He'll tell you nothing.'

'Not us, you're right,' Tayah nodded, before Bram could launch himself into another tirade. 'Kammy, the human girl. She is Semei. She is Simbassi.'

'Simbassi?' Bram's brow furrowed before recognition struck and his eyes grew round with wonder. 'That's impossible.'

Eric shook his head. He understood his father's doubt. He had doubted it too when Jad had first suggested the possibility. But Eric believed it now, he had too.

Somebody screamed.

Eric lurched to his feet and Tayah was already at the door, ready to flee. Only when Bram started laughing did Eric look towards the front of the house and the other door that was hanging open.

His mother, Marie, stood in in the light with a hand pressed to her mouth. A bag lay at her feet, fresh vegetables spilling out of it. Unlike his father, Eric's mother had not changed. Her hair was still yellow and her face still smooth. She pulled her shaking hand away from her face.

'Eric?'

Two smaller figures charged in from behind her, startled by their mother's cry. The smallest, Elvira, was fair. She stared up at Eric, her cheeks round and her mouth forming a perfect circle. Then she flung herself forwards and leapt into Eric's arms. He swept her up, laughing, and Marie followed. She threw her arms around her son's neck and her whole body trembled.

'Please be real...please...' she whispered.

'I am, Ma.'

She planted a flurry of kisses on his cheeks.

Kait, his second sister still stood in the doorway. She was thirteen now and she had grown considerably since Eric had last seen her. She barely looked like a child any more and the eyes that stared at him were too wise for one still young. She shared his bright red hair and she had the same pattern of freckles on her cheeks, but she stared at him as though he were a stranger.

Eric held out an arm to her and her lip trembled. He saw the tears in her eyes and then she charged forwards, to his great relief. She wrapped her arms around his middle and he laughed, planting a kiss on the top of her head. He was sure that his heart was about to explode. He wondered why they were not at school, but decided that - for the moment - he did not care.

'I hated you for leaving us.'

Eric's blood ran cold. Only he heard Kait's whisper.

Marie spotted Tayah and let out a squeal of delight so shrill that Elvira, whose ears were closest, growled at her. His mother let Eric go only to launch herself at Tayah with almost equal gusto. Eric stayed with his sisters. Elvira's head rested on his shoulder as she hummed softly to herself.

Kait smiled up at him, 'But you're back now.'

Marie shrieked something about food and started to bundle them all out of the kitchen, but Eric did not look away from Kait and her eyes that were the same as his own. He tried to smile back at her, but the muscles in his face did not seem to be working. Then Marie was overcome by another surge of emotion and she collapsed back onto her son, choking and laughing all at once. With an almighty roar Bram joined them, slinging out an arm to pull Tayah in too.

Two years before, Eric had abandoned them. He had told himself that he was doing the right thing, a good thing. He was sticking to the pact that he had made and he was helping his friend. But had he helped? Was it worth leaving his family behind?

As they laughed and cried around him, Eric felt a chill. How could he ever leave them again?

CHAPTER TWENTY

AN OLLARION BETRAYED

They could see the Giant's Staircase from where they stood and the palace above it, but Jad did not feel any joy as he gazed upon his old home; he felt only dread. He glanced down at Kammy beside him. Her eyes were wide with wonder and she did not look afraid. He wished he had some of her courage.

'I can't come any further with you,' he said, hating the mere thought of it.

She looked at him and nodded, but he thought he saw a faint flash of anxiety in her eyes. The two of them had waited for five minutes before following Eric and Tayah, but Jad had not dared to move openly. They had crept along the wall, keeping to the shadows as best they could. They had moved in silence, but Kammy let him know, with little touches and smiles, that she was glad he was there. Now, she would have to continue alone.

'Where does she live?' said Kammy, her voice light.

'Ania?' he said, surprised. It felt strange talking about her. He turned, shielding his eyes against the light. They were above the main bulk of the city, amongst the villas and the gardens of Alashdial's most wealthy citizens. Ania's villa could well have been called a palace itself. He pointed at it, sitting atop a rise and shrouded by trees. He realised as he looked that a large portion of his dread was being stored for that upcoming meeting. He had no idea what to expect.

'It's beautiful,' Kammy said with awe. She turned away from him. 'She must be beautiful too.'

'She is,' he said without hesitation. Her beauty had been so important to him once.

'Right then,' Kammy said, 'you better get going.' And just like that she started to walk away from him.

'Whoa,' he jumped forwards, pulling her back. She looked at his hand on her arm and then, reluctantly, she met his eye. He tried to smile at her. 'I still don't like this. This is our last chance to change our minds. We can pick the others up from Eric's and we can think of another way to save Jamie. Just give me some time.'

Her smile came easily and her fingers curled around his. She pulled his hand away and when she let go he felt a rush of cold.

'We don't have time Jad, Jamie doesn't. There is no other way.' They stared at one another until Kammy blinked and looked away. She nudged him lightly. 'We'll be fine.'

Jad sighed. He curled his hands around the strap of his satchel, unsure what else to do with them. He felt awkward and unsure, but there was no point in trying to change her mind now. 'Are you sure you're all right getting up there?'

'I can handle a few steps.'

Jad laughed, 'I know.

She took a step away from him and he was almost overcome by an urge to reach out to her again. He could not shake the feeling that once she was out of sight, he would never see her again. Two weeks before he had not even known that she existed, now the thought of losing her made him cold with terror.

'Jad?'

'Yes?'

'Thank you,' she said, and he thought that her eyes really were such an incredible shade of blue.

Close to the Crystal, she looked different. Her hair shone and her skin glowed. His breath caught as she turned her back on him. He did not reach for her. He stood in silence beneath a tree until she was gone. Then he gathered himself. His friends were relying on him to get something done.

Jad pushed away from the tree and hurried towards Ania's home. He could move more openly among the sheltered paths of the gardens. He ran across the stones and the trees intertwined over his head. He did not see another soul. The rich citizens of Alashdial had descended upon the main hub of the city to work and Jad could only hope that Ania had remained behind. He refused to consider the possibility that she had not. All of their hopes rested upon chance and every muscle in his body was taut with that fact. There had been a time when Jad relished bad odds. He had seen beating them as a way to prove himself. He did not feel that way any more, not now that other lives were forfeit.

He passed a familiar stone bench and his stomach lurched. He could remember the last time he had seen Ania, the day before his life had changed. They had been sitting together on that bench with no idea of what was to come. He had kissed her and he had told her, as he had done countless times, that he loved her. The memory struck him as silly.

He turned off the gravel path and onto smooth flagstone. Here, the trees gave way to an open space, coated with wealth. Jad pushed back his hood as he walked towards her door. He passed ornate fountains and dramatic sculptures. Ania had always implored her father to demonstrate his wealth and her father had never been able to deny her. It had not bothered Jad before, but as he got closer and he saw the extravagant detail of the stained glass windows, he realised that it irked him now.

He paused on the doorstep and stared at it for a couple of minutes, feeling like a fool. He looked down at his clothes and wrinkled his nose; he looked a mess. He ran a hand through his hair, wishing he had thought to smooth it down that morning. He tried to peer at his reflection through the glass, but doing so only made him feel worse so he pulled back and knocked. The seconds dragged and he saw no movement. He could hear nothing but the roar of the twin falls and panic seized his mind. Could he catch up to Kammy in time to tell her that they had failed when they had barely begun?

He was so absorbed in the thought that he did not notice the door open. Only when he heard Ania's muffled cry was he yanked back to himself. The polite smile on her face had frozen and her porcelain skin had turned a faint shade of yellow. Emerald eyes blinked at him and her full lips parted. Jad tried to grin at her and she started to slam the door in his face.

Jad jammed his foot into the closing space and let out a yelp of pain, '*Ania.*'

'Go away,' she growled, sounding very different to the girl he had known.

Jad was not sure if he had expected her to fall into his arms, but he had certainly not expected this. She continued to slam the door against his boot, again and again, but Jad refused to budge. He had the distinct impression that if he let the door close, it would never open to him again.

'Ania,' he pressed an eye to the small gap, '*please.*'

She gave the door one last hefty shove, then she yanked it open with a furious hiss and stepped back, inviting him in with eyes narrowed to slits. He darted inside before she could change her mind.

The entrance hall was cavernous. Marble columns stood at each corner, holding up a mosaic ceiling made of every shade of green. Between each floor tile ran rivulets of water flowing from the mouth of the stone dolphin sprouting out of the far wall. The grandeur was so excessive it looked ridiculous and Jad was about to tease her for it, like he used to, when she slammed the door shut. He turned to face her, swallowing any hint of familiarity.

She was beautiful, but when she was not laughing at one of his terrible jokes or running her long fingers through his hair, it seemed a cold beauty. Even her hair looked severe. It did not wave and curl as Kammy's did, but hung straight to her waist. She lifted a hand to her chest and her jewel encrusted bracelets jangled.

'You cannot be here.'

The room seemed to grow colder with every second, the frost crawled off of her. He tried for levity and smiled, 'I thought you might be happy to see me.'

'*Happy?*' her nostrils flared. 'Do you have any idea what it was like for us when you left? The scrutiny we were under?'

'I did not choose to leave, Ania.'

'Father almost lost his job and we could have lost our home. For the last two years he has worked himself to the bone and only recently has the King,' Jad winced, 'started to reward him. But if he knew that you were *here...*' she drew in a breath and shook her head. 'You have to leave. I should not have let you in. You have to go.'

'Ania, just hear me out. I would not have come to you if it was not important.'

Her eyes flashed, 'Oh, so you want something? How charming. Two years and I did not hear a word from you.'

Jad gaped at her. 'I didn't send word because I feared it might cast suspicion on you, like you just said...'

'You did not send word because you flew away to freedom, forgetting the people that you left behind.'

'Is that what you think?' Jad was stunned. 'That I was free? That I did not care that I had to leave you?' He had cared. He had thought of her every night for months, before the memories had started to fade and to blur. 'Do you think these last two years have been fun for me?'

'The last two years do not matter,' she gasped. She thrust a long nail towards the door, 'All that matters is that you cannot be here. Leave.'

Desperate, Jad swept towards her and grasped one of her hands. She stiffened at his touch, but did not pull away. She smelt of sweets and honey. Once she had doused one of his shirts in her perfume so that he would think of her, always. Jad smiled at the memory and Ania's eyes began to soften.

'You're the only one that can help me, Ania. Please.'

She stared at their hands with pouting lips and Jad held his breath.

'Why are you here?' she said, softly.

Jad gave her hand a squeeze, but she had not relaxed. 'One favour,' he said, 'I need to borrow the key to the palace kitchens.'

Her eyes widened. 'Why?'

'You have heard of Bagor's human prisoner?'

'Of course,' she said, with an arched eyebrow, 'the King now knows that he can trust my father.'

Jad almost sneered at the thought. He could just picture her simpering, red-faced father floundering around behind Bagor. Through clenched teeth, he said, 'The boy's friend has been travelling with us. She...we have to save him.'

Ania snatched her hand back and slapped him across the face. '*How dare you.*'

Jad's cheek burned. 'What...'

'She? *She*?' Ania's voice crackled with fury. 'You want me to risk everything for a human girl?'

'But she's not human, she's...'

'I don't care what she is, Jadanim,' she shrieked, slashing a wild arm through the air.

Jad fell silent. Ania was breathing heavily and a flush spread across her face and down her long neck. He realised that she was jealous, after all this time, but it did not please him. He could feel his chance slipping through his fingers and he could see Bagor smirking as he led Kammy away. Jad could not leave her to that fate.

'She is nothing to me, Ania. All right? But we need her for something, something big. She won't help us if we don't save her friend.' Guilt wormed inside him because of the lie, because of how much he was asking Ania to risk. But she had to help him. It seemed to work, her fury began to retreat.

'Regardless,' she sniffed, 'I cannot do as you ask.'

'Ania...'

'You will get caught and they will know where the key came from.'

'There are countless keys into the kitchens.'

'No. Not any more. Things have changed Jad, in the palace especially. The King does not like people being there. There are only four keys and he has one of them.'

Jad swore. He thought hard. 'I can leave it underneath the step, you know where I mean. You can collect...'

She laughed. 'Because sneaking away from my father as the night is coming and passing beneath the falls to the kitchens, where I

234

hate to be seen, would not be suspicious at all? I would be the first person that Bagor would suspect and even if I could get to the key, I'd never get it home in time.'

'Then I won't get caught. Ania, I won't. I only need to reach the bell. I know the palace better than anyone. I will not get caught.'

'Can you promise that?' she said, her eyes shining.

Jad was about to nod, to insist that he could, but he stopped himself. He was thinking of his own need to help his friends. He was not thinking of the harm that could befall Ania. His scar began to ache, as if reminding him of how unfit he was to help anyone. He ran a hand through his hair and, for the first time, Ania smiled at him. She took a step closer and placed her hand on his right arm. She had always avoided his left.

'You've changed,' she said, looking up at him, 'you are more serious. It's sad.'

He wanted to shout at her, to remind her of all that had happened to him and of what Bagor had done. He wanted to list the things that he had lost. He wanted to tell her of the nightmares that still plagued him and the fears that weighed on him every day, but it was pointless. His head dropped.

'You're right. I should not have come here. I'm sorry for wasting your time.' He started towards the door.

'My father has the key. He will be home an hour past midday.' Her voice trembled and Jad could hardly bear to look at her. If he did get caught, she would pay. She stared at her hands. 'Can you get to Fii's old place, two hours before the light begins to fade?'

Jad nodded.

She met his eye. Her beaded gown and her pale skin made her look doll-like, but her gaze was steel. 'I will do what I can, but I make no promises.'

Jad pulled up his hood, holding her gaze for a long moment. 'Thank you,' he said, before he slipped away through the door.

* * *

Kammy had not known that such beauty could exist, such sprawling, magnificent beauty. From high above on the back of a giant eagle, the city had been impressive. From within, Kammy could hardly blink for staring.

She was sitting on a patch of grass beside a large pond full of vibrant fish. Closed Akasi flowers surrounded her, and a three tiered fountain ahead shot water that glittered like diamonds into the sky. She looked down upon the city and gazed at it in wonder. Three times the size of Emire, it had far more room to breathe. She could see all the way to the wall and the forest beyond. She had walked so far yet she hardly felt tired. The Crystal bathed the city in a soft light despite the clouds that hung overhead. It would have looked ghostly if not for the explosions of green dotted throughout. Even the air in Alashdial tasted different. Kammy felt stronger than she ever had before and with that strength had come a new boldness. It had helped her make it so far, but she had been sitting in the same spot for quite a long time. The minutes continued to stretch on and Kammy feared that no amount of boldness could make her brave enough to continue on her own.

Her back was turned to it, but she was constantly aware of the Giant's Staircase. She could see where it had gotten its name, being wide enough for fifty people to stand across it. And the thundering of the waterfalls drowned out the noise from the city below. Avoiding accepting that she had reached her goal was not going to be possible for long.

Leaving Jad had been difficult enough. Although his impending visit to see the beautiful Ania had helped spur Kammy on her way, she had thought it would be best to appear flippant. She did not want Jad to think that Ania bothered her, because she didn't, not in the slightest. That inner turmoil had given her the courage to walk away from him. She had distracted herself by studying the people that she passed. There were all sorts in Alashdial. She even heard a different language and she knew that she would never be able to learn enough about the Semei to satisfy her. Then the Staircase had loomed larger and no distraction was enough.

It was half a mile of solid stone that led to the palace carved into a cliff. The size and weight of it all was overwhelming. The adrenaline pumping through her stopped her from feeling afraid, but she certainly did not feel confident. She simply could not move. She had even giggled once or twice and feared that she was about to lose her mind to hysteria. Two weeks had passed since she had first woken in a cell inside that palace, but it felt like a lifetime. She had changed,

236

irrevocably, and she feared that returning to that place would cut her old self asunder. She was not sure if she was ready for that.

Kammy took a deep breath and stood. It had been her own insistence that had brought her to this point; nobody else's. If she did not do what she had promised she would, and soon, then her friends would risk everything for nothing.

Kammy forced herself to face the Staircase and the enormity of it struck her all over again. Two Armours stood at its base, their chest plates glinting blue in the light. They had not approached her. She had half hoped that they would, that they would identify her themselves and drag her to see their king, so that she did not need to make herself do it. But even when she stared at them, they showed no special interest in her over the other people lounging on the grass. So Kammy concentrated on breathing as she walked towards them, her eyes fixed on the first step. When it was clear that Kammy intended to climb, the Armour's faces snapped towards her and she froze.

'You,' said the closest one, a mousy haired woman, 'What business do you have at the palace?'

Kammy tried to swallow, but her mouth was too dry. She attempted to recover some of her courage, but the words trembled as they fell out of her. 'My name is Kammy Helseth. I'm the human girl that Bagor is looking for.'

The immediacy of their reaction stunned her. The woman grabbed her arm and yanked her forwards. The man on her right was a dog and he scampered away up the Staircase before she had finished speaking. The woman dragged Kammy after him and she felt a spark of indignation.

'I can walk,' she spat.

The woman pushed her forwards, 'Then walk.'

Kammy had no choice, but to start her ascent. The steps were not steep, but she took her time. She focused on her feet, not wanting to know how far she had to go. She was grateful that the Staircase was wide enough that she could not see over the edge to what lay below. She remembered the sight of the chasm well enough from the flight. She imagined the Staircase crumbling beneath her and carrying her down into oblivion. She had to close her eyes for a moment to gather herself. The woman had no sympathy and gave her another shove, so Kammy stumbled on. She tried not to think of Bagor. She tried to

237

focus all her thoughts on one thing; Jamie. Knowing that he was so close gave her that last spurt of energy she needed to climb the last few steps. She left the Staircase behind her with a relieved groan.

Kammy *had* to look up then and the palace shone before her, stretching high and wide with the Crystal at its centre. She could hardly bear to look at the Crystal, but she did not want to look away either. It bathed the courtyard in a rainbow of colours that shifted and danced through the air. The giant windows cast those colours as fragmented images, the patterns following the paths that wound between the Akasi flowerbeds. The doors stood open, but Kammy could only see darkness within them. Her eyes did not linger on those shadows. They passed across each turret and tower until she saw one that looked a little worse for wear and she laughed. That had been her cell, because there was still a hole in the wall where Eric had blown it up. The Armour behind her heard her laugh and, perhaps offended, grabbed Kammy's arm again. Her painful grip reminded Kammy of what she had come to do. She let the woman propel her forwards, fearing that she would never move again without the help.

A darker shadow shifted beneath the door and Kammy watched as it stepped out into the light. Her fears were confirmed. The terror she had felt when she had last seen that face came flooding back. Dorren strode towards her, his eyes fixed on hers with such hatred that she recoiled. The woman let go of her and snapped to attention as Dorren stopped before them. His whole bulk shook.

Dorren did not take his eyes off her when he spoke. His jaw was clenched so tight she thought it might shatter. 'You say she approached you?'

The woman nodded, relaxing her stance. 'Yes, Sir.'

His nostrils flared. He waved a hand and turned his back, 'Get rid of her.'

'But, Sir...'

'I said,' he growled, 'get rid of her.'

The woman insisted. 'I am sorry, Sir, but his Majesty wants...'

With a roar Dorren spun back towards Kammy. His eyes were bulging with more than just anger. He was afraid.

Kammy backed away from him, 'Bagor...he wants to see me...'

Dorren was not listening. His hands seized Kammy and he swung her up over his head as if she were a rag doll. Kammy screamed and the woman ran at him, trying to pull her down, but Dorren was too tall and too strong.

'Sir, you cannot...'

Dorren ignored the woman. He pushed past her, towards the edge and Kammy could feel his arms trembling. She twisted and she squirmed, but he held on.

'Please,' Kammy cried, 'help me, please...'

But Dorren would not be stopped. In his frenzied state he was deaf to their pleas. He stood at the edge of the courtyard, looking down into the chasm. She realised what he was going to do and her fingers tore at him. This could not happen, not now. She had come to save Jamie. She was going to save Jamie. She reached up to Dorren's face and clawed at his eyes as she struggled with all her strength. Dorren howled and threw Kammy over the edge.

Time stopped. Kammy fell. She stared down at the rocks and the raging water that lay far below. Everything was silent. She knew that she was going to die and her thoughts turned to her Gran. She closed her eyes as the air rushed past her.

She jerked to a halt so suddenly that her head was flung backwards and she cried out in pain. Then she flew. She could feel something on her wrist, but when she opened her eyes, there was nothing there and she had to close them again as the world spun. The next thing she knew, she hit the stone back in the courtyard.

Kammy clung to the stone with her fingertips and lay perfectly still on her back, unable to breathe. Her neck hurt, but she was only faintly aware of it. She was alive, somehow, and she turned her head slowly to see that Dorren had fallen to his knees. His cheeks were bleeding where she had scratched him.

The male Armour had rejoined his female companion and they were both staring at Dorren in mute astonishment. Dorren's eyes were fixed on a point past Kammy's feet and they were wide with fear. She followed his gaze, but there was nothing there.

The air seemed too still and Kammy blinked. *There*. A pocket of space before her was swirling. Her eyes widened as it began to shimmer and solidify. Kammy watched as a man began to form out of nothing. The back of his neck appeared first, a head of thick black hair. Then broad shoulders clad in a white shirt and long legs in black trousers. Kammy knew that this man had just saved her life and she knew who he was; Bagor.

'Your Majesty...'

Bagor held up a hand and Dorren spluttered into silence. Then he turned and his eyes fell on Kammy, sprawled at his feet.

Kammy felt a jolt of shock when she met his gaze. She could see Jad in every inch of his face, from the brightness of his eyes to the line of his jaw. But what was most remarkable was the way that his eyes widened when he saw her and how he staggered back, his face ashen. It took a long moment for the king of Alashdial to find his voice.

'Marianna?'

CHAPTER TWENTY ONE

MARIANNA

He said it again, 'Marianna?'

'No...' Kammy stared at him, unable to move. 'My name is...Kammy Helseth.'

Rust bloomed in his cheeks. He took a step closer, his mouth hanging open, just as Dorren leapt into the air with a flurry of feathers and squawks. Bagor disappeared and Dorren's crow slammed back onto the stone within moments. He flapped his wings feebly, but something held him down and the crow fell away once more, expanding into Dorren's usual shape. He had tears in his eyes as he stared at the empty sky above. A hand appeared, fixed around his thick neck, and then Bagor crouched over him. Kammy shivered. Something in his eyes made her cold. It was not fury. It was something more than rage. There was a stillness to him that was more terrifying than any great show of power. He did not speak and Dorren seemed small beneath him. Bagor hissed a breath through his teeth.

'You are a fool,' Bagor whispered, and it sounded like thunder. 'If you try to run you will only succeed in making things worse for yourself.' He let go and Dorren gasped. Bagor stepped away from him and the pressure of his anger lifted. He turned to the two Armours. 'Get him out of my sight. Find Ria.' The Armours jumped to do as asked. They hauled Dorren to his feet and the big man slumped between them as they led him away.

Kammy still had not moved. She found it hard to breathe and harder to think. Bagor had disappeared right in front of her eyes. One moment he had been there and then he was gone. How was that possible? Was it an illusion? It only made her more sure that Bagor was a monster, yet he looked like a man. Then he turned back to face her and Kammy's confusion deepened. His eyes softened as they fell upon her. He stepped closer, hesitant, and held out his hand. Kammy had no choice but to take it, even as her heart beat for freedom from her chest. His grip was cool but strong as he pulled her to her feet. She staggered and he caught her elbow.

'Are you hurt?'

Kammy continued to stare at him in wonder. He seemed concerned for her. She shook her head and steadied herself. He released her elbow, but he held onto her hand and he smiled.

'You look just like her...'

Kammy closed her eyes. She looked just like her mother, Mary. *Marianna.* It was hard to hide from the truth now. Her mother had come from this place. Her mother had lied to her every day of her life until she had died. Her mother had been Semei and so, in part, was she.

'Come, you are trembling.'

Bagor's arm snaked around her shoulders and he started to lead her across the courtyard. He held her close and Kammy's head screamed at her to push him away, but she stayed where she was, holding herself rigid and unable to comprehend what had just happened. She still felt as though she was falling. The stone beneath her feet tipped and swayed with every step.

'You saved my life,' she whispered.

Bagor stopped walking. After a moment's thought his hand slipped under her chin and he forced her to look at him. His gaze was searching.

'You are afraid.'

Of course she was afraid. As she looked into his eyes, she realised that he did not look like Jad completely. He was taller for one, and his nose was longer. It comforted her that she could see the difference for she knew that Jad would despise it if she could not. Bagor smiled again as her trembling began to ease.

242

'You do not need to fear me,' he said, 'I will not let any harm come to you.'

Kammy could have laughed. Ever since Jad had come to Daleswick to collect her, she had feared Bagor in some distant way. She had known that he would kill her for the Key that she carried. She had heard what the others had told her and she had believed them when they spoke of Bagor and his nature. Yet his words were so soft and his touch so gentle. They started moving again and she could feel her heart pattering with anxiety as they passed out of the light and into the palace.

A cream door dominated her vision. It was ten times as tall as Kammy and bordered with golden flower prints. It was sealed shut and Bagor steered her away from it, down a wide corridor that stretched ahead for what seemed like miles.

'Where are you taking me?'

'There are guest quarters on the second floor. We can talk more comfortably there.'

Yes, they would talk and he would stop this kindly charade. 'You want the Key.'

'I do,' he said, 'but that is not important right now.'

Not important? Was it not the whole reason that Kammy had been dragged into this world? Was it not the whole reason that Jamie had been taken?

Bagor pressed his fingers into her shoulder and looked down at her. 'We have a lot to talk about; Marianna, most of all.'

'Mary. Her name was Mary.'

His grip on her tightened. 'Her name was Marianna.'

Kammy fell silent and watched her feet move. She felt like she was floating and Bagor was the wave that carried her forwards. She tried her hardest to pay attention when they turned corners and passed staircases. She knew she might need to find her way back, but every corridor looked the same. The walls and the floors were unendingly white. The windows were one uniform giant size and the light reflected off the whiteness. Where there were no windows, the walls were hung with curtains and tapestries that were indistinguishable from the next to Kammy's eyes. By the time they began to climb a wide staircase, Kammy's head spun. The beat of their footsteps echoed in her ears, accompanied by Bagor's aimless chatter. Otherwise, the palace appeared empty.

'Where is everybody?'

'They are preparing,' said Bagor.

Kammy felt a chill. 'For what?'

He did not answer straight away. He took the time to smile first. 'For the Festival of the Mother.'

She nodded, she had seen signs of the upcoming celebration as she had made her way through Alashdial.

'You have heard of it? It is always a great event. Perhaps if we celebrate her name, the Mother might return to us. Ah, here we are.' He turned her towards a door and pushed it open. Then he stepped back, releasing her, and held the door so that she could step inside.

The guest quarters of the palace put those of Emire's keep to shame. The room was vast, the furthest wall dominated by a window. The view took Kammy's breath away. Not only could she see the city and the forest, but the mountains beyond and, far in the distance, what she thought must be the Basin. The room itself was also exquisite. The walls were a pale blue, surrounded by drapes of a darker shade. The cream carpet was so spotless that Kammy did not want to walk on it. At one end of the room was a four poster bed that could have slept ten people and ahead of that were three lounging chairs, patterned with gold and circling a glass table. On top of the table were a variety of sumptuous looking cakes and a steaming metal pot.

'When Mathius charged into my office with news of your arrival, I sent ahead for refreshments. Had I not I might have reached you sooner, before Dorren...' his expression darkened, 'please, help yourself.'

Kammy drifted towards the table, her mouth watering. She sank onto one of the chairs and sighed as it moulded around her. Her eyes could hardly take in the assortment of sweets. There were fruit cakes, chocolate cakes, jam cakes and cream cakes. Her stomach growled for she had not eaten properly since the morning of Bagor's arrival in Emire. She plucked up a cupcake smeared in chocolate sauce and bit into it with a satisfied groan. She could hardly believe it, but it tasted better than her Gran's baking. Bagor prepared her a drink from the pot and she grabbed it and poured it down her throat. It was the creamiest hot chocolate she had ever tasted. Kammy stretched for a second cake and Bagor laughed. Her eyes jumped up to his and she shook off the warmth and the sweetness. He sat opposite her with a small smile playing across his lips. Kammy realised with a jolt that she had relaxed. His kind words and the food had been used to disarm her and she had put up no resistance. She had forgotten who it was that she was dealing with. Kammy wiped the crumbs from the corner of her mouth and flushed. She curled her hands in her laps.

'Please,' Bagor urged, 'eat your fill.'

Kammy was suddenly certain that Bagor had poisoned her. Her chest constricted and her eyes widened. He looked concerned, but she recovered herself just in time. He would not poison her yet, not until he had gotten what he wanted. Well, Kammy would get what she wanted first.

'Mary and Marianna,' she began, 'they could be different people.'

Bagor looked disappointed. 'Do you really believe that?'

Kammy hung her head. She did not, but she had decided that one more desperate moment of denial would not harm anyone.

'Then explain to me,' she said, 'if Mum was Semei, why did she end up on Daleswick?'

Bagor started to pour himself a drink. He waited until his cup was full, and then he took a long sip. Each second was agonising and Kammy had to sit on her hands to stop herself from fidgeting. He looked at her and stunned Kammy once more. He looked sad.

'Marianna was banished.'

That was not what she expected. 'Banished? Why?'

His eyes drifted towards the window. 'Because she revealed herself to a human.'

Kammy's hands gripped the chair beneath her. 'That was it?' She thought of her mother and how she had always been so quiet and detached from the things that surrounded her. Kammy had always put it down to her sickness. But now Kammy could see that it had been sadness and longing that had crippled her mother. She felt hot tears sting her eyes, but she blinked them away. She was too angry to cry.

'She was forced out of her own world because one human knew her secret?'

Bagor shrugged. 'It was the law back then and Marianna knew it as well as the rest of us.'

Kammy boiled with fury for her mother and the injustice that had been served to her. Bagor's nonchalance made her brave and she snapped. 'I suppose you thought she deserved it. You hate humans, don't you?'

Bagor's head did not move, but his eyes crawled back to meet hers and Kammy bit her tongue. His pupils were shrinking in just the same way that Jad's did. Once more, his anger manifested itself with a stillness that made Kammy's own die in her throat. He whispered when he spoke, but it was a whisper that carried the strength of a thousand voices.

'I still mourn the loss of Marianna to this day. She was a friend.'

Kammy could not hold his gaze. The emotion that she could see in his eyes confused her. He sounded genuine, but could her mother truly have been friends with such a man? With a rush of bitterness Kammy reminded herself that she had hardly known her mother. How could she have after everything she had learned? Marianna could very well have been friends with a monster, because that was what Bagor was Kammy told herself, again and again.

'She died,' Kammy said, her eyes on her lap.

'I know. She could not have survived for this long away from the Crystals.'

Kammy felt a terrible pain in her chest; her mother's banishment had been a death sentence. She choked it down.

'So how did I survive? Was my father...'

'I know nothing of your father,' Bagor cut in, 'I know nothing of your mother's life on the surface.' Kammy tensed, but he smiled at her again and leaned forwards. 'As for your survival. You must be the first that has ever been born in such a way. Human and Semei. It is fascinating.' His eyes narrowed.

Kammy felt a chill. She licked dry lips. 'Did you know my Gran?'

'Of course,' his lip curled, 'she was a...strong woman.'

'She still is,' Kammy insisted.

Bagor conceded with a nod.

A thought struck Kammy for the first time and she felt a sudden thrill of excitement. 'Is there...anyone else? From my family?'

Bagor's smile turned to pity and Kammy's hope recoiled. 'I am afraid that the recent history of your family is a sad one. The city of Danorrah was struck by a plague and its peoples were scattered. Irena and Marianna appeared in Alashdial with a small group of refugees that were welcomed, under the condition that they did not reveal their origins. We did not want the people to panic, to think they had carried the plague to us. They were the only Simbassi survivors.'

Kammy shook her head. 'Danorrah is...'

He spoke over her. 'It is a long tale for another day, Kammy. The history of your people is something you should tackle when you are rested. For now, we must turn to other matters.'

Kammy almost felt relieved. Was he about to drop the act? She wanted it to be an act. All his talk of time to come made it clear that he had no intention of letting her go. That could only mean that he would soon demand the Key. Then she was sure to see his true colours. Kammy thought of Jad and how Bagor had hurt him. She looked into Bagor's Ollarion blue eyes and felt a pain that she knew Jad must have felt every day of his life. Those eyes were a constant reminder of the ties between them.

'You destroyed Jad's life.'

Bagor nodded. If her turn of conversation surprised him, he did not show it. His gaze was steady. 'I suppose I did, yes.'

Kammy floundered. She had expected him to deny it and to weave an elaborate tale that painted Jad as the villain. He had disarmed her so completely that she wrinkled her nose. 'But you're only king because...'

'Jadanim has his reasons for hating me, it is true, but I am not the one that shed blood on that dreadful day.'

Kammy shook her head, 'You broke free...'

'I did not,' he said with conviction. 'Jadanim did not know of an important detail; I was due to be released. The only thing that saved my life that day was Dorren's complete inability to do anything right. I was meant to stand before the Council as they took my vows and awarded me my freedom. Dorren was late retrieving me from my cell. By the time we reached the Council they had either fled for their lives, or they were dead.'

'Then who killed them, if it wasn't you?'

'The alchemist, Welm.'

Kammy's fingers brushed the lion clasp at her waist. She started to shake her head, but she could not deafen herself to Bagor's words.

'It was an accident, there can be no doubt. I believe he intended for me to die alone, but something went wrong with one of his inventions, as I always feared it would. You see, Welm's great weakness is his unquenchable thirst for knowledge.'

'Knowledge?' Kammy thought of Welm's hideaway and the wonders she had seen there. 'How can knowledge be a weakness?'

'Knowledge in itself is a gift. The more that we know, the less likely it is that we shall make the same mistakes our ancestors did. Knowledge is behind everything that we do and create. But Welm is a glutton for knowledge. He feeds on learning and he pushes the boundaries to breaking point. When he invented Oilblum the Council granted him everything he could ever have wished for. He had the funds, the assistance and the space to work without hindrance. I was the only one that considered keeping a close eye on him. The others were so distracted by the wealth that his Oilblum brought to Alashdial that they did not want to think of ways that things could go awry. When I was imprisoned, Welm was free of me. He was the only one, other than Jadanim, that fought passionately against my release. When it was clear that he would not get his way, he panicked. His need for knowledge had driven him beyond reason and even though he had not intended it, he committed murder that day.'

Kammy would not believe it. No matter how Bagor's words tempted and teased, she refused. Welm was kind and she trusted him, didn't she? He had made this belt, and gifted her the slingshot. Yes, she had felt something strange about him when she had first met him, but that had passed, hadn't it?

248

'It was up to me to put things right.'

Kammy's eyes flashed. 'No. It was up to Jad to put things right.'

'It would have been, but his grief robbed him of his senses...'

'You locked him up.'

'I restricted him and I would again. It was only meant to be for a short while, and I gave him every comfort I could. I feared for him. He was so utterly broken and he had always been a passionate child, prone to acting on impulse. He inherited that from his mother; a brilliant but dangerous woman. I feared that he might do something rash. But he would not listen to my explanations and why should he have? He was the first to find me amongst the dead, cradling my father's body. He already hated me, before his grandfather's death. I can hardly blame him for drawing the conclusions that he did.'

'He hated you because you killed his father,' spat Kammy.

'I did.'

Kammy slumped back against the soft back of the chair.

'I killed his father, but it was an accident.'

'No,' Kammy pressed a hand to her forehead, 'Jad was certain.'

'Because he saw it happen,' said Bagor, his voice cracking, 'My brother and I often trained together. Sometimes we would shift, other times we would stay in our natural forms so as to strengthen our bodies. The Semei are a peaceful people but my brother was always thinking ahead, planning for every possibility. He would tell me that the day would come when our people would be threatened and that we should be strong enough to fight. We owed it to Alashdial to prepare for that day.' Kammy thought of the dying Crystals. Would Jad's father agree with his brother's plan?

'Jadanim would often watch us, delighting in the fact that his father, whom he adored above all others, would always best me. But that day, I had the upper hand. My brother was stronger than me and I was overtaken by a hunger to win, just this once.' There was a haunted look in Bagor's eyes. 'I became over excited. I struck a blow to his temple with all my strength behind it and he crumpled to the floor. It was such a simple way for a great man to die. I still hear Jadanim's screams, even now.' Kammy squeezed her eyes shut. 'I held him. I

249

comforted him, but within minutes he was pulled away from me and in his grief he blurred the truth. But I welcomed my sentence. I had killed my brother and I deserved far worse treatment than what I was given.'

'That's not what Jad told me.'

'Jadanim has always seen things as black or white, but there are shades of grey to every story.'

She thought of Jad and how stubborn he could be. 'Are you going to kill him?'

Bagor closed his eyes. 'No, I just want him to come home.'

'But you locked him up,' Kammy cried, rubbing aching eyes, 'I don't understand...'

'You are tired.'

'No...'

'I should leave you to rest. You have a lot to take in. We have so much time to talk about these things. Please, eat all you like. The chocolate is still warm.' He smiled at her, 'But before I go, I must ask. Where is the Key?'

Kammy stiffened. *This was why she was here.*

'Where is Jamie?'

His expression did not change. 'In a room much like this one. He has been treated well. I hoped to meet with you even before knowing who you were...anyway, it has been quite pleasant having him around. I do not think I have ever met somebody that manages to make every simple interaction amusing.'

Kammy's heart soared; that sounded just like him.

'What about my Gran? I couldn't find her...'

'Irena?' He looked surprised. 'She is not here. I have not seen her...in a very long time.'

A thought hit her and she frowned, surprised it had not been playing on her mind from the moment she had discovered her true heritage. 'If the surface killed my mother...then how did my Gran survive?'

Bagor looked intrigued by that. 'I cannot say. She did not leave with Marianna when the banishment was ordained. I do not know when she first left this layer. That is indeed an interesting question. It is one I would like to know the answer to myself...'

He frowned and his voice trailed off. Kammy bit her lip. She would not let herself fear for her Gran, she could not. Irena was back on Daleswick, no doubt frantic with fear for her granddaughter, but she was safe. Soon, Kammy would take Jamie back too. *Then* she could seek answers.

'I don't have the Key.' She cleared her throat and looked across at him, but he did not react. 'Eric and Tayah have it. They're on their way.'

'Oh?' Bagor raised an eyebrow.

Kammy nodded, clutching clammy hands together. She had never been very good at lying. 'They are tired of running and being away from home. I had to come back for Jamie and they wanted to come with me. Jad was against it, so we...' she paused, 'we left him. It wasn't easy...to do that to him, especially for them, but they are here. They are coming.'

Bagor stood with his smile still intact. 'Ria shall be pleased. They shall be welcomed and perhaps one day, Jadanim will see that he is welcome too.' He stepped around the table and reached for Kammy. She flinched as he placed a cool hand to her cheek. 'I wish you would not fear me. I do not blame you for taking precautions with the Key. I shall have to earn your trust.'

Kammy could not look at him. 'Jamie?'

'One moment.'

Kammy did not watch him leave. She heard the door shut and she wrapped her arms around herself. There was a storm raging in her mind, tearing up roots that she had believed were unbreakable. She tried to remember everything Jad and the others had told her about Bagor. She trusted them. But could they be mistaken? Was it possible? Bagor seemed so sincere. She believed that he had been friends with her mother. Could Welm really have done what Bagor had said? Her instincts told her that he would not, but she hardly knew Welm.

Time passed and she was not sure if it had been seconds, minutes, or even an hour. She looked over her shoulder at the door, but it remained sealed shut. Jamie did not appear and Kammy groaned, clutching her head. She had believed every word that Bagor had said and Jamie was nowhere to be seen. He had died two weeks ago and her hopes had been for nothing. Her shoulders shook as she started to cry; she was a fool.

'Kammy?'

Through her tears she saw a lanky figure standing beside the door. Her grief had descended into hallucination.

'*Kammy*?'

Her breath stuck in her throat. His voice sounded so clear and so real. With trembling hands she wiped her eyes and stared at him. His sandy curls were a little longer than before and there was a shadow of stubble along his jaw, but he was there. He smiled at her, his eyes bright. He was Jamie and he was alive.

They ran for each other, colliding and entangling themselves as they cried.

'You were dead...' Kammy sobbed, pressing her face against him.

His arms gripped her tight. 'I knew you were okay...I knew...'

Words failed them both after that. All Kammy's fears fell away as they stood together. They were reunited and for the moment, that was all that mattered.

CHAPTER TWENTY TWO

THE BELL OF ALASHDIAL

The people of Alashdial had left Fii's home empty. She had touched many peoples lives, and they must have known that she had been driven out of the city. It was a small act of defiance, that they refused to forget her. Their defiance only went so far and it was falling into disrepair. Jad could not help, but feel saddened as he crouched beside the well in her back garden. The walls were dirty, a blemish in an otherwise gleaming city. The windows were fogged with dust and the garden was overgrown. Jad was glad that Fii could not see it; it would break her heart.

Jad huddled as small as he could in the shadow of the well, his eyes fixed on the narrow path that led back to the street. The air held a chill and he turned concerned eyes towards the skies. It had not rained and the clouds were grey rather than the black of the day before, but he could not see a single patch of blue sky. The weather was not helping his mood and then he spotted the dark smudges. He frowned, squinting up at them and he realised that they were birds. There were so many of them that it made him feel uneasy.

Jad pulled his cloak tight around him and tried to focus on something positive. Ania was a little late, but she would bring him the key to the kitchens at any moment. Once inside the palace, he would feel more confident; there would be fewer eyes to watch him. He stared at the path, wishing that Ania would materialise. He could hear the noise of the city moving and he wished he could turn those sounds off so he could hear her approach. She would arrive at any moment, she had to.

He heard the click of a heel against stone. Jad jerked to his feet and darted towards Fii's house. With his back against the wall he peered into the passage.

Ania stood wearing a light shawl wrapped around her shoulders. Her eyes filled with tears when they met his. She shook her head and then she ran back the other way.

'Ania...' he hissed, but she was gone.

A sound split the air and Jad's eyes widened. It reverberated around him, sharp and clear.

The bell of Alashdial was ringing.

Jad crouched paralysed, gaping at the spot where Ania had stood. It felt like the whole world trembled while the bell chimed. Ania had not come to help him; she had given him up to Bagor.

He heard something else, a high pitched whistling. He looked up at the sky. The birds were diving towards him, tearing through the air and looming ever larger. Jad watched in horror as they fell closer; they were Armours.

The innate instinct to survive saved Jad. The wolf roared inside him and burst from his Soul. He caught his satchel around his neck before it struck the earth and then he hit the cobbled pathway at a run. The strength of the wolf surged through him. He exploded out onto the main street and chaos reigned. The bell had sent the people into a frenzy. They panicked, screaming out the names of their loved ones, batting each other aside as they rushed for the relative safety of their homes. The last time the bell had rung had been the day that the Council had fallen.

Jad dove into them, a wolf almost as tall as they were. They screamed when he snarled, but the flood of people still slowed him and he felt a rush of air against his back. He looked over his shoulder and he knew that it was over. The Armours descended, a carpet of feathers against the grey sky. Jad spun to meet them and he howled his fury. He would fight them. He would make it as hard for them as he could. Faces turned to watch as the first Armour flew within his reach. He swiped it aside, but another took its place. He leapt at it, his teeth bared, but then there were two others. The beating of their wings drove him to the ground and sharp talons sunk into his back. He snapped and he struggled, but they swarmed around him and more talons sunk into his flesh.

'Can't you see the scar?'

'It's him. It's Jadanim.'

'He's come back.'

The ground started to move. Jad scrabbled for it, his claws gouging the stone, but the Armours lifted him higher. He howled his agony and a sea of faces turned up towards him.

An old man caught his eye. He dropped the basket that he held and he leapt forwards with a roar of his own. His cry called others. People were shifting every way that Jad looked. All sorts of animals flew into the fray and the Armours were too stunned to withstand it. They dropped Jad and he landed amongst the mass, his back torn and bleeding.

A woman he did not know gripped his muzzle. 'Go,' she said, and then she too shifted.

A path opened before him and Jad pushed towards it. The bell continued to chime but as many people as were running for their homes, were turning to fight. The snarls and the shrieks and the howls surrounded him. He did not dare to stop and look back. The satchel bounced against his legs, threatening to trip him or to fly loose. He ran without knowing where he was going and the path closed behind him as he passed. The people were shielding him as best they could. But more Armours poured from the skies, homing in on the silver wolf.

Jad felt one on him. He could hear its caw and feel its hot breath. The pain in his back was already too much, but he braced himself for more. Too late he saw the black cat charging towards him. He tried to skid to a halt, but then it jumped up over his head and the pressure of the Armour disappeared.

Jad ran on. He turned, twisting down narrow streets, hoping to shake his pursuers. Yet he had nowhere to go. There was nowhere that he could hide where they would not find him and he started to despair. It was then he realised that the black cat was running at his side. Its green eyes stared at him for a long moment before it veered right, glancing over its shoulder. Jad followed it for he had no better plan. The cat leapt down some steps, bounded across a small square and turned into a narrow alleyway.

Light poured out from an open door and Jad hesitated. There was every chance that he was being led into a trap. But he could hear the battle raging around him and he followed the cat inside. The door slammed shut behind him and a woman screamed.

Jad jerked to a halt. Two pale faces stared at him. A woman clutched a man's arm. He stood, panting, in the middle of their kitchen.

'Ma, hush. Or do you want to make it obvious?'

A young girl stepped out from behind Jad. Short and rake thin, she had a mousy bob and deep green eyes. She grinned and saw a gap between her two front teeth. She was the black cat that had led him to safety, for a short while at least.

'Hanna...' the woman's voice was shrill, 'by the Mother, why is there a wolf in my kitchen?'

Hanna rolled her eyes and put her hands on her hips. 'He isn't just any old wolf. Open your eyes.'

The man's eyes narrowed and he took a step forward. Jad, his back lancing with pain, thought that this was as good a time as any to shift back.

Hanna's mother let out a strangled cry and fell back into the chair behind her.

*   *   *

The bell of Alashdial was ringing.

Eric turned cold. His eyes found Tayah's across the table and he dropped his fork with a clatter. The cheerful chatter died and they all grew very still. Tayah watched him, her lips pressed tightly together. She turned to peer out the window and they started to hear the screams.

'That could be anything...' said Marie, her knuckles white as she gripped the edge of the table.

Elvira looked around at their faces. She gulped a breath and then she started to cry. Kait jumped up to put her arms around her sister and she glared at Eric.

'It's too soon for the bell.' He said, still staring at Tayah.

'It's not Jad ringing it,' she replied, her eyes bright with fear.

'Then they must have found him.'

256

'You're leaving us again, aren't you?' Kait spat.

The pain in her voice tore at him. 'Kait...'

Tayah jerked to her feet, spinning away from the table. 'What do we do now?'

Eric's attention split. He could see Kait's eyes burning, but Tayah was on the verge of panic. He started to panic himself. He prayed to the Mother that Jad was okay. 'We go to the palace, as planned. We try and save Kammy. We do what we can.'

'Ria will protect you,' Marie nodded. Her face tightened.

'Go away then,' Kait stepped back from them. Elvira started to cry harder.

'Kait,' said Eric, 'we can't stay here. If the Armours find us they'll know that Da helped us.'

'Don't. Don't make excuses. If you don't want us then we don't want you.'

'Must you go, really?' Bram's voice cracked.

Eric's mouth opened. He wanted to explain to them why it was so important that he leave, but he could no longer remember why himself. What was so important that it was worth his sister staring at him with hatred in her eyes?

Tayah had stopped pacing. 'If they had caught Jad then the bell wouldn't be ringing. Maybe they have only found out that he's in the city. But he's eluding them, somehow.' Eric did not listen to her. She stepped around the table and grabbed his arm. 'You're right. We have to do what we planned. He might not even have to get to the palace. It might still work.'

'Go,' Kait's voice shook, 'and I hope you don't come back.'

'*Kaitlyn,*' Bram boomed.

She ignored her father. She turned her back and she stomped out of the kitchen and up the stairs. Eric stared after her in dumb silence.

'Eric,' Tayah shook his arm gently, 'we need to go now, before the streets empty out and they announce the lockdown.'

257

Eric stood, Kait's face all that he could see. Marie stood, rocking Elvira in her arms even as she cried herself. Bram gripped his son's shoulder and nodded. Then his mother was hugging him, Elvira crushed between them and they were all crying. Tayah pulled him towards the door and he let her lead him. Bram pried Marie away from her son and Eric stepped outside into the rising tumult.

The door slammed shut behind him and Eric felt something grow hard inside. His eyes stared ahead at the street, but he could barely comprehend what was happening. The bell rang in his ears, in time with the pounding of his heart. Faces rushed in all directions, none familiar to him, until he spotted a silver wolf racing through the crowd.

His pulse jumped. Jad was still free of Bagor. Eric focused all of his energy on that one fact, forgetting everything else. So when he saw the raven swooping close behind his friend, he thought only of protecting Jad. He shifted. His fox jumped into the air and latched onto the raven's neck. He pulled it to the ground, his teeth sinking through feathers and flesh and he fell back, panting but exhilarated. Jad had disappeared and Eric had helped him.

The raven lay in the street and then, very slowly, it started to fade. In its place lay a man, his eyes open and still.

Eric was himself again and he scrambled backwards until he hit Tayah and she wrapped her arms around his shoulders. The moment of euphoria passed. He had only meant to slow the raven down.

'I killed him,' Eric breathed, 'I killed him.'

*   *   *

Kammy and Jamie were sprawled on the giant bed, the tray of cakes between them. Kammy lay propped up on an elbow and she stared at her friend, as she had been staring at him since she had found him again.

'You look....'

His eyes rose from the cream cake he was devouring to her face. 'Incredibly handsome?'

She rolled her eyes and laughed. 'I was going to say you look the same as ever.'

'Which *is* incredibly handsome.' Jamie swallowed the rest of the cake in one and sat up. 'You look different.'

Kammy smiled. She knew that he did not only mean because of the clothes she was wearing. She felt different too. 'A lot has happened in two weeks. It feels like a year since I last saw you.'

'Not for me,' he said, 'I've done the same thing here, every day, and it's all just kind of blurred into one. I feel like I saw mum yesterday.'

Kammy closed her eyes at the mention of Helen. 'I'm sorry...'

'It's not your fault.'

'If I hadn't told you about the pebble...'

'Then you would have been a really terrible friend,' said Jamie, tossing her another cake. 'You're my favourite freak in the world. You are obliged to tell me everything about your freakish ways.'

'More of a freak than ever.'

Jamie dropped onto his back and grinned. 'Excellent.'

Kammy lay down too, sinking her head onto the other pillow and turning to face him. 'Has it been awful?'

He shrugged, 'Not really. I mean, it was at first. When that woman took me, I was terrified. And I think they gave me something,' he frowned, 'to knock me out. The first few days I was in and out. But since that passed they've treated me okay. I haven't been able to move about much and not having the internet has been *torture*. But,' he glanced at her, 'they told me that you were coming, and that once you got here we could go home, so I was fine.'

Kammy bit into the cake to distract herself from the hope in his eyes. Bagor was not going to let them go home, not her at least.

'Did you...see my Gran at all?'

'No. Mum was a lot better the next day and I was worried about you. Your phone wasn't ringing so I was heading up to yours. But I only made it halfway. Ria got me just outside the village.'

Kammy nodded. She had not expected to hear any news about her Gran, but she still had to fight the disappointment. She licked the sugar off her lips and was about to speak again when a noise split the air.

Jamie sat bolt upright. 'What is that?'

A loud chiming reverberated from somewhere above them. It echoed around the walls and Kammy winced. Then her eyes widened and she shot off the bed and towards the window.

'What's going on?' said Jamie.

Kammy stared out at the city. She could see people, mere ants from so high up, running along the streets, and dark shapes appeared to be falling from the skies. The sound was the bell that Jad was supposed to ring, but it was too soon. Something had gone wrong. She whirred back to Jamie who stood at the end of the bed, looking very confused.

'What's happening?'

'I don't know,' said Kammy, 'but I came here to rescue you and that is what I am going to do.'

'But Bagor said he'd send us home, Kam. You don't need to rescue me.'

Kammy hesitated. Bagor had treated her with kindness. He had answered her questions and he had saved her life. But then, he had ruined countless other lives and all that he had said of Welm, did she really believe that was true? Answers were not real answers if they were lies.

'He won't Jamie,' she said, squaring her shoulders. 'He lied to you, like he lies to everyone. We need to get out of here to help my friends.'

Jamie held up his hands. 'Wait, hold on...'

Kammy gripped his arms. The loud ringing of the bell threatened to drive her to distraction. She tried to block it out and focused on her best friend. 'I have a lot to explain to you, I know, but we don't have time right now. Jad must be in trouble...'

'Who the hell is Jad?'

Kammy laughed. 'See? There's so much to talk about. Jad is a friend that helped me find you. I can't leave him to suffer after the risk he took coming here.'

Jamie puffed out his cheeks. He looked dazed but he smiled at her and Kammy knew that he would be on her side, no matter what.

She skipped past him and tried the door. With certainty returned her boldness. She could save Jamie and find the others. 'There,' she said, 'if we could trust Bagor, why would he lock us in here?'

'Because you are clearly insane?'

Kammy shot him a look before returning her attention to the door. She chewed on her lip. She stared at the lock and wished that she were Semei enough to shift into a key and unlock it herself. She huffed in frustration and placed her hands on her hips, her fingers brushing against her slingshot. Her eyes brightened as an idea came to her. She had a weapon, thanks to Welm. She took a step back and unhooked her slingshot.

'What is *that*?'

'Jamie,' she said as she opened up her pouch and pulled out one of the marbles, 'you will see a lot of things that are strange to you today. Just know that this is real, this is happening. You just have to go with it.'

'Oh,' Jamie drawled, 'that's brilliant.'

Kammy was no longer listening to him. She lifted her slingshot to her eye, loaded one of the marbles and squinted at the metal keyhole on the door. She took a breath to steady herself, trying to block out the incessant ringing, and she let fly.

The marble hit the wall in a burst of flame and Kammy swore. It burned out, leaving behind a hole roughly the size of a tennis ball. Kammy stared at her marbles in wonder; they were stronger than she had thought.

'Kam,' Jamie started, 'I know you've always been a big fan of the elves in your books, with their bows and arrows, but...'

Kammy grinned, 'Shut up Jamie,' she shot back at him, loading her slingshot again.

Jamie sighed.

This time, when Kammy let fly, the marble struck the metal lock dead on. It hissed, steam rising as the metal flashed orange, then it melted away and the door groaned. Kammy laughed, turning to Jamie with wide eyes.

'I did it.'

He looked from her to the door, utterly dumbfounded. 'You did.'

Kammy felt the adrenaline rush through her. Some part of the plan had failed and she had no idea where Jad and the others were, but she could play her part. She gripped the slingshot tighter and pulled open the door slowly. The corridor outside lay deserted.

Jamie looked out over her head. 'I thought there'd be a guard. I always had a guard.'

'Guess the bell has drawn them all away,' she murmured. Her expression brightened, 'Which is good for us.' She started to step outside, but Jamie placed a hand on her shoulder and she paused.

'Do you have any idea where we're going?'

Kammy shrugged, 'I think I remember the way out.'

'Right...any idea what we're doing?'

'Not really.'

'You fill me with confidence, Helseth.'

Kammy grinned at him. 'We'll be fine. I've got my slingshot and my marbles.'

'No. I'm pretty sure you've lost your marbles.'

Kammy punched him.

CHAPTER TWENTY THREE

HANNA

Three pairs of eyes fixed themselves onto Jad's face and none of them appeared to be blinking. Jad squirmed where he sat, tempted to turn back the way that he had come, but the bell continued to ring. The city would be crawling with Armours searching for him and, without Ania, he had no idea how he could get into the palace.

So he settled quietly into the chair he had been cajoled onto and he waited under their scrutiny. Two young men appeared from an adjoining room, trailed by an elderly woman with a hunched back. Despite the chaos raging outside they all appeared to be rather excited. They crowded around him, hardly able to fit into the same small room and Jad found himself glancing back at the door again. He frowned and his head ached as he tried to stay calm.

The mother had recovered from her shock. She leaned forwards, 'I can hardly believe that it's you.'

Jad shifted on his seat. 'I apologise. I have no intention of burdening you...'

There was outcry. They waved away his concerns with mutterings of how they were happy to help and how it was no trouble at all. Jad stuttered into silence and settled back into his seat, overwhelmed. As he did so, the gouges on his back stretched and he grunted, unable to mask his pain.

The mother clicked her fingers. 'Hanna,' she barked, 'make a bowl of hot water and grab a fresh cloth. We need to clean the young Lord's wounds.'

Jad's cheeks flushed, 'No, please. I...'

Hanna smirked at him as she pushed past the two young men that could only be her brothers. 'It's no trouble,' she called back to him, 'before you say that it is. You won't be no good at whatever it is you're planning on doing if you're bleeding all over the place.'

'But the Armours...'

The mother waved him to silence and turned to the shorter of her two sons. 'Get on the roof. We have time before they start checking houses, but it won't hurt to have eyes on the road.' Her son nodded and disappeared into the next room. After a moment they heard his boots stomping overhead.

Jad clamped his mouth shut. It felt strange sitting around while the city trembled outside, but she was right. Now that he was being sheltered, he had some time to think; to think of Ania and how she had betrayed him. His spurt of anger quickly dwindled. He had seen the pain and the regret in her eyes, and he could not hate her. He sighed and as the adrenaline wore off, the pain in his back intensified. He gritted his teeth and tried not to imagine the patterns that had been carved into his skin. He bowed his head, conceding. 'Thank you.'

'Your grandfather, Rogan...' It was the first time Hanna's father had spoken. 'I must tell you how we mourned him. He was a strong and fair man. It's not right what happened to him. Not right at all.'

Jad looked up at him, wary, 'So you know?' he said, 'The truth?'

The second son, tall enough that he had to stoop to avoid knocking his head on the ceiling, scoffed, 'Know? We know nothing. But we hear the rumours and we're not stupid. We can put the pieces together.'

Hanna returned, whistling softly to herself. She placed a metal bowl beside his chair and stood behind him. 'Take your shirt off then.'

Distracted, Jad started to do as asked but then he froze. He dropped the satchel to the floor as his eyes fell to his left arm and his skin started to burn. 'Can't you do it with the shirt on?'

'Shy, are we?' Hanna giggled and started to tug the shirt off for him.

Jad could only let her do it and he pulled his arm in close, twisting the scar away from them. But it was too prominent to conceal. With shame coursing through his veins, he stared hard into the faces before him and waited for them to recoil. They did not, in fact they hardly seemed to notice his scar at all. Then Hanna pressed a damp cloth to his back and Jad swore, distracted again.

'Watch yer' mouth,' growled the old lady, and Jad's blush deepened.

'We don't know exactly what happened,' said Hanna's father, 'but we know there was murder and trickery. How else could a man like Bagor have found his way to power?'

'The people knew,' said the mother, 'young Lord.'

'Please,' Jad winced every time Hanna dabbed his back, 'just call me Jad.'

Hanna laughed, 'But you are our Lord. More our lord than that murderer who calls himself King, anyway.'

Jad's jaw tightened. 'I'm no lord.' His eyes fell back to his scar and he thought of the friends that he had failed. Eric and Tayah's lives might be spared, but Kammy? What would his failure mean for her? 'I'm just an outlaw.'

Hanna's mother stood, her expression stern. 'The people knew,' she repeated, 'my *Lord*. Bagor told us you had hidden away with your grief, but we wondered. Then when days and months passed with no sign of you, we knew. You're an outlaw because Bagor outsmarted all of us. He outsmarted men and women much wiser than you were then, than you are now. So you stop blaming yourself. You're still our rightful lord and leader, especially now we have no Council.' She let that sink in for a moment and then the tight line of her mouth softened, 'But we can call you Jad, if you insist. Now, let me get you something to drink.'

Jad nodded dumbly.

'She's good at that,' Hanna whispered in his ear, 'guilt tripping you into realising you're being an arse.'

'I 'eard that Hanna,' squawked the old lady.

Jad smiled. Something about this family warmed him. 'Still, Bagor has treated you well. He may have come to power through deceit, but you are risking too much to help me. Perhaps I am the rightful leader, but you do not know that I would lead well. I am barely Semei.'

Hanna dug the cloth into one of his cuts and he cried out, twisting away from her weapon of torture. He glanced back at her, but she was not looking at him.

'That's a stupid thing to say,' she mumbled, all the light gone from her voice.

Her brother frowned at her, 'Don't know if hurting him helps much.'

Hanna sighed, 'Sorry, *my Lord*,' she said as she resumed the gentle prodding of his back.

'She's right though,' said her mother as she re-entered the room, 'you're scarred, not crippled.' With that, she pressed a steaming mug into his hands and settled back into her seat. Jad felt very hot. He had been crippled by his scar, in ways that people could not see.

'Bagor was very good to us because he had no choice. An uprising was always unlikely, but he would have faced one if he had pushed it. He was careful. He lowered taxes and he poured money into housing, especially near the wall. He put in appearances at schools and at the sick bays. He listened to countless complaints and he tried his best to solve them.' Hanna's father shook his head. 'He was very clever. How could those of us with families ever think of standing against him when he was making all those promises? It makes me sick to the stomach, but we did what we thought was best for our children. We were selfish, you could say, but there wasn't much else we could do.'

Jad nodded his understanding. 'But then?' He watched the man's face darken and he felt a twinge of recognition.

'Then he left. Sure, he'd pop up every now and then. But for the last year or so he's been off doing something mysterious and he's left Dorren in charge.'

'Dorren's a bloody fool,' chirped the old lady before sinking back into silence.

'*Gramma.*' Hanna sounded delighted.

'A fool for sure, but a greedy fool,' said the tall brother.

266

'Which makes him dangerous, right Da?' Hanna trilled.

Her father grinned back at her and winked. 'My sons could run this city better than that oaf, and that's saying something.' His son frowned and Hanna snorted a laugh. 'All the promises Bagor made have dissolved into nothing. Taxes are higher than ever and wages are down. The whole city is struggling apart from those in Dorren's pocket; those rich enough to feed his cravings. Anybody that tries to question the way things are run is met with thuggery. We've tried appealing to Bagor, but his head isn't with us. He's concerned with other things. It's easier, and safer, to keep quiet and do the best we can, but people are on edge. We've been waiting, even if we didn't realise it, for a sign to fight back.'

Hanna dumped the blood stained cloth into the copper coloured water and wiped her hands on her thighs. 'That sign is you, in case you didn't get that.'

Jad frowned. 'Me?'

'We never had a reason to fight before,' Hanna's mother beamed at him, 'My Thomas tried to rouse some folk once,' she placed a hand on her husband's arm, 'but with nothing and nobody to rally behind, it was impossible. Now, we have you.'

Jad shook his head. 'You do not understand. I can't stay in the city. I'm here to help a friend and then I have to leave.'

'Nobody would expect you to stay. Not now,' said Thomas, 'Seeing that you are fighting is enough.'

'But I cannot fight Bagor,' Jad snapped in his frustration.

'Not all fights are about physical strength.' Thomas growled over him, staring with a ferocity that Jad recognised. 'We have not seen a soul stand against Bagor since he took power. Yes, we heard that you were out there somewhere, but how could we know for sure? Now we have seen you. Now there can be no doubt. It's all the people need. It's something to inspire them, to bring them together and to show them that there is still something worth fighting for. All that takes is courage. You are an Ollarion. Are you telling me you have no courage?' Thomas's face had turned red beneath the bristles of his beard.

Jad felt his throat tighten. 'I don't know if I can inspire anybody.'

267

Hanna made a frustrated noise and stood in front of him with her hands on her hips. 'Have you already forgotten what happened out there? What happened when the people recognised that scar you seem to hate so much? They fought for you. That was all it took, seeing you, and they were fighting. They know who you are and what you could be. They know you could be our chance to get rid of Dorren and to be free of Bagor. That's why there are women, men and children bleeding in the streets right now. *For you.* So do you have a plan? Or are you gonna repay them by sitting here and feeling sorry for yourself? Cause if you are then I'll go out there right now and tell the Armours we have you.'

'Hanna...' her mother scolded.

'Sorry Ma,' she said, but her blazing eyes told Jad she was not sorry at all.

For somebody so small, she was quite terrifying and she was right. If he closed his eyes he could still hear the people shouting his name, their voices shrill with excitement. He could see the wall of bodies, animal and man, that had closed around him, holding off the Armours. His eyes drifted back to his scar.

He smiled up at Hanna, 'You're good at that guilt tripping thing too.'

Hanna relaxed. Her expression softened and she smirked at him. 'Just because you're marked on the outside, don't mean there's anything wrong with you on the inside. Got it?' She raised an eyebrow and folded her arms. She reminded him of Tayah; a small, short-haired version. He nodded and she grinned. 'So, you do have a plan?'

Jad's smile turned into a grimace. 'I did have one. I need to get into the palace kitchens, through the servant's entrance. I had hoped an old friend would help me. Her father is the servant's taskmaster. But she could not take the risk, it seems.'

'*Ania*?' Hanna snarled. 'You went to *her*? She wouldn't risk a broken fingernail for anyone else, never mind helping an outlaw. She's as bad as her father. They'd shove both their heads up Bagor's arse if they thought they could manage it.'

Her grandmother cackled.

Jad was stunned. 'You know Ania? How?'

Hanna looked smug, 'Cause I sometimes work in the kitchens.'

Jad could hardly bear to hope. Could he really have been so lucky? 'You do?'

'Yup, we all do.'

She glanced back at her father and, finally, Jad made the connection. Thomas had once been a bit rounder, and he had not worn a beard, but Jad knew him. 'That's where I know you from; the kitchens. You're one of the Head Chefs.'

Thomas smiled and bowed his head in acknowledgement. 'Head Chef no longer, but I do work up there still. I wondered if you might recognise me. I shooed you and your friends away from the food enough times.'

Jad laughed. Thomas' glare had struck a note of familiarity because he had seen it so many times before. 'Only when we could smell the sweet pastries. I have still never tasted anything as good. Eric would love to shake your hand.' He chuckled to himself, but then his eyes swept over the cramped home. 'What happened to your quarters in the palace?'

Thomas' expression soured. 'Bagor kicked the servants out. All of them.'

Jad shook his head. He had heard that Bagor preferred to keep the palace quiet, but he had not known it had gone so far. 'Why?'

Hanna's mother shrugged. 'Like we said, things are different now. The palace isn't what it was. It rarely welcomes guests and it no longer gathers a Council. It's almost empty most of the time, from what we can gather. There are a handful of permanent residents, that's all. The rest of us, the servants, are forced to work at strange hours. We work in near silence, as quickly as possible, and we leave. We were told we'd be found somewhere bigger when they first dumped us in here. Still, we make the best of it.'

Jad's fists clenched in fury. He was about to tell them just how furious he was when a loud silence fell. The bell had stopped ringing and Hanna's family drew closer together. Jad stood, ignoring the pain in his back, and stepped towards the window. He peeled back the curtain and peered through. The streets were empty, but his heart would not ease its pounding.

'Todd would have shouted if there was any need to panic,' said his brother.

269

Thomas nodded. 'But we should hurry.'

Hanna's mother turned apologetic eyes to Jad. 'We have no Oilblum, I'm afraid. We can't soak the bandages for your wounds. You'll have to go without.'

'Please, you have done more than enough.'

Thomas stroked his beard as he thought. 'We must come up with some way to get you in the servants entrance. We can give you a key, but as soon as you walk out that door they will be on you.'

'I can get him in,' said Hanna.

Her parents stared at her and stood very still. Jad could feel their anxiety and he shook his head. 'I can't let you take that risk.'

'I'm with our Lord on this, love,' Thomas shrugged, 'you're just fourteen. You can't be getting caught up in this.'

Hanna gaped at him. 'But you just rattled off a whole speech about fighting. I want to fight, Da. I want to do my bit.'

Her mother wrung her hands. 'The risk...'

Hanna rolled her eyes. 'There won't be a risk. I have a plan.' She whistled and called out, 'Annie.'

A black blob began to uncurl itself from the top of one of the cupboards. The cat stretched and yawned, then it hopped down to the floor. Hanna scooped her up and turned back to Jad.

'This is Annie, my sister.'

Jad laughed. 'You call your cat your sister?'

Hanna and Annie hissed in unison and Hanna glared at him. 'Because she is my sister. My twin, actually. She's Abandoned.'

It took a moment to process what she had just said and then the shame hit him. He glanced down at his scar and he wished that he could fold himself up and hide away. No wonder Hanna had scoffed at his self pity, if her twin sister was one of the Abandoned. Annie turned to look at him and it was obvious; such awareness shone from those eyes. He glanced at her parents, but could see no trace of sadness on their faces. He saw none of the shame that he had always felt. Their eyes shone with pride, for both of their daughters.

270

'You could copy her, right?' Hanna said, scratching behind Annie's ears.

'What?' Jad shook himself.

'Now the bell has stopped, we're free to go outside.'

'Hanna,' said Thomas, 'nobody will be out there so soon. You'd draw the attention of the Armours in an instant.'

'Yeah,' Hanna nodded, 'but they know me. They know I'm your daughter and that I'm always backwards and forwards to the kitchens. Most importantly, they know about Annie.' She turned back to Jad. 'We go everywhere together. I'm always seen with a black cat that everyone can sense is Semei.'

Jad started to understand, 'Even if they stopped us, they'd just think I was your sister.'

'Exactly. So, can you do it?'

Jad frowned. Shifting into a cat was simple enough. Annie was black, with one white patch near her tail. It would be difficult to match her exactly on such short notice, but if Hanna was holding him it was possible that nobody would notice. The problem was the pain in his back, but he was sure he could manage the shift for long enough. He nodded.

'Ma,' a voice cried, and they heard Todd's stomping footsteps again. Seconds later he burst back into the crowded room. 'There are Armours at both ends of the street, knocking on doors.'

Hanna's eyes glittered with excitement. She placed Annie on the floor, telling her, 'You stay hidden, right? When they come, get up in the roof. They mustn't see you.'

Annie meowed her understanding and flounced away.

'I'll have to hide my scar, but I can do it,' said Jad, looking at Hanna's parents, 'however, I will not do this without your consent.'

Hanna's mother said nothing. She beckoned her daughter close and planted a kiss on her forehead. Thomas placed a hand on her shoulder and smiled.

'Her plan is sound.' He rummaged around in the pocket of his trousers and pulled out a bronze key. He handed it to Hanna and ruffled her hair, 'She'll be fine and you'll get yourself inside the palace.

Then she can return to us with the key and Bagor will be none the wiser. You'll prove something to the people of Alashdial. You'll prove that we can fight.'

Jad stared into the man's face. He had barely known Thomas when life had been better, and that thought saddened him. Still, his body tingled with exhilaration. He could do this. He could help save Jamie and lead his friends to safety. And he could come back and lead his people, despite his scar. He stooped to pick up his satchel and handed it to Hanna. She slipped it onto her shoulder. It hung right to her knees.

'Thank you,' Jad said, and then Annie had another twin.

Hanna stared at him and clapped her hands with delight. 'You're perfect.'

Jad padded towards her. It did not feel perfect. His back burned and he had not shifted into a cat for a long time, but it would have to be good enough.

'Look a bit more cheerful and nobody would ever be able to tell.' Hanna laughed as she picked him up. He tucked his left foreleg away from sight and growled at her.

'Be careful Hanna,' said her mother.

Her grandmother shouted, 'Keep that mouth in check.'

'I'll be fine.'

Hanna started towards the door and Jad was forced to look over her shoulder at the faces of her family. Her words did little to soothe anybody. Thomas gripped his wife's shoulder and her brothers looked lost. Only her grandmother seemed unconcerned, instead looking like she might have dozed off. Hanna stepped through the door and kicked it shut behind her. The fear on their faces did not leave him, even though those same faces were now hidden. He tried to relax in Hanna's arms, determined not to let them down.

Hanna took a deep breath. 'Right then, Annie,' her chest rumbled as she spoke. She started to scratch Jad behind his ears, which felt quite nice. It distracted him from the pain in his back, the cuts of which were luckily hidden by his fur. He stayed still apart from his whiskers, which twitched out of his control. Hanna did not rush and he silently praised her. She seemed quite at ease.

'Here we go,' she whispered.

They stepped out of the alleyway and onto the main street. Hanna turned left without hesitation and started to whistle. Jad stared at the wide space over her shoulder. It looked much bigger now that he was smaller and he wished that they were some place less open. He could not see what they were heading towards and he hated how defenceless it made him feel. He tried to turn his head, but pain shot through his back and he stayed still. He resigned himself to the torture of waiting and rested his chin on Hanna's shoulder.

Hanna's footsteps started to slow and her grip on him tightened. To his horror she laughed and called out. 'Hello there.'

Jad stiffened, but her grip on him tightened further. There was nothing he could do, other than shift, and shifting would get him nowhere but to a cell.

'Hanna,' cried a distant voice.

'You shouldn't be out here, sweetheart,' said a second voice, moving closer. Jad twitched his ears, thinking it was something an Abandoned cat might do.

'Oh,' Hanna's voice was all innocence, 'but the bell stopped ringing and my Da really needs me to get up to the palace.'

Jad could hear the chiming of their armour, and then they were close enough that he could hear their breathing. He could not afford a lapse in concentration.

'But you finished everything up this morning. Whatever could you be needed for?'

'Well, there were all these cakes we've been making. With all that's gone on my Da is a bit worried that the last batch of cakes might have been forgotten, and so they'll be ruined. If they are then I need to get a new lot going sharpish.'

'Well, it will take you an age to get up there, dear. We're searching for somebody, you see. Any of our fellow Armours spot you and they'll stop you to ask your business.'

Hanna sighed. 'I know. That's why my Da didn't want me to waste any time. The sooner I leave, he said, the sooner I finish.'

There was a moment of silence and Jad checked to see that his scar was hidden. A hand touched his head and he flinched away.

'Oh,' the hand pulled back. 'Annie's not very friendly today.'

Hanna laughed, and for the first time Jad heard her nerves. 'She's been acting strange all day. Maybe she's coming down with something.'

'Poor thing. Well, we best get on. You take care of yourself.'

The Armours were passing by and Jad could see them at last, or the backs of their heads at least. They did not look back. They did not seem even remotely suspicious of the young girl and her cat. He allowed himself to breathe as Hanna started walking again.

Hanna pressed her face into his neck and whispered, 'Remember to purr next time.'

CHAPTER TWENTY FOUR

OBSESSION

'When you insinuated that you had no idea where you were going, I had hoped you were joking.'

Kammy bit her lip and said nothing. She had not thought that it might be difficult to find her friends, because she had not stopped to think at all. She had acted on impulse and as her eyes skittered left and right, her heart sank even further. She had tried so hard to focus on the route that Bagor had taken when he had led her through the palace, but her head had been all over the place and every corridor and staircase looked the same. For all she knew, she was leading her best friend back the way they had come. Or she was leading him away from one prison and into the next.

'Seriously Kam, I think we're walking in circles.'

'If we were walking in circles we would have seen the burnt lock again,' said Kammy, 'and walking somewhere is better than just sitting around waiting, okay?'

To her surprise, Jamie laughed. She looked up at him and felt some of her tension ease. There was an easy smile on his face and his arms swung at his sides. He looked happy despite their predicament because they were together again. Without saying a word Kammy slipped her hand into his. He grinned at her and gave it a little squeeze.

'At least there isn't anybody around.'

In that regard, they were lucky. They had not passed a single soul since their escape, the palace appeared deserted. They walked in the open for there was nowhere they could hide, but silence reigned around them. Silence except for the chiming of the bell that both terrified and reassured Kammy. It meant that something had gone wrong, but she hoped that as long as it was ringing, it meant that Bagor did not have her friends; yet. Still, she was on edge. The chiming was incessant yet she dreaded every second for fear it might stop. Added to that, their freedom was an illusion. As long as they were in the palace they were still prisoners, they just had a little more space.

'You know, it's great seeing you again, but I'd prefer it if you didn't crush my fingers. I might need them.'

'What...' Kammy glanced at their hands. Her knuckles were white and Jamie's fingers were turning purple. She let go with an embarrassed grin, 'Sorry, I just...'

Then the silence was absolute and Kammy ground to a halt.

Jamie looked concerned. 'What?'

'The bell. It's stopped.' It felt like Kammy's heart stopped along with it.

'And?'

'What if that means they've caught one of them?' she turned wide eyes to her friend, 'What if that means they've caught Jad?' She spun away from Jamie, panic rising in her throat, but there were no windows for her to peer through. She let out a small cry and dropped to her knees, squeezing her eyes shut. She felt sick. Her hands began to shake and she clutched at her legs to keep them steady. Her mind had frozen, overwhelmed by the silence.

'It's my fault,' she groaned.

'Hey,' Jamie took her hands and she clung to them, her eyes still closed, 'Kam, don't freak out, okay? None of this is your fault.'

Her eyes snapped open and she laughed. 'No, you don't understand. *Everything* is my fault. You wouldn't be here if it wasn't for me and neither would Jad and the others. I *made* them come back here Jamie, to save you. Their fight is so much bigger than you, but I insisted and if anything has happened to any of them, it's my fault. I will have ruined everything.'

Kammy could see the brightness of her eyes reflected in Jamie's. His gaze softened and he smiled at her.

'First things first, you don't *know* if any of them have been captured. The bell could have been ringing for any number of reasons, right?'

'But...'

'You're looking for all the worst case scenarios Kam, and I get it, but there's no point. What are we going to achieve if we just sit here panicking and waiting around to be found?'

'You're not panicking.'

Jamie's smile stretched into a grin. 'When have I ever lost my cool? I'm unflappable, me.'

'When have you ever been kidnapped by a race of shapeshifters and taken into another world?'

Jamie paused, 'Fair point, yet here I kneel, unflapped.'

Kammy laughed and felt the pressure in her chest ease. Still, she did not release her grip on Jamie's hands.

'I just feel so guilty, for dragging them back here...'

'You didn't force them, Kammy.'

'I did.'

'No,' Jamie's voice was firm, 'you didn't. Look, I know I wasn't there and I know I've never met these people, but unless you've gained a super strength power-up since I last saw you, which I doubt, then you couldn't have forced them.'

Kammy shook her head. 'I told them I'd go without them if I had to.'

Jamie sighed, 'So you stamped your feet and had a tantrum, who cares? If they had really wanted to they could have locked you up somewhere, or they could have just let you go and left you to it. They came with you because they wanted too. Maybe they didn't at first, but in the end they wanted to do this *for you*. They wanted to help. You can't blame yourself for something that was their own choice.'

Kammy stared at Jamie, her heart in her mouth. She saw the three of them: Jad, Eric and Tayah too. She sucked in a breath and let go of Jamie's hands. His ability to remain calm in the worst of situations astounded her.

'You're right.'

'Obviously.'

Kammy hit him and they both laughed. 'I'm pleased to see that captivity hasn't dented your arrogance.'

'Self-confidence,' Jamie corrected.

'Whatever you call it, it's going to help save my friends, right? If they're in trouble, that is. I can't...I can't just leave them. I know it's dangerous, but...'

'It's fine,' Jamie nodded, hopping to his feet. 'These people are helping you to save me; I have to repay the favour really. Besides, I *am* Superman.' He held out a hand and helped Kammy to her feet, even as she scoffed. 'So, do you have any idea what we should do yet?'

Kammy puffed out her cheeks. 'Not really. But maybe if we can get out into the city, we can find out what's going on?'

Jamie looked down at himself and wrinkled his nose, 'Good thing they dressed me all shifter style. I won't stand out too much.'

'They'll work out that you're human, but as long as we move quickly, we should be okay.'

'So,' Jamie folded his arms, 'we just need to find the exit.'

Kammy scowled. Jamie had prevented her from falling into despair, but that did not change the fact that they were lost. Kammy gazed around at the white walls and felt a creeping frustration. She started walking and Jamie followed, but when they turned into another corridor, Kammy sighed. The futility of it all weighed down upon her. How would they ever find the way out? And even if they managed it, the city was massive and unfamiliar. Jamie's positivity comforted her, but even he could not change their situation by force of will alone. They walked and they walked and Kammy hoped that the seconds only *felt* like hours.

'We're screwed,' Kammy mumbled.

Jamie's forehead creased and his mask slipped. She could see the doubt in his eyes.

'You don't recognise anything?' he said.

Kammy shrugged, 'I recognise all of it because everywhere looks the same.' Her eyes roamed over the walls, the curtains and the tapestries. 'We could walk for hours and just be going...' Kammy paused, her eyes widening as something familiar caught her eye.

Jamie skittered closer, 'What?'

Kammy pointed to a tapestry opposite them and walked towards it, her eyes bright and large. 'I've seen this before,' she said, her voice a whisper. The tapestry towered over her, almost double her height and weaved of every shade of blue imaginable. The only thing that stood apart was the image of the silver wolf at its centre; its head thrown back as it howled. Kammy reached out a hand and touched the scruff of the wolf's neck. The last time she had seen it, it had meant nothing to her. Now, she could not help but marvel at how the silver wolf looked so much like Jad. 'When I was first brought here, to this world, the Armours took me past this tapestry to see a man, Dorren.' She stepped back and looked to her right, 'His office is round that corner.'

Jamie followed her gaze, 'Great. So you know the way out from here?'

Kammy shook her head.

Jamie frowned. 'No longer great.'

'He tried to kill me.'

'*What*?'

Kammy waved a hand. 'He tried to kill me and Bagor had him taken away. He must be locked up somewhere. If he's not in his office, maybe we can get in?'

Jamie's eyes lit up. 'We might be able to find something, a map maybe?'

Kammy nodded, trying to beat down the hope inside of her. 'It's the only plan we've got.'

Jamie took her hand again. They did not rush for it was refreshing to feel like they had a goal. Kammy could not help but fear that they would still be stuck after Dorren's office would hold nothing for them. Her heart pounded and Jamie's hand in hers was clammy. They held onto each other and Kammy glanced back at him with a reassuring smile that quickly faded. She heard a voice and she recognised it instantly. It was Ria.

Kammy's eyes bulged and she shot backwards, almost crashing into Jamie. He was about to say something, but Kammy slammed her hand down over his mouth and shook her head sharply. Fear shone from her eyes and she could see that Jamie understood. He nodded and Kammy grabbed his arm, ready to run away, when Ria spoke again. Her voice was muffled and Kammy realised that she was not about to walk around the corner. Ria was inside Dorren's office. Kammy paused, biting down on her lip as she wavered with indecision. She did not want to be anywhere near Ria, but if she could be brave enough for a little while then maybe they could glean something valuable. She looked at Jamie and pointed at her ear, then at the corner. Jamie grinned and gave her a thumbs up, to which Kammy could only roll her eyes.

Taking a deep breath, Kammy crept to the corner and she listened.

'...think that then you are more of a fool than I had thought.'

'Please Ria, you have to. Maybe if you back me up he will...'

Kammy's jaw dropped when she heard Dorren's voice. He sounded so different, so pathetic.

'He will what? Show mercy?' Ria laughed. 'You lied to him and what is worse, you lied to serve yourself. I told you we should wait and I did not even know who she was, or don't you remember? I said as soon as I brought her here that he would want to see her.'

Kammy's stomach twisted; they were talking about her.

'I was only trying to *protect* him...'

'Stop it, just stop it. Your words will do nothing to save you now.'

Dorren shrieked in desperation. 'But his Majesty needs me. I can help with the Key, with the...'

'His Majesty will have the Key by the time the night arrives. My sister, and her friend, Eric, are in the palace now, ready to hand it over. Jadanim is somewhere within the city and it's only a matter of time until we catch him. So you see, the King does not need you at all.'

'Ria...Ria, please...'

280

'Goodbye Dorren.'

All too suddenly, Kammy heard the sharp step of Ria's boots and then a door opening. She flattened herself against the wall, clamped her mouth shut and closed her eyes as she waited to hear which way Ria would turn.

Kammy did not breathe as the moment stretched on. Then Ria started to move and each footstep carried her further away. Kammy glanced at Jamie, whose face was white. They both let out a breath and Ria's footsteps paused. Jamie's fingers tightened painfully around Kammy's, but Ria started moving again and the sound of her boots clacking soon disappeared completely.

Kammy and Jamie did not dare to move or speak for a while. Eventually, Kammy unhooked her fingers from his, flexing them until feeling had returned, and then she straightened, pushing her hair back off her face.

Jamie watched her, his eyes narrowed and wary, 'You're thinking. It concerns me.'

She did not look at him. Instead, she unclipped her slingshot. 'We're going to talk to Dorren.' She stepped around the corner, smiling as Jamie scrambled after her, spluttering expletives.

'Are you sure this is a good idea?' he said.

'You were right. I can't just sit around panicking. I have to do something. Eric and Tayah are somewhere in this palace and I am going to find them. Besides, we wanted to get into his office, right?'

Jamie tangled his fingers in his curls, 'But he tried to kill you...'

Kammy shrugged. 'He's a prisoner. He must be restrained or he would have tried to fight past Ria. He's stronger than her, that's for sure.'

'I don't know...'

'I want to talk to him, Jamie...I,' she shook her head and took a step closer to the door, 'maybe he knows something about...well, me.' When Jamie did not respond she looked at him, but his eyes were warm and understanding. He nodded and she tried the door. 'I figured it would be locked.' She scooped one of the marbles from her pouch and took aim. The marble struck the keyhole with a gust of flame.

Kammy waited for the fire to die out and then, keeping tight hold of her slingshot, she pushed open the door.

Kammy felt the sting of past fears as she stepped inside the dark room. She had been so frightened when she had been pushed to stand before that desk. Kammy's mouth felt dry, but this time was different. This time she was stronger and she had Jamie at her side. She spotted Dorren and her eyes widened at the sight of him. She almost felt pity.

He did not tower over her from his seat behind the desk as he had the last time. Instead, he lay crumpled against the back wall, his wrists and his ankles shackled together. The shackles crackled when he moved and the skin beneath them was raw. One side of his face had swollen and bruised beyond recognition, his eye closed and weeping. His other eye stared at them in disbelief.

He rasped, 'How did you get in here?'

Kammy lifted her chin and glared at him, mustering as much contempt as she could. She would not baulk at the thought of the violence that had been dealt to him. She held up one of her marbles. 'One of these was enough to burn through the metal lock.' She swallowed, feeling foolish, 'And if you don't answer my questions I'll...I'll make sure that they burn...you.' She glanced back at Jamie who, despite everything, seemed to be holding back laughter. Kammy resisted kicking him and turned back to Dorren with a growl.

Dorren *did* laugh. He winced as he did so, but his chest rumbled, 'Get out of here little girl, you will get nothing from me.'

'I'll do it,' said Kammy, her voice squeaking.

Dorren sighed and leant his head back against the wall. 'Even if you could, which I doubt, what difference does it make? Bagor will only kill me anyway.'

'Exactly,' Jamie stepped forward, slipping into the situation with so much ease and grace that Kammy envied him. 'Bagor will kill you anyway, so why not answer Kammy's questions?'

Kammy nodded, 'We heard Ria and you *know* Bagor. He won't spare you.'

Dorren only smiled and said nothing.

Kammy pressed on, 'All these years you've served him, and he's going to kill you over one mistake. You're the only reason he is King at all. If you hadn't helped him, he'd still be stuck in a cell.' Dorren's eye opened a crack and his smile faded. Kammy moved around the desk towards him, 'Why be loyal to him now when he has shown no loyalty to you?'

Dorren's face turned an ugly purple and Kammy thought he looked like something out of a nightmare. The side of his face that had not swollen twisted with rage and his good eye bulged. He looked at Kammy with such hatred that her daring wavered. The muscles in his arms were straining and Kammy realised with a stab of fear that he was trying to break his restraints. Jamie grabbed her arm and pulled her towards him, but Dorren slumped back defeated and breathing hard.

'Why don't you shift?' Kammy asked, gazing at the cuffs on his wrists and ankles. 'Couldn't you get away?'

Dorren gave his wrists a slight shake. 'These are not simple handcuffs girl.' He winced, and Kammy wondered if those red marks she could see were burns. 'All of this is because of you, you know? You are the reason that I am going to die.' He looked at her, bitterness simmering in his gaze, 'I'd crush your pretty little neck if I could.'

Kammy felt Jamie tense beside her, but she cut him off. 'Why?' she said, 'I need to know why?'

Dorren laughed, 'Isn't it obvious? Because of your mother.'

'I don't understand.'

'I tried to kill you because I kept it from him. When Ria first brought you here, she wanted to keep you around because she thought Bagor would be interested in you. She didn't even know the connection. But I refused. I thought, even then, it would be safer if you were dead. I knew as soon as I saw you outside the palace that I was in trouble. I panicked.' He closed his eyes, 'I should have come up with a story...should have thought of something...'

'You're still not telling me why?'

'Because he was obsessed with her.'

Kammy blinked. 'What?'

'He always loved her, from the day that blasted plague sent her here. But his love for her was a disease,' Dorren snarled, 'it ruined him, and when she left it made him mad. He changed and as the years passed it got worse and worse until the accident with his brother. When he was locked up, he seemed to find himself again. He'd tell me of his plans and I listened because I could hear he had the right of things. That's why I helped him. The Council was ineffective, had been for ages. Bagor had a vision.' Dorren's eyes were feverish, 'It was all going to plan, but then I saw your face and I knew that it would all be for nothing if he saw you too. I had betrayed my friends and my family to help Bagor and here you were, the ghost of Marianna come back to haunt him. I knew you'd unhinge him, send him back to what he used to be.'

'But he isn't unhinged,' Kammy protested, denying it with every fibre of her being, 'you must be wrong. He still wants the Key, he...'

'Then why am I in here?'

'Because you lied to him.'

'No.' Dorren shifted onto his knees, leaning towards her. 'This is just the beginning, you'll see. You are his weakness and you will ruin everything.'

Kammy's chest heaved and when Jamie touched her elbow she jerked away from him and towards Dorren, 'What do you mean I will ruin everything?' She did not want to think of love and her mother. She wanted to find a way to help Jad and she did not want to think of anything else. 'What is he planning?'

Dorren only laughed and shook his head. Kammy's eyes blazed with anger and frustration. Without realising it, she aimed her slingshot at him. 'Tell me.'

Dorren's eyes moved from her face to the slingshot and he hesitated, clearly more convinced by this threat than the last.

'You are right, I suppose...why be loyal to him? He believes that the Key opens a Gate to a third layer...another world, and that in that world lies a weapon.'

'A weapon to fight humans?'

Dorren nodded, 'Bagor does not simply seek war. He seeks the destruction of the human race. We Semei do not stand a chance as things are, not against human weaponry. He believes there is a way that he can kill every last one of you.'

Kammy felt her stomach clench. She glanced back at Jamie whose eyes were wide.

'We should go,' he said, his voice low, 'we've been here too long.'

Kammy's head began to throb. She had not talked to Bagor about the war or about the Mother. But how could she be his weakness? She only had her slingshot. She was not strong and she was only ever brave when she had no other choice. How could she stop him from destroying everything?

'Kammy,' Jamie urged.

She nodded and turned to him.

'Wait.'

That same desperate tone that he had tried with Ria crept back into his voice and Kammy found herself looking back at Dorren.

'Please,' he clasped his hands in front of him, 'I've answered your questions. Surely I've earned something in return?'

Kammy's eyes narrowed. 'What do you want?'

He twisted his face into a grotesque smile. 'You can break through my restraints, like you did with the door. You could set me free.'

Kammy looked down at her pouch, she still had plenty of marbles left. She glanced at Jamie who offered her the barest shake of his head. Finally, she looked back at Dorren and his beaten face.

'We heard Ria say that Eric and Tayah are in the palace. Where are they?'

Dorren was in such a rush to answer her that he stumbled over his words. 'The audience...the audience chamber, I would think. I can't say for sure, but it's where I would look.'

'How do we get there from here?'

'You're not far. Turn right outside, then right again at the end of the corridor. You will see a large staircase. Go down that and follow

285

the next corridor around. The chamber is through the doors opposite the entrance, I swear...I swear...'

'Thank you,' said Kammy, her voice small.

'Now, please,' he held up his hands.

The blood rushing in her ears was all that Kammy could hear. She remembered the delight she had seen in Dorren's eyes when he had sentenced her to a death that chance had saved her from. She remembered how it had felt when he had thrown her into the chasm, how she had watched her life fall away from her. *I'd crush your pretty little neck now if I could.*

Kammy turned away from Dorren and followed Jamie out of the room. She pulled the door shut behind them.

It was time to find her friends.

CHAPTER TWENTY FIVE

CONFRONTATION

Jad had never felt so relieved to be back in his natural form. The intense scrutiny of five more pairs of Armours had been practically unbearable to withstand. Somehow, they had made it, but Jad's vision swam every time that he moved and his back burned. His throat felt parched and he darted after Hanna into the kitchens. She stopped just inside the door, but he hurried past to the pump and gulped down some water. It was so cold his teeth ached, but Jad felt it spark a reserve of energy within him. He sighed as he splashed his face, then he turned back to Hanna and smiled.

'Thank you,' he said.

She grinned up at him, showcasing the gap between her teeth. She tossed him his satchel and he caught it with one hand, pulling it back over his shoulder. 'I'll have to hang around here for a bit,' she said, 'they'll be suspicious if I head back too soon.'

Jad cleared his throat, 'I am...not always the best at showing my appreciation, but really - thank you. If there is any way that I can repay you and your family...'

She hopped up to sit on one of the counters. 'Oh, I've already thought of something and I know my Da will approve.'

There was a mischievous glint in her eye and Jad laughed nervously, 'And what is that?'

'In four years I'll be eighteen. Plenty old enough for us to get married.'

Jad gaped at her. He started to blurt a response, but Hanna collapsed crippled with laughter.

'Your face,' she gasped, '*your face.*'

Jad scowled at her, his cheeks the colour of rust. He shook his head and looked towards the turret in the corner where he knew a narrow staircase coiled upwards. 'I cannot wait with you,' he said, changing the subject, 'I have to go now.' Hanna barely seemed to hear him, she was laughing so hard. But her laughter died when they heard a voice drift down towards them.

'Who's there?'

Jad shot a look at Hanna and she mouthed a word at him as footsteps started to clank down the stairs; *hide.*

Jad tried to move silently and as quickly as his back allowed. He grabbed a large pan from the hooks on the wall and then he ducked down behind the nearest counter. He clutched the pan's handle as he held his breath and waited.

He heard Hanna hop back onto the floor with a click just as the Armour entered the kitchens.

'Oh, it's you,' said a young voice.

'Sorry,' said Hanna, and Jad marvelled again at her ability to stay calm under pressure, 'my Da wanted me to get to work early.'

Jad listened to the patter of her feet as she moved around gathering things. The air clattered and clanged and Jad took that chance to draw in a long breath.

'Wait,' the Armours footsteps moved closer and Jad tensed where he crouched, 'I thought you were finished up already.'

'But my Da said...'

'That's right, you were done for the day. And anyway, what are you doing here so soon after the bell?'

'I'm telling you,' Hanna's voice had grown shrill, 'my Da sent me.'

'Then where's your ruddy cat?'

'My *sister.*'

'She hasn't been your sister since the day the Mother abandoned her for rotten.'

Jad did not need to hear Hanna's pained cry for sense to be overwhelmed. He leapt out from his hiding place with a roar and he swung the pan back over his head. Hanna's eyes were wide as saucers as the Armour started to turn, just as the pan smashed into the side of his head.

He dropped like a stone with the sound of the ringing pan echoing around them. Jad stared down at a face he did not recognise and he let the pan slip out of his hand to clang against the floor.

Hanna's voice shook, 'Is he dead?'

Jad glanced at her, breathing heavily. She looked pale, but her eyes were fixed on the Armour with fury. 'I don't think so,' he said, 'but I think you should leave now. I know it's risky, but somebody might have heard that.' He wished he could see her home safely. 'Will you be alright, without Annie?'

Hanna nodded, 'The streets will be a bit busier now and I can always tell them that Annie got moody with me and went off in a huff. She does that a lot.' Hanna said it with great affection. Then she focused, 'If anyone asks, I'll tell them that since the bell, Bagor has changed his mind about his stupid cakes and doesn't need us. That should work. Even if they're suspicious, it's not like they can prove anything. I'll have to lock the door behind me though.'

'Alright,' said Jad, his voice strained. He had a bad feeling in his gut that he could not shake, but Hanna could not stay with him. That would be an even greater risk.

She held out her hand, 'It was a pleasure meeting you, my Lord. I do hope you win.'

Jad took her hand and shook it firmly, 'Thank you again. You have been my saviour.'

Hanna rolled her eyes and pulled her hand free, 'You were supposed to kiss it.'

Jad faltered, 'Oh.'

Hanna giggled, waving a hand at him as she backed away, 'I suppose being your saviour is better than being your wife.' When she reached the door, she looked back at him. 'Good luck.'

289

'And to you. Be careful.'

Hanna flashed him one last gap-toothed grin and then the door clicked shut. He waited until he heard the key turn in the lock; his stomach sinking further by the second, then his eyes fell on the Armour at his feet. A thought gripped him and it turned him cold. He needed this man to be dead, he needed to hit him again to make sure. If he lived, then he would know that Hanna had helped Jad and she would pay the price. He started to reach for the pan, but he could not stop staring at the man's face. He was a boy really, not much older than Jad. He had a family somewhere in the city; he was only trying to earn a living. Jad gripped the pan, but it almost slipped out of his sweaty palm. He had never killed before. In all of his scraps and escapes, he had never killed. It was one thing to kill in the heat of the moment, he assumed, but like this?

He gripped the pan tighter; he had to protect Hanna.

* * *

'This isn't going to work.'

Eric did not respond. He stared at his feet as they waited.

'We're pushing it with Ria,' Tayah paced, her breath rushed, 'she'll know, Eric. Eric?'

He forced his head up. 'Yeah?'

Tayah stopped with her hands on her hips, eyeing him with concern, 'Have you heard a word I've said?'

Eric sighed, 'Look, we're here now. Ria is already on her way. What's the point in worrying? There is nothing we can do.'

Tayah pursed her lips and Eric looked away from her quickly, familiar enough with her moods to know he was irritating her. His eyes swept over the courtyard and he felt a pang of sadness. It had been so long since he had stood at the top of the Giant's Staircase and looked down upon the city. It all looked different to him now. Where once he had only felt wonder, now he felt a constant ache.

'You're still thinking about him, aren't you? The man you killed?'

Eric winced. He turned his back on her and looked beyond the city, to the forest. A part of him wished they had never come back, but then a part of him wished he had never left Alashdial in the first place.

290

'You can't do this to yourself. He was chasing Jad. You were only protecting your friend.'

Eric laughed, 'Yeah.'

'What does that mean.'

'Nothing,' he sighed. His stomach had not stopped turning since the bell had started ringing. 'I didn't have to kill him.'

Tayah rested her hand on his arm, 'It was an accident, that's all.'

Eric jerked away from her, 'Have you ever killed anyone Tay?'

He saw the flash of surprise in her eyes and for a moment he hated himself. He wanted to smile, to laugh and to apologise, but he couldn't and no words came to him. Tayah's gaze fell and she turned away, her hands drifting up to toy with her braid. They stood in silence and for the first time since they had become friends Eric wished she would leave him alone.

Still, he was not so detached from the moment that he did not notice Tayah stiffen. He looked back towards the palace. Ria rushed towards them, her hair streaming behind her shoulders. Her face was split by such a broad grin that Eric glanced back at Tayah and wished he had been kinder.

Ria's gaze never left her sister's face. She stopped a few paces away from them and Eric could hardly bear to look when he realised she had tears in her eyes. Tayah's mouth opened, but she made no sound.

Ria took a step closer. 'Is it true?'

Tayah did not move or speak so Eric nodded.

Ria's eyes brushed over him, then back to Tayah. She seemed to be struggling with something. Her brow pinched and her cheeks flushed. Then she flung herself forward. For one panicked moment Eric thought that she was attacking. Instinct had him twisting towards his friend, but the arms that curled around Tayah were not threatening. Ria was clinging to her little sister with tears glittering on her cheeks. Eric had to turn away when he spotted the tears on Tayah's cheeks too.

'You've made the right choice,' Ria gasped. She pulled back with her hands on Tayah's shoulders. Tayah looked dazed. 'I know it must have been difficult for you, but this is the way it has to be.'

Tayah was still speechless. Eric stepped closer to her and said, 'We know.'

'Good.' Ria could not stop smiling. 'Good, then you must come.' She held out an arm towards the palace, inviting them to follow. 'Bagor is waiting in the audience chamber.'

Eric's legs felt like lead, but he managed to make them move. He could feel Tayah trembling beside him, but he did not reach for her. He did not feel like he could offer her any comfort at all. The two of them walked in silence. Ria, on the other hand, could not seem to stop talking and Eric realised with a start that their sombre mood aided them. She thought that they felt guilty for betraying Jad. She did not realise that their guilt had nothing to do with their friend. Eric saw Kait's face, only she was the one lying dead in the road. He shuddered.

'Now,' Ria said, 'Bagor is very happy to have you back with us, but you must remember that this is a serious situation. Be honest with him. He appreciates honesty.' She looked at both their faces as they stepped across the palace's threshold and her smile faltered. Eric nodded, but his eyes were fixed on the cream doors opposite and the two Armours that stood on either side. Bagor waited beyond those doors and he would not be receiving an ounce of honesty. He would see through their lies straight away.

Ria stopped before the doors and took a deep breath. Eric realised with a growing sense of unease that she was nervous. The Armour just behind Ria seemed to stumble, the loudness of his armour grating into their tense silence. Eric glanced up to meet a pair of eyes through the Armour's visor. Eric's own eyes narrowed, but Ria had gathered herself. She pushed open the heavy doors and all thoughts of the Armour were punched out of his mind as he followed Tayah into the audience chamber.

The audience chamber, once the Council chamber, looked much the same. It was a long hall, with golden walls. The floor looked like fogged glass and the chandelier still hung overhead. But the seven seats of the Council had gone. In their place was a throne, a simple stone seat that had been made for the king that sat upon it.

Jad's eyes looked at him and Eric wanted to run away screaming. He forced himself to keep walking, even though his blood was boiling so hot that it hurt. Bagor slouched on his throne, one leg resting on the other knee. His hands were curled in his lap and his smile was designed to be welcoming, but the hardness of his stare reminded Eric of how much danger they were in. Ria held out a hand to stop them when they were a few paces away and then she positioned herself on Bagor's right-hand side, her face taut.

Bagor stared at them and Eric wondered if he could already see the lies on their faces. Only when Eric looked away from him did he speak. 'Welcome home.'

Eric glanced at Tayah and almost sighed with relief. She was stood straighter and her tears had dried. Her hatred of Bagor had been enough to drag her back to her senses. Ria looked anxiously between them and Eric knew that he needed to say something.

'Thank you,' his voice sounded strange to his own ears, 'your Majesty.'

Bagor's smile flashed teeth. His gaze moved slowly to Tayah who glared at him with a venom she did not care to hide. Eric thought Bagor looked amused. Ria looked sick.

'Would you like refreshment? I'm sure Ria would not mind running off to fetch you something.' The laughter faded from his eyes and Ria's smile looked painful.

'We're fine, thank you.' Eric had to resist the urge to keep looking back at the door.

Bagor shrugged, his eyes fixed onto Eric's with a cold intensity. Eric felt like everything inside of him lay bare underneath that gaze. He clasped his hands behind his back so that Bagor could not see them shaking.

'Forgive me if this sounds rude,' Bagor drawled, 'but I am quite surprised to see you here. I had thought that your loyalty to Jadanim was absolute.'

'It is,' said Tayah, her voice shaking with fierce pride.

Eric's heart skipped a beat. 'It is,' he blurted, though Bagor did not look ruffled. 'We are loyal to him and we would never wish to hurt him.'

Bagor templed his fingers beneath his chin, 'Yet...'

Tayah's hands curled into fists at her sides and Eric knew that she was close to breaking. He spoke quickly, the rehearsed words falling off his tongue in snatches, 'There was a...disagreement, about your prisoner. Kammy, our friend...she was determined to come back for him, but Jad wouldn't have it. Kammy demanded to know what he had planned, but he said nothing. We've abandoned our homes and our families for him, but he hasn't done anything for us. We love him, but we left with Kammy. We're tired of running, of fighting,' the awkwardness fell away and Eric was impassioned, 'it's not fair that we deserted others that needed us. What if it's all just been a waste of time? What if there is only so much you can do for a friend?'

When he finished he was surprised to find that his chest heaved and his cheeks were damp. He did not look at Tayah, but he could feel her eyes on him. His cheeks burned as he held Bagor's gaze.

Bagor leant forwards on his throne, his eyes alight with curiosity, 'Interesting. Very interesting,' he smirked at Eric, and then turned to Tayah, 'and you feel the same?'

Eric peered at her and saw her throat working. He wished he could whisper in her ear and remind her that they needed to buy time. To his relief she managed to nod, but there was that flash of amusement in Bagor's eyes and Eric's skin crawled.

He settled back onto his throne. 'Kammy told me a similar tale. If only my nephew could see things the way that you do.'

'Kammy is safe?' said Eric, anxious to steer talk away from Jad. He did not think that Tayah could withstand it.

'Of course. I am always happy to welcome home one of our own. She has been reunited with her friend, and they are currently relaxing in one of the guest chambers.'

Eric nodded. At least if everything else went wrong, Kammy had found Jamie.

'Now,' Bagor pushed himself to his feet, 'if you could just hand over the Key, then I shall send you along to meet them.'

The chamber felt much smaller all of a sudden and Bagor's words rung in the emptiness around them. Eric had to remind himself to breathe. He reached up a hand to wipe sweat from his brow, but there was nothing he could do to hide the flush beneath his freckles.

'We'd like to see Kammy first.'

Bagor shook his head, his expression eerily calm, 'The Key.'

Eric and Tayah shared a look. She nodded at him and with his whole body pulsing, Eric swung his pack off his back and started to rummage through it. He pulled out the stone they had picked up in the forest and held it out before him.

Bagor looked at it and his smile disappeared. 'Do you think me a fool?'

Eric's arm shook. 'No...'

'Then please put that away before I become angry.'

Eric opened his mouth to insist that the stone he held was the Key, and that they had kept to their word, but one look into Bagor's eyes silenced him. He let the stone drop back into the pack.

'So,' Bagor tapped his boot on the marble floor, 'where is it?'

Tayah folded her arms. 'We don't have it.'

Ria convulsed. 'What?'

Still, Bagor's voice did not rise. 'Then who, may I ask, does have it?'

'We left it with Welm. He's just outside the city,' Eric could hear the desperation in his own voice.

'Welm,' Bagor smirked, 'I see.' He stood with a sigh and took a step closer to them, 'But Kammy told me you would have it on you. I understood that your delayed arrival was simply so that she could see her friend. That then, the Key would be mine.'

Ria looked afraid. 'There must have been a misunderstanding, that is all.'

Eric heard something clatter behind him, but he could not look away from Bagor.

'Is that true?' whispered the King, 'Has there been a misunderstanding?'

'Kammy must have been confused,' Eric shrugged, 'we left it with Welm, but we have every intention of handing it over. It's just... we'd like to see Kammy first, to make sure that she is safe.'

Bagor stopped and stood very still. He waited, letting the pressure of the silence build, his expression unreadable. 'You will take me to the Key now.'

Eric shivered. 'No...Kammy...'

'Tayah,' Ria hissed, striding forwards and grabbing her sister's arm, 'don't be stupid.'

But Tayah glared at her sister and wrenched her arm free, stepping close to Eric.

Bagor laughed. The corners of his eyes crinkled and he pointed at Tayah. 'You are a terrible actress.' He walked closer until Eric had to look up at him. 'You on the other hand...I almost think that I believe you.' His gaze bored into Eric's who felt shame spread through him. Then Bagor laughed again. 'I tire of these games. I am not sure what you hoped to achieve by coming here, but you have no intention of handing me the Key. I know that Jadanim is in the city, no doubt my Armours are closing in on him as we speak, which means that the Key is close. You will take me to it *now*.'

Ria looked wretched. '*Tayah.*'

Tayah shot one last look of contempt at her sister before her lip curled and she spat at Bagor's feet. 'No.'

Eric's eyes fluttered shut; it was over. When he opened them again Bagor was smiling. He moved so fast it was impossible. His hand was around Tayah's throat before Eric could blink. Ria screamed and Eric jumped forwards.

'Do not move,' Bagor's tone was deadly and Eric froze. He stared at Tayah, blood pounding in his ears. Her eyes were blazing and she spat at Bagor again, but he shook her like a doll. She gasped, her fingers pulling at his pale hand. Defiance shone in her eyes, but she could barely breathe and she was no match for Bagor's strength.

'You will bring me the Key, or I will snap her neck.'

'Your Majesty,' Ria had not moved. She clutched at her throat and cried, 'Please...'

'She tried to deceive me, Ria, just as she deceived you,' Bagor spat, 'you have no obligation to protect her. Just because two people are cursed to be siblings, to be family, does not mean that they are

296

doomed to be party to each other's mistakes. Tayah has proven this herself Ria, so I hope you shall not disappoint me in turn.'

Ria wrenched her eyes away from Tayah and turned her back on them, her shoulders shaking.

'The Key,' said Bagor, 'now.'

Tayah tried to say something, but she could only croak and Bagor shook her again, lifting her clean off her feet. She choked. Her eyes started to stream as she kicked feebly at Bagor's chest.

'Alright,' Eric cried, 'I'll tell you.'

'*Where?*'

The doors creaked open and a fifth person entered the chamber.

'I have it.'

Eric spun and he felt his heart stop. The two Armours from outside were nowhere to be seen. Jad strode towards them with the Key in his hand.

CHAPTER TWENTY SIX

THE WOLF'S CRY

When Jad met Bagor's eyes it were as though he lived it all again. He saw the floor of the chamber slick with blood. He felt the pain and his whole body shook with the force of his hatred. Everything moved in slow motion around him and each step rang clear, echoing off the walls. Bagor dropped Tayah, his lip curling into a smile. She crumpled at his feet and Eric ran to her side. Jad's gaze did not waver.

'It has been a long time, nephew.'

Jad stopped. 'Not long enough.' His voice rang strong and clear. He could feel Eric's eyes on him, but he did not dare look away from Bagor. He lingered on the edge of his Soul; he was ready.

'What did you do to my Armours?'

Jad smirked. 'They are incapacitated.'

Bagor's eyes sharpened. Jad's appearance had thrown him.

It was a small victory.

'Hand me the Key now.'

'And my life?'

'Yours is no longer negotiable.'

Tayah hissed at him as Eric helped her back to her feet. They backed away a few steps and Jad stepped closer to Bagor. He laughed bitterly, 'When was it ever?' Bagor simply held out his hand. Jad stared at it and shook his head, 'Of course, you know that I would never value my own life over my friends.'

'Of course.'

'Hand it over, idiot boy.'

Jad's head jerked in surprise and his heart sank when he saw Ria, her face twisted and streaked with tears. He had hoped, desperately, that Bagor might be alone. That way, they might have had a hope. He chanced a quick look at Eric who nodded. He was ready too.

'Come now,' said Bagor, his voice sharp with impatience, 'I am strong enough to fight you by myself, let alone with Ria beside me. Let us not drag this out.'

'Where is Kammy?'

Bagor's smile widened and his eyes flashed. 'You do all seem to have grown rather fond of her. I see the appeal Jadanim, though I feel she could find herself much better company.'

Jad held himself back. The look in Bagor's eyes when he talked about Kammy made him sick. 'Where is she?'

'She is safe, but you shall not be seeing her again. She will remain with me now, under my protection.'

'Your protection?' Jad spat, 'I will only hand this over when Eric and Tayah are free, and when Kammy and her friend have gone home.'

An odd light came into Bagor's eyes. 'This is Kammy's home.'

Jad's grip tightened on the stone. His teeth were clenched as he said, 'That is my only offer.'

Bagor smiled. 'You hand me the Key or I will kill Eric right now, and then I will kill Tayah too. Right here, on the spot that I killed your grandfather.'

Ria whimpered.

Jad looked at his friends. Their faces blazed with courage, but beneath that he saw that they were petrified. All he wanted was for them to be safe, free of the fate that had befallen others he had loved. He stared back at Bagor and he knew that he could buy them time.

Maybe enough time for them to find Kammy and get out. He could see Tayah shaking her head out of the corner of his eye, but he also saw the bruises blooming on her neck. Bagor would kill them, Jad knew for certain. He saw his father, lying still as blood pooled around his head. He saw his grandfather, staring and staring at him long after he was dead. Jad closed the distance between them, his breathing heavy. He dropped the Key into Bagor's waiting palm.

'Run,' Jad bellowed as he charged.

Jad barrelled into Bagor's chest, sending them both crashing to the floor and the Key skittered away. He could not look to see if his friends were doing as he had asked. He thought he heard something behind him, but then Bagor twisted beneath him and Jad did not hesitate a moment longer. He sank into his Soul and leapt at Bagor again. Bagor skipped back and they stopped, staring at one another, snarling. They were two wolves, one black and one silver. Bagor was bigger and stronger and Jad could not win. But he would buy time for Eric and Tayah. They leapt for each other at the same moment. Bagor slammed into Jad, his greater weight bearing him backwards. Jad swung with his paws, but each blow fell away unnoticed and he stumbled, his back in agony. Bagor's large paw slammed into his throat and Jad collapsed to the floor, his strength deserting him. With a grunt of pain, Jad was himself again and Bagor let his Soul drop too. Jad did not struggle as Bagor leant in close, his breath on Jad's face.

'There was once a time when I would have considered sparing your life.' Jad stared into his blue eyes. 'But you are a pitiful excuse for a Semei.'

He was a wolf once more and his teeth bore down on Jad's throat.

*   *   *

Kammy rounded the corner and squealed in delight.

She had found the palace entrance. The doors were still open and the orange beams of the fading light poured in. They kissed the gold patterns on the cream doors opposite, sending light dancing down the corridors. But Kammy's pride quickly faded. The cream doors were open and two Armours lay unconscious beside them.

She was too late.

Jamie caught up to her, gasping for breath, 'Have you gotten even fast-' He faltered when he spotted the two prone figures. 'Oh...'

Then they both heard somebody scream and a voice bellow.

'*Run.*'

'It's them,' Kammy cried, and she ran to the door without pausing to think what she might do when she got there.

She collided with a dark blur and a braid swung up and hit her in the face. They grappled with one another for a moment, Jamie watching them with wide eyes. Then they pulled apart and stared at one another in wonder.

'Kammy, how...'

Kammy had one second to note the dark bruises on Tayah's neck when she heard something that made her blood run cold; a wolf howling. *Jad.*

'Take Jamie,' Kammy roared as she shoved past Tayah and through the doors. Her hands fell to her belt. Strong arms tried to pull her back. She saw a flash of red, but she pushed Eric away. Her eyes were drawn to the giant wolf at the centre of the room, with its teeth inches away from Jad's throat.

She thought she might be screaming as she lifted her loaded slingshot, but she could not hear. She let fly and the wolf, Bagor, looked up just as her marble whistled past his ear. He stared at her and she met that gaze with tears in her eyes. The marble struck the throne behind him and burst into a ball of flame. Bagor glanced back and that split second was all that Jad needed. He kicked out with all of his strength, sending Bagor skidding backwards. Then he grabbed the Key and surged to his feet, running towards Kammy.

'*Go.*'

She did not know who had shouted, but she knew it was Eric's hand on her wrist, pulling her backwards.

'Jad,' she cried.

Bagor was right behind him.

Jad looked up at her and saw the warning on her face. Bagor snarled, leaping forwards, and Jad dived at the last moment, rolling to the side, his face twisting with pain as he hit the floor. Bagor skidded past, still a giant wolf, and Jad was back on his feet. He shoved the Key towards Kammy, took her hand and they were running.

They burst out of the chamber and past the Armours. Eric's fox urged them on. Kammy clung to Jad's hand, but to her horror she realised that she was the one pulling him.

She could feel the heat of Bagor's breath on the back of her neck and she screamed, bracing herself for the blow. But Eric was there. He jumped over her, slashing with his claws and then he spun away again. He had brought them seconds.

They poured out into the evening air. The Akasi flowers were beginning to open and the purple glow mixed with the orange light gave the courtyard an eerie feel. Kammy shot a look at Jad, but his eyes were fixed ahead, his jaw tight. Eric circled them, but Kammy knew that they would never make it. She could hear Bagor behind them. It was only a matter of time. They hit the Giant's Staircase and Kammy felt a wave of relief. She could see Tayah, already halfway down, dragging Jamie behind her. At least they might get away. She could see something else too; a dark mass at the base of the Staircase, but it was too far away for her to make out clearly.

A blur of feathers shot past her shoulder and slammed into Eric. Ria had gathered herself and their chances dwindled further. Kammy tried to run towards them as they tumbled down the stairs, but a shadow fell over her. She glanced back in terror. Jad let go of her hand and shoved her forwards, then he threw himself at Bagor.

Kammy's boots slipped. She twisted and she fell, her hip hitting the stone. The Key and her slingshot bounced away from her. She skidded backwards and she lay, winded, until a scream of agony tore through the air.

Jad had thrown up his left arm to defend himself and Bagor's teeth had sunk into it. Blood poured across his scar.

'No,' Kammy screamed. She stumbled and stood. She stuck a hand into her pouch and she pulled out a marble. Then she whipped her arm back and she threw her marble at Bagor with all the strength that she had. It hit the side of his face.

Bagor's Soul released him and Kammy had never seen anything so terrible. He screamed, his left cheek aflame and he staggered to the side, clawing at his face. His eyes bulged as his skin melted. He was still screaming when he threw himself over the edge.

Kammy stood there, her breathing ragged, and her lip trembling. Bagor's screams faded and the evening was still.

'Kammy?'

His voice shook her free of shock. Jad struggled to stand and she dashed to his side.

'Are you okay?' he managed as she placed a tentative hand on his shoulder.

She laughed. She looked down at his arm, coated in blood and she shook her head. 'Are *you* okay?'

'Yes...yes...' He stared at her, his eyelids fluttering.

Eric's voice drifted towards them, 'Come *on.*'

Eric stood further down the steps, waving them on. Ria had disappeared, but his eyes were wide and Kammy knew that they were still in danger. She pulled Jad's good arm around her shoulders and helped him to his feet. She could see the pain in his eyes, but he did not make a sound. He leaned on her and ran as best he could. When they reached Eric, he helped too and soon Tayah and Jamie's anxious faces came into focus. Kammy smiled, but it was the sight behind them that dumbfounded her.

A sea of hopeful faces looked up at them, filling the gardens and the streets beyond. Amongst them stood the Armours, but they made no move to stop Kammy and the others. At the front of them stood a young girl with a gap between her teeth and a black cat on her shoulder. She jumped up and down, waving frantically. Kammy looked up at Jad to see that his eyes were shining. He did not look like he could believe it. The people were there for him. They would shield them amongst their mass and carry them towards the wall.

They were going to be okay.

CHAPTER TWENTY SEVEN

THE FESTIVAL OF THE MOTHER

His body was on fire.

That was all he knew, other than the darkness. He was floating, but there was a light spot in the distance and it hurtled towards him, faster and faster until it flooded his vision. He blinked, and the burning was no longer all that he felt. He felt the heaviness of his limbs and of his eyes. He felt something stroking his hair. He sucked in a breath.

'You're awake,' said Kammy, pulling her hand back to her side. She beamed down at him, her face flickering in the light from the fire beside them.

Jad turned his head, blinking until his vision began to focus. The fire was only small, but he could feel the warmth soothing the pain in his arm. He spied three shadows bundled around it. They were in the forest.

Jad tried to sit up. 'What happened?'

When he gasped in pain, Kammy scooted forwards and her arm wound around his shoulders. She pushed him back onto the sleeping mat and her hair swung by his face.

'You keep doing that.'

Jad watched her. 'What?'

'Pushing yourself too hard.' Her voice was quiet and he could tell from the shadows under her eyes that she had not slept.

'I'm sorry,' he said.

She pushed her hair back behind her ears and smiled at him. 'Don't be. If you hadn't pushed yourself too hard then we probably wouldn't be here.' Her eyes fell to her lap, 'I just...wish you didn't have to push yourself to this.'

Jad noticed her gaze flicker towards his arm and he felt his heart sink. He could still see Bagor's teeth tearing into his flesh. Swallowing, he braced himself and looked down at it. To his surprise it had been bandaged. He tried to flex his fingers, but it only made the pain worse. Breathing through his teeth, Jad said, 'You act like I'm the one that saved the day,' he let his arm rest and turned back to her, 'it was you that saved my life, twice.' Kammy started to shake her head and Jad raised an eyebrow.

Kammy paused, pressing her lips together, but then she giggled. Her giggle turned into a laugh and her eyes sparkled. 'I did, didn't I?'

Jad smiled. His head was already starting to feel a bit hazy again. 'It was brilliant.'

'To be honest, I was terrified. I had no idea what I was doing. If I hadn't asked you all to come back...' her gaze drifted towards the sleeping bundles.

Jad could barely remember leaving Alashdial. He could see the swarm of people that had surrounded them, he could feel them pressing close, but then nothing. 'Are they all okay?' he said, feeling a sting of guilt for not having asked immediately. He had to tell Eric that Arren had helped. Had any other Armour been at the door to the Audience Chamber, he might never have made it inside.

Kammy nodded, 'Exhausted, but okay. Tayah has just taken over watch. We didn't really want to stop, but we had too. Welm is here,' she said, biting her lip. Jad thought that was curious, but his mind fogged and his thoughts drifted past it. 'He's the one that cleaned up your wounds. He says it should all heal fine, as long as you rest.'

Jad chuckled, 'Rest...'

Kammy did not smile. She looked worried. 'You need to rest, Jad. You've done enough. We have the Key and we're safe for now.'

Without really knowing why, Jad reached forwards to touch Kammy's wrist. He felt her jump and he smiled again, 'I'll be fine.'

He heard her hesitate, taking a breath before she spoke. 'Why did you have the Key on you? That wasn't our plan.'

Jad shrugged and then winced. 'I told Welm it was the only way I would agree. If it came to saving any of you, I'd give it up.'

Her eyelashes fluttered and she looked like she wanted to say something more. Instead, she blushed and pulled her wrist away from his touch.

Jad took a deep breath and let his eyes drifted upwards. The night was silent and still. The fire and the warmth of Kammy's closeness kept away any chill. The trees crowded overhead and he thought he could hear the lapping of water, but he could not see any Akasi blooms.

'Where are we?' he said, softly, 'how did we get out?'

'We're not far from Emire. We'll get there before mid-light tomorrow.'

'Emire?' Jad's shock roused him. He looked at Kammy in surprise, 'I missed a whole day?'

'You passed out as we were leaving the city. Eric carried you. The people stayed with us until we were well beyond the walls. It was incredible. There was nothing Bagor's men could do, without massacring everybody.'

'But there were so many Armours,' Jad frowned at the memory, 'too many.'

'Still not enough to fight the whole city. Plus, I don't think many of them wanted to stop us. They got us out and we went to Welm, but he thought it was best to keep moving while Alashdial was in chaos, before Bagor could regroup and get ahead of us. Jamie wanted to build you a stretcher,' a smile played across her lips, 'but there wasn't time. He and Eric have taken turns to carry you.'

Jad scowled at that. But he swallowed the discomfort. He reminded himself that there was no shame in being helped by others. 'So, have we been followed?'

'Not that we know of. It's strange. We thought Bagor would chase us all the way, but we haven't seen a thing.' She paused and bit her lip again. This time, Jad was alert enough to pick up on it.

'What is it?'

'Could Bagor...' she did not meet his eye, 'could he be dead?'

Jad lay very still, watching the small flames reflect in her dark eyes. 'I think it is safest to assume that he's still alive.'

Kammy let out a breath and Jad thought that she looked relieved.

'Were you afraid that you had killed him?'

Her eyebrows drew together. 'I...I guess so.'

Jad spoke without hesitation. 'He would have deserved it.'

Kammy did not respond and Jad felt something cold crawl into his stomach.

'Did he hurt you?'

Kammy stared at her fingers, tugging through the blades of grass at her knee, 'No,' she said, 'he was nice to me. Or, he pretended to be nice. He actually saved my life.'

Jad almost choked, 'What?'

'It was Dorren. He...' her eyes became distant, 'he threw me into the chasm, but Bagor...he caught me.'

Jad was shot through by such a fury that he sat up before he felt any flicker of pain. Kammy rolled her eyes as he grimaced, and she pressed him back down again, but all Jad could see was the chasm and the rocks that waited in its depths. He stared into Kammy's face and felt sick.

'I should never have let you go,' he hissed between short breaths.

'I'm afraid it's not up to you what I do or don't do,' she said pointedly, 'I'm fine, so it doesn't matter.'

'Because of Bagor...because you had the Key. Imagine if you hadn't?'

'We don't have to imagine that,' she hesitated, glancing at him with apprehension in her eyes, 'but it wasn't like that...he...he could have been a lot crueller to me.'

'He's Bagor, Kammy. He'll treat you like a queen until he gets what he wants. He...'

'Apparently,' she blurted over him, her eyes fixed on a spot past his head, 'he was in love with my mother.'

Jad gaped at her. His anger drowned in a sudden wave of mirth. He laughed and he felt the warmth close in on him again. 'My father mentioned something once...a broken heart...' he yawned, 'but I never believed it. Bagor has no heart.'

'I guess you're right...' he heard Kammy say, but she whispered and it was hard to hear.

'Always.'

He heard her laugh. 'Definitely not always,' she paused and Jad could not stop blinking, 'There was something I wanted to ask...it can wait...'

'Ask, please.'

'Bagor...when he saved my life he shifted, but he did not shift into an animal. It was like...' she frowned, 'it was like he became nothing. Like he was not there. Is that...is that normal?'

Jad felt a darkness stir inside him. He growled, 'It is unnatural what Bagor can do, what he has trained his body to withstand. It is forbidden.'

Kammy was silent. Jad wanted to look at her, to try and gauge what she was thinking, but his eyes would not open. He had to settle for listening to her even breathing, which matched his own. After a while, she spoke again. 'I found something out you know, about why Bagor wants the Key.'

'Tell me...' Jad whispered.

'We can talk about it later, when you've rested. We can talk about everything.'

Jad wanted to protest, but the water lapped in his ears now and the pain in his arm was receding. His eyes drifted closed. 'I'm glad we saved your friend.'

'Sleep,' Kammy's voice hovered around him.

He tried to fight against it. She needed sleep too, and Tayah. It was his turn to watch. But then he felt fingers brushing through his hair again and he slipped away from the fire into a comfortable darkness.

*　　*　　*

'I think I'm going to die.'

Kammy laughed, shooting Jamie a look as he threw himself onto the small bed. Kammy sank into a chair and heaved a sigh.

They had arrived in Emire the day before, half staggering and half crawling through the south gate. Word of their arrival had passed quickly and Seeve had come bounding down to meet them. He had been very conflicted. The furious side of him wanted to make them suffer for their stupidity, but a fierce pride gleamed in his eyes too. In the end he had sent them all straight to bed and only Tayah had refused, insisting that she must find Boo. Jamie had laughed, thinking she was talking about a boyfriend, and he had earned his very first caustic stare. Kammy had slept right through into the next afternoon and she felt much better for it.

Jamie had come barrelling into her room mere minutes after she had awoken. Kammy suspected that he had been sitting outside her door waiting to hear her move.

'Please,' she said, 'you slept as long as I did and I feel fine.'

'One,' Jamie mumbled through the pillow, holding up a finger, 'I don't exercise, *ever*, unlike you. Two,' he held up a second, 'you didn't have to carry a load of dead weight on your back for a day and a half.'

'You probably carried him for two hours in total. Eric did all the work.'

Jamie flipped onto his back and shrugged, 'Details.'

Kammy beamed at him. When she had found him in Alashdial her euphoria had been tempered by the situation that they were in. Now that she felt safe, it really struck her that he was safe too.

He made a face at her. 'What?'

'I'm just so happy you're here.'

309

'See,' he said, stretching his arms up behind his head, 'I'm not sure yet. My quarters in the palace were triple the size of this and the view was incredible.'

Kammy snorted, 'You're an idiot.'

'Shush, freak.'

'A fact now.'

Jamie clucked his tongue. 'Esme was right all along.'

On instinct Kammy frowned, but then she noticed something. Hearing Esme's name no longer made her stomach tighten, nor did her hands clench. She could still picture Esme's face, but it was hazy around the edges, as though she were part of somebody else's life. It was as though she were part of a world that Kammy did not belong too, yet that world was her home. She thought of her Gran and her frown deepened.

'I'll get you home Jamie,' she said, 'I promise.'

'You better,' said Jamie, cracking a yawn, 'I hear humans don't last long in this place.'

Kammy started, 'How did you...'

'That Tay girl told me. She seemed to relish telling me actually. I think she wants me to get stuck here.'

Kammy shook her head, 'Tayah is...difficult, but she's alright once you break her down.'

'Break her down...got it.'

She saw a glint in his eye and Kammy grinned. Watching Jamie in that endeavour would be amusing for the rest of them, less so for him. He yawned again and his eyes fell closed. Kammy watched him and she sat forward. He was the only one she could talk to about what she feared.

'Can I tell you something?'

'Sure,' he mumbled, keeping his eyes closed.

Kammy shifted, struggling to find the words and unsure if she should voice it. Voicing it would make it real. 'When I was with Bagor, he said something that made me think about my...'

There was a knock at the door and Kammy jumped. She gathered herself and shouted a welcome a little too loudly as she got to her feet. She thought it might be Eric and she hoped it would be. She had hardly spoken to him on their journey back to Emire. Their pace had been relentless and they had been too drained to make much conversation. Still, Kammy had not been too exhausted to notice that Eric's smile was gone. It had been a hard day on all of them, so she was not that surprised, but still, it concerned her.

When the door opened it was not Eric, but Kammy's smile stretched so wide that she could not even contemplate feeling disappointed. She could talk to Eric later. Fii bustled into the room, wrapping strong arms around Kammy and squeezing her tight. Kammy hugged the old woman back.

'I am furious with all of you,' said Fii, though there was laughter in her voice, 'furious, but so happy you are okay.' She pulled back to hold Kammy at arm's length, her eyes shining. She tucked a strand of Kammy's hair back behind her ear, 'I wanted to go after you myself, but I could not leave Boo.' She sighed, 'I hear that you were very brave.'

Kammy ducked her head, her cheeks burning with a mixture of embarrassment and pride. 'Have you seen the others?'

Fii nodded, 'Tayah came for Boo as soon as you got here. She was very quiet at first, but Boo doesn't let a person stay sombre for long. I saw Jad this morning and he is the same as ever, determined to ignore everything we say, no matter how much he needs rest.' Kammy fought down the urge to roll her eyes. 'He asked after you, saying you had not slept, so I decided to wait.'

Something fluttered in Kammy's stomach. If Jad remembered that Kammy had not slept then he might remember more. Jamie had caught her stroking his hair and had promised to tease her about it for a very long time. She tried to ignore it and laughed, 'I think we'd have to lock him up and tie him down if he is ever going to rest.' She laughed again at the image of Jad scowling against a gaggle of fluffed up pillows. 'And Eric?' She finished.

Fii hesitated, her smile fading, 'I knocked and there was no answer. I'm sure he's just very tired, but it is quite unlike him.'

'He must be exhausted. He carried Jad most of the way here,' she said, and then her eyes flicked over to the bed, 'with Jamie, too.'

311

Jamie had gotten to his feet and stood in uncharacteristic silence. Kammy had told him about Fii, gushed about her really, and Jamie had always had a healthy respect for his elders.

Fii gasped, horrified with herself, and then her arms were around Jamie, her hands patting his back. Jamie's eyes jerked towards Kammy in alarm and Kammy giggled. He stood rigid for a moment, and then he relaxed, stooping a bit so that he could pat Fii's back in return.

When Fii stepped back, her eyes were twinkling, 'I hope this isn't too overwhelming. You must have been very frightened.'

'Very frightened, but I do my best.'

Fii laughed, 'That is all any of us can do.'

Fii's words hit Kammy and she thought of how since she had found herself in the Semei world, she had been sure that her best would never be good enough. She was sure that she was a burden, but then she *had* saved Jad's life with the slingshot that Welm had made for her. She had experienced a moment of doubt in the palace and she was not sure if she would ever stop feeling guilty about Welm, but she had made a choice to believe in her new friends. She no longer felt that she was a burden. Emire was a place that felt familiar. She could stop and think. She could work through all that she had learned.

'Fii,' she said, 'could we...' she faltered, not knowing exactly what she was asking for, but knowing that she needed something.

Fii understood as Kammy had suspected she would. Fii seemed able to read people better than they could themselves. 'I've heard a little of what happened from the others. I know about your heritage. I can only apologise for not figuring it out myself. I only ever saw your mother from afar.' Kammy shook her head and Fii continued, 'Regardless, you can come to me for anything, whenever you need to talk.'

Kammy smiled at her. Fii would help her figure things out.

Fii clapped her hands together, 'But first, you need to eat and get yourselves ready for tonight.'

'Why?' Jamie looked wary, 'What's tonight?'

'The Festival of the Mother.' She looked at Kammy, 'Had you forgotten?'

Kammy laughed. She had forgotten, completely. The rush to Alashdial and back had pushed everything else from her mind. It felt impossible that they had made it back in time for the Semei's greatest celebration.

'But I have nothing to wear,' Jamie whined.

'I'm sure we can find you something. Now,' she clapped again, 'come. Food.'

*   *   *

Kammy stepped outside feeling a little ridiculous in the best possible way. Her hair had been brushed for what felt like the first time in a century and Fii had even produced a few touches of make up for her to play with. More than that, she wore a dress. It was a simple thing, with a loose skirt that hung just below the knees. It 's deep blue shade was the closest that Fii could find to match Kammy's eyes. She had not worn a dress since her mother had caught her rummaging through her wardrobe when she was ten years old. Not because she had never wanted to, but because she never had the need to, or the money to spare for one. Her sandals were simple as well, but the thin straps made her feet look dainty. Kammy would not have admitted it to anyone, but she felt rather pretty.

'This is awesome.'

Jamie, on the other hand, actually did look ridiculous. His boots, trousers and shirt were fine, but the waistcoat was a monstrosity. Kammy suspected that Fii had only pointed it out as some sort of joke, not knowing, as Kammy did, how much Jamie loved a good joke. He wore the rainbow striped piece with pride and Kammy loved him for it, even though she winced every time she looked at him.

He was right though; it was awesome. Kammy looked out at the streets of Emire, alive with noise and with colour. They had draped banners between the rooftops and hung flags out of their windows. It seemed as though the town was sporting every shade of every colour that Kammy could name against the backdrop of the black night sky. People milled around, laughing and drinking and trying to sing, though most were struggling to form a string of words. The faint sound of music filtered towards them. Fii had told them that the evening's main attractions would be found beneath the Time Tower.

'Come on,' said Kammy, starting off away from the keep.

313

Jamie stuck close to Kammy's side as they slipped into the streets of the mazy town. Jamie's eyes were like orbs, absorbing everything around him. Emire was not as beautiful as Alashdial, but it had its own qualities that mesmerised. He laughed as two men hopped to their feet and started swinging around arm in arm. The mood was infectious. As they hurried over the cobbles the music became louder. The whistling of pipes, light with a high tempo, flew towards them and suddenly Jamie hooked his arm in Kammy's and they were dancing. They were spinning as the people spun around them. Kammy squealed as Jamie turned faster, his waistcoat flapping and the colours blurring. Kammy squeezed her eyes shut and screamed, the music drowning out the sound. They stumbled together, Jamie's arm around her, utterly breathless and elated.

She tugged his sleeve, her jaw aching from laughing so much, 'Let's find the others.'

As she turned, Kammy caught the eye of a man close to her. She did not recognise him, but he glared at her with such venom it took her breath away. Kammy slipped past him, trying to ignore it, but there was another face, shadowed in a doorway. Kammy's smile faded. This second face belonged to an old lady that Kammy had never met in her life. The street pushed in so narrow that she could not help her eyes drifting from face to face. Some paid them no attention, but just as many were staring with disgust and Kammy realised with a start that they were not staring at her, but at Jamie. Kammy grabbed his hand and stepped closer to him, her euphoria seeping away. Jamie glanced down at her, his smile broad, but his attention was drawn away again when they stepped into the Tower Square. He had not noticed.

With a heavy heart, Kammy pulled him off the street and into the square. The tower had been transformed. Crystal lanterns were draped around it and over the roof of the library. A stage had been erected in the centre of the square where the musicians danced and played. Couples and friends twirled around them. A mismatch of tables and chairs had been dragged out and placed around the outside of the square and Kammy spotted a familiar head bobbing up and down to the music, the colours reflecting in his glasses.

'Shall we sit with Welm?' she had to shout at Jamie over the noise.

But Jamie craned his neck over the crowd and a wicked smile crossed his lips.

314

'Do you mind if I abandon you for a bit?'

Kammy was surprised. She could not help worrying about what she had seen, but Jamie looked determined. 'Sure,' she said, 'why?'

Jamie shot her a wink, 'Break her down, right?'

'What...' But Jamie was already off, shimmying through the crowd and disappearing from sight, even with his multi-coloured waistcoat. Kammy shook her head when she realised what he was doing, for she did not rate his chances. Still, as long as he was oblivious to the looks being cast his way, then he would still enjoy himself. She did not want to ruin his mood, not yet. She could not burn the memory from her own mind though, and she found that she felt disappointed more than anything. She had thought that the citizens of Emire had treated her well enough, but then, she was not exactly human. Jamie did not deserve such coldness. Being human was no crime.

When Kammy reached the tables Welm had disappeared, but it did not take her long to spot him. Fii had dragged him from his seat. She looked resplendent in a green gown with her greying hair arranged on top of her head. Welm stumbled all over the place, but his broad grin made Kammy smile. She sank into one of the chairs, watching the pair of them have fun, and tried to lighten her own mood through force of will. When Fii waved, she waved back, smiling as brightly as she could.

'I thought you would be dancing.'

Kammy jumped and her hands flew to her hair. Jad stood beside her and her heart skipped, 'I didn't think you'd be here.'

He shrugged, sitting down opposite her, 'I couldn't stand another moment in that room.'

He looked much better. His arm had been placed in a sling and she could see the bandages beneath his loose white shirt. Yet despite his wounds, there was colour in his cheeks again. He had left his hair a ruffled mess and Kammy noticed that it was still wet at the temples. His appearance must have been quite a spontaneous decision.

'You should have told somebody you were coming.'

He didn't respond and Kammy glanced up at him only to find his eyes glued to her face.

'You look nice,' he said, the healthy glow in his cheeks darkening.

Kammy felt very hot. She laughed because she did not know what else to do and she stared determinedly into the crowd, but she could still feel him watching her.

'You mean I look like a girl, for once?'

'No,' he said, 'I mean you look *clean* for once.'

Kammy's jaw dropped. She stared at him and he smirked, his eyes glowing. Kammy snorted and they were both laughing.

'So,' he said when they caught their breath, 'why aren't you dancing? Where's Jamie?'

Kammy rolled her eyes, 'Jamie is off pursuing somebody in a situation that he has completely underestimated. Where's Eric?'

Jad looked surprised. 'He's not here? Nobody answered when I knocked on his door so I assumed he had already left.'

They shared a look of concern and Kammy wracked her brains trying to remember the last thing that Eric had said to her. Had they not shared a word since leaving Alashdial?

'How was he? On the way here?' Jad's mouth tightened.

'He was quiet, but then we were all quiet,' she reasoned, as much to herself as anything, 'a lot had happened.'

'He has done all of this for me and...' Jad shook his head, unable to find the words.

'It's not your fault. You never forced him.' She thought of Jad agreeing to help her save Jamie. 'It has always been his decision, and he has decided to stick with you.' There was always a choice, and it was an easy one when it came to friends.

Jad sighed, running a hand through his hair and ruffling it some more. 'You're right.' Then he looked at her and his scowl lifted, 'You still haven't told me why you're not dancing?'

Kammy laughed at his persistence. 'I...don't like dancing?'

'Is that why you looked so miserable when I saw you sitting here?'

316

Kammy started to protest, but the look on Jad's face told her it would be pointless. She puffed out her cheeks and shrugged, 'I don't think Jamie is very welcome here.'

'Why do you say that?'

'It sounds silly, but I saw people staring at him and they looked like they hated him. They don't know him, so how can they judge him like that?'

'Maybe they weren't...'

'I saw them, Jad. I saw their faces and it makes me feel sick. When I first heard that Bagor intended to kill humans, I was horrified. But the longer I spent here, the more I doubted that it could ever happen. Nobody cared that I was human. They were kind and welcoming, mostly. But now I realise that it's because I am actually Semei,' she looked at him, 'they could tell that I was like them, or a part of me was. But Jamie *is* human and they hate him for something that is out of his control.'

'It's hard for them Kammy,' said Jad, frowning, 'most Semei don't know anything about the world above.'

'And the humans know nothing of this world, but you don't see them planning a war.'

'Because they don't know that the world is dying.'

'So you still think that killing humans is the answer?'

Jad's eyes narrowed. He stared at her until Kammy felt her flash of anger cool. 'No, I don't. But I had my prejudices and I won't deny it. I thought that humans were stupid and weak. I thought that they were worth less than us Semei.' He paused and his eyes dropped to the table, 'Until I met you.'

Silence stretched between them. Kammy wanted to say something, but her mouth was incredibly dry.

'You know, I recognised you when I saw you in your cell. I don't know if you remember, but...'

'You were the squirrel, in the forest,' she murmured.

Jad's cheeks flushed and he started to fiddle with the material of his sling. 'You knew?'

317

'Well, he told me not to tell you this, but Eric filled me in. I think he was trying to convince me that you were a good guy.'

'I'll kill him.' Jad laughed, then he looked up at her slowly, 'You didn't think I was a good guy? I saved your life.'

Kammy gaped at him. 'Okay, maybe you were a *good* guy, but you weren't *nice.*'

'Well that's because I thought you would be a problem. Saving you the first time got me locked up, and saving you the second time almost resulted in the same. But then...' he stared at her and she could not look away, 'you took everything in your stride. You thought Jamie was dead, but you carried on. You saved us with the stones. You faced your fear of water. Tayah was horrible to you, and neither I nor Eric did much to stop her, but you did not let it get to you. How could I think humans were weak once I had met you?'

'But I'm not human,' Kammy whispered.

Jad leant forward, his eyes bright with conviction. 'Just because you are Semei does not mean you are no longer human. You are special Kammy, you are both. We Semei, maybe we do hate humans, but you can show everyone just like you showed me that our prejudices are wrong. You prove that we are the same. We laugh, we bleed, we cry. We fight the same and we love the same. Just because we are different does not mean that we aren't equal.' She leant towards him too, the air between them charged by his belief. He smiled at her and she smiled back, 'We just need to help other people see that.'

'Will you please control your friend?'

Kammy and Jad jerked away from each other, their faces burning. Tayah stomped towards them, looking quite beautiful despite the bruises on her neck and the scowl that marred her face. She slumped into a seat beside Kammy and it was only then that she spotted Jamie weaving towards them. Boo sat on his shoulders with his arms stretched out wide as Jamie zig-zagged madly. Boo's little face scrunched up in delight.

'If he gets hurt...' Tayah snapped when Jamie stopped before them

'I told you I've got him. Trust me.'

318

'I do *not* trust you.' Tayah huffed. She turned to Jad and Kammy, her back to Jamie. 'What were you talking about anyway? It looked important.'

Kammy shook her head, 'Nothing important,' she said, 'all important talk is banned until tomorrow.'

'So it was just general whisper talk?' Jamie beamed at her and Kammy glared.

Jad cut across them, 'What was that?'

Kammy turned to him. He stood, staring out across the square. Kammy frowned and followed his gaze. Then she noticed it too. Like a current, whispers passed through the crowd. People stopped dancing and the music died, the last note hanging in the air.

In amongst the whispers, Kammy heard a lone voice.

'Jadanim...Jadanim...'

Jad ran and people dodged out of his way. Tayah jumped to her feet and Jamie handed Boo to her without one of his usual quips. Kammy hurried after Jad. That lone voice made her hairs stand on end.

Kammy saw Jad's shoulders stiffen and he slowed. She stopped at his side to see a woman drop to her knees before him. Kammy did not recognise her, but it was clear from the look on Jad's face that he did.

Relief shone from the woman's blue eyes when she looked at him. Her short blonde hair was plastered to her forehead. She was one of Bagor's Armours, but her suit was covered in dirt. Jad rushed to her side and it was only then that she noticed the black bundle in the woman's arms. It was a cat.

'What's going on?' Seeve had pushed through to the front of the crowd that stood in a tight circle around the scene.

Jad did not seem to hear him. He stared at the cat, his eyes bright, 'Annie?'

The woman blinked. She looked confused. 'What?'

Jad placed a hand on her shoulder. 'Eryn, what happened?'

319

Her eyes filled with tears and she gasped, 'He knows. He found out and I...I tried...I tried...'

Jad glared up at the bodies creeping ever closer, 'Get back. Give her some space.'

Seeve took up the call. His loud voice commanded their attention and he moved amongst the crowd, pushing them back. Kammy stayed at Jad's shoulder, her hand over her mouth.

'He killed them,' the woman trembled, 'he killed all of them...I'm sorry...'

'Who?' Jad looked horrified.

She squeezed her eyes shut. 'The ones that helped you...the family...'

Kammy watched Jad sway. He slumped to his knees and his voice cracked, 'But I...all of them?'

'To send a message...to warn...all of them. The old lady...the girl,' she cried out suddenly, gripping Jad's shirt, her eyes wide with terror, 'you must go. You have to get away. He's coming. He's coming...behind me. He's coming.'

Kammy did not need to ask who. Her heart plummeted and the whispers started up again. This time the people backed away of their own accord.

'What's that?' a man shouted, pointing up into the sky.

The townspeople looked up as one and Kammy joined them. Something hurtled through the sky, something that flickered orange. It was a flaming arrow and it sunk into the crowd. Somebody screamed and there was uproar.

Bagor had already arrived.

CHAPTER TWENTY EIGHT
FIRE

Flaming arrows rained down upon them and screams filled the air.

Kammy was swept back. She cried out and Jad started to turn, but then she could no longer see him. Pushed on all sides, she was carried away by a panicked surge. She shouted his name, but her cries were lost. She tried to break free but more faces appeared, pinning her in as they fled the square. She gasped for breath. She tried to shout again, but the words were crushed out of her. She stumbled. The wall of bodies caught her. She thought she could hear Seeve, but there was no way to reach him, she could not turn to look for him. Even if she found a way to break free she would feel that same terror, for Bagor was out there and she did not think he would treat her with the same kindness as he had before.

There was a soft thump and the woman to Kammy's left dropped. She fell so peacefully that Kammy almost missed the arrow protruding from her back. Then the woman was lost beneath the stampede and another face took her place. Bile rose in Kammy's throat. She could only gape with wide eyes. She could only let the horror bear her along.

With a roar, flames burst across the rooftops, jumping from flag to flag. The screams grew louder as the heat bore down on them. It spread in seconds; illuminating tear streaked and frightened faces. Some shifted, shooting into the sky in bird form or snapping at the heels of the slow moving mass. Smoke cascaded towards them and Kammy coughed as she was carried away from the tower, the only comfort being that the crowd started to thin.

When the pressure eased around her, Kammy almost fell. Her knees were shaking, but she dug her nails into her palms and the pain made her focus. Plumes of smoke filled the air, growing thicker by the second. Kammy turned, barely able to see, and ran for a doorway. Bodies bumped her, hands shoved her, but when she pressed herself against the door she could finally breathe. Her chest heaved and she spluttered on the sudden rush of air. She squinted into the haze to see people and animals continuing tó stream past. She saw children, lost and afraid, and she wished that she could help them but she stayed where she was, paralysed by fear.

She had no idea what to do. She could just make out the glow of the tower from where she stood. It loomed out of the murk like a beacon that called to her. Would the others still be there? She peered through the smoke, but she could not make out where she was. There was no way that she would be able to find her way back to the keep, she did not know Emire well enough. The Tower Square was her best and only option, but that was where the attack had fallen. She did not know what she would find there. Kammy closed her eyes and leant her head back against the wood as she tried to calm her racing heart. When she opened her eyes again, her mind was set. Kammy gripped the bottom of her dress and ripped it, tugging off a strip of material. She held it over her mouth and nose and took a moment to gather herself. Then she stepped free of the doorway and she ran. She pushed against the tide. Shadows appeared suddenly from the smoke, lurching around her and groaning as they struggled on. Kammy could hear nothing, but her own desperate breathing and the blood in her ears. Her eyes were stinging and she coughed, the thin material doing little to help. Arrows still fell. Kammy stumbled a few times, but she did not dare look down. She knew what she stumbled over. The tower disappeared completely as she got closer and she turned on the spot, disorientated. She picked a street and almost fell to her knees in relief when she burst out into the Tower Square.

The Time Tower had been struck alight in the chaos. She stared at the flames licking its glass face and she felt her chest tighten until she started to choke. She ducked closer to the ground, hoping she might breathe easier. Her eyes streamed, but even as her vision blurred she could make out the bodies littered across the cobbles, some much smaller than she was. She retched and heaved as she faltered.

The screams were distant now and the square had been abandoned by the living. The Time Tower groaned as the crackling fire ravaged it. The library would burn too; there was no saving it. There was no saving anyone.

Kammy stumbled forward, unsure which way to turn. She tried to call out for her friends, but her voice rasped and arrows still whistled through the night, skittering off the cobbles around her.

Someone grabbed her arm and Kammy screamed and gasped as she tried to pull away.

'Kammy...stop...'

'Fii?' She squinted through the smoke and through her tears. She could barely see the old woman's face. 'Why are you here?'

Kammy could just make out the cloth pulled over Fii's mouth, 'I saw you run back. You didn't hear me shout. Now, we have to go.' Her voice was muffled.

Kammy shook her head, 'No,' she croaked, 'I have to find Jamie.'

'He's with Tayah. Let's go, it's not safe here.'

Still Kammy paused, 'Jad?'

'In the keep. They are all in the keep. *Now*, Kammy.'

The effect of her relief was instantaneous. She let Fii lead her as the Time Tower creaked.

Fii gasped and froze. Kammy jerked to a stop, her eyes darting ahead of them, trying to see what had startled her. She frowned and glanced up at the burning tower. 'What is it?'

Fii turned slowly, her eyes wide and her hand clutching Kammy's. She dropped to her knees. There was an arrow though her heart.

Kammy fell to the floor beside her.

Fii's lips moved, but she did not speak. Kammy's hands hovered over the end of the arrow shaft, but all she could see was the blood. It spilled over Fii's dress and onto Kammy's lap. There was so much blood. It was on Kammy's hands and she did not want to touch Fii's face. She did not want to get blood on Fii's face. It was too hot. Everything was too hot. All the while, Fii's grey eyes were fixed on her, glassy and still.

Kammy screamed, but no sound came out. She pulled Fii up further onto her lap and they sat together in silence as Emire burned around them. Kammy rocked her gently as ash settled into their hair and blood pooled around them.

Hands gripped her shoulders. They were soft hands, comforting hands, but she held onto Fii and shook her head.

A soothing voice whispered in her air, 'It is not safe here. I am sorry Kammy, but you must come.'

'No,' Kammy cried, clutching Fii closer, 'it's my fault...I can't leave her...it's my fault...'

The hands gripped her tighter, not enough to hurt but enough that Kammy needed strength she did not have to resist. She was tugged away from Fii's body and no matter how hard she tried to scream, still no sound would come. Fii slipped from her fingers and pain tore through her. The hands pulled her to her feet, but she could not stand and they caught her before she fell. She was lifted and pulled towards a chest that was hard and warm. Her head leant against it and she could smell something familiar.

'Jad,' she cried, clutching him tight.

'We have to hurry,' he whispered into her hair, and he began to run. His hold on her did not waver. Everything felt very far away apart from the smell of him. The screams were gone. Distantly, she heard something groan and then crash. The ground seemed to tremble, but Jad held on and she trusted him completely. She started to breathe easier, in rhythm with the rise and fall of his chest. She thought that the smoke was getting thinner. She opened her eyes and saw that her fingers, coated in blood and ash, were gripping a black shirt.

Jad whispered in her ear. 'You're safe. You're safe with me.'

Kammy shivered. He sounded strange. She shook her head, trying to clear it, 'Where are we going?'

'Home.'

Kammy pictured a small room with peeling orange wallpaper and a TV that had never had signal. She saw a rickety staircase that always gave her splinters and her Gran waiting at the bottom with a mug of tea. Kammy smiled, but then the image started to dissolve. She saw Ria, her bright hair framing her wild eyes. She saw Jad inside her home, reaching for her.

'I can't go home.'

No answer came and through the haze Kammy remembered something; Jad had been wearing a white shirt.

Certainty hit her and swamped her with revulsion. She stiffened and her hand dropped from his shirt as if it were poison.

'Bagor...'

He was silent. His grip on her did not change. But Kammy's senses were returning and she pushed against him, her arms trembling.

'Put me down,' she croaked, her voice feeble.

'We should get away from the fire.'

Kammy was tempted to let him take her. It was hard to keep her eyes open and her head was swimming. He was holding her so gently. He had saved her life again by carrying her away from the smoke and the flames. Could it really only be because of her resemblance to her mother?

She reached up a hand to her forehead, but her fingers were sticky with blood; Fii's blood. Anger flooded her and she pushed against him again. 'Put me down.'

He slowed. He sighed and she thought she heard him laugh. Then he stopped and he placed her back on the cobbles, holding her for a moment until he was sure she would not fall. When she stopped swaying, he stepped back.

Kammy held herself still, waiting for her legs to stop shaking. She stared at him in shock. His eyes were unreadable. He gazed back at her, his face and his hair iced by flecks of grey ash. But the ash was not enough to cover the damage that she had done. Along the left side of his jaw and across his cheek ran a hideous wound. Kammy hoped that it would make him angry. She hoped it would make him stop.

The town sat still and quiet around them. The arrows had ceased and all she could hear was the roaring of the fire.

'Where are your Armours?'

'Outside the walls.'

'But...the attack. You are attacking.'

'This attack is merely a warning,' he said, as casually as if he were telling her the time, 'a symbol of my strength. Seeve would be a fool to ignore it. I do not want to kill innocent people.'

Kammy's eyes flashed, 'But you have...the family in Alashdial, and so many...so many here...and Fii. You killed Fii.' The fear and the grief became too much and Kammy flew at him. She wanted to hurt him and she swung her small fists against him. He did not fight her and she screamed at him, shredding her throat, because she wanted him to. She wanted him to so badly that she hit him until all her strength was spent, then she stumbled back and slumped to her knees, heaving dry sobs.

'Is that all?'

Kammy glared at him through her tears. 'Why are you doing this? Why are you here...talking to me?'

'I am here because I want to offer you a chance.'

'If you think that I will give you the Key then you're stupid. I won't give you anything.'

Bagor laughed. 'I do not need you to get the Key. That will be mine without your aid.'

Kammy shivered. 'Then why? What do you want?'

He stared at her for a moment, his head tilted to one side. 'I wish for you to come with me, back to Alashdial.'

Kammy could do no more than stare at him.

'You will be safe there. You will be comfortable.'

'You're crazy.'

But he pressed on, stepping towards her, 'I can tell you everything you wish to know about the Semei and about your mother. I can teach you how to shift...'

'Shift?' Kammy breathed.

He nodded, his eyes bright with genuine emotion and that fear that Kammy had carried since meeting him leapt from her tongue.

'Are you my father?'

She snapped her mouth shut and watched his jaw tighten. She did not know what to feel and she hated herself for it. Would any father do? Even if that father was a monster? There was a curious glint in his eyes and Kammy waited.

His voice was steady when he said, 'Would you come with me if I said yes?'

'No,' Kammy spat, not giving herself a moment to wonder.

Bagor smirked. 'I am not your father. He was a human, named John Helseth. That is true. But you are part Semei and you are Marianna's daughter. She would never forgive me if I did not keep you safe.'

Kammy felt a weight fall off of her shoulders. She had never met John Helseth, but those stories that her mother had told her about him had been true. Both her parents were dead, but they were not monsters.

Kammy swallowed. 'You loved her.'

Bagor did not flinch. 'I did.'

Kammy stayed where she was, on her knees, coated in ash, blood and tears. She thought of the others and all that they had suffered. She could not imagine how she would tell them about Fii.

'You have ruined my friends lives,' she said, 'you killed Jad's father and his grandfather and you want to kill him too, your own family. All to wage a war against humans? Yet you think there might be a chance that I would come with you?' Her voice shook and she staggered away from him, 'My Mum fell in love with a human. She would not ever agree with what you are doing. You might have loved her, but she never loved you and she would not want me anywhere near you.'

The smooth side of his face drained of colour. He did not blink as his eyes bored into hers. Kammy tilted her chin and she did not look away.

'You are stubborn,' he said softly, 'you get that from her.'

Kammy said nothing. She waited, aware that nobody knew where she was. Aware that Bagor's body thrummed with tension. She had no way of fighting him.

'Very well,' he said and he smiled, his wound stretching, 'I will return to my Armours. Seeve has three days. If he does not present the Key to me before then, I will enter this town and I will slaughter its inhabitants until he changes his mind. If you change yours, you will be welcomed when we return to Alashdial.'

'I won't,' she said, her eyes blazing, 'not ever.'

His smile stretched and Kammy felt very cold despite the fire. He started to back away, then he paused, and his eyes narrowed. 'I do have an added incentive for you. I have replaced Jamie with another...hostage, you might say.'

Kammy felt all the fight drain out of her.

'This time, I shall not underestimate you as I did before. So, tell Eric that his sister, Kaitlyn, is not the most agreeable captive I have ever housed. In fact, I might tire of her quickly.'

With one last smirk, Bagor walked away. Kammy watched him until he disappeared into the smokey haze, but his words stayed with her. She stood alone, a small grey figure, framed by the glow of the fires that still raged. Her dress was torn and drenched in blood.

She remembered what Dorren had told her. *You are his weakness and you will ruin everything.*

Bagor had no weakness. Bagor was a monster and he was going to win.

The End.

ACKNOWLEDGEMENTS

To all of the parents - Mum and Sped, Dad and Chris. To the siblings - Gabi, Josh and Steve. To Nonna, Gina and to the rest of my family. I am lucky to have you and I thank you for all of your support. You are the ones who never scoffed when my eight-year-old self was writing her first novel. So thank you. Oh, and to Tatiana who I am sure will be just as supportive as she grows up.

A huge thank you to everybody that has ever encouraged or inspired me over the years, including teachers like Mrs Clark, Miss Finch and Mr E. This goes right back to primary school when Verity shared my excitement over the Danshees. Don't worry if you don't remember that Vels! Also to Hannah who unknowingly read the first incarnation of *The Wolf's Cry* on one of our camping trips. And to all of you that have read *this* incarnation or parts of it: Daisy, Rita, Aussie Steph, Val, Anna, Nia, Caro...the list is endless, thank you!

A special thanks to Lucy, Fiona, Tom, Keeley, Paulina and Trisha for the detailed feedback and constant ego boosts you have given me. To Dr Laurence Scott and Dr Harry Whitehead, you guys probably never knew how much your encouragement meant to me. To Lala for being my constant cheerleader and fan, and to Anja for giving the exact emotional responses that I needed at any given time. To Canadian Steph for being my life guru and social media advisor. To Johanna for creating the perfect front cover. To Ellie for blessing me with your editorial ways. To all of you from 'The Thread' and from Twitter. Thank you.

THE LION'S PRIDE

BOOK TWO IN THE SEMEI TRILOGY

COMING SOON

9427691R00184

Printed in Great Britain
by Amazon.co.uk, Ltd.,
Marston Gate.